JULIE GARWOOD

HONOR'S SPLENDOUR

POCKET BOOKS

New York   London   Toronto   Sydney

This book is a work of historical fiction. Names, characters, places and incidents relating to nonhistorical figures are products of the author's imagination or are used fictitiously. Any resemblance of such incidents, places, or figures to actual events or locales or persons living or dead is entirely coincidental.

An *Original* Publication of POCKET BOOKS

 POCKET BOOKS, a division of Simon & Schuster, Inc.
1230 Avenue of the Americas, New York, NY 10020

Copyright © 1987 by Julie Garwood

ISBN -13: 978-0-671-73782-5
ISBN -10:   0-671-73782-1

First Pocket Books paperback printing December 1987

35 34 33 32 31 30

POCKET and colophon are registered trademarks of Simon & Schuster, Inc.

Cover art by Lisa Litwack
Cover photo © John Beatty/Tony Stone Images

Manufactured in the United States of America

For information regarding special discounts for bulk purchases, please contact Simon & Schuster Special Sales at 1-800-456-6798 or business@simonandschuster.com

HONOR'S SPLENDOUR

Chapter One

"Whatsoever things are true, whatsoever things are honest,
Whatsoever things are just, whatsoever things are pure; if
there be any virtue . . . think on these things."

NEW TESTAMENT, PHILIPPIANS, 4:8

England, 1099

They meant to kill him.

The warrior stood in the center of the desolate courtyard, his hands roped together and tied to a post behind his back. His expression was devoid of emotion as he stared straight ahead, outwardly ignoring his enemy.

The captive hadn't offered any resistance, allowing himself to be stripped to his waist without so much as a fist drawn or a word of protest spoken. His rich, fur-lined winter cloak, heavy hauberk, cotton shirt, stockings, and leather boots had all been removed and placed on the frozen ground in front of him. The enemy's intent was clear. The warrior would die, but without a new mark added to his battle-scarred body. While his eager audience watched, the captive could look at his garments while he slowly froze to death.

Twelve men surrounded him. Knives drawn to give them

courage, they circled and jeered, yelling insults and obscenities as they stomped their boot-clad feet in an effort to ward
off the frigid temperature. Yet one and all kept a safe
distance lest their docile captive change his inclination and
decide to break loose and attack. They had little doubt he'd
be capable of the feat, for they'd all heard the tales of his
Herculean strength. Some had even witnessed his superior
prowess in battle a time or two. And if he tore through the
ropes, the men would be forced to use their knives on him,
but not before he sent three, possibly even four of them to
their own deaths.

The leader of the twelve couldn't believe his good fortune.
They had captured the Wolf and would soon witness his
death.

What a reckless mistake their captive had made. Aye,
Duncan, the powerful Baron of Wexton holdings had actually ridden into his enemy's fortress completely alone, and
without a single weapon for defense. He had unwisely
believed that Louddon, a baron of equal land title, would
honor their temporary truce.

He must believe his own reputation, the leader thought.
He must truly think himself to be as invincible as the great
battle stories exaggerated. Surely that was the reason he
seemed so unconcerned over his dire circumstances now.

A feeling of unease settled in the leader's mind as he
continued to watch his captive. They had stripped the man
of his value, shredded his blue and white crest proclaiming
title and worth, making certain that no remnants of the
civilized nobleman remained. Baron Louddon wanted his
captive to die without dignity or honor. Yet the near-naked
warrior standing so proudly before them wasn't complying
with Louddon's wishes at all. He wasn't acting like a man
about to die. Nay, the captive wasn't pleading for his life or
whimpering for a quick end. He didn't look like a dying
man either. His skin wasn't pale or covered with goose
bumps, but sun-bronzed and weather-toughened. Damn, he
wasn't even shivering. Aye, they had stripped the nobleman,
yet under all the layers of refinement stood the proud
warlord, looking as primitive and as fearless as the whispered tales boasted. Before their eyes, the Wolf had been
revealed.

The jeering had ceased. Only the sound of the wind

howling through the courtyard could be heard now. The leader turned his attention to his men, huddled together a short distance away. Every one of them was staring at the ground. He knew they avoided looking at their captive. He couldn't fault them for this show of cowardice as he, too, found it a difficult task to look directly into the warrior's eyes.

Baron Duncan of Wexton land was at least a head taller than the largest of the soldiers guarding him. He was just as massive in proportions, with thick, muscular shoulders and thighs, and with his long, powerful legs braced apart, his stance suggested he was capable of killing them all . . . if he became so inclined.

Darkness was descending, and with it came a curtain of light snow. The soldiers began to complain about the weather in earnest then. "Ain't no need for us to freeze to death right along with him," one muttered.

"He won't die for hours yet," another complained. "Baron Louddon's gone over an hour now. He'll not know if we stayed outside or not."

The agreement by the others with vigorous nods and grunts swayed their leader. The cold was beginning to irritate him too. His unease had grown as well, for he'd been convinced that Baron Wexton wasn't any different from other men. He was sure he would have broken down and screamed in torment by now. The arrogance of the man infuriated him. By God, he looked bored with them all. The leader was forced to admit that he'd underestimated his opponent. It wasn't an easy admission and one that sent him into a rage. His own feet, protected from the harsh weather by his thick boots, were nevertheless stinging in agony now, yet Baron Duncan stood barefoot and hadn't moved or shifted balance once since being restrained. Perhaps there was truth in the tales after all.

The leader cursed his superstitious nature and gave the order to retreat inside. When the last of his men had departed, Louddon's vassal checked that the rope was secure and then came to stand directly in front of his captive. "They say you're as cunning as a wolf, but you're just a man, and you'll soon die like one. Louddon don't want fresh knife cuts in you. Come morning, we'll drag your body miles away from here. No one will be able to prove that Louddon was behind the deed." The leader sneered the words, furious that his captive wouldn't even look down at him, and then added, "If I had my way, I'd cut out your heart and be done with it." He gathered spittle in his mouth to hurl into the warrior's face, hoping this new insult would gain a reaction.

And then the captive slowly lowered his gaze. His eyes met those of his enemy. What the leader saw there caused him to swallow loudly. He turned away in fright. He made the sign of the cross, a puny effort to ward off the dark promise he'd read in the warrior's gray eyes, muttering to himself that he was only doing the bidding of his overlord. And then he ran toward the safety of the castle.

From the shadows against the wall, Madelyne watched. She waited several more minutes to be certain that none of her brother's soldiers were going to return, using the time well to pray for courage to see her plan carried through.

She risked everything. In her heart she knew there was no other choice. She was the only one who could save him now. Madelyne accepted the responsibilities and the consequences, knowing full well that if her deed was discovered, it would surely mean her own death.

Her hands trembled but her steps were quick. The sooner the deed was done, the better for her peace of mind. There'd be plenty of time to worry over her actions once the foolish captive had been released.

A long black cape covered her from head to foot, and the baron didn't notice her until she was standing directly before him. A fierce gust of wind pulled the hood from her head, and a mane of auburn hair fell well past shoulders of a slender frame. She brushed a strand away from her face and looked up at the captive.

For a moment he thought his mind played tricks on him. Duncan actually shook his head in denial. And then her voice reached him and he knew what he was seeing wasn't a figment of his imagination. "I'll have you undone in just a moment or two. Pray don't make a sound until we're away from here."

He couldn't believe what he was hearing. His savior's voice sounded as clear as the truest of harps and as beckoning as one of summer's warm days. Duncan closed his eyes, resisting the urge to shout with laughter over this

4

strange twist in events, considered giving the cry for battle now and be done with the deception, and then immediately decided against that idea. His curiosity was too strong. He determined to wait awhile longer, until his savior revealed her true intentions.

His expression remained inscrutable. He kept silent as he watched her remove a small dagger from beneath her cape. She stood close enough for him to capture with his unbound legs, and if her words proved false or her dagger moved toward his heart, he'd be forced to crush her.

Lady Madelyne had no idea of the danger. Intent only on setting him free, she moved closer to his side and began the task of cutting through the thick rope. Duncan noticed that her hands were shaking. He couldn't decide if it was because of the harsh weather or fear.

The scent of roses reached him. When he inhaled the light fragrance, he decided the freezing temperature had certainly muddled his mind. A rose in the middle of winter, an angel inside this fortress of purgatory . . . neither made sense to him, yet she smelled of the flowers of spring and looked like a vision from above.

He shook his head again. The logical part of his mind knew exactly who she was. The description given to him was accurate in every detail, but misleading too. He'd been told that Louddon's sister was of medium height and had brown hair and blue eyes. And pleasing to look upon, he remembered being informed. Ah, there was the falsehood, he decided. The devil's sister was neither pleasing nor pretty. She was magnificent.

The rope finally gave way, and his hands were freed. He stood where he was, his expression well hidden. The girl came to stand in front of him again and gifted him with a small smile before she turned and knelt to gather his possessions.

Fear made the simple task awkward. She stumbled when she stood up again, straightened herself, and then turned back to him. "Please follow me," she instructed him.

He didn't move, but continued to stand where he was, watching and waiting.

Madelyne frowned over his hesitation, thinking to herself that the cold had surely frozen his ability to think. She clutched his garments to her chest with one hand, letting the

5

heavy boots dangle from her fingertips, and then put her other arm around his waist. "Lean on me," she whispered. "I'll help you, I promise. But please, we must hurry." Her gaze was directed toward the castle doors and the fear sounded in her voice.

He responded to her desperation. He wanted to tell her that they needn't hide, for even now his men were scaling the walls, but he changed his mind. The less she knew, the better his advantage when the time came.

She barely reached his shoulder, yet she valiantly tried to accept some of his weight by taking his arm and draping it around her shoulders. "We go to the visiting priest's quarters behind the chapel," she told him in a soft whisper. "'Tis the one place they'll never think to look."

The warrior paid scant attention to what she was telling him. His gaze was directed to the top of the north wall. The half moon gave the light snow an eerie glow and outlined his soldiers climbing over the top. Not a sound could be heard as his men grew in numbers along the wooden walkway that circled the top of the wall.

The warrior nodded with satisfaction. Louddon's soldiers were as foolish as their lord. The harshness of the weather had sent the gatekeepers inside, leaving the wall unprotected and vulnerable. The enemy had proven their weakness. And they would all die because of it.

He gave the woman more of his weight to slow her progress while he flexed his hands, again and again, trying to force the numbness from his fingers. There was little feeling in his feet, a bad sign, he knew even as he accepted that nothing could be done about it now.

He heard a faint whistle and quickly raised his hand high into the air, giving the signal to wait. He glanced down at the woman to see if she had caught his action, his other hand ready to clamp over her mouth if she gave the least indication that she knew what was happening. But the woman was busy struggling with his weight and seemed oblivious to the fact that her home was being penetrated.

They reached a narrow doorway and Madelyne, believing the captive to be in a dangerously weakened condition, tried to prop him up against the stone wall with one hand while she worked to get the door unlatched.

The baron, understanding her intent, willingly leaned against the wall and watched her juggle his garments and fight the icy chain.

Once she had the door opened, she took hold of his hand and led him through the darkness. A rush of frigid air swirled around them as they made their way to a second door at the end of a long, damp corridor. Madelyne quickly opened it and beckoned him inside.

The room they entered was windowless, but several candles had been lit, casting a warm glow to the intersanctuary. The air was stale. Dust covered the wooden floor and fat cobwebs dangled and swayed from the low-beamed ceiling. Several colorful robes used by visiting priests hung on hooks, and a straw pallet had been placed in the center of the small area with two thick blankets next to it.

Madelyne latched the door and sighed with relief. For the moment they were safe. She motioned for him to sit down on the pallet. "When I saw what they were doing to you, I prepared this room," she explained as she handed him his clothing. "My name is Madelyne and I'm . . ." She started to explain her relationship to her brother, Louddon, and then thought better of it. "I'll stay with you until first light and then show you the way out through a hidden passage. Not even Louddon knows it exists."

The baron sat down and folded his legs in front of him. He pulled on his shirt while he listened to her. He considered that her act of courage certainly complicated his life, found himself wondering how she would react when she realized his true plan, and then decided that his course of action couldn't be altered.

As soon as his hauberk was once again covering his massive chest, Madelyne draped one of the blankets around his shoulders and then knelt down, facing him. She leaned back on the heels of her shoes, motioning for him to stretch out his legs. When he had complied with her wishes, she studied his feet, frowning with concern. He reached for his boots, but Madelyne stayed his hands. "We must warm your feet first," she explained.

She took a deep breath while she considered the quickest way to give life back to the starving limbs. Her head was bent, shielding her face from the watchful gaze of the warrior.

She picked up the second blanket, started to wrap it around his feet, and then shook her head, changing her mind. Without offering a word of explanation, she threw the blanket over his legs, removed her cloak, and then slowly inched the cream-colored chainse up over her knees. The braided leather rope she used as a decorative belt and a sheath for her dagger got caught up in the dark green bliaut that covered her chainse, and she took the time to remove it, discarding it next to the warrior's side.

He was curious about her strange behavior and waited for her to explain her actions. But Madelyne didn't say a word. She took another deep breath, grabbed hold of his feet, and quickly, before she could think better of it, slipped them under her clothing, flattening them against the warmth of her stomach.

She let out a loud gasp when his icy skin touched her own warm flesh, and then adjusted her gown and wrapped her arms around the outside, hugging him to her. Her shoulders began to tremble and the warrior felt it was as if she were drawing all the cold from his body and taking it into her own.

It was the most unselfish act he had ever witnessed.

Feeling was quick to return to his feet. He felt as if a thousand daggers were being thrust into the soles of his feet, burning with an intensity he found difficult to ignore. He tried to shift his position, but she wouldn't allow it, increasing her hold with surprising strength.

"If there is pain, 'tis a good sign," she told him, her voice no more than a husky whisper. "It will go away soon. Besides, you're most fortunate to be feeling anything," she added.

The censure in her tone surprised Duncan, and he raised an eyebrow in reaction. Madelyne glanced up just then and caught his expression. She hurried to explain. "You'd not be in this position if you hadn't acted so carelessly. I only hope you've learned your lesson well this day. I'll not be able to save you a second time."

Madelyne softened her tone. She even tried to smile at him, but it was a puny effort at best. "I know you believed Louddon would act with honor. But that was your mistake.

8

Louddon doesn't know what honor is. Remember that in future and you might live to see another year."

She lowered her gaze and thought about the dear price she'd pay for setting her brother's enemy free. It wouldn't take Louddon long to realize she'd been behind the escape. Madelyne said a prayer of thanksgiving that Louddon had left the fortress, for his departure gave her added time to carry out her own plan of escape.

First, the baron must be taken care of. Once he was safely on his way, she could worry about the repercussions of her bold act. She was determined not to think about it now. "What's done is done," she whispered, letting all the agony and despair echo in her voice.

The baron didn't respond to her remarks, and she didn't offer additional explanation. Silence stretched between them like a growing abyss. Madelyne wished he'd say something to her, anything, to ease her discomfort. She was embarrassed by having his feet nestled against her so intimately and realized that if he moved his toes at all, he'd be touching the undersides of her breasts. That thought made her blush. She dared another quick glance up to see how he was reacting to her strange method of treatment.

He was waiting for her to look at him and quickly, effortlessly, captured her gaze. He thought that her eyes were as blue as the sky above on the clearest of days, and considered, too, that she looked nothing like her brother. He cautioned himself that appearances meant nothing, even as he felt himself becoming mesmerized by her bewitchingly innocent gaze. He reminded himself that she was the sister of his enemy, nothing more, nothing less. Beautiful or not, she was his pawn, his snare to trap the demon.

Madelyne stared into his eyes and thought that they were as gray and as cold as one of her daggers. His face seemed cut from stone, for there was no emotion to be seen there, no feeling at all.

His hair was a dark brown, overly long and slightly curly, but that didn't soften his features. His mouth looked hard, his chin was too firm, and she noticed that there weren't any lines at the corners of his eyes. He didn't look like the kind of man who laughed or smiled. No, she acknowledged with a shiver of apprehension. He looked as hard and as cold as his position demanded. He was a warrior first and a baron second, and she guessed that there wasn't any place in his life for laughter.

She suddenly realized that she didn't have the least idea of what was going on inside his mind. That worried her, not knowing what he was thinking. She coughed to cover her embarrassment, and thought to start the conversation again. Perhaps, if he spoke to her, he would seem less intimidating.

"Did you think to face Louddon alone?" she asked. She waited a long time for his reply, and at his continued silence she sighed with frustration. The warrior was proving to be as obstinate as he was foolish, she told herself. She had just saved his life and he hadn't spoken one word of gratitude. His manner was proving to be as harsh as his appearance and reputation.

He frightened her. Once she admitted that fact to herself, she became irritated. She chastised herself over her reaction to him, thinking that she was now behaving as foolishly as he. The man hadn't said a word, yet she trembled like a child.

It was his size, she decided. Aye, she thought with a nod. In the confines of the small room, he seemed to overpower her.

"Don't think to return for Louddon again. It would be another mistake. And he will surely kill you next time."

The warrior didn't answer. He moved then, slowly sliding his feet from the warmth she provided. He took his time, edging down the sensitive skin on the tops of her thighs with deliberate provocation.

Madelyne continued to kneel in front of him, her gaze downcast as he put on his stockings and his boots.

When he was finished with his task, he slowly lifted the braided belt she had discarded and held it up in front of her.

Madelyne instinctively reached out with both hands to accept her belt. She smiled, thinking his action was a peace offering of sorts, and waited for him to finally speak his gratitude.

The warrior worked with lightning speed. He grabbed her left hand and tied the rope around it. Before she could even think to pull away, he looped the belt around her other wrist and bound her hands together.

10

Madelyne stared in astonishment at her hands and then looked up at him, her confusion obvious.

The expression on his face sent a chill of dread down her spine. She shook her head, denying what was happening.

And then the warrior spoke. "I didn't come for Louddon, Madelyne. I came for you."

Chapter Two

"Vengeance is mine; I will repay . . ."

NEW TESTAMENT, ROMANS, 12:19

"Have you gone daft?" Madelyne whispered. Her voice sounded with astonishment.

The baron didn't answer her, but his scowl suggested he had little liking for her question. He pulled Madelyne to her feet and then grabbed hold of her shoulders to steady her. She would have fallen back to her knees without his aid. Odd, but his touch was gentle for a man of his size, Madelyne thought, and that bit of knowledge confused her all the more.

His trickery was beyond her comprehension. He was the captive and she his savior, and certainly he realized that fact, didn't he? Why, she'd risked everything for him. Dear God, she'd touched his feet, warmed them; aye, she'd given him all she dared.

He towered over her, this nobleman turned barbarian, and wore a savage expression that more than matched his gigantic proportions. She felt the power radiating from him, as forceful and stinging as the touch of a hot poker, and though she tried desperately not to flinch from the chilling look in his icy gray eyes, she knew she was trembling enough for him to notice.

He misunderstood her reaction and reached down for her cloak. When he placed the garment around her shoulders, his hand brushed against the swell of her breasts. She thought the touch was unintentional, yet she instinctively took a step back, clasping the cloak in front of her. The baron's scowl deepened. He took hold of her hands, turned, and led the way down the dark corridor, dragging her behind him.

She had to run to keep up with him, else he'd be dragging her. "Why do you want to confront Louddon's men when it isn't necessary?"

There was no response from the baron but Madelyne wasn't deterred. The warrior was walking toward his own death. She felt compelled to stop him. "Please, Baron, don't do this. Listen to me. The cold has brittled your mind. They'll kill you."

Madelyne pulled against his hold then, hard, using all her strength, but he didn't even slow his pace.

How in God's name was she going to save him?

They reached the heavy door that led to the courtyard. The baron pushed it open so forcefully the hinges unbuckled. The door shredded into planks against the stone wall. Madelyne was pulled through the opening, into an icy wind that slapped her face and made a mockery of her fervent belief that the man she had untied less than an hour past was daft. No, he wasn't daft at all.

The proof surrounded her. Over a hundred soldiers lined the inner courtyard, with more climbing over the top of the stone wall, all as quick as the rising wind and as silent as thieves, and every one of them wearing Baron Wexton's blue and white colors.

Madelyne was so overwhelmed by the sight, she didn't even notice her captor had stopped to look at his men as they gathered in numbers before him. She bumped into his back, instinctively reached out to grab hold of his hauberk to balance herself, and only then realized he'd let go of her hands.

He didn't give the least indication she was there, hovering

behind his back, clutching his garment as if it had suddenly become her lifeline. Madelyne realized she might appear to be hiding, or worse, cowering, and she immediately braved a step to his side so that one and all could see her. The top of her head reached the baron's shoulders. She stood with her shoulders straight, trying to match the baron's defiant stance, praying all the while her terror wasn't discernible.

Lord, but she was scared. In truth, she wasn't overly afraid of death; it was the dying that came before that terrified her. Aye, it was the thought of her own behavior before the foul deed was completed that made her feel so sick inside. Would it be quick or slowly drawn out? Would she lose her carefully nurtured control at the last minute and act the coward? That thought so upset her, she almost blurted out then and there that she wanted to be the first to feel the blade of death. But pleading for a quick end would also make her a coward, wouldn't it? And then her brother's prediction would be fulfilled.

Baron Wexton had no idea of the thoughts racing through his captive's mind. He glanced down to look at her, took in her tranquil expression, and was mildly surprised by it. She looked very calm, almost serene, yet he knew her manner would soon change. Madelyne was about to witness his revenge, beginning with the total destruction of her home. No doubt she'd be weeping and begging for mercy before the deed was done.

One of the soldiers hurried over to stand directly before the baron. It was obvious to Madelyne that he was related to her captor, as he had the identical color of blackish-brown hair and the same muscular bearing, though he wasn't nearly as tall. The soldier ignored Madelyne, addressing his leader. "Duncan? Do you give the call or do we stand here all night?"

His name was Duncan. Odd, but hearing his family name did help lessen Madelyne's fear. Duncan . . . aye, the name seemed to make him a little more human in her mind.

"Well, brother?" the soldier demanded then, giving Madelyne their relationship and the reason the baron allowed such an insolent attitude from his vassal.

The soldier, surely a younger brother from his youthful appearance and lack of battle scars, then turned to look at Madelyne. His brown eyes mirrored his contempt for her.

He looked as though he might hit her. Why, the angry soldier even took a step back, as if he wished to put more distance between himself and the leper she had suddenly become.

"Louddon isn't here, Gilard," Duncan told his brother.

The baron's comment was given so mildly, Madelyne was immediately filled with new hope. "Then you will go home, milord?" she asked, turning to look up at him.

Duncan didn't answer her. She would have repeated her question if the vassal hadn't interrupted her by yelling a litany of crude remarks. His gaze was fixed on Madelyne as he spewed forth his frustration. Though Madelyne didn't understand most of the foul comments, she could tell they were sinful just by the frightening look in Gilard's eyes.

Duncan was about to command his brother to cease his childish tirade, when he felt Madelyne take hold of his hand. He was so astonished by her touch, he didn't know how to react.

Madelyne clung to him and he could feel her trembling, yet when he turned to look down at her, she looked composed. She stared at Gilard. Duncan shook his head. He knew his brother hadn't any idea how terrifying he was to Madelyne. In truth, Duncan doubted Gilard would care if he did know.

Gilard's anger suddenly irritated Duncan. Madelyne was his captive, not his opponent, and the sooner Gilard understood how she was to be treated, the better. "Enough!" he demanded. "Louddon's gone. Your curses won't bring him back."

Duncan suddenly jerked his hand away from Madelyne's. He threw his arm around her shoulders, nearly knocking her over in his haste, and then pulled her up against his side. Gilard was so astonished by the obvious show of protection, he could only stare open-mouthed at his brother.

"Louddon must have taken the south road, Gilard, else you would have spotted him," Duncan said.

Madelyne couldn't stop herself from interfering. "And now you'll go home?" she asked, trying not to sound overly eager. "You can challenge Louddon another time," she suggested, hoping to take the sting out of their disappointment.

Both brothers turned to look at her. Neither answered

her, but the look on their faces implied they thought she had a broken mind.

Madelyne's fear began to intensify again. The chilling look in the baron's eyes nearly made her knees snap. She quickly lowered her own gaze until she was staring at his chest, shamed to the core of her soul that she was proving to be so weak in character. "I'm not the crazed one," she muttered. "You could still get away from here without being caught."

Duncan ignored her comment. He grabbed hold of her bound hands and dragged her over to the very post she'd released him from. Madelyne tripped twice, her legs weak with fear. When Duncan finally released her, Madelyne leaned back against the splintered wood, waiting to see what he would do next.

The baron gave Madelyne a long glare. It was an unspoken command to stay there, Madelyne decided. Then he turned until his shoulders blocked her view of his soldiers. His muscular thighs were braced apart and his big hands were fisted on the tilt of his hips. It was a battle stance that clearly challenged his audience. "No one touches her. She is mine." Duncan's powerful voice rang out, washing over his men with as much force as the icy pellets hurling down from above.

Madelyne turned to look at the door to Louddon's castle. Surely Duncan's voice had reached inside, alerting the sleeping soldiers. Yet, when Louddon's men didn't immediately pour into the courtyard, Madelyne decided that the fierce wind must have swept away the baron's voice.

Duncan started to walk away from Madelyne. She reached out and grabbed hold of the back of his hauberk. The circular steel links cut into her fingers. She grimaced in pain, yet wasn't certain if her reaction was caused by the abrasive links or the infuriated look on the baron's face when he turned back to her. He stood so close, his chest was actually touching hers. Madelyne was forced to tilt her head back in order to see his face.

"You don't understand, Baron," Madelyne blurted out. "If you'd only listen to reason, you'd see how foolish this plan of yours is."

"How foolish my plan is?" Duncan repeated, astonished into bellowing by her brash statement. He didn't understand why he wanted to know what she was talking about, but he did. Hell, she'd just insulted him. He would have killed a man for less. Yet the innocent look on her face, and the sincerity in her voice, indicated she wasn't even aware of her transgression.

Madelyne thought Duncan looked as if he wanted to strangle her. She fought the urge to close her eyes against his intimidating stare. "If you came for me, then you've wasted your time."

"You believe your value isn't worthy enough for my attention?" Duncan asked.

"Of course. In my brother's eyes, I have no value. 'Tis a fact I'm well aware of," she added so matter-of-factly, Duncan knew she believed what she said. "And you are certain to die tonight. Aye, you're outnumbered, by at least four to one by my count. There's a second soldier's keep in the bailey below us, with over a hundred soldiers sleeping there. They will hear the fight. What think you of that?" she asked, aware she was now wringing her hands but unable to stop herself.

Duncan stood there, staring at her with a puzzled expression on his face. Madelyne prayed the news she'd just shared with him about the second soldier's keep would force him to see the folly of his plan.

Her prayers were in vain. When the baron finally reacted, it wasn't at all what Madelyne expected. He merely shrugged.

The gesture infuriated her. The foolish warrior was clearly bent on dying.

"It was a false prayer to think you'd walk away from this, no matter what the odds, wasn't it?" Madelyne asked.

"It was," Duncan answered. A warm glint entered his eyes, surprising Madelyne. It was gone before she could even react. Was the baron laughing at her?

She didn't have the courage to ask him. Duncan continued to stare at her another long moment. Then he shook his head, turned, and started to walk toward Louddon's home. He'd obviously decided he'd wasted enough time on her.

There wasn't the least hint of his intent now. Why, he could have been paying a social call if one judged by the mild look on his face and the slow, unhurried pace.

Madelyne knew better. She was suddenly so filled with

dread, she thought she was going to be sick. She could feel the bile rising, burning a path all the way up to her throat. Madelyne took deep, gulping breaths while she frantically worked to undo the knots binding her hands. Panic made the task impossible, for Madelyne had just realized there were servants sleeping inside. She doubted Duncan's soldiers would concern themselves with killing only those armed against them. Louddon certainly wouldn't have made that distinction.

She knew she was going to die soon. That fact couldn't be undone; she was Louddon's sister. But if she could save innocent lives before her own death, wouldn't that act of kindness give her existence some purpose? Dear God, wouldn't saving one person make her life matter . . . to someone?

Madelyne continued to struggle with the rope while she watched the baron. When he reached the steps and turned back to face his men, his true purpose was obvious. Aye, his expression showed his fury.

Duncan slowly raised his sword into the air. And then his voice rang out with such force as to surely penetrate the stone walls surrounding them. His words of purpose were unmistakable.

"No mercy!"

The screams of battle tortured Madelyne. Her mind pictured what she couldn't see, trapping her within a purgatory of obscene thoughts. She had never actually witnessed a battle before, only heard exaggerated tales of cunning and prowess from boasting victorious soldiers. But none of those stories included the descriptions of the killings, and when the fighting soldiers spilled out into the courtyard, Madelyne's mental purgatory turned into a living hell, with the blood of the victims transformed into her captor's fire of revenge.

Although the numbers heavily favored Louddon's men, Madelyne soon realized they were ill prepared to fight Duncan's well-trained soldiers. She watched as one of her brother's soldiers raised his sword against the baron and lost his life because of it, witnessed another eager soldier thrust his lance forward and then stare in stupefaction when both lance and arm were severed from his body. An ear-piercing scream of agony followed the assault as the soldier pitched forward to the ground now soaked with his own blood.

Madelyne's stomach lurched over the atrocities; she closed her eyes to block out the horror, but the images continued to haunt her.

A boy Madelyne thought might have been Duncan's squire ran over to stand next to Madelyne. He had bright yellow hair and was of medium height, and so thick with muscles as to appear fat. He pulled a dagger and held it in front of him.

He paid her little heed, keeping his gaze directed on Duncan, but Madelyne thought he positioned himself to protect her. She had seen Duncan motion to the boy a short time before.

Madelyne desperately tried to focus on the squire's face. He chewed nervously on his bottom lip. She wasn't certain if the action was caused by fear or excitement. And then he suddenly bolted, leaving her unattended again.

She turned to look at Duncan, noticed that he'd dropped his shield, and then watched the squire race over to retrieve it for his lord. In his haste the squire dropped his own dagger.

Madelyne ran over, took hold of the dagger, and then hurried back to the post in case Duncan came for her. She knelt on the ground, her cloak hiding her action, and began to cut the rope binding her hands together. The acrid smell of smoke reached her. She looked up just in time to see a belch of fire explode through the open doorway of the castle. Servants now mingled with fighting men, trying to gain their freedom as they darted toward the gates. The fire chased after them, scorching the air.

Simon, first son of the Saxon reeve and an old man now, made his way over to Madelyne. Tears streamed down his leathered face, his thick shoulders stooped forward with despair. "I thought they'd done you in, milady," he whispered as he helped her to her feet.

The servant took the dagger from her and quickly cut through the rope. Once she was freed, she cupped the sides of his shoulders. "Save yourself, Simon. This battle isn't yours. Hurry now, away from here. Your family needs you."

"But you . . ."

"Go, before it's too late," Madelyne implored him.

Her voice was harsh with fear. Simon was a good godfearing man who had showed her kindness in the past. He was trapped, as were the other servants, by position and heritage, tied by law to Louddon's land, and that was sentence enough for any man to bear. God couldn't be so cruel as to demand his life as well.

"Come with me, Lady Madelyne," Simon begged. "I will hide you."

Madelyne shook her head, denying him. "You have a better chance without me, Simon. The baron would come after me. Please, don't argue," she hurried to add when she saw he was about to protest again. "Go." She screamed the order and gave it additional emphasis when she pushed against Simon's shoulders.

"The Lord protect you," Simon whispered. He handed her the dagger and turned to make his way to the gates. The old man had gotten only a few feet away from his mistress when he was knocked down to the ground by Duncan's brother. Gilard, in his haste to attack another of Louddon's soldiers, accidentally bumped into the servant. Simon made it back to his knees, when Gilard suddenly turned, as if he'd just realized there was another enemy closer at hand.

Gilard's intent was obvious to Madelyne. She screamed a warning and ran over to stand in front of Simon, using her body to shield the servant from Gilard's blade.

"Stand aside," Gilard yelled, his sword raised.

"Nay," Madelyne shouted back. "You'll have to kill me to get to him."

Gilard immediately raised his sword higher, suggesting he'd do just that. His face was mottled with fury. She thought Gilard was more than capable of killing her without suffering a moment's remorse.

Duncan saw what was taking place. He immediately started running toward Madelyne. Gilard's temper was known to be fierce, yet Duncan didn't worry that his brother would harm Madelyne. Gilard would die before breaking a command. Brother or not, Duncan was Baron of Wexton holdings and Gilard his vassal. Gilard would honor that bond. And Duncan had been most specific. Madelyne belonged to him. No one was to touch her. No one.

The other servants, nearly thirty in all, also witnessed what was happening. Those not close enough to freedom hastened over to stand as a group behind Simon for protection.

Madelyne met Gilard's furious stare with a composed expression, a tranquility that belied the destruction going on inside her.

Duncan reached his brother's side just in time to observe Madelyne's bizarre action. His captive slowly lifted her hand to her hair and then pushed the thick mass of curls away from the side of her neck. In a voice that sounded quite calm, she suggested that Gilard thrust his blade there, and if he pleased, to be quick about it.

Gilard looked stunned over Madelyne's reaction to his bluff. He slowly lowered his sword until its bloodied point was facing the ground.

Madelyne's expression didn't change. She turned her attention to Duncan.

"Does your hatred for Louddon extend to his servants? Do you kill innocent men and women because they're bound by law to serve my brother?"

Before Duncan could form an answer, Madelyne turned her back on him. She took hold of Simon's hand and helped him to his feet. "I've heard that Baron Wexton is an honorable man, Simon. Stand beside me. We'll face him together, dear friend."

Turning back to Duncan, she added, "And we shall see if this lord is honorable or if he be no different from Louddon."

Madelyne suddenly realized she held the dagger in her other hand. She hid the evidence behind her back until she felt a tear in the lining of her cloak, and then slipped the knife inside, praying the hem was strong enough to hold it. To cover her action, she shouted, "Every one of these good people has tried to protect me from my brother, and I'll die before I see you touch them. 'Tis your choice."

Duncan's voice was filled with contempt when he answered her challenge. "Unlike your brother, I don't prey on the weak. Go, old man, leave this place. You may take the others with you."

The servants were quick to comply. Madelyne watched

them run to the gates. His show of compassion surprised her. "And now, Baron, I've one more request. Please kill me now. I know I am a coward for asking, but the wait is becoming unbearable. Do what you must."

She believed he meant to kill her. Duncan found himself astonished by her comments once again. He decided that Lady Madelyne was the most puzzling woman he'd ever come across. "I'm not going to kill you, Madelyne," he announced before turning away from her.

A wave of relief washed over Madelyne. She believed Duncan had given her the truth. He'd looked so surprised when she'd asked him to get the foul deed over with . . . aye, he was giving her the truth now.

Madelyne felt victorious for the first time in her life. She'd saved Duncan's life and would live to tell about it.

The battle was finished. The horses had been released from the stables, and chased after the servants through the opened gates seconds before new flames of destruction devoured the brittle wood.

Madelyne couldn't summon up an ounce of outrage over the destruction of her brother's home. It had never belonged to her. There were no happy memories here.

No, there was no feeling outrage. Duncan's revenge was fitting retribution for her brother's sins. Justice was being served this dark night by a barbarian dressed in knight's clothing, a radical to Madelyne's way of thinking, who dared to ignore Louddon's powerful friendship with the King of England.

What had Louddon done to Baron Wexton to warrant such a retaliation? And what price would Duncan have to pay for his rash action? Would William II, upon hearing of this attack, demand Duncan's life? The king was apt to please Louddon if he commanded that action. Louddon's hold on the king was said to be unusual; Madelyne had heard it said that they were special friends. And only last week had she learned what the whispered obscenities really meant. Marta, the stablemaster's outspoken wife, had taken great delight in revealing the vileness of their relationship late one evening, after she'd swallowed too many swigs of ale.

Madelyne hadn't believed her. She'd blushed and denied

it all, telling Marta that Louddon had remained unmarried because the lady he'd given his heart to had died. Marta had scoffed at Madelyne's innocence. She eventually forced her mistress to admit to the possibility.

Until that evening, Madelyne hadn't realized that some men could act intimately with other men, and the realization that one was her brother and the other reported to be the King of England made it all the more repulsive. Her disgust had turned physical; Madelyne remembered she'd thrown up her dinner, giving Marta quite a laugh.

"Burn the chapel." Duncan's order carried throughout the courtyard, pulling Madelyne's thoughts back to the present. She immediately picked up her skirts and ran toward the church, hoping she'd have time to gather her meager possessions before the command was carried out. No one seemed to be paying her any attention.

Duncan intercepted her just when she reached the side entrance. He slammed his hands up against the wall, blocking her on both sides. Madelyne let out a startled gasp and twisted around to look up at him.

"There isn't any place you can hide from me, Madelyne."

His voice was soft. Lord, he sounded almost bored. "I hide from no one," Madelyne answered, trying to keep the anger out of her voice.

"Then you wish to burn with your chapel?" Duncan asked. "Or perhaps you think to use the secret passage you told me about."

"Neither," Madelyne answered. "All of my possessions are inside the church. I was on my way to fetch them. You said you weren't going to kill me and I thought to take my things on my own journey."

When Duncan didn't respond to her explanation, Madelyne tried again. It was difficult to form a coherent thought, however, with Duncan staring at her so intently. "I'll not ask you for a mount, only my clothing from behind the altar."

"You'll not ask?" He whispered the question. Madelyne didn't know how to react to it, or the smile he now gave her. "You truly expect me to believe you've been living in the church?"

Madelyne wished she had enough courage to tell him she

didn't care what he believed. Lord, she was a coward. Yet years of painful lessons in controlling her real feelings served her well now. She gave him a tranquil expression, forcing her anger aside. Why, she even managed to shrug.

Duncan saw the spark of anger ignite in her blue eyes. Such a mockery it was to the serene expression on her face, and so quickly gone, he was convinced he wouldn't have caught it if he hadn't been watching her so intently. She controlled herself with amazing skill for a mere woman.

"Answer me, Madelyne. Do you wish me to believe you've been living in this church?"

"I haven't been living there," Madelyne answered when she couldn't stand his intense stare a second longer. "I only hid my things so that I could make my escape in the morning."

Duncan frowned over her statement. Did she think him daft to believe such a fool's story? No woman would leave the comfort of her home to journey during these harsh months. And where would she have him believe she was going?

He made the swift decision to prove her story false, just to see her reaction when her lie was discovered. "You may get your things."

Madelyne wasn't about to argue over her good fortune. She believed that by giving his approval, Duncan was also agreeing to her own plan to leave the fortress. "Then I may leave this fortress?" She blurted out the assumption before she could stop herself. And Lord, how her voice shook.

"Aye, Madelyne, you will leave this fortress," Duncan agreed.

He actually smiled at her. Madelyne worried about the change in his disposition. She stared up at him, trying to read his mind. A futile undertaking, she quickly realized. Duncan masked his feelings very well, too well for her to decide if he was telling the truth or not.

Madelyne ducked under his arm and ran down the corridor into the back of the church. Duncan was right behind her.

The burlap satchel was just where she'd hidden it the day before. Madelyne lifted the bundle into her arms and then turned to look at Duncan. She was about to offer her

24

gratitude, yet hesitated when she saw the look of surprise on his face again.

"You didn't believe me?" Madelyne asked. Her voice sounded as incredulous as he looked.

Duncan answered her with a scowl. He turned and walked out of the church. Madelyne followed him. Her hands were shaking now, almost violently. Madelyne decided that the horror of the battle she'd witnessed was just settling in. She'd seen so much blood, so many dead. Her stomach and her mind rebelled, and she could only pray she'd be able to maintain her composure until Duncan and his soldiers left.

The moment she cleared the structure, fiery torches were hurled inside. The flames were like hungry bears, devouring the building with savage intensity.

Madelyne watched the fire a good while, until she realized she was clinging to Duncan's hand. She immediately pulled away from him.

She turned and saw that the soldiers' horses had been led inside the inner bailey. Most of Duncan's men were already mounted and waiting for his order. In the center of the courtyard stood the most magnificent of beasts, a huge white stallion, nearly two hands taller than any of the other horses. The blond-haired squire stood directly in front of the animal, trying without much success to keep the reins in his hands. The fiesty animal no doubt belonged to Duncan, a fitting beast for the baron's stature and rank.

Duncan motioned her toward the stallion. Madelyne frowned over his order, yet instinctively started walking toward the big horse. The closer she got, the more frightened she became. In the corner of her confused mind a black thought crystallized.

Dear God, she wasn't going to be left behind.

Madelyne took a deep breath, trying to calm herself. She told herself she was just too distraught to think clearly. Of course the baron wasn't going to take her with him. Why, she wasn't significant enough to bother about.

She decided she still needed to hear his denial. "You don't think to take me with you, do you?" she blurted out. Her voice sounded strained; she knew she hadn't been able to keep the fear out of her voice.

Duncan walked over to Madelyne. He took hold of her

satchel and threw it to his squire. She had her answer then. Madelyne stared up at Duncan, watched him swiftly mount, and then extend his hand down to her.

Madelyne began to back away. God help her, she was going to defy him. She knew if she tried to climb the distance to the top of his demon horse, she'd disgrace herself by fainting, or worse, screaming. In truth, she believed she preferred death to humiliation.

She was more frightened of the stallion than she was of the baron. Madelyne was sadly lacking in her education, and possessed none of the most basic riding skills. Memories of very young days, when Louddon had used those few riding lessons as a tool to inflict submission, still visited her on occasion. As a fully grown woman, she realized her fears were unreasonable, yet the fretful child inside her still rebelled with stubborn, illogical fright.

She took another step back. Then she slowly shook her head, denying Duncan's assistance. Her decision was made; she'd force him to kill her if that was his inclination, but she wasn't going to get on the stallion.

Without a thought as to where she was going, Madelyne turned and walked away. She was trembling so much, she stumbled several times. Panic was building inside until she was almost blinded by it, yet she kept her gaze directed on the ground and continued on, one determined step at a time.

She stopped when she came to the mutilated body of one of Louddon's soldiers. The man's face was horribly disfigured. The sight proved to be Madelyne's breaking point. She stood there, in the center of the carnage, staring at the dead soldier, until she heard a tortured scream echo in the distance. The sound was soul-wrenching. Madelyne put her hands over her ears to try to block out the noise but the action didn't help. The horrible sound went on and on.

Duncan spurred his horse forward the moment Madelyne started screaming. He reached her side, leaned down, and effortlessly lifted her up into his arms.

She stopped screaming when he touched her. Duncan adjusted his heavy cloak until his captive was completely covered. Her face rested against the steel links of his hauberk, yet he took time and attention to pull some of her own cloak forward so that the side of her cheek was cushioned against the soft sheepskin lining.

He didn't question his desire to be gentle with her. The picture flashed before him of Madelyne kneeling in front of him, taking his near-frozen feet under her own gown to give them warmth. It had been an act of kindness, that. He could do no less for her now. After all, he was the one solely responsible for causing Madelyne such pain in the first place.

Duncan let out a long sigh. It couldn't be undone. Hell, it had started out as such an easy plan too. Leave it to a woman to confuse it.

There was much to reevaluate now. Though he knew Madelyne wasn't aware of it, she had certainly complicated the issues. He'd have to sort it all out, he told himself. The plan was changed now, whether he liked it or not, for he knew with a certainty that both amazed and infuriated him, that he'd never let Madelyne go.

Duncan tightened his hold on his captive and finally gave the signal to ride. He remained behind to form the end of the long procession. When the last of his soldiers had cleared the area, and only Gilard and the young squire flanked his side, Duncan took precious minutes to stare at the destruction.

Madelyne tilted her head back so that she could see Duncan's face clearly. He must have felt her looking up at him, for he slowly lowered his gaze until he was staring directly into her eyes.

"An eye for an eye, Madelyne."

She waited for him to tell her more, to explain what her brother had done to cause such a retaliation, but Duncan just continued to stare at her, as if willing her to comprehend. He wasn't going to make any excuses for his ruthlessness. Madelyne understood that now. The victorious didn't need to justify.

Madelyne turned to look at the ruins. She remembered one of the stories told to her by her uncle, Father Berton, about the Punic Wars of ancient times. There were many tales handed down, most of them frowned upon by the holy church, but Father Berton had repeated them to Madelyne all the same, educating her in the most unacceptable fashion, punishable in fact by severe discipline if the church leaders had any inkling as to what the priest was doing.

The carnage she'd witnessed now reminded her of the story of Carthage. During the third and final war between two mighty powers, the victorious had thoroughly destroyed the city once Carthage had fallen. What had not burned to ashes had been buried beneath the fertile ground. Not a stone was allowed to top another. As a final measure, the fields were covered with salt so that nothing would grow there in the future.

History was being repeated this night; Louddon and all that belonged to him was now being desecrated.

"Delenda est Carthago," Madelyne whispered to herself, repeating the vow made so long ago by Cato, an elder of ancient times.

Duncan was surprised by Madelyne's remark. He wondered how she'd ever come by such knowledge. "Aye, Madelyne. Like Carthage, your brother must be destroyed."

"And do I belong to Loud . . . to Carthage as well?" Madelyne asked, refusing to speak her brother's name.

"Nay, Madelyne, you don't belong to Carthage."

Madelyne nodded and then closed her eyes. She sagged against Duncan's chest.

Duncan used his hand to push her chin up, forcing her to look at him again.

"You don't belong to Louddon, Madelyne. From this moment on, you belong to me. Do you understand?"

Madelyne nodded her head.

Duncan released his hold on her when he saw how frightened he was making her. He watched her a moment longer and then slowly, aye, gently, pulled the cloak up over her face.

From her warm hiding place against him, Madelyne whispered, "I think I would rather belong to no man."

Duncan heard her. A slow smile crossed his face. What Lady Madelyne wanted wasn't the least significant to him. Aye, she belonged to him now, whether she wished it or not.

Lady Madelyne had sealed her own fate.

She'd warmed his feet.

Chapter Three

They journeyed into the north, riding hard and fast through the remainder of the night and most of the next day, pausing only twice to give their horses respite from the furious pace the baron set. Madelyne was allowed a few moments privacy, but her legs could barely hold her weight, making the task of seeing to her personal needs an excruciating ordeal, and before she had a chance to stretch her protesting muscles, she was lifted onto Duncan's steed again.

Because there was safety in their large number, Duncan decided to follow the main road. It was a sorry broken path at best, with overgrown thicket and naked branches making the way a continual challenge to the most fit of knights. The men's shields were up most of the time. Madelyne, however, was well protected, safely embraced beneath Duncan's cloak and armor.

The soldiers were well served by their heavy equipment,

save for those who wore the open-faced conicals and rode with bare hands, and the wilderness had little effect on them other than to slow down their progress somewhat.

The torturous ride didn't let up for almost two days. By the time Duncan announced that they would spend the night in a secluded glen he had spotted, Madelyne was firmly convinced he wasn't human. She had heard the men refer to their leader as a wolf and understood the odious parallel well enough; Duncan wore the outline of that terrible beast of prey in his blue and white crest. She fantasized now that her captor's mother must have been a demon from hell and his father a great, ugly wolf, and that was the only reason he could keep up such a grueling, inhuman pace.

By the time they stopped for the night, Madelyne was sick with hunger. She sat on a boulder and watched the soldiers care for their horses. A noble's first concern, Madelyne decided, knowing that without his steed, the knight would be completely ineffective. Aye, the horses came first.

Small fires were started next, with eight to ten men surrounding each, and when all the fires had been ignited, there were at least thirty separate flames, all outlining the weary shoulders of men ready for rest. Last came the food, a meager offering consisting of crusty bread and yellowed cheese. Horns filled with salty-tasting ale were also passed around. Madelyne noticed the soldiers only drank a sparse portion, though. She thought caution might have overridden their desire to indulge, for they would surely need their wits about them this night, camped as they were in a vulnerable position.

There was the ever-present danger of roving bands of men, displaced misfits who had turned into vultures waiting to pounce on anyone weaker than they, and there were wild animals roaming the wilderness, too, with much the same intent.

Duncan's squire was ordered to see to Madelyne's needs. His name was Ansel, and Madelyne could tell from the frown on his face that he had little liking for his assignment.

Madelyne consoled herself with the knowledge that each mile north was a mile closer to her own secret destination. Before Baron Wexton interfered with her plans, Madelyne had been planning for her own escape. She was going to journey into Scotland to her cousin Edwythe's home. She realized she'd been naive to think she was capable of such an undertaking. Aye, she realized her folly now, even admitted that she wouldn't have lasted more than a day or so on her own, riding the only mare in Louddon's stable that wouldn't unseat her. The mare, swaybacked and quite old, wouldn't have had the stamina for such a journey. Without a strong horse and suitable clothing, the escape would have been a form of suicide. And the hastily drawn map from Simon's faulty memory would have led her in circles.

Though she admitted it was a fool's dream, she decided she'd have to hold on to it. Madelyne grasped at the glimmer of hope simply because it was all she had. Duncan surely lived within shouting distance of Scotland's border. How much farther could it be to her cousin's new home? Perhaps she could even walk there.

The obstacles would overwhelm her if she allowed them leverage. Madelyne pushed reason aside and concentrated instead on the list of what she'd need. A capable horse came first, provisions second, and God's blessing last. Madelyne decided she had the order of importance twisted, put God first and horse last, when she caught sight of Duncan moving to the center of the camp. Lord, wasn't he the biggest obstacle of all? Aye, Duncan, part man, part wolf, would be the most difficult obstacle to get around.

Duncan hadn't said one word to her since they'd left Louddon's fortress. Madelyne had worried herself sick over his fiercely made statement that she now belonged to him. And just what was that supposed to mean? She wished she had the courage to demand an explanation. Yet the baron was so cold, so remote now, and much too frightening for her to approach.

Lord, she was exhausted. She couldn't worry about him now. When she was rested, she'd find a way to escape. It was the duty of a captive, wasn't it?

She knew she was unskilled in such matters. What good was it that she could read and write? No one would ever know of her unusual ability, as it was highly unacceptable for a woman to have such schooling. Why, the majority of noblemen could not write their own names. They relied on the holy men to do such meaningless tasks for them.

Madelyne certainly didn't blame her uncle for her lack of

training. The dear priest had taken great pleasure in teaching her all the ancient stories. Her favorite was the tale about Odysseus. The mythological warrior had become Madelyne's companion when she was a young girl and terribly frightened all the time. She'd pretend Odysseus was sitting beside her during the long, dark nights. He helped her ease her fear that Louddon would come and take her back home.

Louddon! Even his black name made her stomach tighten up. Aye, he was the true reason Madelyne lacked all the skills necessary for survival. She couldn't even ride a horse, for God's sake. He was to blame too. Her brother had taken her riding a few times, when she was six years old, and Madelyne still remembered the outings as clearly as if they'd taken place the day before. Why, she'd made such a fool of herself, or so Louddon screamed, bouncing around the saddle like a clump of hay barely tied in place.

And when he realized how frightened she was, he'd tied her to the saddle and slapped the horse into racing through the countryside.

Her terror had excited her brother. It wasn't until Madelyne finally learned to mask her fear that Louddon stopped this sadistic game.

For as long as she could remember, Madelyne knew her father and her brother disliked her, and she tried every way she knew how to make them love her just a little. When she turned eight years old, she was sent to Father Berton, her mother's younger brother, for a short visitation that turned into long, peaceful years. Father Berton was the only living relative on her mother's side of the family. The priest did his best to raise her, and he constantly told her, until she almost believed him, that it was her father and her brother who were lacking, not her.

Oh, her uncle was a good, loving man, whose gentle ways spilled over into Madelyne's character. He taught her many things, none of them tangible, and he did love her, as much as any real father could love his daughter. He explained to her that Louddon despised all women, but in her heart Madelyne didn't believe him. Her brother cared about his older sisters. Both Clarissa and Sara had been sent to fine manors to gain their proper education, and each had an impressive dowry to take to their marriages, although only Clarissa had married.

Father Berton also told Madelyne that her father wanted nothing to do with her because she looked so much like her mother, a gentle woman he'd married and then turned against almost as soon as the vows had been exchanged. Uncle didn't know the reason for her father's change in attitude, but placed the blame on his soul all the same.

Madelyne barely remembered the early years, though a warm feeling filled her when she thought about her mother. Louddon hadn't been there very often to taunt her, and she'd been well protected by her mother's love.

Only Louddon held the answers to her questions. Perhaps he'd explain it all to her one day and then she'd understand. And with understanding would come the healing, wouldn't it?

Lord, I must put these dour thoughts aside, Madelyne decided. She scooted off the boulder and then walked around the campsite, keeping well away from the men.

When she turned and went off into the dense forest, no one followed, and she was able to take care of her body's demands. Madelyne was on her way back when she spotted a small stream. The top was crusted over but Madelyne used a stick to break through the ice. Kneeling down, she washed her hands and her face. The water was frigid enough to make her fingertips wrinkle, but the clear liquid tasted wonderful.

Madelyne felt someone standing behind her. She turned, so quickly she almost lost her balance. It was Duncan towering over her. "Come, Madelyne. 'Tis time to rest."

He didn't give her time to answer his command but reached down and pulled her to her feet. His big, callused hand enveloped both of hers. His hold was firm, yet his touch gentle, and he didn't let go of her until they'd reached the opening of his tent, a strange-looking affair consisting of wild animal skins braced into an arch by thick, unyielding branches. The skins would block the rising wind. Another gray fur had been placed on the ground inside the tent, obviously meant to be used as a pallet. The glow from the nearest fire cast dancing shadows on top of the skins, making the tent look warm and inviting.

Duncan motioned for Madelyne to get inside. She quickly complied. She couldn't seem to get settled though. The animal skins had absorbed much of the ground's dampness and Madelyne felt as if she were draped upon a block of ice.

Duncan stood there, his arms folded against his massive chest, watching her try to get comfortable. Madelyne kept her expression contained. She vowed she'd die before offering him one word of complaint.

All of a sudden Duncan pulled her to her feet again, very nearly upsetting the tent in his haste. He took her cloak from her shoulders, knelt down on one knee, and spread the garment on top of the animal skins.

Madelyne didn't understand his intent. She had thought the tent was for her, but Duncan settled himself inside, stretching out to his full length, taking up most of the space. Madelyne started to turn away, infuriated over the way he'd claimed her cloak for his own comfort. Why hadn't he just left her back at Louddon's fortress if he meant to freeze her to death, instead of dragging her halfway across the world?

She didn't even have time to gasp. Duncan snared her with lightning speed. Madelyne fell on top of him and let out a groan of protest. She'd barely gotten fresh air and new outrage back into her chest before Duncan rolled to his side, taking her with him. He threw his cape over the two of them, trapping her inside his embrace. Her face was up against the base of his neck, the top of her head caught just under his chin.

Madelyne immediately tried to get away, horrified by such an intimate position. She used every ounce of energy she possessed, but Duncan's hold was too strong to be broken.

"I cannot breathe," she muttered against his neck.

"Yes you can," Duncan answered.

She thought she heard amusement in his voice. That infuriated her almost as much as his overbearing attitude. How dare he decide if she could breathe or not?

Madelyne was too upset to be frightened. She suddenly realized her hands were still free of restraint. Madelyne slapped his shoulders until her palms were stinging. Duncan had removed his hauberk before entering the tent. Only a cotton shirt covered his massive chest now. The thin

34

material was stretched snugly over his wide shoulders, outlining his thick muscles. Madelyne could feel the strength radiating through the soft fabric. Lord, there wasn't an ounce of fat to grab hold of and pinch. His skin was as inflexible as his stubborn nature.

There was one distinct difference, however. Duncan's chest felt warm against her cheek, almost hot, and terribly inviting to snuggle up against. He smelled good, too, like leather and male, and Madelyne couldn't help but react. She was exhausted. Aye, that was the reason his closeness was having such an unsettling effect on her. Why, her heart was racing.

His breath heated the side of her neck, comforting her. How could that be? She was so confused; nothing was making sense to her anymore. Madelyne shook her head, determined to shake the sleepy feeling invading her good intentions, and then grabbed hold of his shirt and began to pull on it.

Duncan must have become bored with her struggles. She heard him sigh just seconds before he trapped her hands and slid them under his shirt, flattening her palms against his chest. The thick mat of hair covering his warm skin made her fingertips tingle.

How could she feel so warm when it was so cold outside? His nearness was an erotic, sensual pull to her senses, flooding her with feelings she hadn't known she possessed. Aye, it was erotic, which certainly made it sinful, obscene, too, because his pelvis was smashed up against the junction of her legs. She could feel his hardness there, nestled so intimately against her. Her gown proved inadequate protection against his manhood, and her inexperience gave her no protection at all against the strange, bewildering feelings he provoked. Why didn't she feel sickened by his touch? In truth, Madelyne didn't feel sick at all, only breathless.

A horrid thought entered her mind and she gasped out loud. Wasn't this the hold a man used when he coupled with a woman? Madelyne fretted over that thought a long moment and then discarded the fear. She remembered the woman had to be flat on her back, and though she wasn't certain of the exact way of it, she didn't believe she was in real danger. She'd overheard Marta visiting with the other servants and remembered that the coarse woman had always begun every lusty adventure with the remark that she had been flat on her back. Aye, Madelyne recalled with acute relief, Marta had been most specific. "Flat on me back I was," she always began. Madelyne regretted now that she hadn't stayed to hear the rest of the woman's bold tales.

Lord, she was lacking in that area of her education too. She got angry then, for a decent lady shouldn't have had such a worry anyway.

It was all Duncan's fault, of course. Did he hold her so intimately just to mock her? Madelyne was close enough to feel the strength in his powerful thighs trying to flatten her own. He could crush her if he had a mind for it. Madelyne shivered over that picture and immediately quit her struggles. She didn't want to provoke the barbarian. At least her hands protected her breasts. She was thankful for that much. Her gratitude was short-lived, however, for as soon as she thought to be appreciative, Duncan shifted his weight, and then her breasts were plastered up against him as well. Her nipples hardened, shaming her all the more.

Duncan suddenly moved again. "What the devil . . ." He roared the unfinished question against Madelyne's ear. She didn't know what caused his outburst, only that she was going to be deaf for the rest of her life.

When Duncan jumped, muttering an expletive she couldn't help but catch, Madelyne moved away. She watched Duncan out of the corner of her eye. Her captor had lifted himself up on one elbow and was searching for something underneath him.

Madelyne remembered the squire's dagger she'd hidden in the lining of her cloak just as Duncan lifted the weapon.

She couldn't help but frown.

Duncan couldn't help but grin.

Madelyne was so surprised by his spontaneous smile, she almost smiled back. Then she happened to notice his smile didn't quite reach his eyes. She decided she'd best not smile after all.

"For a timid creature, you're proving to be resourceful, Madelyne."

His voice was so mild. Had he just given her praise or was he mocking her? Madelyne couldn't make up her mind. She decided not to tell him she'd forgotten about the weapon. He'd certainly think her foolish if she admitted that truth.

"You're the one who captured me," she reminded him. "If I've proven to be resourceful, it is only because I am honor bound to escape. 'Tis the duty of a captive."

Duncan frowned.

"Does my honesty offend you, milord?" Madelyne asked. "Then perhaps it would be best if I didn't speak to you at all. I would like to go to sleep now," she added. "And I'm going to try to forget you're even here."

To prove she meant what she said, Madelyne closed her eyes.

"Come here, Madelyne."

The softly issued command sent a tremor of dread down her spine, and a knot settled in the pit of her stomach. He was doing it again, she decided, scaring the breath right out of her. And she was getting sick of it. Madelyne didn't believe there was much fear left inside her. She opened her eyes to look at him, and when she saw the dagger was now pointed in her direction, she realized she still had quite a store of fear left after all.

What a coward I am, Madelyne thought as she slowly moved closer to Duncan. She rested on her side, facing him, just a few inches away.

"There, does that please you?" she said.

She guessed it hadn't pleased him much at all, when she suddenly found herself flat on her back, with Duncan looming over her. Why, he was so close, she could actually see the silver flecks in his gray eyes.

Eyes were supposed to echo the thoughts of the mind, Madelyne had heard, yet she couldn't tell what Duncan was thinking. That worried her.

Duncan watched Madelyne. He was both amused and irritated by the confusion of emotions she unwillingly showed him. He knew she was afraid of him. Yet she didn't weep or plead with him. And Lord, she was beautiful. There was a sprinkle of freckles on the bridge of her nose. Duncan thought the flaw most appealing. Her mouth was appealing too. He wondered how she'd taste to him and could feel himself becoming aroused just by the thought.

"Are you going to stare at me all night?" Madelyne asked.

"Perhaps I will," Duncan answered. "If I wish to," he added, smiling at the way she tried not to frown at him.

"Then I'll have to look at you all night," Madelyne answered.

"And why is that, Madelyne?" His voice was soft and husky.

"If you think to take advantage of me while I sleep, you're mistaken, Baron."

She looked so indignant. "And how will I take advantage of you, Madelyne?"

He was smiling at her now, a true grin it was, reflected in the depths of his eyes.

Madelyne wished she'd kept silent. Lord, she was putting obscene ideas into his head.

"I'd rather not discuss this issue," she stammered out. "Aye, forget I said anything, if you please."

"But I don't please," Duncan answered. "Do you think I'll satisfy my lust this night and take you while you rest?"

Duncan lowered his head until he was just a scant breath away from Madelyne's face. He was pleased to see her blush, even grunted his approval.

Madelyne was as still as a doe, trapped by her own worries.

"You wouldn't touch me," she suddenly blurted out. "Surely you're too tired to think of such . . . and we are camped out in the open . . . nay, you wouldn't touch me," she ended.

"Perhaps."

And just what did that mean? She saw the mysterious gleam in his eye. Was he gaining true pleasure over her obvious distress.

She decided she wasn't going to be taken advantage of without giving him a good fight. With that thought in mind, she struck him, aiming her fist just below his right eye. Her mark was true, but she thought she received more pain than he did. She was the one who cried out in pain. Duncan didn't even flinch. Lord, she'd probably broken her hand and all for nothing.

"You are made of stone," Madelyne muttered.

"Why did you do that?" Duncan asked, his tone curious.

"To let you know I'll fight you to the death if you try to have your way with me," Madelyne stammered. She thought it was a brave speech, but the force of it was ruined by her shaky voice. She sighed, discouraged.

Duncan smiled again. "To the death, Madelyne?"

From the horrible look on his face, Madelyne decided he found the idea pleasing.

"You jump to conclusions," Duncan commented. "'Tis a flaw, that."

"You threatened," Madelyne countered. "'Tis a bigger flaw, that."

"Nay," he argued. "You suggested."

"I'm sister of your enemy," Madelyne reminded him, pleased by the frown her reminder provoked. "You can't change that fact," she added for good measure.

The tension went right out of her shoulders. She should have thought of that argument sooner.

"But with my eyes closed, I'll not know if you're Louddon's sister or not," Duncan said. "It's rumored that you lived with a defrocked priest and that you played the whore for him. Yet in the dark, that wouldn't bother me. All women are the same when it comes to bedding."

She wished she could hit him again. Madelyne was so outraged over such evil gossip, her eyes filled with tears. She wanted to scream at him, to tell him that Father Berton was in good standing with his God and his church, and that he happened to be her uncle as well. The priest was the only one who cared about her. The only one who loved her. How dare Duncan stain her uncle's reputation?

"Who told you these stories?" Madelyne asked, her voice a hoarse whisper.

Duncan could see how his words wounded her. He knew then that all the stories were just as he suspected. False. Madelyne couldn't hide her pain from him. Besides, he'd already recognized her innocence.

Madelyne was shattered by his malicious words. "Do you think I'm going to try to convince you that the gossip you've heard about me isn't true?" she asked. "Well, think again, Baron. Believe what you will. If you think I'm a whore, then whore I am."

Her outburst was vehement, the first real display of anger Duncan had witnessed since taking her captive. He found himself mesmerized by those incredible blue eyes, flashing with such indignation. Aye, she was innocent all right.

He decided to end their conversation so that Madelyne would be saved further distress. "Go to sleep," he commanded her.

"How can I sleep with the fear you'll take advantage of me during the night?" she asked.

"Do you actually think you'd be able to sleep through it?" Duncan asked. His voice sounded incredulous. Lord, she'd insulted him, yet he realized she was too naive to know it. Duncan shook his head. "If I decide to take advantage of you, as you describe it, I promise to wake you first. Now close your eyes and go to sleep."

He pulled Madelyne into his arms, forcing her back up against his chest. His arm circled her in an intimate way, resting against the swell of her breasts. And then he threw the cloak over both of them, determined to dismiss her from his mind.

It was easier said than done. The scent of roses clung to Madelyne, and she felt so soft against him. Her nearness all but intoxicated him. Duncan knew it would be a long while before sleep claimed him.

"What would you call it?" Madelyne's question came to him from beneath the cover. Her voice was muffled but he caught every word. Duncan had to recount their conversation before he thought he understood what she was asking him.

"Taking advantage?" he asked, clarifying her question.

He felt her nod. "Rape." Duncan muttered the foul word against the top of her head.

Madelyne jerked upward, hitting his chin in her haste. Duncan's patience was wearing thin. He decided he never should have spoken to her. "I have never forced myself on any woman, Madelyne. Your virtue is safe enough. Now, go to sleep."

"Never?" Madelyne whispered her question.

"Never!" Duncan shouted his answer.

Madelyne believed him. Odd, but she felt safe now and knew he wouldn't harm her while she slept. His nearness was starting to comfort her again.

She was soon drugged sleepy by his warmth. She snuggled closer to Duncan, heard him groan when she wiggled her backside against him to get more comfortable, and wondered what was bothering him now. When he grabbed hold of her hips and held them still, she assumed her movement was keeping him awake.

Her shoes had fallen off and she slowly slipped her feet between Duncan's calves to gain more of his heat. She was careful not to wiggle too much for fear she'd irritate him again.

His warm breath heated the side of her neck. Madelyne closed her eyes and sighed. She knew she should resist the temptation, but his warmth pulled at her, lulled her. She remembered one of her favorite stories about Odysseus and his adventures with the Sirens. Aye, Duncan's warmth wooed her just like the song those mythological nymphs sang to lure Odysseus and his soldiers to certain destruction. Odysseus had outwitted the Sirens by stuffing wax into the men's ears to block out the irresistible sound.

Madelyne wished she were as clever and resourceful as the epic warrior.

The wind whistled and moaned a forlorn tune around her, but Madelyne was well protected, held tightly in the arms of her captor. She closed her eyes and accepted the truth then. The Siren's song had captured her.

She awakened only once during the night. The back of her was warm enough, but her chest and arms were freezing. Ever so slowly, so as not to disturb Duncan, Madelyne turned in his arms. She cushioned the side of her cheek on his shoulder and slipped her hands beneath his shirt.

She wasn't completely awake, and when Duncan began to rub his chin against her forehead, Madelyne sighed with contentment and snuggled closer. His whiskers tickled her nose. Madelyne tilted her head back and slowly opened her eyes.

Duncan was watching her. His expression was unguarded, so warm and tender. His mouth looked hard though; she wondered what it would feel like if he kissed her.

Neither said a word, but when Madelyne moved toward Duncan, he met her halfway.

Madelyne tasted as good as he knew she would. God, she was soft, inviting. She wasn't completely awake and therefore didn't resist him, though her mouth wasn't opened enough for him to penetrate. Duncan solved that problem quickly by forcing her chin down with his thumb, and then thrust his tongue inside before Madelyne could guess his intent.

He caught her gasp and gave her his groan.

When Madelyne timidly used her own tongue to stroke his, Duncan rolled her to her back, settling himself between her legs. His hands cupped the sides of her face, holding her still for his tender assault.

Madelyne's hands were trapped under Duncan's shirt. Her fingers began to caress his chest, teasing his skin into a fever.

Duncan wanted to learn all her secrets, to satisfy himself, then and there, and all because Madelyne was so wonderfully responsive.

The kiss turned so hot, so consuming, Duncan knew he was in danger of losing control. His mouth slanted over Madelyne's again and again, his tongue penetrating, stroking, taking. God, he couldn't seem to get enough of her.

It was the most incredible kiss he'd ever experienced, and he wouldn't have stopped if she hadn't started trembling. A soft whimper came from deep in her throat. The sensual sound nearly pushed reason aside.

Madelyne was too stunned to react when Duncan abruptly pulled away from her. He rested on his back, with his eyes closed, and the only indication he gave of their kiss was his harsh, uneven breathing.

Madelyne didn't know what to do. Lord, she was so ashamed of herself. Whatever had come over her? She'd acted so wanton, so . . . common. And she could tell from the frown on Duncan's face that she hadn't pleased him.

Madelyne felt like weeping.

"Duncan?" She thought her voice sounded as if she were already crying.

He didn't answer, but his sigh told her he'd heard her call his name.

"I'm sorry."

He was so surprised by her apology, he turned back to his side to look at her. The ache in his loins was painful and he couldn't keep the scowl from his face.

"Sorry for what?" he demanded, irritated that his voice sounded so harsh.

He knew he'd frightened her again, because Madelyne immediately turned her back to him. She was shaking enough for Duncan to notice too. He was about to reach out and pull her back into his arms, when she finally answered him.

"For taking advantage of you."

He couldn't believe what he'd just heard. It was the most ridiculous apology he'd ever been given.

A slow smile overcame Duncan's scowl. Lord, he felt like laughing now, would have given in to the urge, too, if Madelyne hadn't sounded so damn sincere. His desire to guard her feelings kept his laughter contained, however. Duncan didn't understand his reason for wanting to protect her feelings, but it was there, nagging at him.

He let out a long-drawn-out groan. Madelyne heard him and immediately jumped to the conclusion that he was thoroughly disgusted with her. "I promise you, Duncan, it won't happen again."

Duncan put his arm around Madelyne's waist and pulled her up against him. "And I promise you that it will, Madelyne."

She thought it sounded like a vow.

Chapter Four

Evil is the man who has known honor and discarded it.

Baron Louddon was only a half day's hard ride from where Duncan and his soldiers were camped. Luck was on Louddon's side, for he was able to ride during the night hours by the light of a full, bright moon. His soldiers equaled Duncan's men in loyalty and numbers, and not one complained over this sudden turnabout in plans.

A half-mad servant had chased them down to give them the news of Duncan's foul deed. They had all returned to Louddon's fortress then. All had witnessed the message left by Baron Wexton. Aye, all had seen the mutilated bodies of those soldiers left behind to guard Louddon's domain. The men joined together in outrage and vengeance, and every one of them vowed to be the one to kill Duncan.

The fact that they had all joined with Louddon and acted with treachery toward Baron Wexton was ignored now; they concentrated, instead, on avenging their leader.

Louddon had been quick to decide to go after Duncan.

His reason was twofold. Foremost was the realization that his own plan to destroy Baron Wexton by dishonorable means would be unveiled, making him a coward to be ridiculed in court. Duncan would alert William II, and the king, though he favored Louddon, would nevertheless be forced to issue a battle to the death between the adversaries in order to end what he'd probably deem a petty difference of opinion. The king, called Rufus, the Red, because of his fiery face and disposition, would certainly be irritated over the squabble. Louddon knew, too, that if he had to face Duncan alone on a field of battle, he'd come out the loser. Baron Wexton was an invincible warrior who had shown his ability countless times. Aye, Duncan would kill him if given the chance.

Louddon was a well-skilled man, yet it was in areas that would give him little aid against the likes of Duncan. Louddon was a power to be reckoned with in court. He acted the role of secretary of sorts, though he couldn't read or write and left those mundane matters to the two priests in residence. When the king was holding court, Louddon's primary duty was to sort out those who had true business with the king, and those who didn't. It was a powerful position. Louddon was a master manipulator. He instilled fear into those lesser-titled men who willingly paid for the opportunity to speak to their king. He paved the way for these eager men, lining his pockets with their gold.

Now, if his attempt to kill Duncan became known, he could lose everything.

Madelyne's brother was considered to be a handsome man. Blond hair with nary a crinkle of curl to mar the shine, hazel eyes with chips of gold, tall as well, though reed-thin, with perfectly sculptured lips. And when he smiled, the ladies at court all but swooned. Louddon's sisters, Clarissa and Sara, shared the same color of wheat-white hair and hazel eyes. They were almost as pretty as Louddon was, and just as sought after.

Louddon was known as a most available bachelor and could have his pick of any woman in England. He didn't want just any woman though. He wanted Madelyne. His stepsister was the second reason Louddon chased after Duncan. Madelyne had returned home to him only two months past, and after having forgotten her for most of her growing years, he'd been given a shock when he saw the remarkable changes in her appearance. She'd been such an ugly child. Large blue eyes had swallowed up most of her face. Her lower lip had been too full, her expression set to pouting most of the time, and she'd been so skinny as to look sickly. Aye, Madelyne had been such an awkward child, with long, bony legs that caused her to stumble whenever she tried to curtsy.

Louddon had certainly misjudged her potential. In childhood there had been no sign in her appearance suggesting she might one day look so much like her mother. Madelyne had turned from embarrassment to beauty, so lovely, in fact, as to outshine her stepsisters.

Who would have thought such a miracle could happen? The timid caterpillar had changed into a lovely butterfly. Louddon's friends also had been quite speechless when they'd first seen her. Morcar, Louddon's closest confidant, had even begged him for Madelyne's hand in marriage, putting pounds of gold in front of his petition.

Louddon didn't know if he could let Madelyne go to another man. She was so like her mother. When he first saw her, he'd reacted physically. It was the first such stirring for a woman in so many years, Louddon was all but undone by it. Only Madelyne's mother had been able to affect him in such a way. Ah, Rachael, the love of his heart. She had ruined him for other women. He couldn't have Rachael now; his temper had stolen her from him. Louddon had believed his obsession would end with her death. A foolish hope, he now admitted. No, the obsession lived on. Madelyne. His stepsister could well be his second chance at proving himself a man.

Louddon was a man tormented. He couldn't decide between his greed and his lust. He wanted Madelyne for his own use, but wanted the gold she'd bring too. Perhaps, he thought, if he was shrewd enough, he could have both.

Madelyne awakened in the most awkward position. She was on top of Duncan. The side of her face rested on his hard, flat stomach, her legs were entwined with his, and her hands were wedged between his thighs.

Because of her sleepy state of mind, Madelyne didn't immediately realize exactly where her hands were resting.

46

Duncan felt so warm, though . . . so hard. Oh, Lord, her hands were snuggled against the most private part of him.

Madelyne's eyes flew open. She tensed against her captor, not daring to even breathe. Let him be sleeping, she prayed frantically as she slowly edged her hands away from his heat.

"So you're finally awake."

Duncan knew he'd given her a fright when she jerked against him. Her hands slammed into the junction of his legs. Duncan groaned in reaction. Hell, she'd make him a eunuch if he gave her half the chance.

Madelyne rolled to her side, daring a quick look up at Duncan. She thought she probably should apologize for accidentally bumping him there, but then he'd know she was quite aware of just where her hands had been, wouldn't he?

Oh, heavens, she could feel herself blushing. And Duncan was frowning again this morning. He didn't look disposed to listening to any apology she made anyway, so she put the worry aside.

He looked ferocious. Aye, the new growth of dark brown beard actually made him look more like a wolf than a man, and he was watching her with a curiosity she found unnerving. His hands continued to span her back. She remembered then how he'd warmed her throughout the night. He could have just as easily harmed her. Madelyne realized she was trying to encourage her fear of him, yet was honest enough to admit that the truth was really quite the opposite. Oh, Duncan did frighten her, but not in the same way Louddon did.

Today was the first time in weeks, since she'd returned to her brother's home in fact, that she hadn't awakened with a sick knot of fear lodged in her stomach. She knew the reason too; it was because Louddon wasn't there.

Duncan wasn't like Louddon at all. Nay, a man who wished to inflict cruelty certainly wouldn't have shared his warmth while they slept. And he'd kept his word too. He hadn't taken advantage . . . dear God, she'd kissed him. She suddenly remembered every bit of it with a clarity that sent her pulse racing.

Thank the Lord she'd learned to hide her feelings. Madelyne was certain her expression wasn't giving her horrible thoughts away. That was a bit of grace, wasn't it? Aye, she thought with a little sigh. Duncan couldn't possibly know what she was thinking.

Duncan watched Madelyne, secretly amused by the way she showed him one emotion after another. Her eyes gave her away; in the past few minutes he'd seen fear, embarrassment, and, he thought, relief as well.

He was a man conditioned to finding the flaws in others. As a warrior, knowing what was in his opponent's mind quickened his own reactions. He had also learned to find out what his enemy most valued. And then he would take it away. It was the way of fighting men, yet those lessons had spilled over into his personal relationships as well. It wasn't possible to separate the two. And though Madelyne was unaware of it, she'd already given him important hints about her character. She was a woman who valued control. Keeping her emotions hidden seemed an important quest. Madelyne had already shown him that not all women were ruled by their emotions. Only once during the destruction of her home did she show any outward reaction. She'd screamed in anguish when she saw the mutilated body of Louddon's vassal. Yet Duncan doubted Madelyne even knew she'd lost control.

Aye, Duncan was learning all of Madelyne's secrets, and what he'd learned thus far perplexed him. God's truth, she pleased him too.

Duncan moved away from Madelyne, else the urge to take her back into his arms and kiss her again would become too strong to ignore. He was suddenly very eager to get home. He wouldn't feel at ease until he had Madelyne safely protected behind the walls of his fortress.

Duncan stood, stretched his muscles awake, and then walked away from Madelyne, all but dismissing her from his mind. The sun was climbing into the milky clouds above, clouds that would surely block any heat to melt the night's frost covering the ground. There was much to do before the light was sufficient for their journey. Though the new day was already bitter with chill, the wind was mild enough to please Duncan.

Madelyne knew they'd ride soon. She put on her shoes, brushed the dirt from her gown, and wrapped her cloak around her shoulders. She knew she looked a sight and decided she'd have to do something about it.

Madelyne went in search of Ansel. The squire was readying Duncan's stallion. Madelyne asked him where her satchel was, though she stood a safe distance from the great beast and had to yell her question, and then thanked the boy profusely when he threw the bag over to her.

She was only going to wash the sleep from her eyes, but the clear water was too tempting. Madelyne used the scented soap she'd packed in her satchel to give herself a quick bath and then changed her gown.

Lord, it was cold. Madelyne was shivering by the time she finished dressing. She wore a pale yellow ankle-length chainse with a rich gold-colored knee-length bliaut over it. A band of royal blue needlework circled the long sleeves of the tunic.

Madelyne repacked her satchel and then knelt down by the stream and began to brush the tangles from her hair. Now that she was rested, and her mind wasn't consumed with fear, she had plenty of time to think about her situation. The uppermost question was to find out why Duncan had taken her with him. He had told her she belonged to him. Madelyne didn't understand what he had meant by that remark, yet was too timid to ask him to explain.

Gilard came to fetch Madelyne. She heard his approach and turned in time to watch his approach.

"It's time to ride," Gilard bellowed. The force of his voice nearly pushed her into the water. Gilard hastily reached out and yanked her to her feet, inadvertently saving her from disgrace.

"I've still to plait my hair, Gilard. Then I'll be ready. And you really needn't shout at me," she added, deliberately keeping her voice soft. "My hearing is actually quite good."

"Your hair? You've still to . . ." Gilard was too stunned to continue. He gave Madelyne a look that suggested she'd lost her mind. "You're our captive, for God's sake," he finally managed to stammer out.

"I had surmised as much," Madelyne answered. She sounded as serene as the morning breeze. "But does that mean I may or may not finish arranging my hair before we ride?"

"Are you trying to goad me?" Gilard shouted. "Lady Madelyne, you're in a tenuous position at best. Are you too simpleminded to realize it?"

Madelyne shook her head. "Why are you so angry with me? You shout every word. Is it your usual custom, or is it because I'm Louddon's sister?"

Gilard didn't immediately answer. His face turned a blotchy red though. Madelyne knew she was infuriating him. She was sorry for it, yet decided to continue to bait him all the same. Gilard obviously lacked control over his temper, and if she could nudge him enough, perhaps he'd tell her what was going to happen to her. Gilard was much easier to understand than his brother. And so much easier to manipulate, if she was clever enough.

"Why was I taken captive?" she blurted out. The bluntness of her question made her wince. She hadn't been very clever after all, and was therefore quite surprised when Gilard actually answered her.

"Your brother set the terms of this war, Madelyne. You know that well enough."

"I don't know anything well enough," Madelyne protested. "Explain it to me, if you please. I would like to understand."

"Why do you play the innocent with me?" Gilard demanded. "Everyone in England knows what has taken place over the past year."

"Not everyone, Gilard," Madelyne returned. "I only just returned to my brother's home two months ago. And I lived in a most isolated area for many years."

"Aye, that is right," Gilard sneered. "Lived with your defrocked priest, I understand."

Madelyne could feel her composure slipping. She wanted to scream at the arrogant vassal now. Did everyone in England believe that horrible rumor?

"Very well," Gilard announced. He seemed ignorant of Madelyne's fury now. "I will tell you all the truths, and then you'll not be able to pretend any longer. Louddon's soldiers attacked two holdings belonging to Duncan's loyal vassals. In each attack there was needless slaughter of women and children. The vassals weren't given any warning either; your brother pretended friendship until his men were inside the fortresses."

"Why? Why would Louddon do such a thing? What could he hope to gain?"

She tried not to show how appalled she was by Gilard's words. Madelyne knew her brother was capable of such treachery, yet couldn't understand his motive. "Surely Louddon knew that Duncan, as overlord, would retaliate."

"Aye, that was his hope, Madelyne. He's been trying to kill Duncan," he added with an obscene laugh. "Your brother is greedy for power. He has only to fear one other man in England. Duncan. They are equal in power. Louddon is known to have the king's ear, true, but Duncan's soldiers are the fittest warriors in all the world. The king values my brother's loyalty as much as he values Louddon's friendship."

"The king allowed this treachery?" Madelyne asked.

"William refuses to act without proof," Gilard answered. His voice sounded his disgust. "He defends neither Louddon nor Duncan. I can promise you this, Lady Madelyne. When our king returns from Normandy, he'll not be able to evade the problem any longer."

"Then Duncan hasn't been able to act on his vassals' behalf?" Madelyne asked. "That is the reason my brother's home was destroyed instead?"

"You're naive if you believe Duncan didn't retaliate. He ousted the bastards from his vassals' holdings immediately."

"In kind, Gilard?" Madelyne whispered her question. "Did Duncan also kill the innocent as well as the guilty?"

"Nay," Gilard answered. "The women and children were left alone. We Wextons aren't butchers, Madelyne, regardless of what your brother has told you. And our men don't hide behind false colors when they attack either."

"Louddon has told me nothing," Madelyne protested again. "You forget that I am only a sister. I'm not worthy enough to be privy to his thoughts." Her shoulders sagged. Lord, there was so much to think over, so much to reason out. "What will happen if the king takes Louddon's side? What will happen to your brother?"

Gilard heard the fear in her voice. Why, she was acting as though she cared about Duncan. That made little sense, considering her position as captive. Lady Madelyne would confuse him if he allowed it. "Duncan is a man of little patience, and when your brother dared to touch a Wexton, he sealed his fate. My brother won't wait for the king to return to England so that he can command a battle to the death with your bastard brother. Nay, Duncan is going to kill Louddon, with or without the king's blessing."

"What do you mean when you say Louddon touched a Wexton?" Madelyne asked. "There was another Wexton brother and Louddon killed him?" she surmised.

"Ah, so you pretend you know nothing about Adela either, is that the way of this game?" Gilard demanded.

A knot of dread settled in Madelyne's stomach, for she'd caught the frightening look in Gilard's eyes. "Please," she whispered, her head bowed against his hatred, "I must know all of this. Who is Adela?"

"Our sister."

Madelyne's head jerked up. "You would war because of a sister?" she asked.

She looked quite astonished. Gilard didn't know what to make of such a reaction. "Our sister went to court, and while she was there, Louddon caught her alone. He raped her, Madelyne, and beat her so brutally it is a miracle she survived. Her body has healed, but her mind is broken."

Madelyne's composure snapped. She turned her back on Gilard so he wouldn't see the tears streaming down her cheeks. "I'm so sorry, Gilard," she whispered.

"And you believe what I've just told you?" Gilard demanded, his voice harsh. He wanted to make certain Lady Madelyne wouldn't be able to deny the truth any longer.

"A part of this story, aye," Madelyne answered. "Louddon is capable of beating a woman to death. I do not know if he could rape a woman, though, but if you say it is the truth, I will believe you. My brother is an evil man. I'll not give him my defense."

"Then what is it you don't believe?" Gilard asked, back to shouting again.

"You make me think you value your sister," Madelyne confessed. "That is the confusion."

"What in God's name are you talking about?"

"Do you rage against me because Louddon dishonored the Wexton name or because you actually love your sister?"

Gilard was enraged by such an obscene question. He grabbed hold of Madelyne and jerked her around to face him. His hands painfully gripped her shoulders. "Of course I love my sister," he shouted. "An eye for an eye, Madelyne. We have taken away from your brother that which he most values. You! He'll come after you, and when he does, he'll die."

"So I am responsible for my brother's sins?"

"You are a pawn to draw the demon out," Gilard answered.

"There is a flaw in this plan," Madelyne whispered. Her voice sounded with shame. "Louddon won't come after me. I'm not significant enough to him."

"Louddon isn't a fool," Gilard said, infuriated because he suddenly realized Madelyne meant what she said.

Neither Madelyne nor Gilard heard Duncan approach. "Take your hands off her, Gilard. Now!"

Gilard was quick to comply, even took a step back, putting distance between himself and their captive.

Duncan started toward his brother, intending to find out why Madelyne was weeping. He let Gilard see how furious he was.

Madelyne placed herself between the two brothers. She faced Duncan. "He didn't harm me," she said. "Your brother was only explaining how I am to be used. That is all."

Duncan could see the pain in Madelyne's eyes, yet before he could question her, she turned, picked up her satchel, and then added, "'Tis time to ride."

She tried to walk through Gilard to get back to their camp. Duncan watched his brother hurry to get out of Madelyne's way.

The younger brother was looking worried. "She wants me to believe she's not guilty," he muttered.

"Did Madelyne tell you that?" Duncan asked.

"Nay, she didn't," Gilard admitted with a shrug. "She didn't defend herself at all, Duncan, but she acted so damn innocent. Hell, I don't understand. She seemed surprised that we would care about our sister. I think it was a true reaction too. Why, she actually asked me if we valued Adela."

"And when you answered her?" Duncan asked.

"She seemed all the more perplexed. I don't understand her," Gilard muttered. "The sooner this plan is seen through, the better. Lady Madelyne isn't at all what I expected her to be."

"She is a contradiction," Duncan acknowledged. "God's truth, she doesn't understand her own value." He sighed over his observations and then said, "Come, the hour grows old. We'll be home by nightfall if we make haste."

Gilard answered the command with a nod and fell into step beside his brother.

On her way back to camp, Madelyne decided she wasn't going anywhere. She stood in the center of the clearing, her cloak wrapped around her shoulders. Ansel had taken her satchel and she hadn't argued with the squire. She didn't care if her baggage went with Duncan. God's truth, she didn't think she cared about anything anymore. She just wanted to be left alone.

Duncan started toward the squire, wanting to finish his battle dress. He motioned for Madelyne to get on his stallion, then continued on. He suddenly stopped and slowly turned back to look at Madelyne, however, disbelieving what he thought he'd seen.

She told him no again. Duncan was so amazed by her show of defiance, he didn't immediately react. Madelyne shook her head a third time and then abruptly turned and started to walk back into the forest.

"Madelyne!"

Duncan's roar stopped her. She instinctively turned to look at him, praying inside for the courage to defy him again.

"Get on my horse. Now."

They stared at each other a long, silent moment. Madelyne then realized everyone else had paused in his duties and was watching. Duncan wouldn't back down in front of his men. The way he was staring at her told her that much.

Madelyne picked up her skirts and hurried over to stand directly in front of Duncan. The men might be watching, but if she kept her voice soft, they wouldn't be able to hear what she said to their leader.

"I'm not going with you, Duncan. And if you weren't so .stubborn, you'd realize Louddon won't come after me. You're wasting your time. Leave me here."

"To survive in the wilderness?" Duncan asked, his voice

just as whisper-soft as hers had been. "You wouldn't last an hour."

"I've survived worse situations, milord," Madelyne answered, straightening her shoulders. "My decision's made, Baron. I'm not going with you."

"Madelyne, if a man were to deny my order the way you just have, he wouldn't live long enough to boast of it. And when I give a command, I expect it to be carried out. Don't dare shake your head at me again, else I'll backhand you to the ground in retaliation."

It was a distasteful bluff on Duncan's part, and he regretted it as soon as the words were out of his mouth. He was gripping her arm, knew that he was inadvertently hurting her when she grimaced in pain. He let go immediately, fully expecting her to run as fast as she could to do his bidding.

Madelyne didn't move. She stared up at him, that grand composure back on her face, and calmly said, "I'm used to being knocked to the ground, so do your worst. And when I regain my feet, you may strike me down again if that is your wish."

Her words disturbed him. He knew she was telling the truth. He frowned, infuriated that someone had dared to mistreat her and knew, in his heart, that Louddon was the one who'd meted out the punishment. "Why would your brother—"

"'Tis not important," Madelyne interrupted before Duncan could finish his question. She was sorry now she'd said anything. Madelyne didn't want sympathy or pity. All she wanted was to be left alone.

Duncan sighed. "Get on my horse, Madelyne."

Her temporary bluster of courage deserted her when she saw the muscle in the side of Duncan's cheek flex. The movement accentuated his clenched jaw.

Duncan made a low, growling sound deep in his throat, venting his frustration. He turned her until she was facing the area where his stallion was tethered and gave her a gentle push. "You've given me yet another reason to kill Louddon," he whispered.

Madelyne started to turn around to ask Duncan to explain his remark, but the look in his eyes suggested his patience had worn thin. She accepted the fact that she'd lost this argument. Duncan was determined to take her with him, no matter what she said or did.

She let out a long, sorry sigh and then started to walk toward Duncan's horse. Most of the soldiers still hadn't resumed their tasks. They all watched Madelyne. She tried to appear serene. Inside, her heart was beating fast enough to burst. Though the fear of Duncan's temper weighed heavily upon her peace of mind, there was a greater immediate concern that pricked her now. Duncan's beast. It was one thing to be grabbed and thrown on top of the huge ugly monster, and quite another to mount without aid.

"What a coward I am," Madelyne muttered to herself. She copied Father Berton now, for he often spoke to himself, remembered, too, that he once told her no one was more interested in what he had to say than himself. Madelyne actually smiled over that fond remembrance.

"Oh, Father, if you could see me now, how ashamed you'd be. I've a demon horse to mount and will surely disgrace myself."

The irony of her worry finally penetrated her fear. "Why am I worried about disgracing myself, when Duncan's horse is going to trample me to death? What will I care if they think I'm a coward? I'll already be dead."

Her argument helped lessen her fear. Madelyne was beginning to calm down a little, until she noticed the stallion appeared to be watching her. The animal didn't like what he saw, either, Madelyne concluded, when he began to stomp the ground with his front paws. He even snorted at her. The stupid horse had taken on all the odious characteristics of his master, Madelyne decided.

She gathered her courage and walked over to the stallion's side. He didn't like that much and actually tried to nudge her away with his hind flank. Madelyne reached up to grab hold of the saddle, but the horse let out such a whinny, she jumped back.

Madelyne put her hands on her hips in exasperation. "You're bigger than I am, but certainly not as intelligent." She was pleased to see the horse actually glanced at her. She knew he couldn't possibly understand what she was saying, but it made her feel better all the same just to have his attention.

She smiled at the beast while she timidly edged her way to the front.

Once she faced the animal, she pulled on the reins, forcing his head down. And then she began to whisper to him, her voice low, soothing, as she carefully explained her fears. "I've never learned the way of riding and that is why I'm so afraid of you. You're so strong, you could trample me. I've not heard your master call you by name, but if you belonged to me, I'd call you Silenus. 'Tis the name of one of my favorite gods from the old stories. Silenus was one of the mighty spirits of nature, wild and untamed, very like yourself. Aye, Silenus is a fitting name for you."

When she'd finished her one-sided conversation, Madelyne let go of the reins. "I've been ordered by your master to climb upon your back, Silenus. Please stand still, for I'm still very afraid of you."

Duncan had finished his dress. He stood across the clearing now, watching with growing astonishment as Madelyne talked to his horse. He couldn't hear what she was saying. Lord, she was trying to gain the saddle from the wrong side. He started to shout a warning, certain his horse would bolt, but the words wedged in his throat when he saw Madelyne seat herself on the top of the huge animal. It was all incorrect and certainly strange. He had to sigh over it. Now he understood why Madelyne clung to him when they rode together. She was frightened of his horse. He wondered if her ridiculous fear was confined to his stallion or to all horses.

The skittish stallion hadn't moved a muscle to disrupt Madelyne's awkward climb into the saddle. And damn if she didn't lean down and say something else to the animal once she was settled.

"Did you see what I just saw?" Gilard asked the question from behind Duncan's back.

Duncan nodded but didn't turn around. He continued to stare at Madelyne, a smile catching the corners of his mouth.

"Who do you suppose taught her how to ride?" Gilard asked, shaking his head in amusement. "She doesn't seem to possess the least amount of skill."

"No one taught her," Duncan commented. "That much is

obvious, Gilard. Odd, but my horse doesn't seem out of sorts over Madelyne's lack of education." He shook his head then and began to walk toward the lady under discussion.

The young squire, Ansel, approached Madelyne from the opposite direction. He had a snicker on his freckled face and began to lecture Madelyne on her inferior abilities. "You're to mount on the left," he said with great authority. He took hold of Madelyne's hand, as if he would pull her to the ground so that she could remount correctly. The stallion began to prance just as Duncan appeared. Ansel's hand went flying, as did the rest of his body.

"Don't ever touch her again." Duncan's roar followed Ansel to the ground. The squire quickly regained his feet, apparently unscratched from the fall, and nodded his compliance.

The poor lad looked so horrified over displeasing his lord that Madelyne intervened on his behalf. "Your squire was thoughtful enough to instruct me," she stated. "He wanted to help me back to the ground, for I foolishly forgot in my haste to mount from the proper side."

Ansel gave Madelyne a grateful look before turning back to bow to his lord. Duncan nodded, apparently satisfied with the explanation.

When Madelyne realized Duncan was about to mount Silenus, she squeezed her eyes shut, certain she was about to be hurled to the ground.

Duncan saw Madelyne close her eyes before she turned her face away from him. He shook his head, wondering what in God's name was the matter with her now, and then gained the saddle and lifted Madelyne into his lap in one swift action.

Madelyne was wrapped in his thick cloak and settled against his chest before she could worry over the deed.

"You're no better than Louddon," Madelyne muttered to herself. "Think I didn't notice that you didn't even take the time to bury your dead before you left my brother's fortress? Aye, I noticed all right. You're just as ruthless. You kill without showing any sign of remorse."

It took all of Duncan's self-discipline not to grab hold of his captive and shake some sense into her. "Madelyne, we did not bury our dead, because none of my men died."

Madelyne was so surprised by his answer, she dared a look up at him. The top of her head bumped his but she didn't pause to apologize. "There were bodies all over the ground, Duncan."

"Louddon's soldiers, Madelyne, not mine," Duncan answered.

"Do you expect me to believe that your soldiers are so superior that they—"

"I expect you to quit goading my temper, Madelyne," Duncan answered.

She knew he meant what he said when he slapped the cloak back over her head.

He was a horrible man, Madelyne decided. And he obviously didn't have a heart. Aye, he wouldn't be able to kill so effortlessly if he were gifted with human emotions.

In truth, Madelyne couldn't imagine taking another person's life. Having led such a sheltered existence with only Father Berton and his two companions left her ill prepared for the likes of Louddon or Duncan.

Madelyne had learned that humility was a treasured goal. She forced meekness in front of her brother. Inside, she raged. She prayed she didn't have a dark soul like Louddon. They did share the same father. Madelyne wanted to believe she was given only the goodness from her mother's side of the family and none of the vile traits from her father. Did she fool herself over such a hope?

She was soon too exhausted to worry. This day's journey was proving to be the most difficult to bear. Her nerves were strained to the breaking point. She heard one of the soldiers remark that they were almost home, and perhaps because she believed the end was in sight, each hour seemed much longer.

Rough, hilly terrain slowed their progress. Duncan wasn't able to keep up his usual neckbreaking pace. Several times Madelyne was certain the big stallion was going to stumble, and she spent most of the long, torturous day with her eyes closed and Duncan's arms around her. Aye, she worried herself into exhaustion, convinced that they were about to be thrown into one of the deep, jagged crevices Silenus seemed so fond of getting as close to as possible.

One of the soldiers shouted the news when they finally reached Wexton land. A resounding cheer echoed through-

59

out the hills. Madelyne sighed with relief. She sagged against Duncan's chest and felt the tension ease out of her shoulders. She was too tired to worry over what would happen to her when she entered Duncan's home. Just getting off Silenus was blessing enough for now.

It had turned bitterly cold during the day. Madelyne was growing more and more impatient as the minutes since gaining Wexton land turned into long hours and still not a single glimpse of Duncan's fortress.

Daylight was fading when Duncan called a respite. It was Gilard who nagged him into stopping. Madelyne could tell from the harsh exchange of words that the stop wasn't to Duncan's liking. She noticed, too, that Gilard didn't seem the least offended by his brother's harsh remarks.

"Are you weaker than our captive?" Duncan asked Gilard when he had insisted on taking a few minutes to rest.

"My legs have lost all feeling," Gilard returned with a shrug.

"Lady Madelyne hasn't complained," Duncan commented after raising his hand to signal his men.

"Your captive is too frightened to say anything," Gilard scoffed. "She hides beneath your cloak and weeps against your chest."

"I think not," Duncan answered. He jerked the cloak away so that Gilard could see Madelyne's face. "See you any tears, Gilard?" he asked, amusement in his voice.

Gilard shook his head. Duncan was trying to make him feel inferior to the beautiful woman he held in his arms. He wasn't the least upset by the ploy and actually chuckled. The desire to stretch his legs and taste a bit of ale were his only concerns now. Those, and the fact that his bladder was near to bursting.

"Your captive might be too simpleminded to know fear," Gilard remarked with a grin.

Duncan wasn't amused by the remark. He dismissed Gilard with a frown fierce enough to send his brother running, and then slowly dismounted.

Duncan watched Gilard until he disappeared into the forest, and then turned back to Madelyne. She reached out to him for assistance, placing her hands on the curve of his broad shoulders. She even tried to smile.

Duncan didn't smile back. He took an infinitely long time

getting her to the ground, however. His hands spanned her waist when he pulled her toward him, but as soon as they were eye level with each other, and just a scant space apart, he stopped.

Madelyne straightened her legs with a groan of pain she couldn't quite contain. Every muscle in her backside screamed in agony.

He had the audacity to smile over her distress.

Madelyne decided then and there that Duncan brought out the worst in her. How else could she explain this sudden, overwhelming urge to scream at him. Aye, he nudged the dark side of her character to the front. Why, she never, ever screamed at anyone. She was a gentle woman, gifted with a sweet, even-tempered disposition. Father Berton had told her that often enough.

Now this warrior tried to mock the gentleness right out of her.

Well, she wasn't going to let that happen. Duncan wasn't going to make her lose her temper now, no matter how much he grinned over her aches and pains.

She stared into his eyes, determined not to flinch this time. He was looking at her intently, as if he thought he might find an answer to some unsolved puzzle that was bothering him.

His gaze slowly lowered, until he was staring at her mouth, and she wondered over that until she realized she was staring at his.

She blushed, yet didn't know why. "Gilard is wrong. I'm not simpleminded."

His grin, damn his black soul, widened.

"You may let go of me now." She gave him what she hoped was a haughty look.

"You'll fall on your face if I do," Duncan announced.

"And would that give you pleasure?" she asked, trying her best to keep her voice as whisper-soft as his had been when he made the disgraceful comment.

Duncan shrugged and suddenly let go.

Oh, he was a horrible man all right. He knew exactly what was going to happen. Madelyne would have fallen on her backside if she hadn't grabbed hold of his arm. Her legs could not seem to remember what their duty was. "I'm not accustomed to riding for such long hours."

61

He didn't think she was accustomed to riding at all. Lord, she confused him. Without a doubt Lady Madelyne was the most perplexing woman he'd ever encountered. She was graceful when she walked, but could be incredibly clumsy too. She'd bumped her head against his chin so many times, he thought the top of her head must surely be bruised.

Madelyne didn't have any idea what he was thinking. But he was smiling at her and that was a worry. She was finally able to let go of him. She turned her back on him then and slowly made her way into the forest to find privacy. She knew she was moving like an old woman and prayed Duncan wasn't watching.

When she returned from the dense, wooded area, she circled the men, determined to work the aches and cramps out of her legs before she was forced back on Silenus again. She stopped when she reached the far corner of the triangular area, and stared down at the valley they'd just climbed.

Duncan didn't seem to be in any particular hurry to set out again. That didn't make sense to Madelyne, for she remembered how irritated he'd been when Gilard demanded they stop. Now he acted as though they had all the time in the world. Madelyne shook her head. Duncan of Wexton was the most confusing man she'd ever met.

She decided to be thankful for this respite. She needed a few more minutes alone to clear her mind of her worries; a few precious minutes of peaceful solitude to get her emotions under control.

The day was nearly gone, for the sun was setting now. Glorious streaks of bright orange and faded red lined the sky, arching downward, giving her the impression that they touched the ground in some distant spot. There was such beauty in the starkness of coming winter; each season held its own special treasures. Madelyne tried to ignore the noise behind her and concentrate on the beauty below, when her attention was caught by a spark of light that suddenly appeared through the trees.

The blink of light disappeared a second later. Curious, she moved to the right, until she captured the light again. Odd, but the spark seemed to come from another direction farther down the valley now.

The lights suddenly multiplied, until it appeared as if a

hundred candles had all been lit at the same instant. They flickered and blinked.

The distance was great but the sun acted like a mirror, bringing the sparks closer and closer. Like fire, she thought . . . or metal.

She understood then. Only men wearing armor could account for such reflections.

And there were hundreds of them.

Chapter Five

Dear God, they were going to be attacked. Madelyne was too stunned to move. She started to tremble with fear. That infuriated her, losing her control so quickly. Madelyne threw back her shoulders, determined to think logically. She took a deep, calming breath. There, she told herself, now I can decide what to do.

Oh, how she wished she had courage. Her hands had begun to cramp and she realized she was gripping the folds of her cloak with such force, her fingers ached from the pressure.

Madelyne shook her head, praying for divine help in making up her mind.

It certainly wasn't her duty as a captive to alert Duncan to the approaching threat. She could keep silent, and as soon as the battle began, make her own escape.

That possibility was soon discarded when she realized there'd be more killing. If she told Duncan, perhaps they could hurry to leave this place. Aye, they could gain distance if they left immediately, and the battle would be denied. Wasn't saving lives more important than her own escape plans?

Madelyne made up her mind to intercede. She picked up the hem of her gown and ran in search of her captor. She thought it was ironic that she would be the one to give the warning of the coming attack.

Duncan was standing in a circle of soldiers, Gilard right beside him. Madelyne edged around the men and stopped when she was behind Duncan's back. "Baron, I would have a word with you," Madelyne interrupted. Her voice cracked with tension and held little volume. Surely that was the reason he ignored her petition. He just hadn't heard her.

"I must speak to you." Madelyne repeated her request in a much louder voice. She then dared to nudge his shoulder once.

Duncan continued to ignore her.

Madelyne nudged him again, harder.

Duncan increased his voice as he continued to speak to his men on some subject Madelyne knew had to be paltry in comparison to what she was trying to tell him.

Lord, he was stubborn. Madelyne wrung her hands together, growing more alarmed by the second, sick with worry that the soldiers climbing the hills would be upon them any moment now.

The frustration of waiting for him to acknowledge her suddenly became too much to bear. Anger took control. Utilizing every ounce of strength she possessed, she kicked him quite thoroughly. Her aim was the back of his right knee, her mark most accurate.

Madelyne realized the foolishness of her rash action when excruciating pain shot up her leg. Her toes were surely broken from the impact, and the only consolation for her self-inflicted pain was the fact that she did get his attention. Rather swiftly too. Duncan turned to her with the speed of a wolf ready to pounce.

He looked more astonished than furious. His hands were on his hips, fisted, she couldn't help but notice. Madelyne, grimacing from the pain in her toes, now found it just as painful to look directly up at his face. She turned to stare at Gilard instead, and that did ease her discomfort, for the younger brother had the most ridiculous expression on his face.

"I would like a word with you in private," Madelyne stated when she was finally able to look at Duncan again.

Duncan was curious over the worry he'd heard in her voice. He nodded, took hold of her arm, and dragged her over to the other side of the camp.

Madelyne tripped twice.

He sighed once, long and drawn out it was, and she knew it was all for her benefit.

Madelyne didn't care if he tried to make her feel as unimportant as a splinter under his skin. He certainly wouldn't think her interruption was a nuisance when she explained. Why, he might even be appreciative, though in her heart she doubted he was capable of that reaction.

More important, killing would be averted. That thought gave her courage to look him right in the eye. "There are men coming from the valley," she said.

She expected an immediate reaction to her statement. Yet Duncan just stared at her. He didn't show her any reaction at all.

She was forced to repeat her words. "Soldiers are coming up the hills. I could see the sun reflected from their shields. Think you should do something about it?"

Was it going to be an eternity before action was taken? Madelyne considered that possibility while she waited for Duncan to say something.

He was staring at her in the most disturbing way, his hard, angular face clearly showing his puzzlement. She thought she saw cynicism there as well, in those chilling gray eyes. Madelyne decided then that he was trying to decide if she was telling him the truth.

"I have never spoken a falsehood in my life, Baron. If you'll follow me, I'll show you that I speak the truth."

Duncan watched the lovely woman standing so proudly before him. Wide blue eyes looked up at him with such trust. Tendrils of auburn-colored hair floated across her cheeks. There was a smudge of dirt on the side of her nose, drawing his attention.

"Why do you give me this warning?" Duncan asked.

"Why? So that we could get away from here," Madelyne

answered. She frowned over his bizarre question. "I don't want any more killings."

Duncan nodded, content with her answer. He motioned to Gilard. His younger brother had been standing off to the side, trying to hear what was being said.

"Lady Madelyne has only just realized we're being followed," Duncan remarked.

Gilard showed his surprise. He hadn't realized they were being followed. He turned to look at Madelyne. "We're being followed? How long have you known, Duncan?"

"Since midday," Duncan answered with a shrug.

"They be outcasts?" Gilard inquired. His voice was mild now in an attempt to imitate his brother's nonchalant attitude. Inside, Gilard was irritated over Duncan's silence throughout the afternoon. Yet he was puzzled, too, wondering why Madelyne had given them warning.

"They aren't outcasts, Gilard."

A long, silent moment stretched between the two brothers before a look of comprehension came over Gilard's face. "Does the rat chase after the wolf?" he asked.

"God willing, he'll be leading his men this time," Duncan answered.

Gilard smiled. Duncan nodded. "I'd thought to meet them nearer to home, at Creek Crossing, but the hills below us give much the same advantage. Tell the men to prepare."

Gilard turned and hurried across the clearing, shouting the order to mount.

Madelyne was too appalled to speak. Her plan to give warning so that a battle could be averted evaporated when Gilard's laughter reached her. She hadn't understood what the brothers' exchanges meant though. They spoke in riddles, talking about rats and wolves, making no sense at all.

"Then I was correct," Madelyne blurted out. "You're really no different than Louddon, are you?"

Duncan ignored her angry outburst. "Mount my horse, Madelyne. We'll meet your brother together."

Madelyne was too infuriated to argue. She told herself she should have realized Duncan wouldn't turn his back on a fight. Hadn't she learned that lesson when she'd tried to persuade him into leaving Louddon's land?

Before she realized what she'd done, she found herself

settled on Silenus's back. Her anger had made her forget all about her fear. She couldn't even remember from which side she'd mounted the horse.

Duncan walked over, grabbed hold of the reins, and began to lead the animal across the clearing.

Madelyne held on to the saddle for dear life, her shoulders bent to the task. The stirrups were too long for her feet to catch, and her backside was being slapped with each step the animal took. She knew she looked pitifully untrained and was thankful Duncan wasn't watching her. "By what name do you call this horse?" Madelyne asked.

"Horse," Duncan called over his shoulder. "The animal is a horse and that is what I call him."

"Just as I suspected. You're so cold and heartless, you couldn't even take the time to name your loyal steed. I have given him a name. Silenus. What think you of that?" she asked.

Duncan refused to answer. He should have been irritated that Madelyne had the gall to name his stallion, but his thoughts had already turned to the battle ahead of them. He wouldn't allow himself to be bothered by such insignificant talk.

Madelyne smiled to herself, feeling pleased with the way she'd just goaded him. Then Ansel appeared at her side with another horse, a flecked gray mount that looked much more docile than Silenus. Duncan turned, threw the reins to Madelyne, and mounted the back of the gray.

The smile froze on Madelyne's face. She caught the reins, overwhelmed when it dawned on her that he expected her to direct the animal. The stallion must have caught her worry, for he immediately began to dance to the side. His heavy hooves stomped the ground with enough force to unseat Madelyne. She was sorry now she had done such a good job of pretending to be skilled.

Gilard appeared on Madelyne's other side, riding a brown steed. He forced his mount close to the stallion, effectively blocking the animal's skittish sidestep.

"They still be some distance away," Gilard remarked to his brother over the top of Madelyne's head. "Do we wait for them, brother?"

"No," Duncan answered. "We'll meet them halfway."

The soldiers were lining up behind the threesome, making

a terrible commotion. Madelyne thought Duncan waited until the sound diminished before giving the signal.

"I'll stay here until you return," Madelyne told Duncan. Her voice sounded desperate. Duncan glanced over at her, shook his head, and then turned back to look down into the valley.

"I'm going to stay here," Madelyne announced.

"You are not." He didn't even bother to look at her when he made the harsh denial.

"You could tie me to a tree," Madelyne suggested.

"Ah, Lady Madelyne, you wouldn't want to deny Louddon the sight of your lovely face, now, would you?" Gilard asked the question with a smile on his face. "I promise it will be the last he sees before he dies," the brother added.

"You'll both enjoy this battle, won't you?" Madelyne asked. She was so appalled, her voice shook.

"'Tis a fact I will enjoy it," Gilard answered with a shrug.

"I think you are as crazed as your brother, Gilard."

"You know we've good reason to want your brother dead," Gilard announced. The smile slowly left his face. "Just as you must surely want us dead." He mocked her with his statement, a deliberate sneer in his voice.

Madelyne turned to Duncan to see how he was reacting to his brother's remark, but the baron didn't seem to be paying any attention to their conversation. She turned back to Gilard then. "I understand why you want to kill Louddon. I don't want you or your brother to die in this confrontation, Gilard," she added. "Why would you think that I would?"

Gilard frowned in confusion. "What kind of fool do you take me for, Lady Madelyne? Do you try to tell me you won't take Louddon's side. Louddon is your brother."

"I will not take sides," Madelyne argued. "I don't want anyone to die."

"Oh, I see your plan now," Gilard returned. He was almost shouting at her. "You'll wait to see who is the winner and then make your choice. 'Tis very cunning of you."

"Believe what you will," Madelyne answered. "You're very like your brother," she added, shaking her head.

When Gilard grinned at her, she realized he was pleased by her comment.

"'Tis not praise I give you, Gilard. Just the opposite.

You're proving to be as stubborn and ruthless as your Duncan. I think you enjoy killing as much as he does," she ended.

Madelyne was horrified inside over the way she tried to goad Gilard into losing control, but God help her, she couldn't seem to stop herself.

"Can you honestly look me in the eye and tell me you don't hate me?" Gilard asked. He was so angry, the vein stood out on the side of his neck. Madelyne thought he wanted to strike her.

"I do not hate you," Madelyne said. "I would like to, I'll admit that to you, but I don't, Gilard."

"And why not?" Gilard asked.

"Because you love your sister."

Gilard was about to tell Madelyne he thought she was the most simpleminded woman he'd ever come across, when Duncan caught his attention. The younger brother immediately dismissed Madelyne and turned to reach for his sword.

Duncan finally gave the signal. Madelyne was suddenly so terrified, she couldn't even remember any of her prayers.

Was it going to be a fight to the death? Madelyne knew enough about Duncan's stubborn character to know he didn't care about the odds.

She tried, but couldn't count the number of soldiers coming up the hills. They covered the ground like locusts.

Were Duncan's men outnumbered again?

It would be a massacre, she thought, and all because Duncan would challenge with honor and Louddon would not. Such a simple realization, but one that was lost on the likes of the baron. He'd obviously forgotten Louddon had tricked him into believing he'd honor their temporary truce. That was how he'd captured Duncan, by simple trickery.

Madelyne knew Louddon better than Duncan did. Her brother would fight like an animal if he smelled the scent of victory on his side.

Madelyne told herself she didn't care who claimed victory. If they all killed each other, so be it. Their wills would prevail, not hers.

"I will not care," she whispered over and over until it became a desperate chant.

Yet no matter how many times she said the words, she couldn't make them true.

Chapter Six

"The wisdom of this world is foolishness with God."

NEW TESTAMENT, I CORINTHIANS, 3:19

Baron Wexton obviously didn't care to have the element of surprise on his side. His battle cry echoed throughout the countryside, all but rocking the withered leaves from their branches. A trumpet sounded, giving additional message to the soldiers advancing from below, and if those were not enough, the thunder from the horses racing down the slopes surely alerted Louddon and his men to the approaching threat.

Madelyne was caught between Duncan and his brother as they made their descent. Soldiers surrounded them as well, their shields raised. Although Madelyne held no such protection, both Duncan and Gilard blocked the branches that would have plucked her from her seat, using their kite-shaped shields as barriers against the gnarled branches barring their path.

When the soldiers reached a small ridge high above the

site Duncan had chosen for the confrontation, Duncan jerked on the stallion's reins and shouted a command to the animal. The stallion immediately stopped. Duncan used his free hand to grab hold of Madelyne's jaw. He applied pressure as he forced her to look up at him.

Gray eyes challenged blue. "Do not dare move from this spot."

He started to let go of her, but Madelyne stayed his hand. "If you die, I'll not weep for you," she whispered.

He actually smiled at her. "Yes, you would," he answered, his voice both arrogant and gentle.

Madelyne didn't have time to answer him. Duncan spurred his steed into motion and raced toward the battle already unfolding below. Madelyne was suddenly alone atop the stark ridge as the last of Duncan's soldiers moved past her at a furious speed.

The noise was shattering. Metal clashed with metal, ringing with ear-piercing intensity. Screams of torment mingled with shouts of victory. Madelyne wasn't close enough to see individual faces, but she kept her attention on Duncan's back. The gray he rode was easily visible. She watched him wield his sword with accuracy, thought him surely blessed by the gods when the enemy all but surrounded him and he unseated each with deadly slaps from his blade.

Madelyne closed her eyes for just a moment. When she looked to the scene again, the gray had disappeared. She frantically scanned the area, looking for Duncan, and Gilard as well, but she couldn't find either brother. The battle edged toward her.

She never looked for her brother, knowing full well that he wouldn't be in the thick of battle. Louddon, unlike Duncan, would be the last one to raise his sword. There was too much risk involved. No, he placed too much value on his life, whereas Duncan didn't seem to value his own at all. Louddon left the fighting to the men who pledged him fealty. And if the battle turned against him, he'd be the first to run away.

"This is not my fight," Madelyne screamed at the top of her lungs. She pulled on the reins, determined to leave with as much speed as possible. She wouldn't watch another minute. Aye, she would leave them all.

"Come, Silenus, we go now," she said, nudging the animal as she had seen Duncan do. The stallion didn't move. She jerked on the reins, hard, determined to get the animal to do her bidding. The soldiers were fast climbing the crest and haste was suddenly becoming imperative.

Duncan was infuriated. He had searched but couldn't find a trace of Louddon. The victory over his enemy would be hollow indeed if their leader escaped again. He glanced a quick look up toward Madelyne and was shocked to see that the battle was circling her. Duncan realized then that he had been so consumed with finding Louddon, he hadn't given sufficient thought to Madelyne's safety. He admitted the mistake, damning himself for not having the foresight to leave men to guard her.

Duncan threw his shield to the ground and gave a shrill whistle he prayed would reach his stallion. His heart lodged in his throat as he ran toward the crest. It was a logical reaction, he told himself, this fierce need to protect Madelyne, for she was his captive, and he had the responsibility to keep her safe. Aye, that was the reason he ran to her now, roaring his outrage with as much force as any battle cry.

The stallion responded to the whistled signal, charging forward. The animal would have allowed Madelyne control now, but she lost the reins when he bolted.

Silenus jumped over two soldiers just climbing the top of the ridge, clipping both their heads with his hind legs. The soldiers' screams carried them back down the hill.

Madelyne was soon in the thick of battle, with men on horseback and more crowding the ground around her, all fighting for their lives. Duncan's stallion was blocked by the soldiers. Madelyne clung to the animal's neck and prayed for a quick end.

She suddenly spotted Gilard making his way toward her. He was on foot, holding a bloody sword in one hand and a scarred shield in the other, fending off attack from the left while he thrust his blade forward with the right.

One of Louddon's soldiers lunged at Madelyne, his sword raised against her. There was a crazed look glazing his eyes, as if he had passed the point of knowing what he was doing.

He meant to kill her, Madelyne realized. She screamed Duncan's name, yet knew her safety depended upon her own wits. There wasn't any escape other than the hard ground, and Madelyne quickly threw herself over the side of the horse. She wasn't quick enough. The blade found its target, slashing a deep path down the length of Madelyne's left thigh. She screamed in agony, but the sound died in her throat when she hit the ground. The air was knocked out of her.

Her cloak followed her to the ground, landing in a heap on top of her shoulders. Stunned, and in a state of near shock, Madelyne's concentration suddenly focused on pulling the garment around herself, a slow, arduous process she became obsessed with completing. The pain in her thigh was so consuming at first that she thought she would die from it. And then a blessed numbness settled in her thigh and in her mind, giving Madelyne new strength. She stood, feeling dazed and confused, clutching her cloak to her breasts as she watched the fighting men around her.

Duncan's stallion nudged Madelyne between her shoulder blades, nearly knocking her back down to the ground. She regained her balance and leaned against the animal's side, finding comfort in the fact that the horse hadn't bolted away when she had fallen. The animal acted as a barrier as well, protecting her back from assault.

Tears streamed down her face, an involuntary reaction to the scent of death that permeated the air. Gilard yelled something to her but Madelyne couldn't understand what he was shouting. She could only watch as he continued to make his way toward her. He yelled again, his voice more forceful, but the order mingled with the clash of metal scraping metal and became too garbled to comprehend.

Her mind rebelled over the carnage. She began to walk toward Gilard, believing that was what he wished her to do. She stumbled twice over the legs and arms of slain warriors spewed like discarded garbage upon the ground, her thoughts only of getting to Gilard, the one man she recognized in this forest of destruction. In the back of her mind lived the hope that he would take her to Duncan. And then she would be safe.

Madelyne was only a few feet away when Gilard was challenged from behind. He turned to meet the new opponent, his back unprotected. Madelyne saw another of

Louddon's men grasp the opportunity, raising his blackened sword into the air as he rushed toward the vulnerable target.

She tried to scream a warning but her voice failed her and only a whimper escaped.

Dear God, she was the only one who was close enough to aid him, the only one who could make a difference. Madelyne didn't hesitate. She grabbed one of the discarded weapons from the stiff fingers of a faceless corpse. It was a heavy, cumbersome mace thick with spikes and dried blood.

Madelyne held the weapon in both her hands, struggling over its weight. Clutching the blunt end, she half dragged, half carried the weapon as she hurried to position herself behind Gilard, her back nearly touching his. And then she waited for the enemy to make his attack.

The soldier wasn't daunted, as Madelyne presented a weak defense against his armor and strength. A glimmer of a smile soured his face. Yelling a defiant shout, he rushed forward, his long, curved weapon slicing the air with deadly intent.

Madelyne waited until the last possible second and then swung the mace off the ground in a wide arc. Terror lent her strength. She meant only to deter his attack, but the spikes protruding from the circular bulb of the weapon severed the chain links of the soldier's coat of mail and entered tender flesh concealed beneath.

Gilard finished his fight against the frontal attack, turned swiftly in his bid to get to Madelyne, and very nearly knocked her down. He was just in time to see the killing, watched, as Madelyne did, the enemy soldier drop to the ground with a scream trapped in his throat and spikes of the club embedded in his middle. Gilard was so astonished over what he had just witnessed, he was momentarily speechless.

Madelyne let out a low moan of anguish. She folded her arms in front of her waist and doubled over. Gilard thought she acted as though she had been the one to receive the injury. He sought to help her, reached out to gently touch her shoulder.

Madelyne was so consumed with horror over what she had just done, she wasn't even aware of Gilard any longer. The battle had ceased to exist for her.

Duncan had also witnessed the killing. In one swift action he mounted his stallion and goaded the animal toward Gilard. The brother jumped out of the way just as Duncan reached down and grabbed hold of Madelyne. He lifted her up with one powerful arm and all but slammed her into the saddle in front of him. God proved merciful, for her right side took the force of the impact and her injured thigh was barely jarred.

The battle was almost over. Duncan's soldiers were chasing Louddon's retreating forces down the valley.

"Finish it," Duncan yelled to Gilard. He jerked on the reins, directing his mount up the hills again. The animal raced away from the battlefield, his breeding and strength obvious now as he galloped with amazing speed up the treacherous terrain.

Duncan had discarded his cloak and his shield during the fight. He used his hands now to protect Madelyne's face from the branches swaying into their path.

She wanted none of his thoughtfulness. Madelyne shoved against him, trying to make him let go of her, preferring the hard ground to his loathsome touch.

Because of him she'd killed a man.

Duncan didn't try to quiet her. Safety was his primary concern now. He didn't let up his pace until they were well away from the threat. He finally reined his stallion to a halt when they entered a cluster of trees. It was quiet there, and protected as well.

He was furious with himself for placing Madelyne in such danger. Duncan turned his attention to her now. When he saw the tears streaming down her face, he let out a frustrated groan.

And then he sought to soothe her. "You can quit crying, Madelyne. Your brother wasn't among the dead. Save your tears."

She hadn't even been aware she was crying. When his words registered, Madelyne became so enraged over his misinterpretation of her distress, she could barely form an answer. The man was despicable.

Madelyne wiped the tears away from her cheeks, took a deep breath, gathering fresh air and new fury. "I didn't know what true hate was until today, Baron. But you've given the vile word new meaning. As God is my witness, I'll hate you until the day I die. I might as well," she continued, "I'm damned to hell anyway and all because of you." Her voice was so low that Duncan was forced to lean forward until his forehead was touching Madelyne's just to hear her words.

She wasn't making any sense at all.

"Aren't you listening to me?" he demanded, though he kept his voice as soft as hers had been. He felt the tension in her shoulders, knew she was close to losing control, and sought to calm her again. He wanted to be gentle with her, an unusual reaction to his way of thinking, but he excused his conduct by telling himself that it was only because he felt responsible for her. "I've just explained that your brother is safe, Madelyne. For the moment," he added, deciding to give her honesty as well as comfort.

"You're the one who isn't listening to me," Madelyne returned. Tears began to fall again, interrupting her speech. She stopped to brush them aside. "Because of you I've taken a man's life. It was a grave sin and you're just as much to blame as I am. If you hadn't dragged me along with you, I wouldn't have been able to kill anyone."

"You're upset because you killed?" Duncan asked, unable to keep the astonishment out of his voice. Duncan had to remind himself that Madelyne was only a woman, and the strangest things did seem to upset the weaker sex. He also weighed all that he'd put Madelyne through in the past two days. "I've killed many more," he said, thinking to ease her conscience.

His plan failed. "I don't care if you've killed legions of soldiers," Madelyne announced. "You don't have a soul, so it doesn't matter how many lives you take."

Duncan didn't have a ready answer to that statement. He realized that it was pointless to argue with her. Madelyne was too distraught to think logically, and surely just as exhausted. Why, she was so upset, she couldn't even raise her voice to him.

Duncan cradled her in his arms, tightening his grip until she stopped struggling. With a weary sigh he muttered, more to himself than to her, "What am I to do with you?"

Madelyne heard him, and her answer was swift. "I don't care what you do with me." She jerked her head back and looked up at him. Madelyne noticed the jagged cut just below Duncan's right eye then. She used the cuff of her gown to mop the stream of blood away, but she contradicted her gentle action with angry words. "You can leave me here, or you can kill me," she informed him as she dabbed at the edges of his cut. "Nothing you do makes any difference to me. You shouldn't have taken me with you, Duncan."

"Your brother came after you," Duncan pointed out.

"He did not," Madelyne contradicted him. "He came after you because you destroyed his home. He doesn't care about me. If you'd only open your mind, I know I could convince you of the truth. But you are too stubborn to listen to anyone. I find it pointless to speak to you. Aye, pointless! I vow I'll never speak to you again."

Her tirade took the last of her strength. Madelyne finished cleaning his abrasion as best she could and then sagged against his chest, dismissing him.

Lady Madelyne was a paradox. Duncan was nearly undone by the tender way she touched his face when she tried to repair his injury. Duncan didn't think she had even been aware of what she was doing. He suddenly remembered how Madelyne had faced Gilard when they were back in Louddon's fortress. Aye, she'd been a contradiction then too. Madelyne had given Gilard a serene look while he shouted his frustration, yet all the while she'd clung to Duncan's hand.

Now she raged at him while she ministered to him. Duncan sighed again. He rested his chin against the top of Madelyne's head and wondered how in God's name such a gentle woman could be related to the devil.

The numbness was wearing thin. Now that the surge of anger had abandoned her, Madelyne's thigh began to throb painfully. Her cloak hid the damage from Duncan. She believed he was unaware of her injury and found perverse satisfaction over that fact. It was an illogical reaction but Madelyne couldn't seem to think with much reason. She was suddenly so tired, so hungry, and in such pain, she couldn't think at all.

The soldiers joined their leader and within minutes they were headed for the Wexton fortress. An hour later it became gritty determination that kept Madelyne from voicing complaint.

Duncan's hand accidentally brushed against her injured

thigh. Her cloak and gown offered little cushion against the burning agony. Madelyne held her scream. She slapped his hand away, but the fire from his touch lingered, inflaming the injury to an excruciating level.

Madelyne knew she was going to be sick. "We must stop for a moment," she told Duncan. She wanted to scream at him, to weep, too, but she had vowed he wouldn't destroy what was left of her gentle disposition.

Madelyne knew he'd heard her. His nod acknowledged that he had, yet they continued to ride, and after a few more minutes she came to the conclusion he had decided to ignore her request.

What an inhuman beast he was! Though it offered her little comfort, she mentally listed all the vile names she wished to yell at him. She summoned up every foul word she could remember, though her vocabulary of crude words was limited. It satisfied her, until she realized she was probably sinking to Duncan's level. Damn, she was a gentle woman.

Her stomach wouldn't settle. Madelyne remembered her vow never to speak to him again, but she was forced, by circumstances, to repeat her request. "If you don't stop, I'm going to be sick all over you."

Her threat got an immediate reaction. Duncan raised his hand, giving the order to halt. He was off his horse and lifting Madelyne to the ground before she could brace herself in preparation.

"Why are we stopping?" The question came from Gilard, who had also dismounted and was hurrying over to his brother. "We're almost home."

"Lady Madelyne," Duncan answered, giving Gilard no further information.

Madelyne had already begun the torturous walk toward the privacy the trees offered, but she paused when she heard Gilard's question. "You can just stand there and wait for me, Gilard."

It sounded like an order. Gilard raised an eyebrow in surprise, turning to his brother. Duncan was frowning as he watched Madelyne, and Gilard concluded his brother was irritated by the way Madelyne had just spoken to him. "She has been through an ordeal," Gilard rushed out in excuse, lest Duncan decide to retaliate.

Duncan shook his head. He continued to watch Madelyne until she had disappeared into the forest. "Something's wrong," he muttered, frowning as he tried to figure out what was bothering him.

Gilard sighed. "She is ill perhaps?"

"And, and she threatened to . . ." Duncan didn't finish his comment, but started out after Madelyne.

Gilard tried to stay him with his hand. "Give her some privacy, Duncan. She'll return to us," he said. "There isn't anyplace she can hide," he reasoned.

Duncan shook his brother's hand away. He'd seen the look of pain in Madelyne's eyes, noticed, too, the extreme stiffness in her gait. Duncan instinctively knew an unsettled stomach wasn't the cause. She wouldn't have favored her right side if that was the case. And if she was about to throw up, she would have run, not walked away from the soldiers. Nay, something was wrong and Duncan meant to find out what it was.

He found her leaning against the side of a gnarled oak tree, her head bent. Duncan stopped, not wishing to invade upon her privacy. Madelyne was weeping. He watched as she slowly lifted the cloak away and let it drop to the ground. And then he understood the true reason for her distress. The left side of her gown was shredded to the hem, and soaked with blood.

Duncan didn't realize he'd shouted until Madelyne let out a frightened whimper. She didn't have the strength to back away from him, nor did she fight him when he forced her hands away from her thigh and knelt down at her side.

When Duncan viewed the damage, he was filled with such rage, his hands shook as he pried the garment away. Dried blood made it a slow task. Duncan's hands were big and awkward and he was trying to be as gentle as possible.

The injury was deep, nearly as long as his forearm, and embedded with dirt. It would need to be cleaned and sewn together.

"Ah, Madelyne," Duncan whispered, his voice gruff. "Who did this to you?"

His voice sounded like a warm caress, his sympathy obvious. Madelyne knew she'd start crying again if he showed her any more kindness. Aye, her control would break then, just like one of the brittle branches she was clinging to now.

Madelyne wouldn't allow it. "I don't want your sympathy, Duncan." She straightened her shoulders and tried to give him a look of dismissal. "Take your hands off my leg. It isn't decent."

Duncan was so surprised by the show of authority, he almost smiled. He glanced up, saw the fire in her eyes. Duncan knew then what she was trying to do. Pride had become her defense. He'd already noticed how Madelyne valued control.

Looking back at her injury, he realized there was little to be done about it now. He decided then to let Madelyne have her way.

Duncan forced a gruff voice when he stood up and answered her. "You'll get no sympathy from me, Madelyne. I'm like a wolf. I don't suffer human emotions."

Madelyne didn't answer him, but her eyes widened over his comment. Duncan smiled and knelt down again.

"Leave me alone."

"Nay," Duncan replied, his voice mild. He pulled his dagger free and began to cut a long strip of her gown.

"You are ruining my gown," Madelyne muttered.

"For God's sake, Madelyne, your gown is already ruined," Duncan answered.

With as much tenderness as possible he wrapped the strip of material around her thigh. He was tying a knot, when she shoved against his shoulder.

"You're hurting me." She hated herself for admitting it. Damn, she was going to cry.

"I am not."

Madelyne gasped, forgetting all about weeping. She was infuriated over his comment. How dare he contradict her! She was the one suffering.

"Your flesh will need needle and thread," Duncan remarked.

Madelyne slapped his shoulder when he dared shrug over his announcement.

"No one is putting a needle to me."

"You're a contrary woman, Madelyne." Duncan said as he bent to pick up her cloak. He draped it around her shoulders and then lifted her into his arms, careful to shield her injury.

Madelyne instinctively put her arms around his neck. She considered scratching his eyes out because of the terrible way he was treating her. "You're the contrary one, Duncan. I'm a sweet-tempered maiden you would try to destroy if I gave you the chance. And I swear to God, this is the last time I'll speak to you."

"Ah, and you're so honorable you'd never break your word. Isn't that true, Lady Madelyne?" he asked as he carried her back to the waiting men.

"That is correct," Madelyne immediately answered. She closed her eyes and leaned against his chest. "You have the brains of a wolf, do you know that? And wolves have very small brains."

Madelyne was too tired to look up to see how he was reacting to her insults. She bristled inside over the way he was treating her, and then realized she should be thankful for his cold attitude. Why, he had made her angry enough to forget her pain. Just as important, his lack of compassion had helped her overcome the urge to break down and weep in front of him. That would have been undignified, crying like an infant, and both her dignity and her pride were cherished cloaks she always wore. It would have been humiliating to lose either. Madelyne allowed herself a little smile, certain Duncan couldn't see it. He was a foolish man, for he had just saved her pride and didn't even know it.

Duncan sighed. Madelyne had just broken her promise when she spoke to him. He didn't feel the urge to point that fact out to her, but it made him feel like grinning all the same.

He wanted the details from Madelyne, to learn how she'd been injured and by whose hand. In his heart he couldn't believe one of his own had harmed her; yet Louddon's men would also try to protect her, wouldn't they?

Duncan decided to wait for his answers. He needed to get his anger under control first. And Madelyne needed care and rest now.

It had been difficult to banter with her. Duncan wasn't a man used to masking his anger. When he was wronged, he attacked. Yet he had understood how close Madelyne was to breaking down. The retelling would upset her now.

When they were once again on their way, Madelyne found escape from her pain, snuggled against Duncan's chest. Her face rested under his chin.

Madelyne was feeling safe again. Her reaction to Duncan confused her. In her heart she admitted that he wasn't anything like Louddon, though she'd take to her deathbed before she told him that. She was still his captive, after all, his pawn to use against her brother. Yet she really didn't hate him. Duncan was merely retaliating against Louddon, and she was caught in the middle.

"I'll escape, you know."

She hadn't realized she'd spoken the thought aloud until Duncan answered her. "You will not."

"We are home at last," Gilard shouted. His gaze was directed on Madelyne. Most of her face was hidden from view, but what he could see showed a very tranquil expression. He thought she might be sleeping and was thankful. In truth, Gilard didn't know how to proceed with Lady Madelyne now. He was in a damn awkward position. He'd treated her with contempt. And how had she repaid him? Why, she'd actually saved his life. He couldn't understand why she'd come to his assistance and longed to ask. He didn't though, because he had a feeling he wouldn't like her answer.

When Gilard saw the walls looming into the sky ahead of them, he nudged his mount ahead of Duncan's so that he could be the first to enter the lower bailey. By rite and tradition, Duncan chose to be the last of his men to enter the safety provided by the thick stone walls. The soldiers liked this ritual, for it reminded each of them that their overlord placed their lives above his own. Though each man had pledged fealty to Baron Wexton, and each willingly met the call to join him in battle, every one also knew he could depend upon his lord for protection as well.

It was an easy alliance. Pride was the root. Aye, each man could also boast of being one of Duncan's elite soldiers.

Duncan's men were the best-trained soldiers in England. Duncan measured success by inflicting trials ordinary men would have found impossible to meet. His men were considered to be the chosen few, though they numbered near to six hundred in all when an accurate count was taken and all were called to fulfill their forty-day requirement.

Their might was revered, whispered about by lesser men, and their feats of remarkable strength recounted without need of exaggeration to liven the telling. The truth was interesting enough.

The soldiers reflected the values of their leader, a lord who wielded his sword with far greater accuracy than all challengers. Duncan of Wexton was a man to be frightened of. His enemies had given up trying to discover his weakness. The warrior showed no vulnerability. He didn't appear to be interested in worldly offerings. No, Duncan had never taken gold as his second mistress as others of his rank had so done. The baron presented no Achilles heel to the outside world. He was a man of steel, or so it was sadly believed by those who wished him harm. He was a man without conscience, a warrior without a heart.

Madelyne had little knowledge of Duncan's reputation. She felt protected in his arms and watched the soldiers file past. She was curious over the way Duncan waited.

She turned her attention to the fortress in front of her. The massive structure sat atop a stark hill, without benefit of a single tree to give relief from the severity. A gray stone wall circled the fortress and must have been at least seven hundred feet in width. Madelyne had never seen anything so monstrous. The wall was tall enough to touch the bright moon, or so it seemed to Madelyne. She could see a portion of a circular tower protruding from inside, so tall that the top was hidden from view by heavy clouds.

The road to the drawbridge curved like a serpent's belly up the rocky climb. Duncan nudged his mount forward when the last of his men had cleared the wooden planks spanning the moat. The stallion was eager to get to his destination, prancing a nervous sidestep that jarred Madelyne's thigh into aching again. She grimaced against the sting, unaware she was squeezing Duncan's arm.

He knew she was in pain. Duncan looked down at Madelyne, took in her exhausted expression, and scowled.

"You'll be able to rest soon, Madelyne. Hold on just a little longer," Duncan whispered, his voice ragged with concern.

Madelyne nodded and closed her eyes.

When they reached the courtyard, Duncan quickly dismounted and then lifted Madelyne into his arms. He held

84

her firmly against his chest, and then turned and started walking toward his home.

Soldiers lined the way. Gilard was standing with two men in front of the castle doors. Madelyne opened her eyes and looked at Gilard. She thought he looked perplexed but couldn't reason why.

It wasn't until they'd gotten closer that Madelyne realized Gilard wasn't looking at her. Why, his attention was drawn to her legs. Madelyne glanced down, saw then that her cloak wasn't hiding her injury any longer. The tattered gown trailed behind her like a shredded banner. Only blood covered her, flowing a stream down the length of her leg.

Gilard hurried to open the doors, a double entry that dwarfed the men. A rush of warm air greeted Madelyne when they reached the center of a small hallway.

The area around her was obviously the soldiers' keep. The entryway was narrow, the floor wooden, and the men's quarters located on the right. A circular stairway took up all of the left wall, curving wide steps that led to the housing above. There was something oddly disturbing about the structure, but Madelyne couldn't figure out what bothered her until Duncan had carried her halfway up the steps.

"The stairs are on the wrong side," Madelyne suddenly said.

"Nay, Madelyne. They are on the correct side," Duncan answered.

She thought he sounded amused. "'Tis not on the correct side," she contradicted him. "The stairway is always built on the right side of the wall. Anyone knows that well enough," she added with great authority.

For some reason, Madelyne was infuriated that Duncan wouldn't admit the obvious flaw in his home.

"It's built on the right unless it is deliberately ordered built on the left," Duncan answered. Each word was carefully enunciated. Why, he acted as though he was instructing a dimwitted child.

Why Madelyne found this discussion so important was beyond her. She did though, and vowed to have the last word on the subject. "It's an ignorant deliberation then," she told him. Madelyne glared up at him and was sorry he wasn't looking down at her to see it.

"You're a stubborn man."

"You're a stubborn woman," Duncan countered. He smiled, pleased with his observation.

Gilard trailed behind his brother. He thought their conversation ridiculous. Yet he was too worried to smile over their foolish banter.

Gilard knew Edmond would be waiting for them. Aye, the middle brother would certainly be inside the hall. Adela might be there as well. Gilard realized he was concerned for Madelyne now. He didn't want her to have any unpleasant confrontations. And he hoped there'd be time to explain Madelyne's gentle nature to his brother Edmond.

Gilard's worry was temporarily put aside when Duncan reached the second level and didn't turn to enter the great hall. He took the opposite direction, climbed another stairway, and then entered the mouth of the tower. The steps were narrower and the procession slowed somewhat by the sharp curves.

The room at the top of the tower was freezing. There was a hearth built into the center of the circular wall. A large window had also been added, right next to the fireplace. The window was wide open, the wooden shutters flapping loudly against the stone walls.

There was a bed against the inside wall. Duncan tried to be gentle when he placed Madelyne on the covers. Gilard followed behind them and Duncan issued his orders to his brother as he bent to pile chunks of wood into the fireplace. "Send Gerty with a trencher of food for Madelyne, and tell Edmond to bring his medicines. He'll have to use his needle on her."

"He'll argue over it," Gilard commented.

"He'll do it all the same."

"Who is Edmond?"

The softly spoken question came from Madelyne. Both Duncan and Gilard turned to look at her. She was struggling to sit up, and frowning over the impossibility of the task. Her teeth started chattering from the cold and the strain, and she finally collapsed against the bed again.

"Edmond is middle brother to Duncan and me," Gilard explained.

"How many Wextons are there?" Madelyne asked, frowning.

"Five in all," Gilard answered. "Catherine is oldest sister,

86

then Duncan, then Edmond, then Adela, and lastly me," he added with a smile. "Edmond will care for your injury, Madelyne. He knows the ways of healing, and before you know it, you'll be as fit as ever."

"Why?"

Gilard frowned. "Why what?"

"Why would you want me fit as ever?" Madelyne asked, clearly puzzled.

Gilard didn't know how to answer her. He turned back to look at Duncan, hoping he'd give Madelyne answer. Duncan had started the fire and was now closing the shutters. Without turning around, he commanded, "Gilard, do as I've instructed."

His voice didn't suggest argument. Gilard was wise enough to obey. He made it to the door before Madelyne's voice caught up with him. "Don't bring your brother. I can take care of my injury without his aid."

"Now, Gilard."

The door slammed.

Duncan turned to Madelyne then. "For as long as you are here, you'll not contradict any of my orders. Is that understood?"

He was advancing upon the bed with a slow, measured stride.

"How can I understand anything, milord?" Madelyne whispered. "I am but a pawn, isn't that the way of it?"

Before he could frighten her, Madelyne closed her eyes. She folded her arms across her chest, an action meant to ward off the chill in the room.

"Let me die in peace," she whispered quite dramatically. Lord, how she wished she had the strength and the courage to yell at him. She was so miserable now. There'd be more pain coming if Duncan's brother touched her too. "I do not have the stamina for your brother's ministrations."

"Yes, you do, Madelyne."

His voice had sounded gentle, but Madelyne was too angry to care. "Why must you contradict everything I say to you? 'Tis a terrible flaw, that," Madelyne muttered.

A knock sounded at the door. Duncan yelled out as he walked back across the room. He leaned one shoulder against the mantel above the hearth, his gaze directed on Madelyne.

Madelyne was too curious to keep her eyes closed. The door protested with a squeak as it was opened and an elderly woman appeared. She carried a trencher in one hand and a jug in the other. There were two animal skins tucked under her arm. The servant was a plump woman with worried brown eyes. She darted a hasty look at Madelyne and then turned to curtsy awkwardly to her lord.

Madelyne decided the servant was afraid of Duncan. She watched the poor woman, feeling great compassion for her as she tried to balance the items in her hands and genuflect.

Duncan wasn't making it any easier on the woman either. He gave her a curt nod and then motioned her to Madelyne's side. Not a word of encouragement or kindness did he utter.

The servant proved to be quick on her feet, because as soon as Duncan commanded the task, she all but ran to the bed, stumbling twice before she was there.

She placed the trencher of food next to Madelyne and offered her the jug. "By what name are you called?" Madelyne asked the woman. She kept her voice low so Duncan wouldn't overhear.

"Gerty," the woman answered.

The woman remembered the covers she held under her arm then and quickly moved the trencher to the wooden chest next to the bed. She covered Madelyne with the blanket.

Madelyne smiled her appreciation and that encouraged Gerty to tuck the sides of the animal skins against Madelyne's legs. "I can see you're shivering to death," she whispered.

Gerty had no knowledge of Madelyne's injury. When she pushed the fur against her injured thigh, Madelyne squeezed her eyes shut against the excruciating insult and didn't say a word.

Duncan saw what had happened, thought to yell a rebuke to the servant, but the deed was already done. Gerty was handing Madelyne her food now.

"Thank you for your kindness, Gerty."

Madelyne's approval amazed Duncan. He stared at his captive, took in her tranquil expression, and found himself shaking his head. Instead of lashing out at the servant, Lady Madelyne had given her praise.

The door suddenly flew open. Madelyne turned, her eyes wide with fright. The door bounced against the wall twice before settling. A giant of a man stood in the doorway, his hands resting on his hips and a fierce scowl drawn across his face. Madelyne concluded with a weary sigh that this, then, was Edmond.

Gerty scooted around the big man and hurried out the doorway just as Edmond advanced into the room. A trail of servants followed, carrying bowls of water and an assortment of trays with odd-shaped jars on them. The servants placed their trays on the floor next to the bed and then turned, bowed to Duncan, and left. They all acted like scared rabbits. And why wouldn't they? Madelyne asked herself. After all, there were two wolves in the room with her and wasn't that enough to scare anyone?

Edmond still hadn't said a word to his brother. Duncan didn't want a confrontation in front of Madelyne. He knew he'd become angry, and that would frighten Madelyne. Yet, he wasn't about to back down either.

"Have you no greeting for your brother, Edmond?" Duncan asked.

The ploy worked. Edmond looked surprised by the question. His face lost some of its anger. "Why wasn't I informed of your plan to bring Louddon's sister back with you? I have only just learned that Gilard understood the way of it from the beginning."

"I suppose he boasted of it too," Duncan said, shaking his head.

"He did."

"Gilard exaggerates, Edmond. He had no knowledge of my intentions."

"And your reason for keeping this plan secret, Duncan?" Edmond asked.

"You would have argued over it," Duncan remarked. He smiled over his own admission, as if he would have found pleasure in the fight.

Madelyne observed the change in Duncan's manner. She was truly amazed. Why, he looked so ruggedly handsome when he smiled. Aye, she thought, he looked human. And that, she scolded herself, was all she would allow herself to think about his appearance.

"When have you ever turned your back on an argument?" Edmond shouted at his brother.

The walls surely rocked from the noise. Madelyne wondered if both Edmond and Gilard suffered from a hearing problem of some sort.

Edmond wasn't as tall as Duncan, not when they stood so close together. He looked more like Duncan than Gilard did though. He was just as mean-looking when he scowled. The facial features were almost identical, down to their frowns. Edmond's hair wasn't black though; it was as brown as a newly plowed field and just as rich in thickness. And when he turned to look at her, Madelyne thought she saw a smile light those dark brown eyes before they turned as cold as stone.

"If you think to yell at me, Edmond, I must tell you I'm not up to listening," Madelyne said.

Edmond didn't reply. He folded his arms across his chest and stared at her, long and hard, until Duncan told him to see to her injury.

When the middle brother walked over to the bed, Madelyne began to get frightened again. "I would prefer that you leave me alone," she said, trying to keep her voice from shaking.

"Your preferences do not concern me," Edmond remarked. His voice was now as soft as hers had been.

She admitted defeat when Edmond motioned for her to show him which leg he was to tend. He was large enough to force her, and Madelyne needed to keep her strength for the ordeal ahead of her.

Edmond's expression didn't change when she lifted the covering. Madelyne was careful to shield the rest of her body from his view. She was a modest lady, after all, and it was best that Edmond understand that from the beginning.

Duncan walked over to the other side of the bed. He frowned when Edmond touched Madelyne's leg, and she grimaced in pain.

"You'd best hold her down, Duncan," Edmond remarked. His voice was mild now, his concentration obviously centered on the task ahead of him.

"Nay! Duncan?"

She couldn't keep the frantic look from her eyes.

"There isn't any need," Duncan instructed his brother.

He looked at Madelyne and added, "I'll hold her down *if* it becomes necessary."

Madelyne's shoulders sagged against the bed again. She nodded and a look of calm settled on her face.

Duncan was certain he'd have to restrain her, else Edmond wouldn't be able to complete the task of cleaning the wound and sewing her flesh back together. There'd be pain, intense but necessary, and it would be no disgrace for a woman to scream during the ordeal.

Edmond lined up his supplies and was finally ready to begin. He looked at his brother, received his nod, and turned to look at Madelyne. What he saw surprised him into stillness. There was trust in those magnificent blue eyes, and not a trace of fear in evidence. She was quite beautiful, Edmond admitted, just as Gilard had claimed.

"You may begin, Edmond," Madelyne whispered then, interrupting Edmond's thoughts.

Edmond watched Madelyne wave her hand in a regal gesture indicating she was waiting. He almost smiled over her show of authority. Her husky voice surprised him too. "Would it be easier if you just used a hot knife to seal the wound?"

Before Edmond could answer her, Madelyne hastened on. "I do not mean to tell you the way of it," she said. "Please don't take offense, but it does seem barbaric of you to use a needle and thread."

"Barbaric?"

Edmond looked as if he were having trouble following the conversation.

Madelyne sighed. She decided she was too exhausted to try to make him understand. "You may begin, Edmond," she repeated. "I'm ready."

"I may?" Edmond asked, looking up at Duncan to catch his reaction.

Duncan was too worried to smile over Madelyne's conversation. He looked grim.

"You're a bossy bit of goods," Edmond told Madelyne. The rebuke was softened by his smile.

"Get on with it," Duncan muttered. "The waiting is worse than the deed."

Edmond nodded. He closed his mind to everything but his duty. Bracing himself against the screams he knew

91

would start as soon as he touched her, he then began the cleaning.

She never made a sound. Sometime during the ordeal, Duncan sat down on the bed. Madelyne immediately turned her face into his side. She acted as though she were trying to squeeze underneath him. Her fingernails dug into his thigh, but he didn't think she was aware of what she was doing.

Madelyne didn't think she'd be able to bear the pain much longer. She was thankful Duncan was there, though she couldn't understand why she felt that way. She couldn't seem to think much at all now, only accepted that Duncan had become her anchor to hold on to for dear life. Without him her control would collapse.

Just when she was certain she was going to start screaming, she felt the needle pierce her skin. Sweet oblivion claimed her, and she felt nothing more.

Duncan knew the second Madelyne fainted. He slowly pried her hand away from his thigh and gently turned her cheek until her entire face was visible to him. Tears wet her cheeks and he slowly wiped them away.

"I think I would have preferred her yelling," Edmond muttered as he worked the ragged flesh together with his needle and thread.

"It wouldn't have made it any easier for you," Duncan answered. He stood when Edmond finished and watched his brother wrap a thick cotton strip around Madelyne's thigh.

"Hell, Duncan, she's probably going to get the fever and die anyway," Edmond predicted with a scowl.

His comment infuriated Duncan. "Nay! I'll not allow it, Edmond."

Edmond was shocked by Duncan's vehement statement. "You would care, brother?"

"I would care," Duncan admitted.

Edmond didn't know what to say. He stood with his mouth open and watched his brother walk out of the room.

With a weary sigh Edmond followed his brother.

Duncan had already left the castle and was making his way to the lake located behind the butcher's hut. The bitterness of the weather was welcomed, for it took his mind off the questions nagging him.

The ritualistic nightly swim was yet another demand

Duncan made on his mind and his body. Aye, it was a challenge meant to toughen him against discomfort. He neither looked forward to the swim nor avoided it. And he never wavered from this ritual either, be it summer or winter.

Duncan stripped off his garments and made a clean dive into the frigid water, hoping the cold would be enough to put Madelyne out of his thoughts for just a few minutes.

A short time later Duncan ate his supper. Edmond and Gilard kept him company, an unusual occurrence to be sure, as Duncan was in the habit of taking all his meals in solitude. The two younger brothers talked of many things, but neither dared question Duncan about Lady Madelyne. Duncan's silence and perpetual scowl throughout the meal didn't lend itself to discussion of any issue.

Duncan couldn't remember what he'd eaten. He determined to get some rest, but when he finally took to his bed, the picture of Madelyne kept intruding. He told himself he'd become accustomed to having her near, and surely that was the only reason he couldn't sleep. An hour passed and then another, and still Duncan continued to toss and turn.

By the middle of the night Duncan gave up the battle. He cursed himself all the way up to the tower room, telling himself he wanted only to look in on Madelyne, to make certain she hadn't defied him by dying.

Duncan stood in the doorway a long while, until he heard Madelyne cry out in her sleep. The sound pulled him inside. He shut the door, added more logs to the fire, and then went to Madelyne.

She was sleeping on her good side with her gown bunched up around her thighs. Duncan tried, but couldn't get her clothing adjusted to his satisfaction. Frustrated, he used his dagger to slit the material. He didn't stop until he'd removed both her bliaut and chainse, telling himself she'd be far more comfortable without them.

She wore only her white chemise now. The scooped neck showed the swell of her breasts. There was a wide yoke of delicate embroidery around the neckline; threads of red and yellow and green had been meticulously worked into a border of springtime flowers. It was such a feminine accomplishment, and one that pleased Duncan, because he knew she'd spent long hours working on the task.

Madelyne was as exquisite and as feminine as the flowers on her chemise. What a gentle creature she was. Her skin was flawless, dappled now into a golden hue by the flickering light from the fire.

Lord, she was lovely. "Hell," he muttered to himself. Madelyne was a sight better than lovely without her gown obstructing his view.

When she started to shiver, Duncan got into bed beside her. The tension slowly ebbed from his shoulders. Aye, he was used to having her next to him, and surely that was the reason he now felt such contentment.

Duncan pulled the cover up over the two of them. He was about to put his arm around her waist and move her closer to him, but Madelyne was quicker. She scooted up against him, until her backside was snuggled up most intimately against the junction of his thighs.

Duncan smiled. Lady Madelyne had obviously become accustomed to having him near, too, and his arrogant grin was all because he knew she wasn't aware of it . . . yet.

Chapter Seven

"A soft answer turneth away wrath."

OLD TESTAMENT, PROVERBS, 15:1

Madelyne slept almost twenty-four hours. When she finally opened her eyes, the room was cast in afternoon shadows with only a few streamers of sunlight filtering through the wooden shutters. Everything looked hazy to Madelyne, and she felt so disoriented that she couldn't remember where she was.

She tried to sit up in bed, grimaced against the sting that movement caused her, and remembered every bit of it then.

Lord, she felt awful. Every muscle in her body ached. Madelyne thought someone might have taken a stick to her backside, or glued a hot iron rod against the side of her leg. Her stomach grumbled, but she didn't want anything to eat. No, she was just terribly thirsty and blazing hot. All she wanted was to tear off her clothes and stand in front of an open window.

That idea seemed perfectly wonderful. She tried to get out of bed to open the shutters, yet was too weak even to kick the covers out of her way. She kept on trying until she realized she wasn't wearing her own clothes. Someone had removed them, and while that fact did offend her sense of modesty, it wasn't nearly as alarming as the realization that she had absolutely no memory of the deed.

Madelyne was now wearing a white cotton shirt of some kind, an indecent garment to be sure, for it barely covered her knees. The sleeves were too long though. When she tried to fold the fabric back to her wrists, she remembered where she'd seen such a garment before. Why, it was a man's shirt, and from its gigantic proportions around the shoulders, obviously belonged to Duncan. It was the same all right; Duncan had been wearing an identical shirt when he slept beside her in the tent the night before . . . or was it two nights past now? Madelyne was too sleepy to remember. She decided to close her eyes for another minute to think about it.

She had the most peaceful dream. Madelyne was eleven years old again and living with her dear uncle, Father Berton. Father Robert and Father Samuel had come to Grinsteade manor to visit her uncle and to pay their respects to old man Morton, lord of Grinsteade manor. Aside from the peasants who worked Baron Morton's small land holding, Madelyne was the only young person in residence. She was surrounded by gentle, kind men, and all old enough to be her grandfather. Both Father Robert and Father Samuel had come from the overcrowded Claremont monastery. Lord Morton offered them permanent quarters. The old man had taken quite a liking to Father Berton's friends. Both were excellent chess players, and both enjoyed listening to the baron recount his favorite stories of the past.

Madelyne was surrounded by doting old men who believed her to be a most gifted child. They took turns teaching her how to read and write, and Madelyne's dream centered on one particularly peaceful evening. She sat at the table and read to her "uncles" from the writings she had transcribed. A fire blazed in the hearth and there was a warm, tranquil atmosphere in the room. Madelyne was retelling an unusual story, that of the adventures of her favorite hero, Odysseus. The mighty warrior kept her company during her dream, standing over her shoulder and smiling down at her as she recounted the wonderful events of his long journey.

The next time she awakened, and surely only a few minutes had passed since she had decided to rest for just a bit, Madelyne immediately realized that someone had actually tied her eyelids shut. "How dare I be treated this way?" She muttered the outrage aloud, to no one in particular.

The binding was wet too. Madelyne ripped the offending restraint off her with an expletive worthy of a bawdy peasant. Odd, but she thought she heard someone laugh then. She tried to concentrate on the sound, when her mind was turned again. Damn if another binding wasn't slapped against her forehead. That didn't make sense at all. Hadn't she just removed it? She shook her head over the confusion of it all.

Someone spoke to her, but she couldn't understand what he was saying. If he would stop whispering and quit garbling every word, it would make it so much easier. She thought whoever was speaking to her was being terribly rude and yelled just that opinion.

Madelyne suddenly remembered how hot she was, when another cover was weighed down on her shoulders. She knew she had to get to the window and breathe some of the healing cold air. It was the only thing that would save her from this heat. Why, if she hadn't known better, she would have thought she was in purgatory. But she was a good girl and that couldn't be true. No, she was going to heaven, damn if she wasn't.

Why couldn't she open her eyes? She felt someone tug on her shoulders and then a drink of cool water touched her parched lips. Madelyne tried to take a long gulp, but the water suddenly vanished after she had tasted only a small, puny portion. Someone was out to play a cruel trick on her, she decided, frowning as ferociously as she could manage under the circumstances.

All of a sudden, everything became crystal-clear. Why, she was in Hades, not purgatory, and at the mercy of all the monsters and demons who tried to trick Odysseus. Now they tried to trick her. Well, she told herself, she was having none of it.

The idea of these demons didn't upset Madelyne at all.

Quite the contrary. She became absolutely infuriated. Her uncles had lied to her. The stories of Odysseus weren't falsehoods or legends passed down from generation to generation. The monsters did exist. She could feel them surrounding her, just waiting for her to open her eyes.

And just where was Odysseus? she demanded to know. How dare he leave her alone to fight his demons? Didn't he understand what he was supposed to do? Hadn't anyone told him about his own triumphs?

Madelyne felt someone touch her thigh, interrupting her disgruntled thoughts. She knocked off the new binding scorching her eyes and turned her head just in time to see who was kneeling beside her bed. She screamed then, an instinctive reaction to the horrible one-eyed giant looking at her with such a smirk on his distorted face, and then she remembered she was angry, not frightened. It was one of the Cyclops all right, maybe even their leader, Polyphemus, the most despicable of them all, and out to get her if she'd allow it.

Madelyne made a fist and struck the giant a powerful blow. She aimed for his nose, missed it by an inch or two, but was just as satisfied. The action exhausted her and she fell back against the mattress, suddenly as weak as a kitten. There was a smug smile on her face, however, for she had heard Polyphemus let out a howl of distress.

Madelyne turned her head away from the Cyclops, determined to ignore the monster poking at her thigh. She looked over at the hearth. And then she saw him. Why, he was standing right in front of the fire, with light shining all around his magnificent body. He was much bigger than she had imagined him to be, and much more attractive. But then, he wasn't mortal, she tried to remind herself. She guessed that fact accounted for his giant proportions and the mystical light glowing all around him. "And just where have you been?" she demanded with a yell meant to gain his attention.

Madelyne wasn't sure if mythological warriors could converse with mere mortals, quickly surmised that this one didn't, or wouldn't, because he just continued to stand there and stare at her, and didn't offer a single word in answer to her demand.

She thought to try again, though she found it a terribly

exasperating task. There was a Cyclops right beside her, for God's sake, and even if the warrior couldn't speak to her, he could see that there was work to be done. "Get on with it, Odysseus," Madelyne demanded, pointing her finger at the monster kneeling beside her.

Damn if he didn't just stand there and look confused. For all his size and might, he didn't appear to be overly intelligent. "Must I fight every battle on my own?" she demanded to know, raising her voice until the muscles in her neck began to ache from the strain. Tears of frustration clouded her vision, but she couldn't help that. Odysseus was trying to vanish into the light. How very rude of him, she thought.

She couldn't allow him to disappear. Dimwitted or not, he was all she had. Madelyne tried to placate him. "I promise to forgive you for all the times you let Louddon hurt me, but I'll not forgive you if you leave me alone now."

Odysseus didn't seem overly concerned with gaining her forgiveness. She could barely see him now, knew he'd soon be gone, and realized she'd have to increase her threats if she was going to get any help from him.

"If you leave me, Odysseus, I'll send someone after you to teach you some manners. Aye," she added, warming to her threat. "I'll send the most fearsome of all warriors. Just you leave and see what happens! If you don't get rid of him," she declared, pausing in her threat to point dramatically at the Cyclops a long moment, "I'll send Duncan after you."

Madelyne was so satisfied with herself that she closed her eyes with a sigh. She had surely put the fear of Zeus into the most magnificent of creatures, the powerful Odysseus, by pretending to send Duncan after him. She let out a rather inelegant snort over her cleverness.

She peeked a quick look back out of one eye to see how her threat was being taken, and smiled with victory. Odysseus looked worried. And that, Madelyne suddenly decided, wasn't good enough. If he was going to fight a Cyclops, he'd need to be good and angry. "Duncan is really a wolf, you understand, and he'll tear you to shreds if I tell him to," she boasted. "He'll do anything I ask," she added, "Just like that." Madelyne tried to snap her fingers together but couldn't quite manage the feat.

She closed her eyes again, feeling as though she'd just won

an important battle. And all with gentle words, she reminded herself. She hadn't used any force at all. "I am ever a gentle maiden," she shouted. "Damn, if I'm not."

For three long days and nights Madelyne fought the mythological monsters who appeared and try to snatch her away to Hades. Odysseus was always there, by her side, helping her ward off each attack when she demanded it.

At times the stubborn giant even conversed with her. He liked to question her about her past, and when she understood what he was asking, she'd immediately answer him. Odysseus seemed most interested in a specific time of her childhood. He wanted her to tell what it had been like after her mother had died and Louddon had taken over her guardianship.

She hated answering those questions. She wanted to talk only about her life with Father Berton. Yet she didn't want Odysseus to become angry and leave her either. For that reason, she suffered through his gentle interrogation.

"I don't want to talk about *him.*"

Duncan was jarred awake by Madelyne's vehement outburst. He didn't know what she was ranting about now but quickly went to her bed. He sat down next to Madelyne and took her into his arms. "Hush now," he whispered. "Go back to sleep, Madelyne."

"When he made me come back from Father Berton's home, he was so horrible. He'd sneak into my room every night. He'd just stand there, at the foot of the bed. I could feel him staring at me. I thought that if I opened my eyes . . . I was very afraid."

"Don't think about Louddon now," Duncan said. He stretched out on the bed as soon as she began to cry and pulled her into his arms.

Though he was careful to hide his reaction, inside he was shaking with rage. He knew Madelyne didn't understand what she was telling him, but he understood well enough.

Soothed by his touch, Madelyne fell asleep again. She didn't rest long, however, and awakened to find Odysseus was still there, keeping vigil. She wasn't afraid when he was by her side. Odysseus was the most wonderful warrior. He was strong, arrogant, though she didn't fault him for that flaw, and filled with a good heart.

He was full of mischief too. His favorite game was to change his appearance. It would happen so quickly, Madelyne didn't even have time to draw a breath of surprise. One minute he pretended to be Duncan and the next he was back to being Odysseus again. And once, during the dark hours of the night, when Madelyne was most afraid, he actually changed himself into Achilles, just to amuse her. He was sitting there, in a straight-back wooden chair that was entirely too little for his size and bulk, just looking at her in the most peculiar way.

Achilles wasn't wearing his boots. That worried her and she immediately cautioned him to protect his heels from injury. Achilles looked confused by her suggestion, forcing Madelyne to remind him that his mama had dipped him headfirst in the magical waters of Styx, making all of him invincible, save for the tiny bit of flesh on the backs of his heels, where she'd held on to him so he wouldn't be swept away by the swirling waters.

"The water didn't touch your heels, and that is where you are most vulnerable," she instructed him. "Do you understand my meaning?"

She decided he didn't understand at all. His puzzled look told her as much. Perhaps his mama hadn't taken the time to tell him the story. Madelyne sighed and gave him a sad, pitying look. She knew what was going to happen to Achilles, yet didn't have the heart to tell him to beware of stray arrows. She guessed he'd find out soon enough.

Madelyne started to weep over Achilles's future, when he suddenly stood up and walked over to her. But he wasn't Achilles now. Nay, it was Duncan taking her into his arms and soothing her. Odd, but his touch felt just like Odysseus's.

Madelyne nagged Duncan into getting into bed beside her, then immediately rolled on top of him. She propped her head on his chest so she could look into his eyes. "My hair is like a curtain," she told him, "hiding your face from everyone but me. What think you of that, Duncan?"

"So I am Duncan once again, am I?" he answered. "You don't know what you're saying, Madelyne. You burn with fever. That is what I think," he added.

"Are you going to call a priest?" Madelyne asked. Her question upset her and tears filled her eyes.

"Would you like that?" Duncan asked.

"Nay," Madelyne bellowed right into his face. "If a priest be called, I'll know I'm dying. I'm not ready to die yet, Duncan. There's too much to do."

"And what would you like to do?" Duncan asked, smiling over her ferocious expression.

Madelyne suddenly leaned down and rubbed her nose against Duncan's chin. "I think I would like to kiss you, Duncan. Does that make you angry?"

"Madelyne, you must rest," Duncan said. He tried to roll her to her side, but she proved to be as clinging as a vine. Duncan didn't force her, concerned he might accidentally hurt her. In truth, he liked her just where she was.

"If you kiss me just once, then I'll rest," she promised. She didn't give him time to respond but slapped her hands on both sides of his face and pressed her face against his.

Lord, did she kiss him then. Her mouth was hot, open, and thoroughly arousing. It was such a lustful, passionate kiss, Duncan couldn't help but respond. His arms slowly slipped around her waist. When he felt warm skin, he realized her skirt had ridden up. His hands stroked her soft buttock and it wasn't long before he was caught up in a fever of his own.

Madelyne was wild and thoroughly undisciplined when she kissed him. Her mouth slanted over his, her tongue penetrated and stroked until she was breathless.

"When I kiss you, I don't want to stop. 'Tis sinful, isn't it?" she asked Duncan.

He noticed she didn't look particularly remorseful over her admission and assumed the fever had rid her of her inhibitions. "I have you flat on your back, Duncan. I could have my way with you if I wanted."

Duncan sighed in exasperation. The sigh turned into a groan, however, when Madelyne snatched his hand and boldly placed it over one of her breasts.

"Nay, Madelyne," Duncan muttered, though he didn't take his hand away. God, she felt so warm. The nipple hardened when his thumb instinctively rubbed against it. He groaned again. "'Tis not the time for loving. You don't know what you're doing to me, do you?" he asked then. Lord, his voice sounded as harsh as the howling wind outside.

Madelyne immediately started to cry. "Duncan? Tell me that I matter to you. Even if it's a lie, tell me anyway."

"Aye, Madelyne, you matter to me," Duncan answered. He wrapped his arms around her waist and rolled her to his side. "'Tis the truth."

He knew he had to put some distance between them, else lose this battle of sweet torture. Yet he couldn't help but kiss her once again.

The action seemed to placate her. Before Duncan could draw another shaky breath, Madelyne had fallen asleep.

The fever ruled Madelyne's mind and Duncan's life. He dared not leave her alone with Gilard or Edmond. When her passionate nature asserted itself, he didn't want either of his brothers to be the recipient of her kisses. No one was going to offer comfort to Madelyne in those uninhibited moments but him.

The demons finally left Madelyne during the third night. On the morning of the fourth day she awakened feeling as wrung out as one of the damp cloths littering the floor. Duncan was sitting in the chair beside the fireplace. He looked exhausted. Madelyne wondered if he'd taken ill. She was about to ask him that question, when he suddenly noticed she was staring at him. He bounded to his feet with the quickness of a wolf and came to stand beside the bed. Odd, but she thought he looked relieved.

"You've had the fever," Duncan announced. His voice was gruff.

"So that is why my throat aches," Madelyne said. Lord, she barely recognized her own voice. It sounded hoarse, felt raw.

Madelyne looked around the room, took in the clutter surrounding her. She shook her head in confusion. Had a battle taken place here while she slept?

When she turned back to ask Duncan about the chaos, she caught his amused expression.

"Your throat is paining you?" he asked.

"You find it amusing my throat hurts?" Madelyne asked, disgruntled over his unkind reaction.

Duncan shook his head, denying her accusation. Madelyne wasn't at all convinced. He was still grinning.

Heavens, he did look fit this morning. Duncan was dressed in black, an austere color to be sure, yet when he smiled, those gray eyes didn't look cold or intimidating. He reminded her of someone, but she couldn't think who that would be. Madelyne was certain she'd remember meeting anyone who remotely resembled the Baron Wexton. Still, there was an elusive memory of someone else . . .

Duncan interrupted her concentration. "Now that you're awake, I'll send a servant to tend to you. You're not going to leave this room until you're healed, Madelyne."

"Was I very ill?" Madelyne asked.

"Aye, you were very ill," Duncan admitted. He turned and walked to the door.

Madelyne thought he was in quite a hurry to get away from her. She pushed a clump of hair out of her eyes and stared at Duncan's back. "Lord, I must look as messy as a mop," she muttered to herself.

"Aye, you do," Duncan answered.

She could hear the smile in his voice. She frowned over his rudeness and then called out, "Duncan? How long did I have the fever?"

"Over three days, Madelyne."

He turned back to catch her reaction. Madelyne looked astonished. "You don't recall any of it, do you?" he asked.

Madelyne shook her head, totally bewildered now, because Duncan was smiling again. He was such a strange man, finding humor in the oddest things.

"Duncan?"

"Aye?"

She caught the exasperation in his voice and bristled over it. "Were you here all three days? In this room with me?"

He began to pull the door closed behind him. Madelyne didn't think he was going to answer her question until his voice rang out, firm and insistent.

"I was not."

The door slammed shut behind him.

Madelyne didn't think he was telling the truth. She couldn't remember what had happened, yet instinctively knew Duncan hadn't left her side.

Why had he denied it? "What a contrary man you are," Madelyne whispered.

There was a smile in her voice.

Chapter Eight

"Prove all things, hold fast that which is good."

NEW TESTAMENT, 1 THESSALONIANS, 5:21

Madelyne sat on the side of her bed, willing strength back into her legs. A timid knock sounded at the door just a few minutes after Duncan had left. Madelyne called out and a servant entered the room. The woman was parchment-thin and haggard-looking, with stooped shoulders and lines of worry creasing her wide forehead. As the servant approached the bed, her steps became labored.

The servant looked ready to bolt, and it suddenly dawned on Madelyne that she might be afraid. The woman kept giving longing glances toward the door.

Madelyne smiled, trying to ease the servant's discomfort, though she was puzzled over her timid behavior.

The woman held something behind her back. She slowly made the satchel visible and then blurted out, "I've brung your baggage, milady."

"'Tis most kind of you," Madelyne answered.

She could tell her compliment pleased the woman. She didn't look as worried now, only a bit confused.

"I don't know why you are so afraid of me," Madelyne said, deciding to face the problem head on. "I'll not harm you, I can promise you that. What have the Wexton brothers told you to make you so frightened?"

Madelyne's bluntness eased the tension in the woman's posture. "They didn't tell me nothing, milady, but I ain't deaf. I could hear the yelling going on up here all the way down to the buttery, and you was doing the most of it."

"I was yelling?" Madelyne was horrified over such a suggestion. Surely the woman was mistaken.

"You was," the servant answered, nodding her head vigorously. "I knew you had the fever and couldn't help what you was doing. Gerty's bringing you food in a minute. I'm to help you change your clothes, if that be your want."

"I am hungry," Madelyne remarked. She flexed her legs, testing their strength. "I'm also as weak as an infant. By what name are you called?"

"Me name's Maude, after the queen," she announced. "The dead one, of course, since our King William ain't taken a wife yet."

Madelyne smiled. "Maude, do you think I might manage a bath? I feel so sticky."

"A bath, milady?" Maude looked horrified by the idea. "In the dead of winter?"

"I'm accustomed to taking a bath every day, Maude, and it does seem an eternity since I last—"

"A bath a day? Whatever for?"

"I just like to feel clean," Madelyne answered. She took a good long look at the servant and decided the kind woman would benefit from a bath of her own, though she didn't offer her comment lest she offend the kind woman. "Do you think your lord would permit me this vanity?"

Maude shrugged. "You're to have anything you want, so long as you stay in this room. The baron doesn't want you getting sick trying to overdo. I guess I could find a tub around here and have my man haul it up the steps."

"You have a family, Maude?"

"Aye, a good man and a lad nearly five summers now. The boy's a wild one."

Maude helped Madelyne stand up and walked with her

over to the chair by the hearth. "My boy's named William," she went on. "Named him after our dead king though, and not the one who's running things now."

The door opened during Maude's recitation. Another servant hurried inside, carrying a trencher of food. Maude called out, "Gerty, ain't no need to be nervous. She ain't daft like we supposed."

Gerty smiled. She was a bulky woman with a pure complexion and brown eyes. "I'm cook here," she informed Madelyne. "Heard you was pretty. Skinny though, much too skinny. Eat every bit of this food, else you'll blow away with the first good wind."

"She's wanting a bath, Gerty," Maude announced.

Gerty raised an eyebrow. "Guess she can have it then. Can't be blaming us if she gets chilled."

The two women continued to visit with each other as they cleaned Madelyne's room. They were obviously fast friends and Madelyne thoroughly enjoyed listening to their gossip.

They helped her with her bath too. By the time the tub was removed, Madelyne was exhausted. She'd washed her hair, but it was taking an eternity to dry. Madelyne sat on a soft animal skin in front of the hearth. She lifted strands of her long hair close to the heat so that it would dry faster, until her arms began to ache. With a loud, unladylike yawn, Madelyne stretched out on the furry skin, thinking she'd rest for just a minute or two. She wore only her chemise, yet didn't want to dress until her hair was dried and plaited.

Duncan found Madelyne sound asleep. She made an enticing picture, sleeping on her side in front of the fire. Her golden legs were drawn up against her chest, and her glorious hair covered most of her face.

He couldn't help but smile. Lord, she reminded him of a kitten, curled up so snugly. Aye, she was enticing all right, and she was probably going to freeze to death if he didn't do something.

Madelyne didn't even open her eyes when Duncan picked her up and carried her over to the bed. He smiled over the way she instinctively cuddled up against his chest. She sighed, too, as if she were most content, and damn, she was smelling like roses again.

Duncan placed her on the bed and covered her. He tried to keep his manner distant, but he couldn't seem to stop himself from brushing his hand against the smoothness of her cheek.

Madelyne looked so vulnerable when she was sleeping. Surely that was the reason he didn't want to leave. The urge to protect her was overwhelming. She was so innocent and so trusting. In his heart he knew he'd never let her go back to her brother. She was an angel and he'd not allow her near the demon Louddon, ever again.

The rules had turned upside down on Duncan. With a frustrated groan he walked over to the door. Hell, he thought, he didn't know his own mind anymore.

It was Madelyne's doing, though she certainly couldn't be aware of that fact. She drove him to distraction, and when he was near her, he couldn't think much at all.

Duncan decided he'd have to put distance between himself and Madelyne until he settled the issues bothering him. Yet, as soon as he made up his mind to avoid Madelyne, his mood blackened. Duncan muttered an expletive, turned, and slowly closed the door behind him.

Madelyne was still weak enough that the enforced isolation didn't bother her. Yet after two more days, with only Gerty and Maude making an occasional visit, she was feeling the effects of her prison. She paced the room until she knew every inch of it by heart, and then began to drive the servants to distraction when she insisted on doing what they deemed was common work. Madelyne scrubbed the floor and the walls. The physical exercise didn't help much. She felt as caged as an animal. And she waited, hour upon hour, for Duncan to come to her.

Madelyne kept telling herself that she should be thankful Duncan had all but forgotten her. Lord, wasn't she used to being forgotten?

When another two days had passed, Madelyne was close to throwing herself out the window just to diversify her routine. She was bored enough to scream.

She stood by the window and stared out into the fading sunset, thinking about Duncan.

Madelyne thought she might have conjured him up in her mind, for even as she thought about how much she wanted to see him, he suddenly appeared. The door opened, bouncing against the stone wall announcing his arrival, and there he stood, looking fierce and powerful, and altogether too handsome for her peace of mind. God's truth, she could have stared at him for the rest of the evening.

"Edmond is going to remove the threads now," Duncan told her.

Duncan walked into the room and over to stand in front of the hearth. He folded his arms across his chest, giving Madelyne the idea that he was bored with this mission.

She was hurt by his cold manner, yet determined he'd never know it. She gave him what she hoped was a most tranquil expression.

Lord, she was a sight to behold. Madelyne was dressed in a cream-colored gown and a blue overtunic. A braided rope was wrapped around her slender waist, accentuating her feminine curves.

Her hair wasn't pulled away from her face but rested against the swell of her breasts. Such a thick, curly mass of hair it was, worthy of any queen, the color of sable, Duncan thought, though intertwined with threads of red as well. He remembered the feel of it, so soft and silky.

He scowled, irritated over the way she continued to disturb him. He couldn't quit staring at Madelyne either, admitting that he'd missed having her by his side. A foolish thought, and one he'd never openly acknowledge, but there all the same, prickling him into a new awareness.

It suddenly dawned on him that Madelyne was wearing his colors, and he grinned. He doubted she was aware of that fact, and had she not looked so damn kissable, he might have mentioned it just to see her reaction.

Madelyne couldn't look at Duncan long. She was afraid he'd see how much she'd missed him. And then he'd have a good gloat, she thought to herself.

"I would like to know what you are going to do with me, Duncan," she said. She turned her gaze to the floor, not daring to look up to see how he was taking her question, else completely lose her train of thought.

Aye, her ability to concentrate was always in jeopardy whenever she was around Duncan. She didn't understand her reaction to him, but accepted it all the same. The baron was able to worry her without speaking a word. He disturbed her peace of mind, confused her too. When he was close to her, she wanted him to leave. Yet when he was away from her, she missed him.

Madelyne turned her back on Duncan and looked out the window again. "Do you think to keep me locked in this room for the rest of my life?"

Duncan smiled over the worry he'd heard in her voice. "Madelyne, the door wasn't barred," he said.

"Are you jesting?" Madelyne asked. She turned around and gave him the most incredulous look. "Do you mean to tell me I haven't been locked in this tower all week?" Lord, she felt like yelling. "I could have escaped?"

"Nay, you couldn't have escaped, but you could have left the room," Duncan answered.

"I don't believe you," Madelyne announced. She folded her arms in front of her, mocking his stance. "You would lie just to make me feel foolish. You have an unfair advantage, Duncan, for I never, ever lie. Therefore," she concluded, "it is an uneven match."

Edmond appeared in the open doorway. The middle brother was wearing his usual frown. Yet he looked wary, too, and stared at Madelyne a good while before he walked inside.

"You'll hold her down this time," he told Duncan.

Madelyne gave Duncan a worried glance and saw him smile. "Madelyne doesn't have a fever now, Edmond, and is as docile as a kitten," he remarked. He turned to Madelyne then and instructed her to go to the bed so that Edmond could remove the bandage.

Madelyne nodded. She knew what needed to be done, but shyness overcame common sense. "If you would both leave, I would have a moment's privacy to prepare."

"Prepare what?" Duncan asked.

"I am a gentle lady," Madelyne stammered. "I'll not let either of you see anything but my injury. That is what I would prepare."

She was blushing enough to make Duncan realize she'd meant every word. Edmond started to cough but Duncan's sigh was louder. "'Tis not the time for modesty, Madelyne. Besides, I've seen . . . your legs already."

Madelyne straightened her shoulders, gave him a good

glare, and then hurried over to the bed. She grabbed one of the animal skins that had fallen to the floor, and when she was situated on top of the bed, she draped the skin over her and then wiggled her garments up to the top of her thighs.

Edging the exposed bandage to the side, she began the slow task of unwinding the material.

Edmond knelt down beside her when the bandage was removed. Madelyne noticed a dark shadow beneath his left eye then. She wondered how he'd come by the bruise, and then jumped to the conclusion that one of his brothers was probably responsible. What hateful people, she told herself, even when she noticed Edmond was being very gentle as he removed the sticky threads from her skin.

"Why, it doesn't feel any worse than a pinch, Edmond," Madelyne said with relief.

Duncan had walked over to stand next to the bed. He looked ready to pounce if she moved.

And it was awkward, having both men staring at her thigh. She soon became embarrassed again. Thinking to turn Duncan's attention, she said the first thing that came into her mind. "Why are there locks on each side of the door?"

"What?" He did look perplexed.

"The slat of wood that slides into the loops to lock the door," Madelyne rushed on. "You've built loops on both sides. Why is that, do you suppose?" she asked, feigning great interest in such a ridiculous topic.

Her strategy worked, however. Duncan turned, stared at the door, and then looked back at her. He was staring at her face now, ignoring, for the moment, her exposed thigh.

"Well?" she challenged. "Were you so confused when you built the door you couldn't decide on which side to put the bars?"

"Madelyne, 'tis the same reason the staircase is built on the left," Duncan bantered. There was a definite sparkle in his eye. Madelyne was pleased by the change it made in his appearance. He wasn't nearly as worrisome when he smiled.

"And what is that reason?" Madelyne asked, smiling in spite of herself.

"Because I prefer it."

"A paltry reason, that," Madelyne announced.

She kept smiling until she realized she had hold of his hand. Madelyne quickly pulled free and turned to stare at Edmond.

The middle brother was looking at Duncan. He stood up then and said, "It has healed."

Madelyne looked down at the ugly jagged line that marked her thigh. She grimaced over the horrible scar. Yet she quickly gained control, ashamed by her shallow reaction. Why, she wasn't a vain woman. "Thank you, Edmond," she said as she pulled the cover over her leg.

Duncan hadn't seen the results of Edmond's work. He leaned forward to pull the animal skin away. Madelyne pushed his hand away and then pressed the edge of the cover against the bed. "He said it has healed, Duncan."

He obviously wanted to see for himself. Madelyne let out a startled yelp when Duncan ripped the cover away. She tried to push her gown down, but Duncan grabbed hold of her hands and slowly, deliberately, pushed the chainse up until all of her thigh was exposed.

"There isn't any infection," Edmond remarked to Duncan, watching the scene from the other side of the bed.

"Aye, it has healed," Duncan announced with a nod.

When he let go of Madelyne's hands, she smoothed her gown and asked, "You didn't believe your own brother?" She sounded appalled.

Duncan and Edmond exchanged a look Madelyne couldn't interpret. "Of course you don't," she muttered. "Probably gave him the black eye as well," she added, letting her disgust show. "'Tis what I would expect from the Wexton brothers."

Duncan showed his exasperation by turning and walking toward the door. His loud sigh followed him. Edmond stood there, frowning at Madelyne for another minute or so, and then followed his brother.

Madelyne repeated her gratitude. "I know you were ordered to care for my injury, Edmond, but I thank you all the same."

Madelyne was certain the sour man would abuse her compliment, and readied herself for his insults. No matter what vile thing he said to her, she'd humbly turn the other cheek.

Edmond didn't bother to say anything. Madelyne was

disappointed. How could she show the Wextons that she was a gentle maiden if they didn't give her the chance?

"Dinner will be in one hour's time, Madelyne. You may join us in the hall when Gilard comes for you."

Duncan walked out the doorway after making his announcement. Edmond, however, paused and then slowly turned around to look at Madelyne again. He seemed to be pondering some decision.

"Who is Polyphemus?"

Madelyne's eyes widened. What a strange question. "Why, he was a giant, the leader of the Cyclops in Homer's ancient tale," she answered. "Polyphemus was a horribly deformed giant with one huge eye right in the center of his forehead. He ate Odysseus's soldiers for his supper," she added with a dainty shrug of her shoulders.

Edmond didn't like her answer. "For God's sake," he muttered.

"You shouldn't be taking God's name in vain," Madelyne called out. "And why would you be asking me who Polyphemus was?"

Madelyne surmised, by the sound of fading footsteps, that Edmond wasn't going to answer her.

Yet even the rudeness of the middle brother didn't diminish Madelyne's pleasure. She bounded off the bed and let out a laugh. Lord, she was finally going to get out of this room. She did not believe for one second that the door had been unlocked all week. Duncan had told her that only to get her upset. Yes, he'd have me believe I'm dimwitted if I allowed it.

Madelyne dug through her satchel. She wished she had a pretty gown to wear and then realized the foolishness of the wish. She was their captive, for heaven's sake, not their invited guest.

It took her all of five minutes to prepare. She paced the room a long while and then walked over to the door to see how securely it was barred. With the first pull, the door opened wide, nearly knocking Madelyne down.

Duncan had obviously left the door open just to trick her. She wanted to believe that story—until she remembered that he'd left before Edmond.

Sounds floated up through the open stairway, drawing Madelyne to the landing. She leaned over the railing, strained to hear the conversation, but the distance proved too great to catch a clear word. Madelyne finally gave up and turned back to go into her room. She spotted the long wooden slat propped against the stone wall and on impulse took hold of it and dragged it inside her bedroom. She hid the slat beneath her bed, smiling to herself over her bold action. "I just might be inclined to lock you out, Duncan, instead of letting you lock me in."

As if she could allow much of anything, she thought. Lord, she'd been confined in this room for too long a period and surely that was the pitiful reason she found such amusement in her thoughts.

Gilard did take forever to come for her. Madelyne had already jumped to the conclusion that Duncan had lied to her. He was just being cruel.

When Madelyne heard the sound of footsteps, she smiled with relief and ran over to stand next to the window. Smoothing her gown and her hair into place, she forced a tranquil expression.

Gilard wasn't frowning. That was a surprise. He looked fit this evening, attired in the color of the forest in spring. The warm green made him look handsome.

There was tenderness in his voice when he spoke. "Lady Madelyne, I would have a word with you before we go downstairs," he announced in lieu of a greeting.

Gilard gave her a worried glance, clasped his hands behind his back, and proceeded to pace a path directly in front of her.

"Adela will probably join the family. She knows you're here and she—"

"Is unhappy?"

"Aye, though more than just unhappy. She hasn't said anything, but the look in her eyes makes me uneasy."

"Why are you telling me this?" Madelyne asked.

"Why, I tell you because I felt I owed you an explanation so that you could prepare yourself."

"Why are you concerned? You've obviously done a turn-around in your opinion of me. Is it because I helped you during the battle against my brother?"

"Well, of course," Gilard stammered.

"It's a sorry reason," Madelyne told him.

"You're sorry you saved my life?" Gilard asked.

"You misunderstand, Gilard. I'm sorry I was forced to take another man's life in order to aid you," she explained. "I'm not sorry I was able to help you though."

"Lady Madelyne, you contradict yourself," Gilard told her. He was frowning and looking confused.

He couldn't possibly understand. He was just too much like his brother. Aye, like Duncan, Gilard was used to killing, she supposed, and he'd never comprehend the shame she felt over her behavior. Lord, he probably viewed her aid as heroic. "I think I'd prefer you had found something good in me and that was the reason you've changed your opinion."

"I don't understand you," Gilard remarked, shrugging his shoulders.

"I know." The words were said so sadly Gilard felt like comforting her.

"You're an unusual woman."

"I try not to be. It is difficult, though, when you consider my past."

"I give you a compliment when I tell you I think you're unusual," Gilard returned, smiling over the worry he'd caught in her voice. Did she think unusual meant a flaw of some sort, he wondered.

He shook his head and then turned and led the way down the stairs, explaining as he went that if she slipped, she was to grab hold of his shoulders for support. The steps were wet, slick in spots.

Gilard kept up a steady monologue, but Madelyne was too nervous to listen to him. She was a bundle of worry inside over the possibility of meeting Adela.

When they reached the entrance to the hall, Gilard moved to her side. He offered her his arm. Madelyne denied the gallant gesture, concerned that Gilard's change of heart might not sit well with his brothers.

With a small shake of her head Madelyne folded her hands in front of her and turned her attention to the hall. Lord, it was gigantic in proportions, with a stone hearth taking up a fair portion of the wall facing her. To the right of the fireplace, yet some distance away, was a massive table, long enough to sit at least twenty. The table squatted atop a wooden platform. Scarred stools lined the length on both sides, some upright, more overturned.

A rather peculiar odor reached Madelyne, and she wrinkled her nose in response. She took a good look around her then and immediately spotted the cause. The rushes littering the floor were mottled with age. Why, they were ripe with staleness. A fire blazed in the hearth, heating the stench, and if that wasn't enough to turn a stomach, a dozen or so dogs added their own unwashed scent as they slept against each other in a contented pile in the center of the room.

Madelyne was appalled by the mess, but she was determined to keep her thoughts to herself. If the Wextons wished to live like animals, so be it. She certainly didn't care.

When Gilard nudged her, Madelyne started to walk toward the platform. Edmond was already seated at the table, his back to the wall behind him. The middle brother was watching her. He looked as if he were brooding over something. He tried to look right through her, just as she pretended to act unconcerned.

Once she and Gilard had taken their places at the table, soldiers of diverse rank and size filed into the room. They took up the remaining stools, save for the one at the head of the table, adjacent to Madelyne. She assumed the empty chair belonged to Duncan, for he was head of the Wexton clan.

Madelyne was about to ask Gilard when Duncan was going to join them, when Edmond's voice rang out. "Gerty!"

The bellow washed away Madelyne's question. The shout was promptly answered by a loud response, coming from the buttery to the right. "We hear you."

Gerty appeared then, juggling a stack of empty trenchers on one arm and a large platter of meat on the other. Two other serving girls followed in Gerty's wake, carrying additional platters, all brimming with food. A third servant appeared, ending the procession, with crusty loaves of bread in her hands and tucked under her arms.

What happened next was so revolting, Madelyne was struck speechless. Gerty slammed the platters down in the middle of the table, and motioned to the other servants to do the same. Trenchers flew like discs propelled on a battlefield, landing and spinning all around her, followed by fat jugs of ale. The men, led by Edmond, immediately began to eat.

This was obviously some sort of signal to the sleeping dogs, for they bounded to their feet and raced over to take up positions along the length on both sides of the table. Madelyne didn't understand the reason for this strange behavior until the first bone went flying over one of the soldiers' shoulders. The discarded bone was immediately snatched up by one of the larger dogs, a Levrier nearly twice the size of the greyhounds on either sides of him. Fierce growling came next, until another bit of garbage was thrown over another shoulder, and then another and another, until all the dogs were in a frenzy of feeding, just like the men surrounding her.

Madelyne stared at the men. She couldn't hide her repulsion and didn't even try. She did, however, lose her appetite.

Not a decent word was exchanged throughout the meal; only obscene grunts from men thoroughly enjoying their food could be heard over the snapping of the dogs at her backside.

She thought, at first, that it was all some sort of trick to make her sick, but when it continued on and on, until all the men had filled their bellies and belched their satisfaction, she was forced to reevaluate her way of thinking.

"You're not eating anything, Madelyne. Aren't you hungry?" Gilard asked with a mouth full of food. He had finally noticed that Madelyne hadn't touched any of the meat that had landed between them.

"I've lost my hunger," Madelyne whispered.

Madelyne watched Gilard take a long swig of ale, then wipe his mouth on the sleeve of his tunic. She closed her eyes. "Tell me this, Gilard," she finally managed, "why didn't the men wait for Duncan. I would think he would demand it."

"Oh, Duncan never eats with us," Gilard answered. He ripped a piece of bread from a long loaf and offered Madelyne a share. She shook her head.

"Duncan never eats with you?"

"Not since our father died and Mary took ill," Gilard qualified.

"Who is Mary?"

"Was," Gilard corrected her. "She's dead now." He belched before continuing. "She was housekeep. It was years past her time to die," he went on, rather callously in Madelyne's opinion. "I thought she'd outlive all of us. Adela wouldn't hear of replacing her, said it would hurt her feelings. Toward the end, Mary's eyes went bad on her and she couldn't find the table half the time."

Gilard took another huge bite of meat and casually flipped the bone over his shoulder. Madelyne was forced to dodge the garbage. A fresh spurt of anger washed over her.

"Anyway," Gilard continued, "Duncan is lord of this manor. He separates himself from the family as much as possible. I think he prefers to eat alone too."

"I don't doubt it," Madelyne muttered.

To think she'd actually looked forward to getting out of her room. "Do Duncan's men always eat with such enthusiasm?" she asked.

Gilard looked confused by her question. He shrugged his shoulders and said, "When they put in a full day, it would seem so."

When Madelyne thought she couldn't watch the men a moment longer, the ordeal abruptly came to an end. One by one the soldiers stood, belched, and took their leave. Had it not been so disgusting, she might have found the ritual humorous.

The dogs also retreated, lazily making their way back to form a new pyramid in front of the fireplace. Madelyne decided the animals were better disciplined than their masters. None of them belched their farewell.

"You didn't eat anything," Gilard said. "Didn't you enjoy the meal?" he asked. His voice was low. Madelyne thought he kept it that way so Edmond wouldn't hear.

"Was it a meal?" Madelyne asked, unable to keep the anger out of her voice.

"What would you call it?" Edmond interjected with a scowl the size of the hall.

"I would call it a feeding."

"I don't understand your meaning," Edmond said.

"Then I will be most happy to explain," Madelyne answered. "I've seen animals act with better manners." She nodded, emphasizing her comment. "Men of breeding eat their food, Edmond. What I have just witnessed wasn't a meal. Nay, it was a feeding by a pack of animals dressed as men. Is that clear enough for you?"

Edmond's face had turned flushed during her speech. He looked as if he wanted to leap across the table and throttle her. Madelyne was too angry to care. It had felt good to let go of some of her anger.

"I believe you've made your position quite clear. Wouldn't you agree, Edmond?"

Oh, Lord, it was Duncan speaking, and his deep voice came from right behind her back. She didn't dare turn around, else lose her newfound courage.

He felt terribly close. She leaned back just a little and felt his thighs touch her shoulder blades. Madelyne realized she shouldn't have touched him, remembering all too well the power in those muscular thighs of his.

She decided to knock him off the platform. Madelyne stood up, turned at the same time, and found herself plastered up against Baron Wexton. He hadn't given an inch, and it was Madelyne who was now forced to edge around him. She lifted her skirt and stepped off the platform, turned again, fully intending to tell Duncan just what she thought of his barbaric dinner. Then she made the mistake of looking up at him, stared into his gray eyes, and felt her courage run right out of her.

It was unfortunate, this mystical power he seemed to have over her mind. He was using it now, she told herself, robbing her of her thoughts. God help her, she couldn't even remember what she wanted to say to him.

Without a word of farewell, Madelyne turned and slowly walked away. She considered that victory enough, because she really would have preferred running.

Madelyne made it halfway to the entrance of the hall before Duncan's command stopped her. "Madelyne, I did not give you permission to leave." Each word was slowly enunciated.

Her back stiffened. Madelyne turned, gave him an insincere smile, and returned her answer with the same exaggerated tone.

"I didn't ask it."

She saw his astonished expression before she turned her back on him again. Madelyne started walking, muttering to herself that she was nothing but a pawn, after all, and pawns certainly didn't have to do the bidding of their captors. Aye, the injustices dealt out to her were so unfair. She was a good, gentle lady.

Because she was busy muttering to herself, she never heard Duncan move. He acted just like a wolf, she thought a little frantically when she felt his big hands settle on her shoulders.

Duncan applied subtle pressure to stop her, but it really hadn't been necessary. As soon as he touched her, he felt the stiffness leave her shoulders.

Madelyne sagged against him. Duncan felt her tremble. He realized then that she wasn't paying him the least attention. Nay, Madelyne was staring at the entrance of the hall. She was staring at Adela.

Chapter Nine

"Abhor that which is evil;
Cleave to that which is good."

NEW TESTAMENT, ROMANS, 12:9

Madelyne was horrified by the sight standing before her.
She recognized Adela immediately, for the woman looked
remarkably like her brother, Gilard. She had his brown-
colored hair, brown eyes too. But she wasn't nearly as tall as
Gilard, and she was much too thin, with a sallowness to her
complexion that indicated to Madelyne she hadn't been
well.

Adela was dressed in a gown that might have been a pale
color at one time. It was so covered with dirt and filth now,
the true color wasn't recognizable. Her hair, long and
stringy, appeared to be just as filthy as her gown. Madelyne
thought there might be more than dirt living in the sticky-
looking mess.

Madelyne wasn't repelled by Adela's appearance once her
initial shock had eased. She could see the haunted look in
the poor girl's eyes. There was pain there, and such despair.
Madelyne felt like weeping. Dear God, her brother had

caused this. Madelyne knew then that Louddon would spend eternity in hell.

Duncan wrapped his arm around Madelyne's shoulders and pulled her roughly up against his side. She didn't understand his motive, yet quit trembling in his embrace.

"I'll kill her, Duncan." Adela shouted the threat.

Edmond suddenly came into view. Madelyne watched him hurry over to his sister and take hold of her arm.

Adela slowly followed her brother to the table. Edmond was speaking to her but his voice was too low for Madelyne to hear what he was saying. He did seem to soothe his sister though. Her gait lost its stiffness and she nodded several times in response to her brother's words.

When Adela was seated next to Edmond, she suddenly screamed her threat again. "It is my right to kill her, Duncan."

There was such hatred in those eyes. Madelyne would have taken a step back had Duncan not held her so firmly.

She didn't know how to respond to the threat. Madelyne finally nodded, indicating to Adela that she understood what she promised, and then considered it might look as though she were in agreement. "You may try, Adela," she answered.

Her answer seemed to push Adela into a full rage. Duncan's sister stood up, so quickly the stool toppled off the platform and crashed to the stone floor.

"When you turn your back, I'll—"

"Enough." Duncan's voice echoed off the walls. The command got an immediate reaction from Adela. She seemed to wilt right before Madelyne's eyes.

Edmond obviously didn't like the way Duncan had shouted at their sister. He gave his brother a scowl before regaining Adela's chair and helping her sit down.

Duncan muttered an expletive. He let go of Madelyne's shoulders but kept her prisoner by taking hold of her hand. And then he walked out of the hall, pulling her behind him. Madelyne had to run to keep up.

Duncan didn't let up his pace or his grip until they had reached the narrow landing outside her tower bedroom.

"How could you let her get that way?" Madelyne demanded.

"Your brother is responsible," Duncan answered.

She knew she was going to start to cry. Madelyne straightened her shoulders. "I am very tired, Duncan. I would like to go to bed now."

She slowly walked into the room, praying he wouldn't follow. When she heard the clip of his boots against the steps, she knew he'd left.

Madelyne turned and closed the door, and almost made it to the bed before she started to weep.

Duncan immediately went back to the hall. He intended to command cooperation from his brothers on his plan for Madelyne.

Edmond and Gilard were still sitting at the table, sharing a jug of ale between them. Adela had, thankfully, already left the hall.

When Duncan sat down, Gilard passed the jug to Duncan just as Edmond challenged him. "Are we Wextons now going to have to protect Louddon's sister from one of our own?"

"Madelyne hasn't done anything to Adela," Gilard defended. "She's nothing like her brother and you damn well know it, Edmond. We've treated her shamefully, yet she hasn't spoken a single word of protest."

"Don't play Madelyne's champion to me," Edmond returned. "She *is* courageous," he admitted with a shrug. "You've already recounted the story of how she saved your backside during the battle, Gilard. God, you've retold it so many times, I know it by heart," he added, looking at Duncan now. "The issue isn't Madelyne's character, however. Her presence upsets Adela."

"Aye," Duncan interjected. "And that pleases me."

"What say you?" Edmond demanded.

"Edmond, before you lose your temper, answer me this. When did Adela last speak to you?"

"In London, right after we found her," Edmond answered. His voice sounded with irritation, but Duncan wasn't offended by it.

"Gilard? When did your sister last speak to you?"

"'Tis the same as Edmond," Gilard answered, frowning. "She told me what happened and that was all. You know she hasn't spoken a word to anyone since that night."

"Until this evening," Duncan reminded them. "Adela spoke to Madelyne."

"And you view this as a good sign?" Edmond asked, his voice incredulous. "Adela finally speaks, aye, but only of murder, brother. Good God, our sweet sister vows to kill Madelyne. I don't see this as recovery."

"Adela is coming back to us," Duncan explained. "There's anger now, so fierce it all but consumes her mind, but I think, with Madelyne's help, Adela will begin to heal."

Edmond shook his head. "When our sister Catherine came to visit, Adela wouldn't even look at her. Why do you think Madelyne can help when Adela's own sister couldn't?"

Duncan was hard pressed to put his feelings into explanation. He wasn't at all accustomed to discussing anything of significance with his two younger brothers. Nay, his usual custom was to issue commands, expecting each and every one to be carried out to his satisfaction. Duncan ruled his house just as he ruled his men, and in much the same manner as his father had ruled. The only exception to this sacred law was when he trained with his men. Then Duncan became an active participant as well as their instructor, demanding only from each soldier those feats he'd already accomplished himself.

Yet this was certainly not a usual circumstance. His brothers deserved to know what Duncan thought to do. Adela was also their sister. Aye, it was also their right to voice their opinions.

"I say we send for Catherine again," Edmond interjected, a stubborn set to his jaw.

"It isn't necessary," Duncan stated. "Madelyne will help Adela. We've only to give her direction," he added with a hint of a smile. "Madelyne is the only one who'll understand what's going on inside Adela's mind. Eventually our sister will turn to her."

"Aye, Duncan, Adela will turn to your Madelyne all right, but with a dagger in her hand and killing in her mind. We'll have to take every precaution."

"I don't want Madelyne placed in jeopardy," Gilard remarked. "I think we should have left her behind. Louddon would have found her soon enough. And she isn't Duncan's Madelyne, Edmond. We are all equally responsible for her."

"Madelyne is mine, Gilard," Duncan announced. His

voice was soft but the challenge was there, in the set of his shoulders and the way he stared at his brother.

Gilard reluctantly nodded agreement. Edmond watched the exchange between his brothers. He wasn't at all pleased by the possessive tone in Duncan's voice.

Edmond was suddenly in complete agreement with Gilard, a rarity, for Gilard and Edmond usually took opposing viewpoints in nearly all matters of substance. "Perhaps Madelyne should have remained behind," he said, thinking to next bring up the possibility of returning her as soon as possible.

Duncan's fist hit the table with enough force to overturn the ale. The jug would have toppled off the table had Gilard not reacted so quickly.

"Madelyne isn't going anywhere, Edmond. I'll not ask again, brother. Do you back me in this decision?"

A long moment of silence stretched between the two brothers.

"So that's the way of it," Edmond finally said.

Duncan nodded. Gilard watched the exchange, perplexed. He'd obviously missed something but couldn't understand what it was.

"Aye, that is the way of it," Duncan acknowledged. "Do you think to challenge me on this?"

Edmond sighed. He shook his head. "I do not. I stand behind you, Duncan, though I would advise you of the problems this decision will bring."

"It wouldn't sway me, Edmond."

Duncan didn't look disposed to explaining the conversation. Gilard decided to wait until he had Edmond alone, and then find out what was going on. Besides, another comment had nagged him into a quick question. "Duncan? What did you mean when you said Madelyne only need be directed toward helping Adela?"

Duncan finally turned to look at Gilard. He was pleased by Edmond's support, and his mood was therefore lightened. "Madelyne has had experiences that will help her with our sister. My suggestion is to place the two together as often as possible. Edmond, it will be your duty to escort your sister to dinner each night. Gilard, you'll bring Madelyne. She isn't as frightened of you."

"She's afraid of me?" Edmond sounded incredulous.

Duncan ignored the question, though he gave Edmond an irritated look to let him know he'd little liking for being interrupted. "It isn't significant if either Adela or Madelyne wishes to decline. Drag them if you have to, but eat together they will."

"Adela will destroy our gentle Madelyne," Gilard rushed out. "Why, sweet Madelyne could never hold her own against—"

"Sweet Madelyne has a temper as fierce as a winter gale, Gilard." Duncan's voice sounded exasperated. "We have only to direct her to lose a bit of it."

"What say you?" Gilard all but shouted, clearly astonished. "Madelyne is a gentle maiden. Why . . ."

Edmond's usual scowl deserted him. He actually started to chuckle. "She's got a sweet left hook as well, Gilard. And we know well enough what a gentle little maiden she is. She bellowed it loud enough for all of England to hear."

"The fever ruled her mind then. I told you we should have cut her hair to let the demons out, Duncan. Madelyne wasn't herself, I tell you. Why, she doesn't even know she blackened Edmond's eye."

Duncan shook his head. "You needn't defend Madelyne to me," he said.

"Well, what are you going to do with Madelyne?" Gilard couldn't keep the demand out of his voice.

"She will have a safe haven here, Gilard." He stood then and was about to walk out of the room, when Edmond's comment reached him. "It won't be safe until Adela comes to her senses. Madelyne's going to be put through an ordeal."

"An ordeal for all of us," Duncan called out. "God willing, it will all be over soon enough."

Duncan dismissed his brothers. He made his way to the lake for his swim.

His thoughts kept turning to Madelyne. The truth was inescapable. By an ironic twist of fate, Madelyne had remained unblemished by Louddon's black nature. She was a woman to be reckoned with. She hides her true character from herself, Duncan thought with a smile. Yet he'd been given treasured glimpses of the real Lady Madelyne. It had taken a raging fever to bring out her passionate spirit though. Aye, she was sensual, with a thirst for life that pleased him considerably.

Perhaps, Duncan thought, Adela will aid Madelyne as well. His sister might unknowingly help rid Madelyne of some of her cloaks.

The frigid water finally bothered Duncan enough to push all thoughts aside. He'd finish his swim and go to Madelyne. That singular motive aided him through the ritual in quickened time.

Madelyne had just opened the shutters to her window, when she caught sight of Duncan walking toward the lake. His back was to her and she watched him remove every bit of clothing and dive into the water.

She felt no shame in seeing him without his clothes on. Aye, his nudity didn't embarrass her at all. She was too stunned by what the daft man was doing to blush over his nudity. Besides, his back was facing her, saving her true discomfort.

She wouldn't believe he was actually going to dive into the water, but he did just that, and without a moment's hesitation.

The full moon gave her sufficient light to follow him across the lake and back again. Madelyne never lost sight of him, but out of a sense of modesty she closed her eyes when he climbed out onto the bank. She waited for what she thought an adequate length of time, and then looked again.

Duncan stood by the edge of the water, the lower half of his body covered. He looked just like an avenging godchild of Zeus, for he was gifted with a most magnificent body.

He hadn't bothered to put his tunic back on, but threw it carelessly over one shoulder instead. Didn't he feel the cold? Madelyne was already shivering from the breeze that came through the window. Yet Duncan acted as if it were a warm spring day. Why, he was walking back toward his home with a lazy, unhurried stride.

Madelyne's heart quickened as Duncan drew closer. He certainly was well proportioned. The man was long in flank, lean in waist, extremely broad in shoulders. The strength in his upper arms was clearly outlined by the light. Madelyne could see muscles all but rippling across his chest. Power radiated from him, even from such a distance, drawing her and worrying her at the same time.

Duncan suddenly stopped and looked up, catching Madelyne staring at him. She instinctively raised her hand in greeting, then faltered in the attempt. Madelyne couldn't see the expression on his face, but she guessed he was scowling. Lord knew that was his usual expression.

Madelyne turned away and went back to her bed, forgetting in her haste to close the shutters.

She was still angry. Every time the picture of Adela came into her mind, she wanted to scream. She'd wept instead, for almost a good hour, until her cheeks were raw and her eyes swollen.

Adela was the initial reason for her fury. The poor girl had been through such an ordeal.

Madelyne understood what it felt like to be at the mercy of another. She knew the rage inside Adela and pitied the girl.

Yet she was also furious with the Wexton brothers. They had made the situation far worse by treating Adela so poorly.

Madelyne made the decision that she'd accept responsibility for Adela now. She didn't think she wanted to help Duncan's sister because Louddon had caused her pain. Even though Madelyne was Louddon's sister, she wasn't going to feel guilt because of relation. She would help Adela because the sister was so vulnerable and lost.

She would be gentle with the girl, kind, too, and surely in time Adela would accept her comfort.

God help her, Madelyne started to cry again. She felt so trapped. She was so close to the border and to her cousin Edwythe's home, but now she'd have to wait to make her escape. Adela needed love and guidance, and her barbarian brothers didn't know how to give either. Aye, she was needed here, Madelyne thought, until Duncan's sister was given new strength.

The air in the room had turned freezing. Madelyne huddled under the covers, shivering, until she remembered the shutters were wide open. She got out of bed, wrapped an animal skin around her shoulders, and hurried over to the window.

It had started to rain, fitting weather for her mood, Madelyne decided. She looked down at the lake just to make certain Duncan wasn't still there, and then glanced over to look at the crest on the lower hill visible over the top of the battlements.

Madelyne saw the animal then. She was so startled by the sight, she rose up on tiptoe and leaned out the window, afraid to take her gaze away for even a second, lest the huge beast up and vanish on her.

The animal seemed to be looking up at her. Madelyne knew then that her mind had broken, just like Adela's. Good God, the beast looked just like a wolf. And Lord, he was magnificent!

Madelyne shook her head, yet continued to watch, mesmerized by the sight. When the wolf arched his neck back, she thought he might be howling. The sound never reached her though, probably snatched away by the wind and the rain pelting against the stones.

She didn't know how long she stood by the window watching the animal. She did close her eyes, deliberately, but when she opened them again, the wolf was still there.

"'Tis only a dog," she muttered to herself. Aye, a dog, not a wolf. "A very large dog," she added.

If Madelyne had been given to a superstitious nature, she would have jumped to the conclusion that the wolf was an omen.

Madelyne closed the shutters and went back to her bed.

Her mind was filled with images of the wild beast, and it took a long time before sleep claimed her. Her last thought was a stubborn one. She hadn't seen a wolf after all.

Sometime during the cold night Madelyne shivered enough to wake up. She felt Duncan put his arm around her and pull her toward his warmth.

She smiled over her fanciful dream and fell asleep again.

Chapter Ten

"There were giants in the earth in those days."

OLD TESTAMENT, GENESIS, 6:4

If Madelyne lived to the ripe old age of thirty, she vowed she'd never forget the week that followed her decision to help Adela.

It was a week like none other, save the invasion by Duke William perhaps, but then, she hadn't been born yet to witness that event, so she guessed it didn't count. The week all but destroyed her gentle nature and her sanity. Madelyne wasn't sure which she coveted more, however, and therefore determined to keep both.

Why, the strain was enough to set a saint's teeth to gritting. The Wexton family was, of course, the sole reason.

Madelyne was given freedom to roam the castle grounds, with only one soldier trailing behind her like a loud shadow. She had even gained permission from Duncan to utilize the waste of foodstuff by feeding the animals. And since the soldier had also heard her request approved, he actually argued in her favor to the men in charge of the drawbridge.

Madelyne walked all the way to the top of the hill outside the walls, her arms filled with a burlap bag containing meat, fowl, and grain. She didn't know what her wild dog would eat and carried a selection sure to entice him.

Her shadow, a handsome soldier named Anthony, muttered over the distance. He had suggested they ride, but Madelyne was against the plan, forcing the soldier to walk beside her. She told him the walk would do them good, when in fact she hoped to hide her lack of riding skills.

When Madelyne returned from her chore, Duncan was waiting for her. He didn't look too pleased. "You weren't given permission to go outside the walls," he stated quite emphatically.

Anthony came to her defense. "You did give her permission to feed the animals," he reminded his lord.

"Aye, you did," Madelyne agreed, and with such a sweet smile and soft voice, she was certain he thought her most composed.

Duncan nodded his head.

The look on his face was chilling. Madelyne thought he wished he was rid of her. Yet he didn't even yell at her now. In truth, he rarely raised his voice. He didn't have to. Duncan's size gained immediate attention, and his expression, when he was as displeased as he was now, seemed just as effective as any bellow.

Madelyne wasn't afraid of him anymore. Unfortunately, she had to remind herself of that fact several times a day. And she still didn't have enough courage to ask him what he'd meant by telling her she now belonged to him. She kept putting that confrontation off, in truth fearing what his answer would be.

Besides, she told herself, there'd be time enough after Adela was feeling better to find out her own destiny. For the time being, she'd attack each battle as it presented itself.

"I only walked to the top of the hill," Madelyne finally answered. "Are you worried that I'll just keep on walking until I've reached London?"

"What is the point of this walk?" Duncan asked, ignoring her comment about escape. He thought it too ludicrous to respond to.

"To feed my wolf."

His reaction was most satisfactory. For once he wasn't

able to keep his expression contained. He was looking at her in astonishment. Madelyne smiled.

"You may laugh if you've a mind to, but I saw either a very large dog or a wild wolf, and I did feel it was my duty to feed him, just until the weather improves and he can hunt again. Of course, it will mean an entire winter ahead to see to his food, but come next spring, with the first warm breeze, I'm certain my wolf will be able to fend for himself."

Duncan turned his back on Madelyne and walked away.

Madelyne felt like laughing. He hadn't denied her walks outside his fortress, and that was victory enough to gloat over.

In truth, Madelyne didn't think the wild dog was in the area any longer. She looked out her window every night since first sighting the animal, but he was never there. The dog had left, and sometimes, late at night when she was huddled under the covers, she'd wonder if she'd really seen the animal or if he'd just been a figment of her overactive imagination.

Madelyne would never admit that to Duncan, however, and gained perverse pleasure each time she walked across the drawbridge. The food she had left the day before was always gone, indicating that there were animals feeding during the night. She was happy knowing the food wasn't wasted. And she was even happier vexing Duncan.

Aye, she did it just to irritate him. And from the way Duncan avoided her, she thought she had succeeded.

The days would have been enjoyable if Madelyne hadn't had to worry about the dinner hours. That did put a weight on her shoulders and a strain on her gentle nature.

She stayed outside as much as possible, ignoring the rain and the cold. Gerty had given her cast-off clothing that had belonged to Duncan's older sister, Catherine. The garments were too large, but Madelyne put her needle and thread to them and the result was more than adequate for her needs. She didn't care if she was fashionable. The clothes were faded but clean, and felt soft against her skin. Most important, they kept her warm.

Each afternoon Madelyne walked to the stables with a clump of sugar to give to Duncan's stallion, the white beauty she'd named Silenus. She and the horse had formed a bond of sorts. The stallion would set up a terrible fuss, pretending to try to knock the wooden stall apart whenever he caught sight of Madelyne approaching. Yet as soon as she spoke to him, Silenus would settle down. Madelyne understood the animal's need to show off for her, and she always praised his spirit after giving him his treat.

Silenus, for all his size, was becoming affectionate. He'd nudge her hand until she petted him, and when she'd stop and rest her hand on the railing, a trick to gain a reaction, Silenus would immediately nudge her hand back on his head.

The stablemaster didn't like Madelyne visiting and stated his opinion loud enough for her to hear. He also thought she spoiled Duncan's horse and even threatened to tell the lord what she was up to. He was all bluster though. Aye, the stablemaster was amazed by Madelyne's gifted way with the horse. He was still a wee bit nervous whenever he saddled Duncan's stallion, but this mite of a girl didn't seem the least afraid.

On the third afternoon, the stablemaster spoke to Madelyne, and by week's end, they were fast friends.

His name was James, Madelyne learned, and he was married to Maude. Their son, William, was still attached to his mama's skirts, but James was patiently awaiting the time when the boy would be old enough to become apprentice under him. The child would follow tradition, James explained with an air of importance.

"Silenus would let you ride him bareback," James announced after he'd given Madelyne a tour of his domain.

Madelyne smiled. James had accepted her name for Duncan's mount. "I've never ridden bareback," she said. "'Tis the truth, James, that I've not ridden much at all."

"Perhaps," James suggested with a kind smile, "when the rain eases a bit, you could learn the proper way."

Madelyne nodded.

"Now, if you've never learned, how'd you get from one place to the next, I'm wondering," James admitted.

"I walked," Madelyne told him. She laughed over his look of surprise. "'Tis not a sin I'm confessing."

"I've a gentle mare you could start your practicing with," he suggested.

"Nay, I think not," Madelyne answered. "Silenus wouldn't like that much. I think his feelings might be injured, and we can't allow that, now, can we?"

"We can't?" James looked confused.

"I'll do well enough with Silenus."

"'Tis the lord's stallion you're wanting to ride, milady?" James stammered. He sounded as if he were strangling.

"I know whom he belongs to," Madelyne returned. "Don't concern yourself over the animal's size," she said, trying to ease the incredulous look off his face. "I've ridden Silenus before."

"But do you have the lord's permission?"

"I shall gain it, James."

Madelyne smiled again, and all the logical arguments went right out of the stablemaster's mind. Aye, he told himself, from the look in her pretty blue eyes and the way she smiled up at him so trustingly, James suddenly found himself in complete agreement.

When Madelyne left the stable, the guard walked beside her. He was a constant reminder to her and to everyone else that she was not an invited guest. Anthony's attitude toward her had softened considerably though. He wasn't nearly as irritated by his duty.

From the way Anthony was greeted by the other soldiers, Madelyne surmised he was well thought of. He had an attractive smile, a boyish grin it was, which was at great odds with his size and age. She couldn't understand why he'd been ordered to watch her, thinking that someone of lesser stature, such as Ansel, the squire, would have been better suited for the placid duty.

Her curiosity increased, until she finally decided to question him. "Have you done something to displease your lord?"

Anthony didn't seem to understand her question.

"When the soldiers return from their work, I can see the envious way you watch them, Anthony. You'd like to be training with them instead of walking with me in circles."

"'Tis no trouble," Anthony protested.

"Still, I don't understand why you've been given this duty unless you've displeased Duncan some way."

"I've an injury needing to heal a bit more," Anthony

explained. His voice was hesitant, and Madelyne noticed the blush that slowly crept up from his neck.

She thought it most odd that he would be embarrassed. Seeking only to put him at ease, she said, "I've also suffered an injury, and not too mild, I can tell you that." It did sound like a boast, but her goal was to make Anthony realize he had nothing to be ashamed of. "Almost did me in, Anthony, but Edmond took care of me. I've a horrid scar now, down the length of my thigh."

Anthony continued to look uncomfortable with their topic. "Don't soldiers think it noble when they're injured in battle?" Madelyne asked.

"They do," Anthony answered. He clasped his hands behind his back and increased his pace.

It suddenly dawned on Madelyne that Anthony might be embarrassed about just where he'd sustained his wound. His arms and legs looked fit enough, and that left only his chest and his . . .

"We'll not speak of this again," Madelyne blurted out. She felt her face warm. When Anthony immediately slowed his pace, Madelyne knew she was right. The injury was in an inappropriate place.

Though she never questioned Anthony about it, Madelyne thought it curious that the soldiers trained such long hours every day. She supposed that defending their lord was difficult work, considering the fact that their leader had so many enemies. She didn't think she was jumping to conclusions either. Duncan wasn't an easy man to like; he certainly wasn't given to being tactful or diplomatic. Why, he'd probably collected more enemies than friends in William II's court.

She was, unfortunately, given plenty of time to think about Duncan. She wasn't at all accustomed to having so much unstructured time on her hands. When she wasn't outside walking with Anthony, she drove Gerty and Maude to distraction with suggestions for making Duncan's home more pleasing.

Maude wasn't as guarded as Gerty. She was always eager to set her chores aside and visit with Madelyne. Little Willie, Maude's four-year-old son, proved to be as talkative as his mother once Madelyne was able to coach his thumb out of his mouth.

When the day's sunlight began to fade, however, Madelyne's stomach would tighten up and her head would start pounding. It was little wonder, she told herself, when one considered that the evenings spent with the Wexton family were trials of endurance Odysseus would have turned his back on.

Madelyne wasn't allowed to turn her back though. She had all but gotten down on her knees and begged to take her meals in her room, too, but Duncan wouldn't allow it. Nay, he demanded her attendance at the family meal and then had the gall to remove himself from the disgusting ordeal he forced on her. The baron always ate alone, and made a brief appearance only once the table had been cleared of the clutter the men hadn't already thrown to the floor.

Adela provided the stimulating conversation. While the men hurled bones over their shoulders, Duncan's sister hurled one obscenity after another at Madelyne.

Madelyne didn't think she could stand the torment much longer. Her smile felt as brittle as dry parchment.

On the seventh evening Madelyne's composure did crack, and with such violent force that those who witnessed it were too astonished to intervene.

Duncan had just given her permission to leave the hall. Madelyne stood up, excused herself, and began to walk toward the entrance.

Her head was pounding, and she thought only to give Adela a wide path. Madelyne wasn't up to another round of screaming. Duncan's little sister was walking toward her.

Madelyne warily glanced over at Adela and saw little Willie peeking out from the doorway to the kitchens. The little boy smiled at Madelyne and she immediately stopped to speak to him.

The child responded to Madelyne's smile. He darted out in front of Adela just as the sister swept her hand out in one of the grand gestures she always made when she was about to start in abusing Madelyne again. The back of Adela's hand struck Willie's cheek. The little one toppled to the ground.

Willie started to wail, Gilard shouted, and Madelyne let out an ear-piercing scream. The sound of rage she made stunned everyone in the hall, even Adela, who actually backed up a step, the first real retreat she'd ever made from Madelyne.

Gilard started to stand. Duncan grabbed hold of his arm. The youngest brother was about to argue over the restraint, but the look in Duncan's eyes stopped him.

Madelyne rushed over to the little boy, soothed him with a soft word and a tender kiss on the top of his head, and then bade him to go to his mother. Maude, upon hearing her son's wails, had appeared in the doorway, with Gerty at her side.

Madelyne turned to confront Adela then. She might have been able to control her anger if Duncan's sister had shown any sign of remorse. Adela, however, didn't look the least bit sorry for her conduct. And when she muttered that the boy was a nuisance, Madelyne let go of her control.

Adela called Willie a brat a scant second before Madelyne lashed out and slapped her right where she thought Adela most deserved it, across her mouth. Adela was so stunned by the attack, she lost her balance and stumbled to her knees. Without realizing it, she gave Madelyne added advantage.

Before Adela could stand up, Madelyne grabbed hold of her hair and twisted the mass behind her head, making the sister vulnerable and unable to strike back. She forced Adela's head back. "You've spoken your last word of filth, Adela. Do you understand me?"

Everyone stared at the two women. Edmond was the first to come out of his stupor. "Unhand her, Madelyne," he shouted.

Without taking her attention away from Adela, Madelyne shouted back to Edmond. "Keep out of this, Edmond. You hold me responsible for what happened to your sister, and I've decided 'tis high time I took a hand to right this mess. Starting now."

Duncan never said a word. "I do not hold you responsible," Edmond yelled. "Let go of her. Her mind is—"

"Her mind needs but a good cleaning, Edmond."

Madelyne saw that Maude and Gerty were both watching from the doorway. She kept a firm hold on Adela when she turned to speak to them. "I think we'll have need for two tubs to rid the filth covering this pitiful creature. See to it, Gerty. Maude, find clean clothes for your mistress."

"You're going to have a bath now, milady?" Gerty asked.

"Adela is going to get a bath," Madelyne announced. She turned back to glare at Adela and said, "And soap in your mouth every time you say an unladylike word to me."

Madelyne let go of Adela's hair then and helped her stand. Duncan's sister tried to pull away, but Madelyne wouldn't allow it. Her anger had given her the strength of Hercules. "You're taller than I am, but I'm stronger, and meaner right this minute than you could ever imagine, Adela. If I have to kick you all the way up to the tower, I'm more than up to the task." She pulled on Adela's arm, dragging her toward the entrance, muttering loud enough for all three brothers to hear. "And I'm smiling over the thought of kicking you, that's the truth of it."

Adela burst into tears. Madelyne was heartless. The sister wasn't going to get any more sympathy from her. Edmond and Gilard had given Adela too much of that already. Without realizing it, the brothers hurt their sister with their pity and their compassion. What was needed now was a firm hand. And Madelyne's were firm enough. Odd, but her head was not aching anymore.

"Cry all you want, Adela. It won't help your cause. You dared to call little Willie a brat, when the name belongs to you. Aye, you're the brat. That's all going to change now. I promise you that."

Madelyne kept up a constant chatter all the way to her room. She didn't have to kick Adela once.

By the time the wooden tubs were filled to spilling with steaming water, the fight had gone out of Adela. Gerty and Maude stayed to lend a hand getting Adela's clothes off her. "Burn these," Madelyne ordered after handing the offensive garments to Gerty.

When Adela was pushed into the first tub, Madelyne thought she tried to mimic Lot's wife. Duncan's sister sat like a sculptured piece of stone and stared off into the distance. The look in her eyes told another story, however. Aye, it was plain to see that Adela was seething with rage.

"Why was there need for two tubs?" Maude asked. She wrung her hands with worry. Adela had suddenly changed tactics and had just grabbed hold of Lady Madelyne's hair. It looked as though she meant to rip Madelyne's pretty locks right out of her scalp.

In retaliation, the lady who Maude had come to view as a sweet, gentle woman, shoved Adela's face under the water. Did she think to drown the baron's sister?

"I don't think Lady Adela can breathe under there," Maude said.

"Aye, and she can't spit at me either," Madelyne answered, snapping out each word.

"Well, I never . . ." Gerty gasped the protest before turning. Maude watched her friend run out the doorway.

Gerty was always one for telling the news before anyone else had a chance, Maude knew. Next Baron Wexton would probably be wanting to know what was going on.

Maude wished she could chase after Gerty. Lady Madelyne frightened her now; she'd never seen such a ferocious temper. Still, she'd stood up for little Willie, Maude admitted, and for that reason she'd stay and lend a hand as long as Lady Madelyne demanded it.

"We need two tubs because Adela is so filthy, she'll need two baths."

Maude had difficulty hearing what Lady Madelyne was telling her. Adela had started kicking and scratching. Lord, there was water everywhere, most especially on Lady Madelyne.

"Hand me the soap, if you please," Madelyne ordered.

The next hour was an incredible ordeal worthy of retelling until next spring. Gerty kept poking her head in to check on the progress. She'd then hurry back downstairs to report to Edmond and Gilard.

When the commotion was over, Gerty was a bit disappointed. Lady Adela was sitting quietly in front of the fireplace while Lady Madelyne combed her hair. The fight had gone out of the baron's sister, and the excitement was over.

Maude and Gerty left the tower after the tubs had been emptied and carried away.

Neither Adela nor Madelyne had spoken a civil word to each other. Maude suddenly appeared in the doorway again and rushed out. "I've still to tell you my gratitude for helping my boy."

Madelyne was about to answer Maude, when the servant continued. "Mind you, I don't hold it against Lady Adela.

She can't help the way she is. But you went out of your way to comfort Willie and I'm grateful to you."

"I didn't mean to hit him."

The admission came from Adela. It was the first decent sentence she'd spoken. Maude and Madelyne shared a smile.

As soon as the door closed behind Maude, Madelyne pulled up a chair and sat down, facing Adela.

Adela refused to look at Madelyne. Her hands were folded together in her lap and she stared intently at them.

Madelyne was given plenty of time to study Duncan's sister. Adela was actually very pretty. She had large brown eyes, golden brown hair, a surprise that, but once the dirt had been removed, the strands of blond were most noticeable.

She didn't look much like Duncan, yet she certainly shared his stubborn streak. Madelyne forced herself to be patient.

At least an hour passed before Adela finally looked up at Madelyne. "What do you want from me?"

"I want you to tell me what happened to you."

Adela's face immediately turned red. "Do you want all the details, Madelyne? Will that give you pleasure?" Adela began to twist the cuff of the freshly laundered sleeping gown she wore.

"Nay, I won't gain pleasure," Madelyne answered. Her voice sounded sad. "But you've a need to tell it. There's poison inside of you, Adela, and you need to get rid of it. You'll feel better afterward, I promise you. And you won't have to keep up your childish act in front of your brothers anymore."

Adela's eyes widened. "How did you . . ." She suddenly realized what she was giving away.

Madelyne smiled. "It's obvious to the most simple-minded that you don't hate me. We've crossed paths each day and you never screamed at me then. Nay, Adela, you've been too deliberate in your hatred."

"I do hate you."

"You do not," Madelyne announced. "You've nothing to hate me for. I've done nothing to harm you. We are both innocent and both caught in this war between our brothers. Aye, we are both innocent."

"I'm no longer innocent," Adela answered. "And Duncan has gone to your bed every night, so I doubt that you're innocent either."

Madelyne was astonished by Adela's words. Why did she think that Duncan had spent his nights with her? She was mistaken, of course, but Madelyne forced herself to concentrate on Adela's problem now. She could protest her own innocence later.

"I would kill your brother if I had a chance," Adela announced. "Why don't you just leave me alone? I want to die in peace."

"Don't speak such sinful thoughts," Madelyne returned. "Adela, how can I help you if you . . ."

"Why? Why would you want to help me? You're Louddon's sister."

"I've no loyalty toward my brother. He destroyed that long ago. When did you meet Louddon?" she asked most casually then, as if it really held no importance.

"In London," Adela answered. "And that is all I'm going to tell you."

"We *are* going to speak of this, no matter how painful it is. We've only each other, Adela. I'll keep your secrets safe."

"Secrets? There are no secrets, Madelyne. Everyone knows what happened to me."

"I will hear the truth from you," Madelyne announced. "If we have to sit here and stare at each other all night, I'm more than willing."

Adela looked at Madelyne a long while, obviously trying to make up her mind. She felt ready to burst into a thousand fragments. God, she was so tired of the deception, and so very lonely. "And will you tell Louddon every word when you return to him?" she asked, though her voice was a hoarse whisper now.

"I'm never going back to Louddon," Madelyne said. Her voice sounded her anger. "I've a plan to go and live with my cousin. I don't know the way of it yet, but I'll get to Scotland even if I have to walk."

"I believe you, you'll not tell Louddon. But what about Duncan? Will you tell him?"

"I'll tell no one unless you give me permission," Madelyne answered.

"I met your brother when I was at court," Adela whispered. "He is a handsome man," she added. "He told me he loved me, pledged himself to me."

Adela started to cry, and several minutes elapsed before she could regain control.

"I was already betrothed to Baron Gerald. The arrangement was made when I was ten years old. I was content until I met Louddon. I haven't seen Gerald since I was a little girl. God's truth, I'm not even sure I'd recognize him now. Duncan gave permission for me to go with Edmond and Gilard to court. Gerald was supposed to be there, and since the marriage vows were to be exchanged next summer, my brothers thought it a good idea for me to get to know my future husband. Duncan believed that Louddon was in Normandy with the king, you see. Else he'd never allow me near the court."

Adela took a deep breath and then continued. "Gerald wasn't there. He had reason enough," she added, "one of his vassals' homes had been attacked and he had to retaliate. Still, I was angry and disappointed."

She shrugged then. Madelyne reached out and clasped her hands. "I would have been disappointed too," she offered.

"Everything happened so quickly, Madelyne. We were in London only two weeks. I knew how much Duncan disliked Louddon, but I didn't know why. We kept our meetings secret. He was always kind and considerate to me. I liked the attention. The meetings were easy to arrange, too, because Duncan wasn't there."

"Louddon would have found a way," Madelyne said. "I think he used you to hurt your brother. You're very pretty, but I don't think Louddon loved you. He's not capable of loving anyone but himself. I know that now."

"Louddon didn't touch me."

The statement fell between them. Madelyne was stunned. She forced herself to keep her expression contained and then said, "Please go on."

"We agreed to meet in a chamber Louddon had found vacant the day before. It was well away from the rest of the guests, quite isolated. I knew what I was doing, Madelyne. I agreed to this meeting. I thought I loved your brother. I knew it was wrong, but I couldn't help how I felt. Lord, he was so handsome. Dear God, Duncan would kill me if he knew the truth."

"Don't torment yourself, Adela. He won't know anything unless you tell him."

"Louddon came to meet me," Adela said. "But he wasn't alone. His friend was with him and he was the one who . . . violated me."

All of Madelyne's training in hiding her feelings saved her now. She showed no outward sign at Adela's shocking admission.

Duncan's sister watched Madelyne. She waited to see repulsion. "This doesn't make you—"

"Finish it," Madelyne whispered.

The full sordid story poured out, haltingly at first and then with increased speed, and when Adela was finished, Madelyne gave her a few minutes to calm herself.

"Who was this man with Louddon? Give me his name."

"Morcar."

"I know the bastard," Madelyne answered, unable to keep the rage out of her voice. Adela looked frightened by the outburst. Madelyne tried to push her anger aside. "Why didn't you tell Duncan all of this? Not the part about making the choice to meet Louddon, of course, but about Morcar's involvement?"

"I couldn't," Adela answered. "I was so ashamed. And I was so badly beaten, I truly thought I was going to die. Louddon was as responsible as Morcar was . . . Oh, I don't know, but once I'd said Louddon's name to Gilard and Edmond, they didn't want to hear any more."

Adela started weeping, but Madelyne quickly stopped her. "All right then," she said most matter-of-factly. "You're to listen to me now. Your only sin was falling in love with the wrong man. I wish you could tell Duncan about Morcar, but that decision is yours to make, not mine. For as long as you bind me, I vow I'll keep your secret."

"I trust you," Adela answered. "I've been watching you all week. You're nothing like your brother. You don't even look like him."

"Thank God for that," Madelyne muttered with such gusto in her voice, Adela smiled.

"One more question, Adela, if you please," Madelyne said. "Why have you been acting so crazed? Was it all for your brothers' benefit?"

Adela nodded. "Why?" Madelyne asked, confused.

"When I came home, I realized I wasn't going to die. And then I began to worry that I might be carrying Morcar's child. Duncan would force a marriage, and—"

"You can't believe Duncan would bind you to Louddon?" Madelyne interrupted.

"No, no," Adela said. "But he'd find someone. His only concern would be to help me."

"And are you with child?" Madelyne asked. She felt her stomach lurch over the possibility.

"I don't know. I've missed my monthly but I don't feel any different and they've never been orderly fluxes." Adela blushed after making her confession.

"Perhaps it is too soon to tell," Madelyne advised. "But if you are, how did you think to keep it from Duncan? He may be stubborn, Adela, but he certainly isn't blind."

"I thought I'd keep to my room until it was too late, I guess. It sounds so foolish now. I haven't been thinking too clearly. I just know I'll kill myself before I am forced to marry anyone."

"What about Baron Gerald?" Madelyne asked.

"The contract is broken now," Adela said. "I'm no longer a virgin."

Madelyne sighed. "Did the baron announce this?"

"Nay, but Duncan says he'll not have to honor it now," Adela said.

Madelyne nodded. "Is your main worry that Duncan will force a marriage?"

"It is."

"Then let us face this worry first. We'll form a plan to rid you of that concern."

"We will?"

Madelyne heard the eagerness in Adela's voice, saw the spark of hope in her eyes too. That made her all the more determined. Unable to sit still a moment longer, Madelyne bounded to her feet and began to pace a slow circle around the chairs. "I don't believe for one minute that your brother would be so heartless as to demand that you marry anyone." She raised her hand when Adela looked as if she were going to interrupt, and then continued. "However, what I believe isn't important. What if I gained a promise from Duncan that you could live here for as long as you wanted to, no matter what the circumstances? Would that ease your fear, Adela?"

"Would you have to tell him I might be carrying a child?"

Madelyne didn't answer immediately. She continued to pace her circle, wondering how in God's name she'd ever get Duncan to promise her anything.

"Of course not," Madelyne answered. She stopped when she was directly in front of Adela and smiled down at the girl. "I'd get his promise first. He'll find out the rest soon enough, won't he?"

Adela smiled. "You've a devious mind, Madelyne. I understand your plan now. Once Duncan agrees, he won't go back on his word. But he'll be furious with you for tricking him," she added, her smile fading over that worry.

"He's always furious with me," Madelyne answered with a shrug. "I'm not afraid of your brother, Adela. He blusters like the wind, yet there's a soft core underneath. I'm sure of it," Madelyne said, praying to herself that she was correct. "Now then, promise me you'll not worry about the possibility of carrying a child. You've had an ordeal, and that could well be the reason you've missed your monthly," she advised. "I know all about this, you see, because Frieda, the woodcutter's wife, suffered a terrible upset when her boy fell down the drinking well and couldn't be gotten out for the longest time. The lad was unharmed, and thank God for that, but I heard Frieda tell another servant some two months later that she wasn't having her monthly. The other servant did explain that it was a natural enough condition considering the fright she'd had. I don't remember the wise woman's name now, else I'd share it with you, but she turned out to be right on the subject. Aye, Frieda was back to her usual flux the following month."

Adela nodded. "And if you do carry a babe," Madelyne went on, "we'll see it through, won't we? You'll not hate the child, will you, Adela?" Madelyne couldn't keep the worry out of her voice. "The baby would be as innocent as you are, Adela."

"He'd have a black soul, like his father," Adela said. "They would share the same blood."

"Then if that is the way of it, I'm damned to hell just as Louddon is, aren't I?"

"Nay, you're not like your brother," Adela protested.

"And your child won't be like Morcar either. You'd see to it," Madelyne said.

"How?"

"By loving the baby and helping him make the right choices when he's old enough to understand."

Madelyne sighed then and shook her head. "You may not be with child anyway, so let's put the matter aside for now. I can see how tired you are. Since your room must still be cleaned before you can sleep there, you're to have my bed this night. I'll find another."

Adela followed Madelyne over to the bed and watched as her new friend pulled the covers back. "When will you ask Duncan for his promise?"

Madelyne waited until Adela got into bed before answering. "I'll speak to him tomorrow. "'Tis most important to you, I can see that. I won't be forgetting."

"I don't ever want another man to touch me," Adela said.

Her voice was so harsh, Madelyne began to worry she'd get herself upset again.

"Hush, now," Madelyne soothed as she tucked the covers around Adela. "Rest now. Everything is going to be all right."

Adela smiled over the way Madelyne was pampering her. "Madelyne? I'm sorry for the way I've treated you. If I thought it would help, I'd ask Edmond to speak to Duncan about taking you to Scotland."

Madelyne noticed Adela thought to talk to Edmond and not go directly to Duncan. That comment reinforced her belief that Adela was afraid of her eldest brother.

Adela sighed and then said, "I really don't want you to go anywhere just yet. I've been so lonely. Is that selfish of me to admit?"

"Only truthful," Madelyne returned. "A trait I most admire," she added. "Why, I've never told a lie in all my days," she boasted.

"Not ever?"

Madelyne caught Adela's giggle and smiled over it. "Not that I can recall," she said. "And I promise to stay here just as long as you need me. I've no wish to travel in this harsh weather."

"You've also been dishonored, Madelyne. Everyone will think . . ."

"'Tis nonsense you speak," Madelyne said. "Neither one of us is responsible for what has happened. We are both honorable enough inside our hearts. That is all that matters to me."

"You've the most unusual attitudes," Adela said. "I would think you should hate all of us Wextons."

"Well, it is a fact that your brothers aren't easy men to like," Madelyne admitted. "But I don't hate them. Do you know I feel safe here? It's remarkable, isn't it? To be a captive and feel so safe at the same time. Now, that's a truth to mull over."

Madelyne frowned, her mind filled with her amazing admission. "Well now," she said to herself. "I'm going to have to think about this a bit longer."

She patted Adela on her arm and then turned to walk to the door.

"You won't do anything foolish about Morcar, will you, Madelyne?"

"Now, why would you ask such a thing?" Madelyne asked.

"Because of the look that came over you when I told you his name," Adela answered. "You won't do anything, will you?"

Adela sounded scared again. "You've an overactive imagination," Madelyne told her. "That gives us something else in common," she added, neatly avoiding the issue of Morcar.

Her ploy worked, for Adela was smiling again. "I don't think I'll have nightmares tonight. I'm too tired. You better come to bed soon, Madelyne. You'll need to be rested for your talk with Duncan."

"Do you think he'll drain the strength out of me?" Madelyne asked.

"Not you," Adela answered. "You can get Duncan to promise you anything."

Lord, the sister held such confidence. Madelyne felt her shoulders slump.

"I see the way Duncan watches you. And you did save Gilard's life. I heard him tell Edmond the story. Remind

Duncan of that and he wouldn't be able to deny you anything."

"Go to sleep, Adela."

Madelyne was just about to pull the door closed, when Adela's next words caught her. "Duncan never looks at Lady Eleanor the way he looks at you."

Madelyne couldn't resist. "Who is Lady Eleanor?" she asked, trying not to sound too interested. She turned and looked over at Adela, and from the way the sister was smiling at her, she thought she might not have fooled her.

"The woman Duncan is thinking to marry."

Madelyne showed no visible reaction. She nodded, indicating she'd heard Adela.

"Then I'm good and sorry for her. She'll have her hands full living with your brother. Do not take offense, Adela, but I believe your brother is too arrogant for his own good."

"I said he was thinking about marrying her, Madelyne. But he won't."

Madelyne didn't answer. She closed the door behind her and made it across the landing before she burst into tears.

Chapter Eleven

"He is best who is trained in the severest discipline."

KING ARCHIDAMUS II OF SPARTA

Madelyne didn't want anyone to catch her crying. When she left Adela, she really didn't have any clear destination in mind. She only wanted to find a quiet place where she could sort out her emotions.

The hall was her first choice, but when she approached the entrance, she heard Gilard talking to someone. She continued on, down the next flight of stairs, collected her winter cloak from the peg adjacent to the soldiers' keep, and then struggled to get the heavy doors opened just enough for her to squeeze through.

The air was cold enough to make a bear shiver. Madelyne pulled her cloak around her shoulders and hurried on. The moon gave sufficient light for her walk, and when she'd circled the butcher's hut, she leaned against the stone fortress wall and began to weep like an infant. She was loud, undisciplined, unfortunate, too, because she didn't feel the least bit better afterward. Her head hurt, her cheeks stung, and she was consumed with hiccuping.

The rage wouldn't go away.

Once Adela had begun her story, she told every bit of it. Madelyne hadn't shown any visible reaction to the horror, but her heart felt close to bursting with pain. Morcar! The bastard was just as guilty as Louddon was, yet no one would ever know of his involvement.

"What are you doing out here?"

Madelyne let out a gasp. Duncan had frightened the breath right out of her, appearing out of nowhere to stand next to her.

She tried to turn her back on him. Duncan wouldn't let her. He took hold of her chin and forced her to look up at him.

He'd have to be blind not to notice she'd been crying. Madelyne thought to give him a curt excuse, but the moment he touched her, she started weeping again.

Duncan pulled her into his arms. He seemed content to hold her until she gained control of herself. He'd obviously just finished his swim, as he was dripping from head to waist. Madelyne wasn't helping him dry either; she was crying and gasping and hiccuping all over the soft mat of hair covering his chest.

"You're going to freeze to death walking around half naked," she told him between sobs. "And I'll not warm your feet this time."

If Duncan answered her, she didn't hear him. Her face was pressed against his shoulder. She was stroking his chest too. Duncan thought she didn't even realize what she was doing, or understand the effect she was having on him.

Madelyne suddenly tried to push away from Duncan. She bumped his chin, muttered an apology, and then made the mistake of looking up at him. His mouth was entirely too close. She couldn't quit staring at it, remembering all too clearly the way he'd felt when she'd blatantly kissed him that night in the tent.

She wanted to kiss him again.

Duncan must have read her intentions, for he slowly lowered his mouth to hers.

He meant only to give her a gentle kiss. Aye, he meant to comfort her, but Madelyne's arms went around his neck and her mouth immediately opened to him. His tongue took advantage, mating with hers.

God, she was good. She could make him so hot so quickly. She wouldn't let him be gentle either. The sound she made, way in the back of her throat, pushed all thoughts of comfort aside.

He felt her shiver and only then remembered where they were. Reluctantly he pulled away from Madelyne, though he fully expected an argument from her. He'd have to kiss her again, he decided, and then went ahead and did just that before his soft, sensual woman even had the chance to ask.

Duncan was making her burn. She didn't think she had the strength to stop, until his hand brushed the side of her breast. It felt wonderful, and when she realized how much more she wanted, she pulled away from him.

"You'd best get inside before you turn to a block of ice," Madelyne said. Her voice sounded ragged.

Duncan sighed. Madelyne was at it again, trying to order him around. He picked her up into his arms, ignoring her protests, and started to walk toward the castle. "Did Adela speak to you about what happened to her?" Duncan asked when his mind could focus again.

"She did," Madelyne answered. "But I'll not retell a single word, no matter how insistent you become. You can torture me if you've a wish to, yet I'll—"

"Madelyne." His long-drawn-out sigh stopped her.

"I promised Adela I wouldn't say anything to anyone, especially you. Your sister is afraid of you, Duncan. 'Tis a sorry state of affairs, that," she added.

She thought her announcement would anger Duncan and was surprised when he nodded. "It's the way it should be," Duncan said, shrugging. "I'm lord as well as brother and the first must take preference over the second."

"It isn't the way it should be," Madelyne argued. "A family should be close. They should eat all their meals together and never fight with each other. They should—"

"How the hell would you know what a family should or shouldn't do? You've lived with your uncle," Duncan said, shaking his head in exasperation.

"Well, I still know how families should act," Madelyne argued.

"Madelyne, don't question my methods," Duncan said in

a low growl. "Why were you weeping?" he asked, swiftly changing the subject.

"Because of what my brother did to Adela," Madelyne whispered. She rested her face on Duncan's shoulder. "My brother will burn in hell for eternity."

"Aye," Duncan answered.

"He's a man in need of killing. I don't condemn you for wanting to kill him, Duncan."

Duncan shook his head. "Does it make you feel better not to condemn me?" he asked.

She thought she heard amusement in his voice. "I have changed my views on killing. I was weeping because of that loss," she whispered. "And for what I must do."

Duncan waited for Madelyne to explain. They reached the doors. Duncan pulled one open without unsettling her. The strength in him amazed her yet again. It had taken all her determination, both hands, too, to work one of those doors open enough to slip through without catching her backside, yet Duncan hadn't shown the least bit of strain.

"What must you do?" Duncan asked, unable to contain his curiosity.

"I must kill a man."

The door slammed shut just as Madelyne whispered her confession. Duncan wasn't sure he'd heard her correctly. He decided he had enough patience to wait until they had reached his bedroom before questioning her further.

He carried Madelyne up the steps, ignoring her protests that she was able to walk, didn't pause when they reached the hall level, but continued on, up to the next. Madelyne believed he was taking her back to the tower room. When they reached the mouth of the circular structure, Duncan turned in the opposite direction and continued on down a dark corridor. It was too dark to see where it led.

She was highly curious, for she hadn't even noticed the narrow hallway. They reached the end of the corridor, and Duncan opened a door and carried Madelyne inside. It was obviously his sleeping quarters, Madelyne realized, even as she considered it most kind of him to give up his bedroom to her for this night.

It was warm and cozy inside the bedroom. A full fire blazed in the hearth, giving heat and a soft glow to the otherwise stark room. A single window was centered in the opposite wall, covered with an animal skin in lieu of shutters. A wide bed took up most of the stone wall adjacent to the hearth, with a chest beside it.

The bed and chest were the only pieces of furniture in the room. It was clean, though, almost spotless. That fact made Madelyne smile. She didn't know why it pleased her but was glad that Duncan didn't like clutter any more than she did.

Why then did he allow the main hall to be so ill attended? That didn't make sense to her, now that she'd seen his own quarters. She decided to question him about it just as soon as she caught him in a good mood. Madelyne did smile then, for she realized she might very well be an old woman before Duncan achieved such a remarkable change in disposition.

Duncan didn't seem to be in any particular hurry to release her. He walked over to the hearth, leaned his shoulders against the edge of the thick mantel, and began to rub back and forth, obviously appeasing a sudden itch. Madelyne held on to him for dear life. Lord, she wished he were wearing a shirt. It wasn't decent, she told herself, because she liked touching his skin too much. Duncan was like a bronze god. His skin felt warm, and with her palms resting on his shoulders, she could feel the rippled muscles play beneath her fingertips.

She wished she could understand her reaction to him. Why, her heart was pacing a wild beat again. Madelyne dared a quick look up and found Duncan was watching her intently. He looked so handsome. She wanted him to be ugly. "Are you going to hold me the rest of the night?" she asked, sounding ridiculously disgruntled.

Duncan shrugged, almost unsettling Madelyne. She grabbed hold of him again, and when he smiled at her, she realized he might have jarred her just to get her to cling to him.

"Answer my question first, then I'll release you," Duncan commanded.

"I'll answer your question," she told him.

"Did you tell me you thought to kill a man?"

"I did." She stared at his chin when she answered him.

Madelyne waited a long minute for Duncan to comment on her admission. She thought he'd probably lecture her on her weakness for the task of killing anyone.

She was, however, totally unprepared for his laughter. It started as a low rumble in his chest, yet quickly gained in sound, until he was all but choking with true joy.

He'd heard her correctly after all. Madelyne did tell him she was going to kill. That statement was at first so astonishing, he believed she was jesting. Yet the serious look on her face indicated she really meant what she said.

His reaction didn't please her much. God help him, he couldn't quit laughing. He let Madelyne slip out of his grasp but kept his hands settled on her shoulders so she couldn't bolt. "And who is the unfortunate man you plan to kill?" he finally managed to ask. "One of us Wextons perchance?"

Madelyne pulled away from him. "Of course it isn't a Wexton, though to give you the full truth, if I had an evil soul, you'd be the first on my list of those I'd do in, milord."

"Ah," Duncan returned, smiling still. "If it isn't one of us, my sweet, gentle lady, then who do you wish to 'do in'?" he asked, using her ridiculous expression for killing.

"Aye, 'tis the truth, Duncan. I am a sweet, gentle maiden and it's high time you understood that," Madelyne answered. Her voice didn't sound particularly sweet now.

Madelyne walked over to the bed and sat down on the side. She took a long time smoothing her skirt and then folded her hands in her lap. She was truly appalled that she could speak so easily of taking another's life. But then, the man she had in mind was certainly in need of killing, wasn't he?

"You'll not get his name from me, Duncan. 'Tis my own affair, not yours."

Duncan wasn't in agreement but decided to wait before he forced the truth.

"And when you kill this man, Madelyne, will you lose your food from your stomach again?"

She didn't answer him. Duncan thought she might be realizing just how foolish her plan was. "And will you cry as well?" he asked her, repeating her reaction after killing the soldier who attacked Gilard.

"I'll remember not to eat anything before I kill him, Duncan, so that I won't become ill, and if I cry after I've done it, then I'll just find a private place so that no one will see me. Is that explanation enough for you?"

Madelyne took a deep breath, trying desperately to keep

her expression contained. Lord, she already felt like a sinner. "Death is not to be taken lightly," she said then. "But justice shouldn't be cheated either."

Duncan started laughing again. That infuriated her. "I'd like to sleep now, so please leave."

"Do you think to tell me to leave my own quarters?" Duncan asked.

He wasn't laughing now, and Madelyne didn't have the nerve to look at him.

"I was," she admitted. "If I'm being disrespectful, I'm sorry for it. But you know I don't lie. It's kind of you to give up your bed for this one night. I really do appreciate it. And I'll return to the tower tomorrow, after Adela's room has been scrubbed."

She was out of breath after she finished her explanation.

"Your honesty is refreshing."

"It gets me into mischief." Madelyne sighed. She continued to look down at her hands, wishing Duncan would hurry up and leave. Then she heard a soft thud. That noise did draw her attention, and when she glanced up, she was just in time to watch Duncan remove his second boot and drop it to the floor.

"'Tis indecent to stand before me without your shirt on," Madelyne stated. "And now you're taking off the rest of your garments before you leave? Do you parade around Lady Eleanor like this?"

Madelyne could feel herself blushing. She was determined to ignore Duncan. If he wanted to strut around half naked, then she'd just close her eyes. And he'd get no parting words from her either.

She was a bit slow to catch on to Duncan's intentions. Madelyne continued to watch him out of the corner of her eye. Duncan knelt down in front of the fire, added another fat log. She almost thanked him for that courtesy, until she remembered she was bent on ignoring him. Lord, he did make her lose her train of thought, didn't he?

Duncan stood up and walked over to the door. Before Madelyne knew what he was about to do, he pushed the thick slat of wood through the metal loops.

Her eyes widened in astonishment. She was locked inside the bedroom, but the true problem, as she viewed it, was that Duncan was on the wrong side of the door. And not even a sweet, gentle lady of breeding could misinterpret the meaning of that action.

Madelyne let out a gasp of outrage, bounded off the bed, and ran over to the door. Her intention was single-minded. She was going to get out of this room and away from Duncan.

He watched her struggle with the latch for a moment. When he was satisfied she'd never be able to figure out the unusual lock beneath the bar, he walked over to the bed. He decided to leave his pants on out of deference to Madelyne's feelings. She looked close to the brink of losing her control again.

"Come to bed, Madelyne," Duncan demanded as he stretched out on top of the covers.

"I'll not sleep next to you," Madelyne stammered.

"We've slept together . . ."

"Only once, in that tent, Duncan, and that was for necessity's sake. We shared each other's heat."

"Nay, Madelyne, I've slept beside you every night since," Duncan announced.

Madelyne turned to glare at Duncan. "You have not!"

"Aye, I have."

He was smiling at her. "How can you lie so easily?" Madelyne demanded.

She didn't give him time to answer but turned around again and began to work on the latch.

A sliver of wood under the tender skin on her thumb was her reward for her efforts. She yelped in anger. "And now I've most of this damn wood under my skin, thanks to you," she muttered as she bent her head to look at the damage.

Duncan sighed. Madelyne heard the exaggerated sound all the way across the room, but she didn't hear him move, and when he suddenly grabbed hold of her hand, she jumped back, clipping the top of her head against the bottom of his chin. "You move just like a wolf," she announced as she allowed him to drag her toward the light of the fire. "'Tis no compliment I'm giving you, Duncan, so you can quit smiling."

Duncan ignored her mutterings. He reached up on the mantel and took hold of a sharp, almost needle-pointed dagger. Madelyne closed her eyes until she felt the first prick. She had to open her eyes then, for if she didn't watch him, he'd probably cut her thumb clean off. Madelyne leaned down until she inadvertently blocked Duncan's view of her thumb.

He pulled her hand upward to get it in a better light. He bent his head to finish his task. Madelyne's forehead touched Duncan's. She didn't move away, and neither did he.

He smelled nice.

She smelled like roses again.

The splinter was removed. Madelyne didn't say a word to him, but she was looking up at him with such a trusting expression on her face. Duncan frowned in frustration. When she looked at him like that, all he could think about was taking her into his arms and kissing her. Hell, he admitted with disgust, all she had to do was look at him and he wanted to bed her.

Duncan threw the dagger back on the mantel and then went back to bed. He hadn't let go of Madelyne's hand and now dragged her behind him. "Can't even get a splinter out and you think to kill a man," he muttered.

"I am not sleeping with you," Madelyne stated most emphatically. She stood beside the bed, determined to win. "You're the most arrogant, the most stubborn man. My patience is running as thin as water. I'll not put up with much more."

Madelyne realized her error was in getting too close to Duncan when she shouted her threat. He reached up and literally lifted her on top of him. She landed with a thud. Duncan shrugged her to his side, his hand still locked on her wrist.

He closed his eyes, obviously trying to dismiss her. Madelyne faced him.

"You hate me too much to sleep next to me. You lied, didn't you, Duncan? We haven't been sleeping together. I'd remember it."

"You can sleep through a battle," Duncan remarked. His eyes were still closed but he was smiling. "And I don't hate you, Madelyne."

"You most certainly do hate me," Madelyne retorted. "Don't you dare change your mind now."

She waited a long while for Duncan to answer her. When he didn't say a word, she started in again. "It was a sorry deed that brought us together. I saved your life. And how am I repaid? Why, you drag me to this godforsaken place, constantly abusing my good nature, I might add. I imagine you've conveniently forgotten all about my saving Gilard's life too."

Lord, she wished he'd open his eyes so she could see his reaction. "Now I've taken on caring for Adela. I'm wondering, though, if you hadn't planned that all along."

Madelyne frowned over that thought and then continued. "You should admit by now that I'm the innocent in this scheme of yours. I'm the one who is being wronged. Why, when I think of all I've been through—"

Duncan's snore stopped her cold. Madelyne was suddenly so furious, she wished she had the courage to scream right into his ear.

"I'm the one who should hate you," she muttered to herself. She adjusted her gown and settled herself on her back. "If I didn't have satisfactory plans of my own, I'd be angry over what you've done to ruin my good name, Duncan. I can't ever make a suitable marriage now. That's a certainty, but I'll admit Louddon will be the loser, not me. He was going to sell me to the highest bidder. At least that's what he told me he was going to do. Now he'll only kill me if he gets near enough," she muttered. "And all because of you," she added with gusto.

She was exhausted when she finished her complaints. "How am I ever going to get you to promise me anything? And I've already given my word to poor Adela," she added with a weary yawn.

Duncan moved then. Madelyne was caught unprepared. She only had time to open her eyes before Duncan was leaning over her. His face was close to hers, his breath warm and sweet against her cheeks. One of his heavy thighs trapped her.

Good God, she was flat on her back.

"I'll find a way to tell your Lady Eleanor if you take advantage of me," Madelyne blurted out.

Duncan rolled his eyes heavenward. "Madelyne, your mind is consumed with my taking . . ."

She slapped her hand over his mouth and held it there. "Don't dare say it," she returned. "And why else would you be draped over me like a blanket if you didn't want to . . ."

Madelyne matched his sigh with one of her own. "You try to make me daft," she accused him.

"You already are," Duncan announced.

"Get off me. You weigh more than the doors to your home."

Duncan shifted his weight until his bulk was cushioned by his elbows. His pelvis rested against Madelyne's. He could feel the heat in her.

"What promise do you want from me?"

Madelyne looked confused by the question. "Adela," Duncan reminded her.

"Oh," Madelyne said, sounding breathless. "I had thought to wait until tomorrow to speak to you about Adela. I didn't realize you'd make me sleep with you though. And I'd hoped to catch you in a better mood. . . ."

"Madelyne." The last of her name was drawn out in a long, controlled groan and she knew from the way he clenched his jaw that his patience was gone.

"I wish you to give me your word Adela may live here with you for as long as she wants, and that you'll not force a marriage on her, no matter what the circumstances. There, is that specific enough for you?"

Duncan frowned. "I'll speak to Adela tomorrow," he stated.

"Your sister is too frightened to speak freely to you, but if I may tell her you've given your word, then I believe you'll see a remarkable change in her. She's so worried, Duncan, and if we can ease her burden, she'll feel much better."

He felt like smiling. Madelyne had taken on the role of mother to Adela, just as he suspected she would. He was enormously pleased his plan had worked. "Very well. Tell Adela I've given my word. I'll have to speak to Gerald," he added, almost as an afterthought.

"Gerald will just have to find someone else to marry. Adela believes the contract isn't binding now, anyway. Besides, Gerald will want an unblemished woman, and that makes me dislike him immensely."

"You never even met the man," Duncan said with exasperation. "How can you judge him so easily?"

Madelyne frowned. Duncan was right though it was almost painful to give him that admission. "Does Gerald know all of what happened to Adela?"

"By now all of England knows. Louddon would have made certain."

"My brother is an evil man."

"Does your uncle Berton feel the same way about Louddon?" Duncan asked.

"How did you know my uncle's name?" Madelyne asked.

"You told me," Duncan supplied, smiling over the way her eyes widened.

"When? I've an excellent memory and I don't recall mentioning it."

"When you were sick, you told me all about your uncle."

"If I spoke to you, I don't remember. It was rude of you to listen to anything I said."

"It wasn't possible to block out your voice," Duncan told her, grinning over the memory. "You shouted everything you said."

He exaggerated, just to increase her reaction. When Madelyne wasn't guarded, her expressions were so innocently refreshing to see. "Tell me what else I said," Madelyne demanded. Her tone sounded with suspicion.

"The list is too long. Suffice it to say that you told me everything."

"Everything?" She looked horrified now.

Lord, she was embarrassed. What if she'd told him how much she liked him kissing her?

There was a sparkle in Duncan's eyes. Perhaps he was only teasing her. That didn't sit well. Madelyne decided to remove that smile. "Then I gave you all the names of the men I've taken to my bed, didn't I? The game is up, I suppose," she ended with a sigh.

"Your game was up the moment we met," Duncan told her. His voice was soft.

Madelyne felt as though she'd just been caressed. She didn't know how to react. "And just what does that mean?"

Duncan smiled. "You talk too much," he told her. "'Tis yet another flaw you should work on."

"That's ridiculous," Madelyne returned. "I've said little enough to you all week and you've ignored me altogether. How can you suggest I talk too much?" she asked, daring to poke his shoulder.

"I don't suggest anything, I state facts," Duncan answered. He watched her closely, saw the flash of fire in her blue eyes.

Baiting her was easy work. He knew he should stop but he was actually enjoying the way she responded. He could find little harm in it. She was suddenly as feisty as a hellcat.

"It displeases you when I speak what's on my mind?"

Duncan nodded.

She thought he looked every bit the rascal now. A lock of dark hair had fallen forward to rest against his forehead. He was grinning too. Why, it was enough to rattle a saint into cursing. "Then I'll just quit talking to you. I vow I'll never speak to you again. Does that please you?"

He nodded again, though much slower this time. Madelyne took a deep breath, preparing to tell him what she thought about his rudeness, but Duncan silenced her. He lowered his head and brushed his mouth against hers, startling her into temporary submission.

With barely any coaching, she opened her mouth to his insistent tongue. Duncan began to make slow love to her with his tongue. Lord, he could feel the fire in her. His hands spread wide against the sides of her face, his fingers tangling in her glorious hair.

God how he wanted her. The kiss quickly changed from gentle caress to wild passion. Their tongues mated again and again until Duncan was almost mindless with wanting more. He knew he should stop and was about to pull away, when he felt Madelyne's hands touch his back. A soft, hesitant caress it was and at first as skittish as a butterfly, but when Duncan growled and delved again into the sweetness of her mouth, the caress gained in pressure. Their mouths were hot, wet, clinging.

He felt a shudder pass through her, heard her ragged moan escape when he reluctantly eased himself away from her.

Madelyne's eyes were misty with passion and her lips, red and swollen, beckoned him to taste her again. Duncan knew he shouldn't have started what he couldn't finish. His loins throbbed with want and it took a supreme act of will to move away from her.

With another groan of frustration Duncan rolled to his side. He wrapped his arm around Madelyne's waist and pulled her up against him.

Madelyne wanted to weep. She couldn't understand why she kept letting him kiss her. More important, she couldn't seem to stop herself from kissing him. She was as wanton as a wench.

All Duncan had to do was touch her and she went to pieces. Her heart raced, her palms turned hot, and she was filled with a restless yearning for more.

She heard Duncan yawn and concluded then that the kiss hadn't meant much to him at all.

The man irritated her just like a rash. Madelyne determined to keep her distance from him even as she contradicted the decision by adjusting herself into the curve of Duncan. When she was almost settled to her satisfaction, Duncan let out a harsh groan. His hands moved to her hips and he held her firmly.

What a contrary man he was! Didn't he realize how awkward it was to sleep in her walking gown? She moved again, felt him shudder, and thought then that he might be getting ready to snap at her.

Madelyne was too weary to worry about his temper. With a yawn of her own, she fell asleep.

It was, without a doubt, Duncan's most difficult challenge. And if she moved her backside just one more time, he knew he'd fail this test.

Duncan had never wanted a woman the way he wanted Madelyne. He closed his eyes and took a deep, ragged breath. Madelyne wiggled against him again, and he began to count to ten, promising himself that when he reached that magic number, he'd be more controlled.

The innocent cuddled up against him had absolutely no idea of her jeopardy. Her derriere had driven him to distraction all week long. He pictured the way she walked, saw again the gentle sway of her hips as she strolled around his fortress.

Did she affect others the way she affected him? Duncan frowned over that question, admitting that she most certainly did. Aye, he'd seen the looks his men had given her when her attention was directed elsewhere. Even faithful Anthony, his most trusted vassal and closest friend, had changed his attitude toward Madelyne. At the beginning of the week Anthony had been silent and taken to frowning, but by week's end Duncan noticed his vassal was usually the one speaking. And he didn't trail behind Madelyne any longer either. Nay, he was always right by her side.

Just where Duncan wanted to be.

He couldn't fault Anthony for his weakness in falling under Madelyne's charms.

Gilard, however, was of a different cloth altogether. It appeared that the youngest brother was taken with Madelyne. That could present a problem.

She started squirming again. Duncan felt as though he'd just been branded. A painful longing claimed his full attention. With a growl of frustration he threw off the covers and got out of bed. Though Madelyne was jarred by the sudden movement, she didn't wake up. "Sleeps like an innocent babe," Duncan muttered to himself as he walked over to the door.

He was going back to his lake and realized with a hefty shake of his head that he'd find true pleasure in this second swim.

Duncan wasn't a patient man. He wanted the issues resolved before he claimed Madelyne for his own though. He resigned himself to the fact that he'd probably be swimming in his lake more often. It wasn't a challenge that sent him outside now, but a release from the fire burning in his loins.

With a mutter of disgust, Duncan closed the door.

Chapter Twelve

A flower among thorns, an angel among thorns . . .

"And sometimes, Adela, if a babe was born with any noticeable flaw, why, the Spartan fathers would just throw the newborn child out a convenient window or off the top of a nearby cliff to get rid of him. Aye, I can see you're properly shocked, but my uncle Berton did relate the tales about those fierce warriors of times gone by, and he'd not exaggerate the telling just to please me. It was his duty to recount them with accuracy, you understand."

"What were the Spartan ladies like? Did your uncle Berton tell you all about them?" Adela asked, her voice quite eager. Duncan's little sister sat on the edge of her bed, trying her best to stay out of the way while Madelyne rearranged the furnishings in her bedroom. Adela had given up trying to convince Madelyne that it wasn't at all usual for her to work like a serving wench. Her new companion had a stubborn streak and it was useless to argue with her.

It had been over three weeks since Madelyne had forced

the confrontation with Adela. Once Adela had told the truth about her ordeal, the pain and guilt had truly lessened. Madelyne had been right about that. Madelyne hadn't seemed the least shocked by the story. Odd, but that helped Adela as much as the telling. Madelyne sympathized with Adela, yet she didn't pity her.

Now Adela followed Madelyne's lead, trusting her to know what was best. She accepted that the past couldn't be undone and tried to put it behind her, just as Madelyne suggested. That was easier said than done, of course, but Madelyne's friendship, so unrestrictive and so giving, helped Adela take her mind off her problems. Adela had finally started her monthly flux a week ago, and that was one less worry to concern her.

Madelyne had opened a new world to Adela. She told the most wonderful stories. Adela was amazed by the wealth of information in Madelyne's memory and eagerly awaited each day's new tale.

Adela smiled as she watched Madelyne now. Her friend did look a sight. A smudge of dirt had settled on the bridge of her nose, and her hair, though tied with a piece of blue ribbon behind her neck, was gradually gaining freedom from the binding.

Madelyne stopped sweeping the dust from the corner and leaned against the handle of her broom. "I can see I've caught your interest," she remarked. She paused to brush a stray curl away from her face, making a new mark of dirt on her forehead, and then continued on with her story. "I do believe the Spartan ladies were most undignified. They'd have to be as horrible as their men, Adela. How would they ever have gotten along if they weren't?"

Adela answered the question with a giggle. The sound warmed Madelyne's heart. The transformation in Duncan's sister was most pleasing. There was a sparkle in her eyes now and she smiled quite often.

"Now that the new priest has arrived, we must be careful not to talk like this in front of him," Adela whispered.

"I've yet to meet him," Madelyne answered. "Though I'm looking forward to it. It's high time the Wexton brothers had a man of God looking after their souls."

"They used to," Adela said. "But when Father John died, and then the church caught fire, well, no one did much of anything about it." She shrugged and then said, "Tell me more about the Spartans, Madelyne."

"Well now, the ladies had probably all gone to fat by the time they were twelve or so, though that is just a supposition on my part and not a dictate from my dear uncle. I do know, however, that they took more than one man to their beds."

Adela gasped and Madelyne nodded, thoroughly satisfied by her friend's reaction. "More than one at a time?" Adela asked. She whispered the question and then blushed with embarrassment.

Madelyne nibbled on her lip while she considered if that was possible.

"I don't think so," she finally announced. Her back was to the door, and Adela's full attention was centered on her friend. Neither noticed Duncan now stood in the open doorway.

He was about to announce his presence, when Madelyne spoke again.

"I don't believe it's possible to be flat on your back with more than one man at a time," she admitted.

Adela giggled, Madelyne shrugged, and Duncan, having heard most of Madelyne's dissertation on the ways of the Spartans, rolled his eyes heavenward.

Madelyne had propped the broom against the wall and was now kneeling in front of Adela's chest. "We'll have to empty this if we're going to move it across the room," she said.

"You must finish your story first," Adela insisted. "You do tell the most unusual tales, Madelyne."

Duncan started to interrupt again and then discarded the notion. In truth, his curiosity was caught.

"In Sparta there wasn't any such thing as celibacy. Why, it was considered a crime not to wed. Gangs of unmarried women would take to the streets. They'd search for unmarried men and when they found them, they fell upon them."

"Fell upon them?" Adela asked.

"Aye, they'd fall upon the poor man and beat him to a bloody pulp," she yelled out. Her head had completely disappeared inside the trunk. "'Tis the truth I'm telling you," Madelyne added.

"What else?" Adela asked.

"Did you know that the young men were locked in a dark

room with the women they'd never seen in the light of day and they were supposed to . . . well, you get my meaning there," she ended.

Madelyne took a breath, sneezed over the dust inside the chest. "Some of the women had babies before ever seeing their husbands' faces." She straightened up then, bumped her head on the lid of the chest, and promptly rubbed the ribbon off her head.

"It sounds horrible, but I'll tell you this. When I think of your brother Duncan, I can imagine his Lady Eleanor might prefer a dark room."

Madelyne made the statement as a jest. Adela let out a gasp of dismay. The little sister had just noticed Duncan was leaning against the door.

Madelyne misunderstood Adela's reaction and was immediately contrite.

"'Tis common talk I've taken up," she announced. "Duncan is your lord, after all, and brother, too, and I've no business teasing you about him. I do apologize."

"I will accept it."

It was Duncan giving her forgiveness. Madelyne was so surprised by his booming voice, she bumped her head again when she turned to look up at him.

"How long have you been standing there?" she asked, blushing with mortification. She stood up and faced him.

Duncan didn't answer her, he just stood there, making her nervous. Madelyne smoothed the wrinkles from her gown, noticed a large stain right above her waist, and immediately folded her hands in front of it. A lock of hair swayed in front of her left eye, but if she moved her hand to push the hair away, he'd see what a mess she'd made of her gown, wouldn't he?

Madelyne had to remind herself that she was only his captive and he her keeper. What difference did it make if she looked messy or not? She blew the hair out of her vision and struggled to give Duncan a serene look.

She failed miserably, and Duncan, knowing what was in Madelyne's mind, smiled over her failure. It was getting more difficult for her to hide her feelings. That fact pleased him almost as much as her disheveled appearance.

She thought he smiled over her sorry-looking gown. Duncan reinforced her belief by giving her a thorough inspection. His gaze moved slowly from the top of her head to the dust on her shoes. His smile widened until the attractive dent was back in the side of his cheek.

"Go up to your room, Madelyne, and stay there until I come for you."

"May I finish this task first?" Madelyne asked, trying to sound humble.

"You may not."

"Duncan, Adela wanted to rearrange her room to look more like . . ." Lord, she was about to tell him Adela wanted her room to be as cozy as the tower room. He'd find out what she'd done then, and probably pitch a fit.

Madelyne glanced over to look at Adela. The poor girl was clutching her hands together and staring at the floor. "Adela, you have forgotten to give your brother a proper greeting," she instructed her.

"Good day, milord," Adela whispered immediately. She didn't look up at Duncan.

"His name is Duncan. Lord or not, he is your brother." Madelyne turned to Duncan then and glared at him. He'd better not snap at his sister.

Duncan raised an eyebrow when Madelyne frowned at him. When she motioned with a vigorous tilt of her head toward Adela, he shrugged. He didn't have the faintest idea what she was trying to tell him. "Well? Aren't you going to give your sister a greeting, Duncan?" she demanded.

His sigh bounced off the walls. "Are you instructing me?" he asked.

He looked irritated. Madelyne shrugged. "I'll not have you frightening your sister," she said before she could stop herself.

Duncan felt like laughing. It was true then, just as Gilard had praised and Edmond had protested. Timid Madelyne had become Adela's protector. One kitten trying to protect another, except that Madelyne was acting more like a tigress now, he decided. There was blue fire in her eyes, and oh, how she tried to keep her anger hidden from him.

Duncan gave Madelyne a look that told her what he thought of her dictate. Then he turned to his sister and said, "Good morning, Adela. Are you feeling well today?"

Adela nodded and then looked up at her brother and

smiled. Duncan nodded, surprised that such a simple greeting could change his sister's manner.

He turned to leave then, determined to get as far away from his fragile little sister as possible before letting Madelyne have a piece of his mind.

"Couldn't Madelyne stay here and—"

"Adela, please don't challenge your brother's order," Madelyne interrupted, fearing that Duncan's patience was near the shouting point. "It wouldn't be honorable," she added with a smile of encouragement.

Madelyne picked up her skirt and hurried after Duncan, calling over her shoulder, "I'm certain he has good reason for his order."

She had to run to catch up with him. "Why do I have to return to the tower?" she asked when she was certain Adela couldn't hear her.

They'd reached the landing when Duncan turned to her. He wanted to shake her teeth loose, but the smear of dirt on the bridge of her nose drew his attention. He used his thumb to wipe the dirt away.

"Your face is covered with dirt, Madelyne. Aye, you're flawed now. Should I throw you out a convenient window, do you suppose?"

It took Madelyne a moment to understand what Duncan was talking about. "The Spartans didn't throw their captives out windows," she answered. "Only ill-formed babies. They were mighty warriors with mean hearts," she added.

"They ruled with complete control," Duncan said. His thumb slowly moved to her lower lip. He couldn't stop himself from rubbing his thumb against her mouth. "Without compassion."

Madelyne couldn't seem to move away. She stared up into Duncan's eyes while she tried to follow their conversation. "Without compassion?"

"Aye, 'tis the way a leader should rule."

"It isn't," Madelyne whispered.

Duncan nodded. "The Spartans were invincible."

"See you any Spartans now, Duncan?" Madelyne asked.

He shrugged, though he couldn't help but smile over her ridiculous question.

"They might have been invincible, but they're all dead now."

Lord, her voice shook. She knew the reason well enough. Duncan was looking at her so intently and pulling her toward him ever so slowly.

He didn't kiss her. It was a disappointment. Madelyne sighed.

"Madelyne, I'll not deny myself much longer," Duncan whispered. His head was bent, his mouth bare inches away from her own.

"You'll not?" Madelyne asked, sounding breathless again.

"Nay, I'll not," Duncan muttered. He sounded angry now. Madelyne shook her head in confusion.

"Duncan, I would allow you to kiss me now," she told him. "There's no need to deny yourself."

His answer to her honest admission was to grab hold of her hand and drag her up the stairs to the tower.

"You'll not be captive here much longer," Duncan announced.

"Then you admit it was a mistake bringing me here?" she asked.

He could hear the fear in her voice. "I never make mistakes, Madelyne."

He hadn't bothered to turn around and look at her, and he didn't speak again until they reached the door to her room. When Duncan reached for the handle, Madelyne blocked the door by leaning against it. "I can open my own door," she said, "and you most certainly do make mistakes. I was your biggest mistake of all."

She really hadn't meant to phrase her statement that way. Lord, she had actually insulted herself.

Duncan smiled. He'd obviously caught her blunder. Then he pulled her out of the way and opened the bedroom door. Madelyne rushed inside and tried to slam the door shut behind her.

Duncan wouldn't let her. The fat's in the fire now, Madelyne thought, bracing herself for his reaction to the changes she'd made.

He couldn't believe what he was seeing. Madelyne had changed the stark cell into an inviting retreat. The walls had been washed and a large beige-colored tapestry was centered on the wall facing him. The hanging told the story of the final battle of William's invasion; the colors were vivid, the figures of the soldiers stitched in red and blue. It was a simple design, but pleasing too.

The bed was covered with a blue quilt. Across the room were two large chairs, both covered with red cushions. They were set at an angle to the hearth. There were footstools in front of each chair. Duncan noticed an unfinished tapestry propped up against one of the chairs. Brown threads dangled to the floor. The outline of the design was sufficiently stitched for him to recognize what it was going to be. It was the design of Madelyne's imaginary wolf.

The muscle in the side of his jaw flinched. Twice. Madelyne wasn't sure what that meant. She waited, her temper gaining timber for a blazing retort when he started yelling at her.

Duncan never said a word. He turned and pulled the door closed behind him.

The scent of roses followed him down the stairs. He held his temper until he reached the entrance to the hall. Gilard spotted him and immediately rushed over to speak to him. His voice was filled with youthful eagerness when he asked, "Is Lady Madelyne receiving visitors yet this morning?"

Duncan's bellow could be heard all the way up in the tower.

Gilard's eyes widened. He'd never heard Duncan yell like that. Edmond strolled into the hallway just in time to watch Duncan leave.

"What's got him so riled?" Gilard asked.

"Not what, Gilard, but who," Edmond remarked.

"I don't understand."

Edmond smiled and then whacked his brother on the shoulder. "Neither does Duncan, but I wager he will soon enough."

Chapter Thirteen

"The race is not to the swift nor the battle to the strong. . . ."

OLD TESTAMENT, ECCLESIASTES, 4:2

Madelyne worked on her tapestry. Her mind wasn't on the task, however; she kept repeating Duncan's remarks. What had he meant when he told her she wasn't going to be his captive much longer?

She knew she'd have to confront him soon. She'd been acting like such a coward and was honest enough to admit the truth. She was frightened of hearing his answers.

The door suddenly flew open. Adela rushed into the room. Duncan's little sister was terribly distressed. She looked close to weeping.

Madelyne jumped to her feet. "Who has upset you so?" she demanded to know, already jumping to the conclusion that Duncan was responsible.

Adela burst into tears. Madelyne hurried to close the door. She put her arm around Adela then and led her over to one of the chairs. "Sit down and calm yourself. Why, it can't possibly be as terrible as you're carrying on," she soothed her.

Madelyne prayed she was right. "Tell me what has caused such tears and I'll make it right again."

Adela nodded, but once she looked up at Madelyne, she started crying again. Madelyne sat down on the stool facing Adela and patiently waited.

"Your brother has sent men to fetch you, Madelyne. Duncan allowed the messenger inside. That's why you've been ordered back to your room. Duncan didn't want the soldier to see you."

"Why? Everyone knows I'm captive here. Louddon—"

"You misunderstand," Adela interrupted. "Edmond told Gilard he thought Duncan didn't want the messenger to see that you're being treated well." She paused to dab at the corners of her eyes with the cuff of her gown. "You do think you've been treated well, don't you, Madelyne?"

"Good God, is that why you're crying?" Madelyne asked. "Of course I've been treated well. Just look around you, Adela," she added with a little smile. "Doesn't my room look comfortable enough?"

"I shouldn't have listened to what the messenger was telling Duncan, but I did. Gilard and Edmond were there and they heard every word too. Duncan didn't make them leave. And no one noticed me, Madelyne. I'm certain of it."

"Was the messenger from the king or from my brother?" Madelyne asked. She was so frightened inside now, yet knew she'd have to hide her fear from Adela. Aye, the sister depended on Madelyne's strength, and she couldn't fail her now.

"I don't know who the message came from. I didn't hear the beginning of what he was saying."

"Tell me what you did hear," Madelyne suggested.

"You're to be taken to the king's court immediately. The messenger said that even though you've been . . . soiled . . ." Adela's voice cracked then and she paused to compose herself. Madelyne bit on her lower lip until it numbed. She fought the urge to grab Adela by her shoulders and shake the rest of the story out of her.

"You're to be married as soon as you reach London."

"I see," Madelyne whispered. "We knew it was coming,

Adela. We knew Louddon would do something. Did you catch the name of the man I'm to wed?"

Adela nodded. "Morcar."

The sister covered her face with her hands, weeping uncontrollably now. Madelyne didn't have to hide her expression now. She thought she was going to be sick. "What about Duncan, Adela?" she managed to ask. "What did he say to this messenger? Was he in agreement?"

"He didn't say a word. The soldier recited his message and then returned to the others waiting outside the walls."

"How many soldiers did Louddon send?"

"I don't know," Adela whispered. "Edmond and Gilard were shouting at each other once the soldier had left. Duncan didn't say anything. He just stood there in front of the fire with his hands clasped behind his back."

"He separates himself," Madelyne said.

"I don't understand."

"Your brother must assume two positions in his household, Adela. He is lord and he is brother. I can imagine what Edmond and Gilard were arguing about. Edmond would want me given over to Louddon as soon as possible, while Gilard would argue in favor of a battle to keep me here."

Adela was shaking her head before Madelyne finished her suppositions. "Nay, Edmond doesn't want you handed over to Louddon's men," she said.

"Edmond championed my cause?"

"He did," Adela said. "And he suggested that I be sent to my sister, Catherine, for a brief visit. He's worried that all of this will be too much for me. I don't want to go anywhere. Catherine's so much older than I am, and her husband is most unusual. . . ."

Madelyne stood up and slowly walked over to the window. She opened the shutters and stared out into the wilderness. She knew she needed to gain control of the seething anger building inside her. "Did you know, Adela, that a Spartan child was taken from his mother at a very early age and sent to live with the soldiers? The little boys were taught to steal. It was considered cunning to be a good thief."

"Madelyne, what are you talking about? How can you tell me stories now?"

Madelyne turned around, letting Adela see the tears

174

streaming down her cheeks. Adela had never seen Madelyne cry before.

"I find comfort in the old stories, Adela. They're familiar to me. Once I've calmed my mind, I'll be able to think clearly. Then I can decide what's to be done."

Adela, stunned into submission by the pain she saw in her friend's eyes, quickly nodded.

Madelyne turned back to look out the window. She stared at the lower crest. And who will feed my wolf when I'm gone, she asked herself. Odd, but the picture of Duncan came into her mind. She confused him with her wolf, realized then that he needed as much taking care of as her wild beast. Probably more.

It didn't make sense to her, this need to straighten out Duncan's bleak life until she was satisfied with it.

"My uncle and I would sit before the fire every evening. I learned to play the psaltery. Uncle would join in with his viele some evenings when he wasn't too tired. It was a most peaceful time, Adela."

"Weren't there any young people there, Madelyne? Every time you tell a story, you speak of such old, frail people."

"Uncle Berton lived at the Grinsteade holding. Baron Morton was very old. And then Fathers Robert and Samuel came to stay with us as well. They all got along but I was the only one who'd play chess with Baron Morton. He cheated something fierce. Uncle said it wasn't a sin, just cantankerous, ornery behavior because he was so old."

Madelyne didn't speak again for a long while. Adela stared into the fire while Madelyne stared out into the night.

It wasn't working this time. Madelyne's bid to gain control wasn't going to happen. She could feel her composure cracking. Fury was building inside her.

"We must find someone to protect you," Adela whispered.

"If I am forced to return to Louddon, all my plans will be ruined. I was going to go to Scotland. Edwythe would have welcomed me into her home."

"Madelyne, Scotland is where—" Adela was about to explain that Catherine lived in Scotland and was married to a cousin of Scotland's king.

She wasn't given a chance to explain. "Why in God's name am I worrying about my plans being ruined? Louddon will kill me or give me to Morcar. Then Morcar will kill me." Madelyne let out a harsh laugh, sending a shiver down Adela's legs. "I still can't believe Louddon is bothering with me. When he chased after Duncan after his fortress was destroyed, I thought he wanted to kill only Duncan. Yet now he has sent men for me." Madelyne paused, shaking her head. "I don't understand any of this."

Before Adela could offer comfort, Madelyne suddenly turned and started for the door. "Madelyne. You must stay here. Duncan hasn't given you permission—"

"I must find a protector, Adela, isn't that the way of it?" she shouted over her shoulder. "Well, Duncan's fit enough for the task."

"What are you going to do?"

"Your brother is going to send Louddon's men away. And I am going to instruct him on the matter now."

Before Adela could caution Madelyne, her friend was out the door and running down the steps. Adela hurried after her. "Madelyne, you think to instruct my brother?" Her voice squeaked with worry.

"I do," Madelyne shouted.

Adela had to sit down on the step. She was stunned by the change in Madelyne. Her dear friend had lost her mind. Adela watched Madelyne continue down the circular stairs, her hair flying out behind her. Only when Madelyne had disappeared down the next level did Adela realize she should try to help her. No matter how frightening the prospect, she was determined to face Duncan by Madelyne's side. Why, she might even be able to speak up to him.

Madelyne reached the entrance to the hall and paused to gain a breath. Edmond and Gilard were seated across from each other at the dining table. Duncan was standing with his back to the entrance, directly in front of the blazing fire.

Edmond was just finishing his comments to his brothers. Madelyne only heard the last of what he was saying. "Then it's agreed that Duncan will take her—"

Madelyne immediately jumped to the conclusion that everyone thought it a good idea to give her over to Louddon's men.

"I'm not going anywhere."

Her bellow got an immediate reaction. Duncan slowly

turned around and looked at her. She watched him a long moment and then turned her attention to his brothers. Gilard had the audacity to smile, as if he found her outburst amusing, while Edmond, true to his contrary nature, scowled.

Duncan didn't show any reaction. Madelyne picked up her skirts. She slowly walked over to stand directly in front of him. "You captured me, Duncan. That was your decision," she announced. "Now I've a decision to tell you. I'm staying caught. Do I make myself clear on that issue?"

His eyes showed his surprise. Aye, he'd heard every word. And why wouldn't he? she asked herself. She'd fairly roared her decision right into his face.

When he just continued to stare at her, Madelyne thought he might be trying to frighten her. Well, it wasn't going to work this time. "You're stuck with me, Duncan."

Damn, her voice shook.

Edmond stood up, upsetting his chair. The sound turned Madelyne's attention. She slowly walked over to the table, her hands on her hips. "You can rid yourself of that frown, Edmond, or I promise God I'll smack it right off your face."

Gilard watched Madelyne. He'd never seen her this angry. Did she actually think Duncan would send her back to Louddon? The realization made Gilard smile. Poor Madelyne. She obviously didn't know Duncan very well. She wasn't aware of her own importance either, he concluded. She'd worked herself into a fine state. Such a gentle little thing, yet hadn't he just seen her challenge Duncan? If he hadn't seen it, he wouldn't have believed it possible. God help him, he started to laugh.

Madelyne heard him. She rounded to glare at him. "You find this amusing, Gilard?"

He made the mistake of nodding. He looked up at Madelyne just in time to see her hurl one of the jugs of ale at his head. Gilard dodged the jug, and when Madelyne picked up another, Edmond reached over her head and took it from her grasp. The two were standing side by side on the edge of the platform. Madelyne gave Edmond a hard shove with her hip. The middle brother promptly lost his balance and fell backward.

He landed on his backside. Edmond might have been able to stop the fall if the stool hadn't gotten caught up in his feet. Madelyne watched his puny efforts before turning back to Gilard. "Don't you ever laugh at me again," she demanded.

"Madelyne, come here," Duncan ordered. He was leaning against the mantel, looking bored enough to fall asleep.

She obeyed without question and was almost across the room before she realized what she was doing. She stopped then, shaking her head. "I'm no longer taking orders from you, Duncan. You've no hold over me. I'm only a pawn to you. Kill me if you wish. I would prefer it to being sent back to Louddon."

Her fingernails were digging into her palms. She couldn't keep her hands from shaking.

He never took his gaze off her. "Edmond, Gilard, leave us now." His command was softly given, yet there was an unmistakable edge of steel in his tone. "And take your sister with you."

Adela had been hiding behind the wall next to the entrance. When she heard Duncan's order, she rushed into the room. "I would like to stay here, Duncan, in the event Madelyne needs me."

"You'll go with your brothers," Duncan stated. His voice had gone cold now, effectively stopping further argument.

Gilard took hold of Adela's arm. "If you want me to stay, Madelyne—"

"Don't contradict your brother's order," Madelyne interrupted. She hadn't meant to shout the command.

Adela started to cry, renewing Madelyne's anger. She reached over and patted Adela on her shoulder. She couldn't manage a smile though. "I'm not going to marry Morcar," she said. "'Tis a fact I'm not marrying anyone."

"Aye, but you are," Duncan said. He actually smiled at her when he made his promise.

Madelyne felt as if he'd just slapped her. She took a step away, shaking her head in denial.

"I'll not marry Morcar."

"No, you'll not."

His answer confused her into temporary submission.

Duncan wasn't looking at Madelyne now. He watched his brothers walk with Adela toward the entrance. The three of them were taking their own sweet time, acting as though they had armor nailed to the bottoms of their shoes. It was obvious they were bent on hearing as much of his conversation with Madelyne as possible. Duncan placed the blame for their sudden show of insubordination directly on Madelyne's shoulders. Aye, it was all her fault. They'd been obedient enough before she entered their lives.

From the moment Lady Madelyne had set foot inside his home, everyone and everything had gone upside down.

Duncan told himself he didn't like the changes, even as he acknowledged there were still more to come. He was sure to meet with resistance, especially from Gilard. The youngest brother was Madelyne's greatest ally. Duncan sighed over it. He much preferred a good battle to the dealings of family.

"Edmond, find our new priest and bring him to me," Duncan suddenly called out.

Edmond turned, a question in his expression. "Now," Duncan snapped.

His command was frigid enough to chill Madelyne to the bone. She started to turn around to speak to Edmond, when Duncan's next command stopped her. "Don't you dare instruct him to obey me, Madelyne, or so help me God, I'll take hold of your red hair and bind your mouth shut with it."

Madelyne let out a gasp of outrage. Duncan was satisfied, thinking that his crude threat had made her realize her vulnerable position. His goal was her submission. Aye, he wanted her docile for what was to come.

When Madelyne began to walk toward him with a murderous look in her eye, Duncan decided his threat hadn't bothered her much. She wasn't acting the least bit docile. "How dare you insult me? My hair isn't red, and you damn well know it. It's brown," she shouted. "'Tis unlucky to have red hair, and mine isn't."

He couldn't believe what he was hearing. Her contradictions were becoming a usual occurrence.

Madelyne stopped her advance when she was a scant foot away. Close enough to grab, he thought.

The woman was brave but innocent about the world. It was the only excuse Duncan could find for her comments. There were over a hundred of Louddon's men waiting outside the walls, threatening to attack if Madelyne wasn't handed over to them by tomorrow morning. She should have been raging about that situation, he told himself.

Instead, she argues about the color of her hair. It was more red than brown, and why in God's name she couldn't see that was beyond him.

"Your insults know no bounds," she told him. Then she started to cry. She couldn't look up at him anymore, and surely that was the reason she allowed him to take her into his arms.

"You're not going back to Louddon, Madelyne," Duncan said, his voice gruff.

"Then I'm staying here until spring," she said.

Edmond appeared at the entrance with the new priest. "Father Laurance is here," he announced to get Duncan's attention.

Madelyne pulled away from Duncan. She turned to look at the priest. Why, he was so young. That surprised her. He looked vaguely familiar to her, too, though she couldn't put her finger on just where she might have met him. Very few young priests visited her uncle Berton.

She shook her head, deciding then that she couldn't have met him before.

Duncan suddenly pulled Madelyne up against his side. They stood so close to the fire, Madelyne forgot about the priest and began to worry her gown would catch flame. When she tried to move away, Duncan tightened his hold. His arm was draped across her shoulders, anchoring her to him. Odd, but after a moment or so, his closeness calmed her, and she was able to fold her hands in front of her and regain her composed expression.

The priest seemed worried. He wasn't a very appealing-looking man, for his face was pock-marked into scars. He looked unkempt too.

Gilard rushed into the room. The look on his face suggested he was ready to do battle. He and Edmond had suddenly changed dispositions. Edmond was smiling now while Gilard scowled.

"Duncan, I'll be the one to marry Lady Madelyne. I'm more than willing to make this sacrifice," Gilard announced. His face was red and he'd deliberately used the word sacrifice so that Duncan wouldn't know the depth of his true feelings for Madelyne. "She did save my life," he added when Duncan didn't immediately answer him.

Duncan knew exactly what was going on inside Gilard's

mind. The brother was as transparent as water. He thought himself in love with Madelyne. "Don't give me argument, Gilard. My decision is made and you will honor it. Do you understand me, brother?"

Duncan's voice was soft but menacing, and Gilard, after giving a loud, angry sigh, slowly shook his head. "I'll not challenge you."

"Marriage?" Madelyne whispered the word as if it was a blasphemy.

She shouted the next. "Sacrifice?"

Chapter Fourteen

"Giving honor unto the wife, as unto the weaker vessel."

NEW TESTAMENT, I PETER 3:7

"I'm not marrying anyone." Madelyne meant to shout her decision, but the words came out strangled. She couldn't help that, for she finally understood what Duncan meant to do. Gilard might not challenge that decision, but *she* certainly was going to.

Duncan did seem determined in the matter. He ignored Madelyne's struggle to get away from him and motioned for the priest to begin the ceremony.

Father Laurance was so flustered, he couldn't even remember most of the standard phrases, and Madelyne was so incensed, she wasn't paying the least attention. She was too busy yelling at the man trying to squeeze her to death.

When Madelyne heard Duncan promise to take her as wife, she shook her head. The priest then asked her if she'd have Duncan for husband. Madelyne gave an immediate answer. "Nay, I will not."

182

Duncan didn't care for her answer. He gripped her so tightly, Madelyne thought he was trying to push the bones right out of her.

Duncan grabbed hold of her hair, twisted it back until she was looking up at him. "Answer him again, Madelyne," Duncan suggested.

The look in his eyes almost changed her determination. "Let go of me first," she demanded.

Duncan, believing she meant to obey him, released her. His arm settled on top of her shoulders again. "Ask her again," he told the frazzled priest.

Father Laurance looked ready to faint. He stuttered out the question again.

Madelyne didn't yell a denial or an acceptance. She didn't say anything at all. Let them stand there until morning, she didn't care. No one was forcing her into this mockery.

She hadn't counted on Gilard's interference. Madelyne thought he looked as if he wanted to kill Duncan. When his hand went to the handle of his sword, and he took a threatening step forward, she let out an involuntary gasp. Good God, he was going to challenge Duncan. "I do take you, Duncan," she blurted out. She continued to stare at Gilard, saw the indecision in his eyes, and added, "Willingly do I pledge myself."

Gilard's hands dropped back to his sides. Madelyne's shoulders sagged with relief.

Adela walked over to stand between Edmond and Gilard. She smiled at Madelyne. Edmond was grinning too. Madelyne wanted to scream at both of them. She didn't dare, what with Gilard looking so crazed.

The priest rushed through the rest of the ceremony. After giving an awkward, backward blessing, he excused himself and rushed out of the room. His color had turned green. The man was obviously terrified of Duncan. She understood that feeling well enough.

Duncan finally let go of Madelyne. She rounded on him then. "This marriage is a mockery," she whispered so that Gilard wouldn't hear. "The priest didn't even give us a proper blessing."

Duncan had the audacity to smile at her. "You told me you never make mistakes, Duncan. This time you certainly have. Now you've gone and ruined your life. And for what purpose? Your vengeance against my brother is endless, isn't it?"

"Madelyne, the marriage is real enough. Go up to my room and wait for me, wife. I'll join you soon."

He deliberately stressed the word *wife.* Madelyne stared up at him in astonishment. There was a warm glint in his eye now. His room?

Madelyne jumped when Adela touched her on the shoulder, trying to tell her everything would be all right. That was certainly easy enough for her to say; she wasn't the one bound to a wolf.

She had to get away from all the Wextons. There was so much to think through. Madelyne lifted the skirt of her gown and slowly started to walk out of the room.

Edmond stopped her when she reached the entrance by putting his hand on her arm. "I would welcome you into our family," he said.

The brother actually looked as though he meant what he said. That infuriated Madelyne almost as much as his horrible smile. She much preferred him scowling at her. "Don't you dare smile at me, Edmond, or I'll hit you. Just see if I don't."

He looked surprised enough to satisfy her.

"I seem to remember your threat to hit me for just the opposite reason, Madelyne."

She didn't have the faintest idea what he was talking about. Nor did she particularly care, for her mind was filled with far more important matters. Madelyne pulled away from Edmond, muttering to herself that she hoped he'd choke on his dinner, and then he walked out of the room.

Gilard tried to go after Madelyne but Edmond grabbed him. "She's your brother's wife now, Gilard. Honor that bond." Edmond kept his voice low so Duncan wouldn't overhear. The eldest brother had turned his back on them and was staring at the fire again.

"I would have made her happy, Edmond. Madelyne has had so much pain in her life. She deserves to be content."

"Are you blind, brother? Haven't you seen the way Madelyne looks at Duncan and the way he stares at her? They care for each other."

"You're mistaken," Gilard answered. "Madelyne hates Duncan."

"Madelyne doesn't hate anyone. She isn't capable of it." Edmond smiled at his brother. "You just don't want to admit the truth. Why do you think I've been so angry with Madelyne? Hell, I could see the attraction from the beginning. Why, Duncan never left her side when she was so ill."

"That was only because he felt responsible for her," Gilard argued.

The youngest brother was trying desperately to hold on to his anger, yet Edmond's argument was staring to sound reasonable.

"Duncan married Madelyne because he wanted to. You know, Gilard, it's quite remarkable that our brother married because of love. In these times, that is a rarity. He'll not gain any lands, only the king's displeasure."

"He doesn't love her," Gilard muttered.

"Aye, he does," Edmond contradicted his brother. "He just doesn't know it yet."

Duncan's mind wasn't on his brothers. He ignored them as he reviewed his plans for tomorrow. The messenger had hinted they'd attack with first light if Madelyne wasn't given to them. Duncan knew it was a bluff. He was almost disappointed. Aye, he was aching for another battle with anyone pledged to Louddon. However, the paltry assembly freezing their backsides outside his walls wouldn't be foolish enough to challenge their leader's petition. They knew they were outnumbered, outskilled. Louddon had probably sent them so that he could stand before his king and show he'd tried to regain his sister back without involving his leader.

Satisfied with his conclusions, Duncan put the matter aside and turned his thoughts to his new life. How long would it take her to accept him as husband? It didn't make the least difference to him how long it took, he told himself, but the sooner she came to terms with her new life, the better for her own peace of mind.

He felt honor bound to keep her safe. She'd given him her courage and her trust. He couldn't turn his back on her. Aye, it was a sense of duty that propelled him into this hasty decision. Sending her back to Louddon would be like sending a child into a cage to fight a lion.

"Hell," he muttered to himself. He'd known from the beginning, when he first touched her, that he'd never let her go. "She is making me daft," he said, uncaring who overheard.

She did please him. He hadn't realized just how rigid his life had been, until Madelyne began to interfere. She could get reactions from him with just an innocent look. When he wasn't thinking about strangling her, he was obsessed with kissing her. It didn't matter that Louddon was her brother. Madelyne didn't have his black soul; she was gifted with a pure heart and a capacity for love that rocked all of Duncan's cynical beliefs.

Duncan smiled. He wondered what state he'd find Madelyne in when he went upstairs. Would she be terrified or would she give him one of her practiced serene expressions again? Would his new wife be a kitten or a tigress?

He left the hall and went in search of Anthony. After listening to his vassal's congratulations on his marriage, he gave Anthony additional instructions for the night's watch.

The nightly ritual of swimming in his lake came next. Duncan took his time, giving Madelyne a bit longer to prepare herself for him. It had been over an hour since Madelyne had stormed out of the hall.

Duncan decided that was time enough. He took the steps two at a time. It wasn't going to be easy to convince Madelyne that he meant to bed her. He wouldn't use force, however, no matter how she tried his patience. It would take time, but she would willingly give herself to him.

His vow to keep his temper under control was strained somewhat when he reached his room and found it empty. Duncan sighed in exasperation and immediately went up to the tower.

Did she actually think she could hide from him? He found that thought amusing and smiled. His smile faded, however, when he tried to open the door and realized it was barred against him.

Madelyne was still a little worried. She'd returned to her room in a nearly hysterical state and then had been forced to wait until her tub was filled with water. Maude had already begun the nightly task. Madelyne tried to be appreciative, but the servant and the two men carrying the buckets of steaming water did take the longest time, until

Madelyne was sick with fear that Duncan would find her before she could lock him out.

The slat of wood was right where she'd hidden it, tucked underneath the bed. Once she slid the heavy panel through the metal loops, she let out a loud sigh of relief.

The muscles in Madelyne's shoulders throbbed. She was tense and out of sorts, and no matter how she tried, she couldn't seem to reason anything through. Had Duncan married her just to infuriate Louddon? What about Lady Eleanor?

Madelyne took a long time soaking. Her hair had been washed the night before so she didn't have that chore to do. She tied the curls on top of her head, using a strip of ribbon to anchor them in place. Yet most of the strands had fallen back to her shoulders before her bath was finished.

God's truth, she didn't feel the least bit calmer after her bath. Her mind was consumed with worry. She wanted to scream in anger, yet weep with humiliation too. The only reason she didn't do either was that she couldn't make up her mind.

She heard Duncan coming up the steps just as she was getting out of the tub. Her hands shook when she reached for her robe, but it was only because it was so cold in her room, she told herself.

The footsteps stopped. Duncan was right outside the door. Madelyne reacted with a fresh spurt of fear, shamed she was acting so cowardly when she ran over to the far corner of the room and stood there trembling like an infant. She frantically knotted the belt of her robe even as she reasoned Duncan couldn't see through the wood, for God's sake, and there wasn't any need to work herself up into such a fit.

"Madelyne, get away from the door."

His voice had sounded so mild. That surprised her. Madelyne frowned, waiting for him to start threatening. And why didn't he want her standing by the door?

She had her answer soon enough. The sound was so explosive, she jumped back, bumping her head against the stone wall. Madelyne let out a yelp when the slat of wood snapped like a twig, and would have made the sign of the cross if she'd been able to get her hands undone from each other.

The door shredded, and what puny strips remained, Duncan easily ripped apart.

He fully intended to drag Madelyne down to his room, yet when he saw how she cowered in the corner, his heart softened. Duncan also had the real concern she'd jump out the window before he could get to her. She looked frightened enough to try it.

He didn't want her frightened. Duncan deliberately sighed, a long-drawn-out affair it was, and then casually leaned against the doorway. He smiled at Madelyne, waiting for her to regain her control.

He'd use reason and soft words to make her come to him.

"You could have knocked, Duncan."

The change in her happened so swiftly. She wasn't cowering in the corner now but standing there frowning at him with a look that told him she wouldn't be throwing herself out any windows. She might, however, be thinking of trying to push him out.

He tried not to laugh, recognizing her pride was important to both of them. Damn, he didn't like her cowering away from him. "And would you have opened the door for me, wife?" he asked, his tone soft, coaxing.

"Don't call me your wife, Duncan. I was forced to say those vows. Now look what you've done to my door. I'll be sleeping with a draft flying around my head, thanks to your ill consideration."

"Ah, then you *would* have opened the door for me?" Duncan asked, grinning. He was thoroughly enjoying her outrage. Edmond was right, Madelyne was a bossy bit of goods. Her door, indeed.

She was a lovely sight to be sure. Her hair fell below her shoulders. The fire from the hearth cast a deep red glow to her curls. Her hands were back on her hips, her back as straight as a lance, and the opening of her robe gaped almost to her waist, giving him an ample view of the cleft between her full breasts.

He wondered how long it would be before Madelyne realized her vulnerable position. The oversized robe was slowly working its way loose. Duncan had already realized she wasn't wearing anything underneath the covering. Her knees peeked out at him.

The grin slowly faded from Duncan's face. His eyes

darkened as well. His concentration was strained, and all he could think about was touching her.

Whatever was the matter with him? Madelyne wondered. His expression had turned as black as his tunic, and heavens, she did wish he didn't look so handsome.

"Of course I wouldn't have opened the door, Duncan, but you should have knocked all the same." She blurted out the ridiculous statement, feeling like a fool. If only he'd quit looking at her as if he wanted to . . .

"Have you never told a lie?" Duncan asked when he saw fear return to her eyes.

His question caught her off guard, as was his intention. Duncan slowly straightened and walked into the room.

"I've always told the truth, no matter how painful," Madelyne answered. "And you know that well enough by now." She gave him a disgruntled look and began to walk toward him so that he'd hear her next rebuke clearly. Madelyne was determined to give Duncan a piece of her mind, and she certainly would have done just that if she hadn't forgotten the robe was too long and the wooden tub was directly in her path. She tripped over her hem, stubbed her toe on the base of the tub. She would have pitched forward into the water if Duncan hadn't grabbed her in time.

He took hold of Madelyne's waist when she bent to rub the sting from her toe. "Every time I'm near you, I get injured."

She was muttering to herself, but Duncan heard every word. He took immediate exception. "I've never harmed you," he insisted.

"Well, you threatened to," Madelyne said. She stood up then, realized his arm was around her waist. "Let go of me," she demanded.

"Do I carry you like a sack of wheat to my room or will you walk beside me like a new wife should?" he asked.

He slowly forced her to turn around and face him.

She was staring at his chest. Duncan gently pushed her chin up. "Why don't you leave me alone?" Madelyne asked, finally meeting his gaze.

"I have tried, Madelyne."

She thought his voice sounded like a caress, as soft as any summer's breeze.

His thumb was slowly stroking the curve of her chin. How could such an insignificant little touch have such a devastating effect on her? "You try to bewitch me," Madelyne whispered, yet she didn't pull away when his thumb moved to stroke her sensitive lower lip.

"'Tis you who bewitches me," Duncan admitted. His voice had gone hoarse. Madelyne's heart started pounding. She could barely catch her breath. Her tongue touched the tip of his thumb. It was all she'd allow herself, this one small pleasure that sent a shock down her legs. She bewitched him? The thought was as pleasing as his kisses. She did want him to kiss her. Just one kiss, she told herself, and then she'd demand his dismissal.

Duncan seemed content to stand there all night. Madelyne quickly grew impatient. She pushed his hands away and then rose up on tiptoe to place a single chaste kiss on the cleft of his chin.

When Duncan didn't react, she grew a bit bolder and put her hands on his shoulders. He was looking down at her and that made the task easier, yet she hesitated when she felt him stiffen against her. "I would kiss you good night," she explained, barely recognizing her own voice. "I do like to kiss you, Duncan, but that is all I will allow."

He didn't move. Madelyne couldn't even feel him breathing. She didn't know if her admission angered him or pleased him, until her lips touched his. Then she knew he liked kissing almost as much as she did.

Madelyne sighed, content.

Duncan growled, impatient.

He wouldn't give her his tongue until she demanded it, using her own to push him into responding. Then he took control, thursting his tongue deep into her mouth.

Madelyne didn't want to stop. When she realized that, she pulled away from him.

Duncan's hands rested on her hips. He let her pull back, waiting with great curiosity to see what she'd do next. She was unpredictable.

Madelyne couldn't quite look up at him. A true blush covered her cheeks. She was obviously embarrassed.

Duncan suddenly lifted Madelyne up into his arms, smiling over the way she grabbed the edge of her robe where it parted at the knees. He almost mentioned that her modesty was ill placed, since he'd taken care of her when she was so sick. But Madelyne was rigid in his arms and he decided not to bring up that subject.

When they were halfway down the steps, Madelyne realized how unprepared she was to spend the night with Duncan. "I've left my sleeping gown upstairs," she stammered. "'Tis one thing to sleep in my day gown but this is so bulky and—"

"You won't need anything," Duncan interrupted.

"I will," Madelyne muttered.

Duncan didn't answer her. Madelyne knew she'd lost the argument when the door to his bedroom slammed shut. They were, unfortunately, inside his room.

Duncan placed Madelyne on his bed and went back to the door. He pushed the wooden slat through the loops. And then he turned, slowly folded his arms across his chest, and smiled at her.

The attractive dent was back in the side of his cheek. Madelyne would have called it a dimple, yet that was an incorrect description for a man of his size and might. Warriors didn't have dimples.

Her mind was rambling. It was his fault, of course. Why, he just stood there, staring at her. She felt like a little mouse cornered by a hungry wolf.

"Are you deliberately trying to frighten me?" Madelyne asked, sounding terrified.

Duncan shook his head. He caught her fear, realized then that his forced smile hadn't aided his cause at all. "I don't want you frightened."

He started to walk toward her. "I'd prefer you unafraid, though I can understand the first time would be frightening for a virgin."

His bid to soothe her failed. Duncan reached that conclusion when Madelyne bounded off the bed. "First time? Duncan, you're not going to bed me," she shouted.

"I am," he answered.

"'Tis one thing to be forced to sleep beside you, but that is all that's going to take place this night!"

"Madelyne, we're married now. 'Tis a usual occurrence to bed one's wife on the wedding night."

"And is it a usual occurrence to force a lady to marry?" she asked.

He deliberately shrugged. She looked ready to cry. Duncan decided to make her angry again. He preferred it over tears. "It was necessary."

"Necessary? You mean expedient, don't you? Tell me this, Duncan. Will it also be necessary to force yourself on me tonight?"

She didn't give him time to answer her. "You didn't even bother to take the time to explain your reasons for this marriage. That is unforgivable of you."

"You actually expected me to explain my actions to you?" he roared. He was almost immediately sorry for his lack of control because Madelyne was back to sitting on the edge of the bed, wringing her hands.

Duncan attempted to cool his temper. He walked over to stand in front of the fire. With deliberate slowness he began to unfasten the lacings at the neck of his tunic. He never took his gaze off Madelyne, wanting her to see what he was doing.

She tried not to look at him, but he was an overwhelming presence, and she could not ignore him. His skin was bronzed by the sun, golden now by the glow of the fire. The play of muscles showed when he bent to remove his boots.

God's truth, she wanted to touch him. It was such an appealing admission, she shook her head. Touch him, indeed. She wanted him out of this room. But that, she thought with a sigh that reached her toes, wasn't the truth at all.

"You think I'm a whore," Madelyne suddenly blurted out. "Aye, living with a defrocked priest . . . those were your words, Duncan," she reminded him. "You'd not want to bed a whore."

She prayed she was right.

Duncan smiled over the way she thought to sway him. "Whores do have certain advantages over unskilled virgins, Madelyne. You, of course, understand my meaning."

No, she most certainly didn't understand his meaning, but she couldn't tell him that, now, could she? Her deception was getting out of hand.

"They do not have certain advantages," Madelyne muttered.

"Don't you mean to say we?"

She gave up. She wasn't a whore and knew he realized it too.

When she didn't answer him, Duncan concluded she'd be forced to lie if she continued. "A whore knows all the ways to please a man, Madelyne."

"I'm not a whore and you know it."

Duncan smiled. Oh, how her honesty pleased him. He was a man conditioned to betrayals, yet he knew with a certainty he'd stake his life on that Madelyne would never lie to him.

Duncan removed the rest of his clothes and walked over to the other side of the bed. Madelyne's back faced him. He saw her shoulders stiffen to the snapping point when he threw back the covers and got into bed. He turned, smothered out the candle flame, and then let out a loud yawn. If Madelyne had been watching him, she would have known the yawn was a blatant lie. His arousal was obvious, even to someone as naive as his skittish wife. It was going to be a long night.

"Madelyne."

She hated the way he called her name when he was irritated with her. Duncan always drew out the last until it sounded as though her name was actually Lane.

"My name is not Lane," she muttered.

"Come to bed."

"I'm not tired." It was a stupid remark, but Madelyne was too frightened to be clever. She should have listened to more of Marta's tales. It was too late to do anything about that now. Oh, God, she thought she was going to be sick right this minute. And wouldn't that be humiliating—to lose her dinner in front of him. The thought made her stomach lurch, intensifying her worry.

"I don't know what to do."

The anguished whisper tore at Duncan's heart. "Madelyne, do you remember the first night we spent together in my tent?" Duncan asked.

His voice was soft, husky too. Madelyne thought he might be trying to calm her.

"I promised you that night I'd never force you. And have I ever broken my word to you on any matter?" he asked.

"How would I know?" Madelyne returned. "You've never

given me your word on anything." She turned to see if he was going to try to grab her. That was a mistake, because Duncan hadn't bothered to pull the cover over himself. He was as naked as a wolf. Madelyne grabbed the blanket and threw it toward him. "Cover yourself, Duncan. It isn't decent to let me see your . . . legs."

She was blushing again. Duncan didn't know how long he could keep up this nonchalant facade. "I want you, Madelyne, but I want you willing. I'll have you begging, even if it takes all night."

"I'll never beg."

"You will."

Madelyne stared into Duncan's eyes, trying to discover if he was trying to trick her or not. His expression told her nothing of what he was thinking. She nibbled on her lower lip while she worried. "You promise me?" she finally asked. "You really won't force me?"

Duncan let her see his exasperation even though he nodded. He decided that tomorrow he'd let her know she wasn't to question him in such a manner. For tonight, however, he'd allow her transgression.

"I trust you," she whispered. "'Tis strange, yet I think I've always trusted you."

"I know."

She actually smiled over his arrogant remark. Then she let out a sigh of relief. She felt safe again. "Since you wouldn't let me bring my sleeping gown, I'll just have to use one of your shirts," she said.

Madelyne didn't wait to gain his permission. She went over to his chest, opened the lid, and rummaged through the clothing until she found one of his shirts. She didn't know if Duncan was watching her or not, so she kept her back to him when she pulled her robe off and put his shirt on.

The garment barely covered her knees. She hurried to get under the blankets. And surely that was the reason she accidentally bumped into Duncan.

She took an infinitely long time adjusting the covers to her satisfaction. Madelyne didn't think it would be proper to touch him, but she wanted to get close enough to feel some of his warmth. At last she was settled. She let out a sigh. She had hoped that Duncan would have grown weary of her motions by now. In truth, she wanted him to grab hold of her and pull her up against him. Lord knew she was used to being grabbed and hauled around, and if the truth were admitted, she actually liked it a bit. She always ended up cuddled against him, feeling snug and safe. And almost loved. It was a fantasy, that, but she allowed the pretense anyway. There wasn't any sin in pretending, was there?

Duncan had no idea what was going on inside Madelyne's head. It had taken him far longer than he had anticipated just to get her into bed. His nightly ritual of swimming in the freezing lake was a paltry effort compared to the trial he was presently undergoing. The prize was worth the torment, however. With that thought in mind, Duncan turned to his side. Propping his head up on his elbow, he looked down at his wife. He was surprised to find her staring up at him, for he truly expected her to be hiding under the covers. "Good night, Duncan," she whispered to him, giving him another smile.

Duncan wanted much, much more. "Kiss me good night, wife."

His tone was arrogant. Madelyne wasn't upset by it. She gave him a frown. "I've already kissed you good night," she reminded him sweetly. "Was it so insignificant that you've forgotten it already?"

Was she baiting him? Duncan decided she was, and probably because she felt so safe. Victorious too. Ah, she trusted him, and while he was pleased by that fact, the throbbing increased in his loins, bothering his concentration. He couldn't take his gaze away from her mouth, was powerless to stop himself as he slowly, inevitably, lowered his mouth to hers. His arm circled her waist, blocking any retreat if she tried to leave him. He promised himself that he wouldn't force the kiss, only keep her next to him until he could find a way to reason with her.

His mouth settled on hers in a kiss meant to melt any resistance. His tongue plunged into her mouth, hungry, almost savage in the quest to mate with her. He wanted to give her pleasure and knew he had succeeded when her tongue touched his and her hand gently brushed the side of his cheek.

Duncan captured her sigh when he deepened the kiss. His hand caressed the side of her neck while his thumb rubbed a lazy circle above the wild pulse he felt.

Madelyne wanted to get a little closer to his warmth. Kissing him felt so right. Her hands slipped around Duncan's neck, and when he showed his pleasure over her aggression by emitting a low growl, she smiled against his mouth.

He lifted his head to look at her. Madelyne looked thoroughly satisfied. Her lips were dewy and swollen and there was a sparkle in her eye that warmed his heart. He found himself smiling back and couldn't explain the reason. When he felt her fingers tentatively brush the nape of his neck, he couldn't resist kissing her again. Her lower lip was easily captured between his teeth; he tugged, bringing Madelyne up to him. She laughed, delighted. Duncan groaned, tormented.

The kiss turned fierce and hot. His hands captured the sides of her face, and when she began to respond, he let her feel the hunger in him.

Madelyne moaned and moved closer, until her toes were rubbing against the crisp hair on his legs.

Duncan stopped her restless motions by trapping her legs between his heavy thighs. His mouth never left hers. He feasted on her, using his tongue to plunder the sweet interior she so willingly offered.

He couldn't get enough of her. The kiss turned wild, ravenous. His hands were as undisciplined as his mouth, taming and exciting as he stroked a warm path from her shoulders to the base of her spine. Shivers of ecstasy made her tremble all the more. She couldn't seem to catch a thought and hold on to it. Madelyne felt as if she were spinning out of control. She couldn't seem to save herself. Her mind was being ruled by such new, erotic sensations flooding her body.

Madelyne squirmed within his hold. She was drawn to the heat, until she felt his hard arousal against the junction of her thighs. She uttered a gasp and tried to pull away, but Duncan's hot kiss was pushing away all her fear. The heat was incredible. Her mind rebelled against the intimacy, but her body knew how to respond. She instinctively captured him and held him there, using her thighs to cuddle him. She let the warmth penetrate, but when Duncan began to move his hips and his arousal rubbed against her, she tried to stop him. Her hands grabbed hold of his thighs and she pushed him. She thought she was making him stop, but the more he moved, the weaker her struggle became. His touch ignited the embers of desire deep inside her, and it wasn't long before she was actually clinging to him, her nails digging into his backside to keep him firmly against her.

Duncan realized she was frightened by the longing that had taken her, but he was determined to make her respond with equal passion. His hands cupped her buttocks, almost roughly. He lifted her and pulled her against him, letting her feel all of him. A low mating sound came from deep in his chest, a primitive, erotic sound, and as magical as the song of the Sirens calling to Madelyne, mesmerizing her. She couldn't resist and she kissed him with wild, free abandon.

Madelyne's uninhibited response nearly pushed Duncan over the brink of sanity. He tore his mouth away from hers and began to press hot kisses down the column of her neck. He tried to gain control but the effort cost him. It had turned painful holding back, and he wanted nothing more than to plunge inside her, to fill her body and her soul completely. He couldn't, of course, it was too soon for her. Duncan told himself to go easy, to give her a little more time, but his mouth and his hands refused to listen to the dictates of his mind. God help him, he couldn't stop touching her. Her scent drove him to distraction; Duncan had never experienced such overwhelming passion. The realization that there was still much more to come made him feel close to exploding.

Madelyne knew she should stop his liberties. She was clinging to Duncan, her arms wrapped tightly around his waist. She took a deep breath, trying desperately to control herself. It proved an impossible task; Duncan was tantalizing her neck with his mouth and his tongue, and whispering such bold, sexy, unrepeatable words into her ear, she couldn't think much at all.

He called her beautiful, told her in erotic detail what he wanted to do to her. He said she made him crazed with desire, and she could tell from the way his hands shook when he pushed her hair away from her face and kissed her brow that he meant what he said.

She knew he could easily crush any resistance she offered him. Yet his strength didn't frighten her now. All she had to do was tell him to stop. He wouldn't force her. Duncan always kept his power contained when he was with her, whenever he touched her; he used an even greater method of winning her. Aye, he wooed her with tender caresses and soft, forbidden promises.

If she could just find the strength to put a little distance between them, perhaps she could think again. With that intent in mind she rolled away from him.

Duncan followed her. She realized then that the blankets were gone. He covered her now, most thoroughly. Their bare legs were entwined and only a thin shirt protected her virginity from him.

He removed that barrier as well, slowly edging the material up over her breasts. He was determined, and had the shirt off before she could utter a single word of denial. In truth, she might have helped him.

All thoughts of caution left when Duncan's chest touched her breasts.

The thick mat of hair rubbed against her nipples. She moaned with true pleasure. His breathing excited her almost as much as his touch did. It was harsh, uncontrolled, as ragged with need as her own.

Duncan lifted his head to look at her. Madelyne's eyes were dark, slumberous.

"Do you like kissing me, Duncan?"

He wasn't prepared for the question and answered her only when he'd found his voice. "Aye, Madelyne, I like kissing you." He smiled then. "As much as you like kissing me."

"I do," Madelyne whispered. She shivered with heat, nervously rubbed the tip of her tongue along her lower lip. Duncan watched her. He groaned and had to close his eyes for a second before he could look at her again.

She was making him frantic. This wooing was difficult work. He wanted her. Now. He knew she still wasn't ready for him. He'd have to continue this trial of endurance even if it killed him. He thought it just might.

Duncan took a deep breath and placed a kiss on the tip of one of Madelyne's finely arched eyebrows. He kissed the bridge of her nose next, right in the center of her attractive freckles, the ones he knew she probably would have denied she had.

Madelyne held her breath, waiting for him to reach her

mouth. When Duncan turned and moved to the side of her neck, she tried to get him back where she wanted him.

"I want to kiss you again, Duncan," she whispered.

She knew she was being brazen. Aye, she was playing with forbidden fire. Madelyne told herself she acted so bold because she was so unprepared. No one had ever explained the ways of men and women. No one had ever cautioned her about the intense pleasure. And the pleasure warred with her ability to reason.

Madelyne suddenly realized that the make-believe battle she fought with herself was just that, make-believe. She was trying to force Duncan into taking the decision away from her. Then he alone would be responsible for this act. She'd remain an innocent, trapped by the pleasure he forced on her.

The truth shamed her. Duncan wasn't forcing her at all. "I'm a coward," she whispered.

"Don't be afraid," Duncan soothed her. His voice was filled with tenderness.

Madelyne tried to explain, to give him all the words, to tell him how much she wanted him. Just for tonight she wanted to belong to him. She didn't believe he could ever love her, but for one glorious night she wanted to pretend the promises he gave her were true. If Duncan could give her only a part of himself, she'd make herself believe it was enough.

"Put your arms around me, Madelyne," Duncan ordered her. His voice was controlled, yet his hands were gentle as they played against the swell of her breasts.

The palms of his hands cupped her breasts fully then. Madelyne instinctively arched against him, thinking the pleasure he gave her was excruciatingly sweet.

Duncan ignored her surprised gasp. He used his thumbs to coax her nipples into responding. When they were hard and straining, he moved downward and took one into his mouth. His tongue was velvet torture. He used suction to drive her mad. She twisted and moaned while her hands clung to his shoulders.

Both breasts felt swollen when he finished with them. Duncan covered them with his chest again and captured her mouth in a long, searing kiss that only made her desperate for more.

He couldn't wait any longer. In the back of his mind he knew she still hadn't given him permission. He lifted his head to look at her, saw the tears shimmering in her eyes. "Do you want me to stop?" Even as he asked the question he wondered how in God's name he'd ever be able to accomplish that feat.

"Tell me why you're crying, Madelyne." He caught the first tear that escaped from her lashes with his thumb.

She didn't answer him. Duncan roughly took hold of her hair. His fingers twisted into the silky strands. "Give me your honesty now, wife, full measure. I can see the passion in your eyes. Say the words, Madelyne."

His demand was as forceful as his need. Duncan could feel the heat in Madelyne. Her body moved restlessly against him.

"'Tis wrong of me to want you, but I do," Madelyne whispered. "I want you so much, I ache."

"You're my wife now, Madelyne," Duncan answered, his voice raspy. "What we do isn't wrong." He leaned down and kissed her again, a hot, searing kiss that held nothing back. She responded with equal passion. When her fingernails dug into his shoulder blades, he abruptly pulled back.

"Tell me you want me inside you. Now. Say it, Madelyne." Duncan stared into her eyes as he slowly pushed her legs apart with his thigh. Before Madelyne understood his intention, his hand slid into the soft mount of curls covering the most sensitive part of her. His fingers gentled and stroked until her heat was wet and slick with desire. And all the while he watched her passionate response.

His finger slowly penetrated her. Madelyne instinctively arched against his hand, giving him so much pleasure by her uninhibited action, he thought he was going to die. She was so incredibly hot. And the heat belonged to him.

"Cease this torment, Duncan. Come to me."

He moaned her name just before his mouth took hers again. As slowly as he could manage, he settled himself between her silky thighs, lifted her hips, and began to penetrate. She twisted, driving Duncan forward.

Duncan paused when he felt the shield proving her virginity. "Put your legs around me." He groaned the instruction. His face fell against her neck. When he felt her move to obey him, he plunged forward. Madelyne cried out in pain and tried to pull back. "It's all right, love. The pain is over now, I promise. Hush now," he whispered.

Duncan wanted to wait until her body had adjusted to his invasion, but the throbbing was unbearable now. He couldn't stop. He began to move, slowly at first, and then with growing need and force. His hand moved between them, arousing her to a fevered pitch when his fingers rubbed against her.

The pain was soon forgotten. Duncan filled her completely. Madelyne began to move with him, arched her hips to take him deeper inside, and felt the change that overcame her husband then.

The power uncoiled, surrounded, penetrated. She glorified in the sensations, allowed her softness to become the sheath for his power. They were so much a part of each other now; each belonged to the other, body, mind, and soul.

Her control deserted her. She was wild, as free as a tigress now, reaching to attain the mystery of fulfillment just outside her grasp. She gave herself up to the feelings, surrendering herself to her husband, her lover. And all because he surrendered himself to her.

He whispered bold words into her ear, but she was soon too mindless to understand what he was saying. She couldn't think, only feel the power pulling at her, stroking, demanding.

The climax was so overwhelming, she cried out. His name. She was terrified, vulnerable, safe. She was loved.

Duncan answered her with an explosive climax and a harsh growl. He called out to her, held her so tightly she thought he might absorb her. And then he collapsed against her, sighing her name with true satisfaction.

Their bodies were damp with perspiration. The musky smell of loving surrounded the haze of their passion. Madelyne touched his shoulder with her tongue, licked the salty taste of him.

Duncan didn't think he had the strength left in him to roll away from her. He decided he'd stay right where he was forever.

He had never experienced such contentment. When he was finally able to gather his wits, he leaned up on his elbows to look at her. Madelyne's eyes were closed. Her cheeks were pink. She was back to being a timid kitten, Duncan concluded with a smile. Lord, how could she be embarrassed now, after the way she'd responded to him. He thought he'd carry her scratches on his shoulders for at least a week.

"Did I hurt you?"

"Yes." She sounded shy.

"Very much?" He sounded worried.

"Very little."

"And did I pleasure you, Madelyne?" Duncan asked.

Madelyne dared a look up at him. His arrogant smile captured her. "Yes," she admitted.

"Very little?"

She shook her head, smiling now. Madelyne suddenly realized he needed to hear her tell him how much he'd pleased her almost as much as she needed to hear of his satisfaction. "Very much, Duncan."

He nodded, thoroughly satisfied. Though he'd known he'd given her fulfillment, his contentment was intensified because of her honesty. "You're a passionate woman, Madelyne. You've nothing to be embarrassed about." He kissed her long and hard, and when he next looked at her, he was pleased to see her shyness gone. Her eyes had turned a deep blue. Lord, he could lose himself in her again.

Duncan suddenly felt vulnerable. He couldn't give a reason for the feeling. It was too foreign to his nature to understand. If he didn't guard against her, Madelyne could turn him into Samson. He thought she was more enticing than Delilah. Aye, she'd snatch his strength away if he allowed it.

With a frown Duncan rolled onto his back, clasped his hands behind his head, catching some of Madelyne's hair under his elbow. He ignored her, staring at the ceiling while she struggled to get free of the restriction.

Duncan was trying to come to terms with all the truths demanding his attention. He'd ignored the facts too long. The only time he'd been honest with himself was when he touched Madelyne. He couldn't control his reactions then, no matter how valiantly he tried. She had come to mean a good deal to him. The power she had over him actually worried him. And Duncan wasn't a man given to worry much or easily.

Madelyne pulled the covers up to her chin. She rested on her back but glanced over to catch the ferocious frown on her husband's face.

She immediately became frightened. Had she failed him some way? She knew she'd been a little timid, awkward too. "Do you have regrets now, Duncan?" she asked, her voice hesitant.

She couldn't look at him. Madelyne closed her eyes, letting her fear and shame build.

"None."

He snapped out the denial. His voice was harsh. Madelyne wasn't the least comforted. She felt hurt and humiliated. The glow of their lovemaking was gone now, replaced by such a desolate, desperate feeling of failure. God help her, she started to cry.

Duncan wasn't paying Madelyne much attention, for he had only just accepted the full truth.

The admission staggered him. The disrespectful, unpredictable woman weeping loud enough to wake the dead had tripped her way right into his heart.

He suddenly felt as vulnerable as this Achilles warrior Madelyne told him about. Aye, Achilles couldn't have been too pleased to find out his heels were vulnerable. He'd probably been infuriated, as infuriated as Duncan suddenly was.

Duncan didn't have the faintest idea how he was going to protect himself from her. He decided he needed time to think through this situation. Aye, time, and distance, too, because it just wasn't possible to think about all the ramifications when Madelyne was near him. Hell, that infuriated him.

Duncan sighed, long and loud. He knew what Madelyne wanted, what she needed from him now. With a groan of frustration he jerked the covers away and pulled her into his arms. He told her to quit crying, but she blatantly disobeyed him and continued on until his neck was soaking wet from where her face rested.

Madelyne fully intended to tell him she despised him and that she was never going to speak to him again, that he was the most insensitive, overbearing man she'd ever encountered. She needed to quit crying first, else she'd just sound pitiful instead of angry.

"Do you have regrets now, Madelyne," he asked her when he couldn't stand the sound of her weeping any longer.

She nodded, bumping his chin. "I do," she told him. "I obviously didn't please you. I know that's true because you're frowning and snapping at me, but it was only because I didn't do what I was supposed to do, Duncan."

Lord, she was unpredictable. She cried because she thought she hadn't satisfied him. The realization made him smile.

Madelyne suddenly pulled out of his arms, bumping him again. "I don't want you to touch me ever again."

In her anger she forgot all about her nakedness. Duncan's body reacted swiftly to the lovely view. Madelyne faced him, her legs tucked beneath her, and her breasts, magnificent, full and rosy-tipped, were too irresistible to ignore. Duncan reached out and circled the nipple of one with his thumb. The nipple hardened before Madelyne could slap his hand away.

She tried to deny him then by pulling the covers over her bosom, but Duncan easily won the spontaneous tug-of-war when he ripped the blanket out of her grasp and flung it to the floor. She would have followed it if he hadn't grabbed hold of her arm and yanked her back on top of his chest.

Duncan trapped her hands with his and grinned. The grin left quite abruptly when her knee found a vulnerable target between his legs.

He groaned, captured her legs by locking his own around her ankles, effectively stopping her struggles. He let go of her hands and then slowly pulled her head down to him. He could feel her heart pounding against his chest, wanted nothing more than to kiss her anger away, but when she was just a breath away, he stopped. "Listen well, wife. You weren't awkward, only innocent. And you have pleased me more than I had thought was possible."

Madelyne stared at him a long moment. Tears flooded her eyes again. "The truth, Duncan? I did please you?"

He nodded, exasperated. He vowed to lecture her first thing in the morning about questioning him, and then remembered he'd already made that vow.

She was appeased. "You pleased me too," she whispered.

"I know I did, Madelyne." He wiped the tears away from her cheeks and sighed over the disgruntled look that came over her face. "Don't frown at me," he ordered.

"How do you know you pleased me?"

"Because you screamed my name and you begged me to—"

"I never beg, Duncan," Madelyne interrupted. "You exaggerate."

He smiled most arrogantly. Madelyne opened her mouth to tell him just how arrogant she thought he was, but his mouth caught hers, effectively stopping her rebuke.

It was a hot kiss. Madelyne could feel his arousal pressed against her. She moved her hips against him restlessly, teasingly, too, arousing him all the more.

Duncan gently pulled away. "Go to sleep now. It would be too painful a second time."

She stopped his protest with another kiss. Madelyne decided she liked being on top of him, shyly whispered that fact to him.

He smiled, yet still insisted she sleep. "I command it," he told her.

"I don't want to sleep," Madelyne said. She nibbled on the side of his neck, shivering with new awareness. "You smell so good," she told him. Her tongue played with his earlobe, driving him to distraction.

Duncan decided to put an end to her game now, before he was unable to stop himself from taking her again. He didn't want to hurt her, but he knew that she was too innocent to understand.

He'd have to show her how uncomfortable it would be for her.

With that intent in mind, his hand moved between them. When he thrust his finger inside, Madelyne moaned. Her fingernails dug into his shoulders. "Now tell me you want me," Duncan demanded, his voice harsh with his desire.

Madelyne slowly arched up. Pain and pleasure blended into confusion. She rubbed her breasts against his chest. "I do want you, Duncan," she whispered.

Duncan suddenly felt his control desert him. He felt strong enough to conquer the world. When Madelyne tried to roll onto her back, he shook his head.

"Do you really force me to beg you, Duncan?" she asked, though it sounded more of a demand to her husband. He thought her voice quavered because she ached with as much need as he did.

He kissed the frown away from her face while he slowly began to penetrate her.

Madelyne straddled his hips, moaning with contentment. Her last coherent thought was a revelation. She didn't have to be flat on her back.

Chapter Fifteen

"Where your treasure is, there will your heart be also."

NEW TESTAMENT, LUKE, 12:34

Duncan had always believed himself to be a practical man. He knew he was stubborn, set in his ways, too, but didn't look at either of those as flaws in his character. He liked his days to follow the same rigid pattern, believing there was safety and comfort in predictability. As a leader of such vast numbers, it was imperative to maintain order and discipline. Why, without a well-constructed plan for each day, there'd be chaos.

Ha, chaos. The word reminded Duncan of his gentle little wife. Though he didn't voice his opinion, he thought Madelyne gave the word *confusion* new meaning. Lord only knew how chaotic, how unpredictable his life had become since he had made the decision to marry the woman. He admitted, but only to himself, of course, that his marriage was the first impractical thing he had ever done.

Duncan truly believed he'd be able to continue his

routine without interruption. He also thought he'd be able to ignore Madelyne just as thoroughly as he had before they had exchanged those binding vows. And he had been vastly mistaken in both beliefs.

Madelyne was far more stubborn than he had thought. It was the only excuse he could find to explain the blatant way she disregarded his position.

Duncan hated changes. In the back of his mind he thought Madelyne knew it. She gave him innocent looks when he demanded she cease her constant meddling and then blithely went on her way to change something else.

Oh, his pretty wife was still timid enough around him. At least she gave the appearance that she was. She blushed quite easily. Duncan only had to give her a good long stare to get her immediate reaction. He puzzled over it, yet didn't question her about her obvious embarrassment. But when he was not paying attention, she did anything she pleased.

The changes Madelyne instituted weren't even subtle. Most impressive and the least to complain about was the radical change in his hall. Without gaining permission, Madelyne had ordered the wobbly platform removed. The old scarred table was carried down to the soldiers' keep, and a new, unblemished, smaller table was built by a carpenter Madelyne had commissioned, again without asking his permission.

Madelyne drove the servants ragged over what they referred to as her cleaning fits. The servants probably thought Madelyne was demented, though none would openly declare such in front of their lord. Yet Duncan also noticed how each hurried to comply with Madelyne's orders, as though pleasing his mistress was a treasured goal.

The floors had been scrubbed, the walls stained and decorated. New rushes, smelling suspiciously like roses, lined the floor. A gigantic banner, primarily the color of royal blue, with white stitching of Duncan's impressive crest, hung above the hearth now, and Madelyne had placed two tall-backed chairs right in front of the fireplace. The room mimicked the tower room in some ways. Madelyne had reduced the size of the hall by making several small sitting areas. Why anyone would want to sit in the hall was beyond Duncan's comprehension. Even though it looked inviting, the hall was just a place to eat a meal, and perhaps to stand before the roaring fire for a few minutes to gain warmth. No one was supposed to linger there. Yet his wife didn't seem capable of comprehending that simple fact and transformed his hall into a room that beckoned laziness.

Duncan also noticed that the soldiers made certain their boots were clean before walking into the hall. He didn't know if that pleased him or not. Why, even his men were bending to Madelyne's silent dictates.

The dogs had proven to be Madelyne's greatest challenge. She kept dragging them downstairs. The dogs kept coming back. Madelyne had gotten around that problem too. Once she had established which animal was the leader of the pack, she wooed him down the stairs by dangling a piece of mutton in front of his face to gain his compliance. She then had him barred from the stairwell until the pattern of feeding downstairs was firmly established.

No one threw their discarded bones over their shoulders anymore either. Gilard told Duncan how Madelyne stood at the head of the table and sweetly explained they were all going to eat like civilized men or not eat at all. The men didn't complain. They seemed as eager as the servants to please Madelyne.

Aye, she was more tigress than kitten now. If she thought any of the servants were being the least disrespectful to any Wexton, she lectured them into humiliation.

Now that he thought about it, Duncan realized she lectured him too. His wife was a little more subdued with him but she still spoke her mind often enough.

She constantly challenged his opinions. Duncan remembered an incident that had taken place the day before, when Madelyne was listening to a conversation he was having with Gilard about King William and his brothers, Robert and Henry. As soon as Gilard left the hall, Madelyne told Duncan she was worried about the king's brothers. She said in a voice that reeked with authority that neither brother had been given sufficient responsibility. In her mind, since the two men were so unappreciated, both would certainly become discontent and cause problems for their king.

She hadn't known what she was talking about, of course. How could a woman understand politics? Duncan had patiently taken time to point out to her that the oldest brother, Robert, had been given Normandy, for God's sake, a far greater treasure than England, and had already shown his lack of responsibility by bonding the land to his brother for enough coins to go crusading.

Madelyne ignored his logical argument, insisting that he himself acted just like King William because he kept his own brothers under his wing and wouldn't allow either of them to make any decisions. She was lecturing him then, explaining her worry that both Edmond and Gilard would soon feel as restless as the king's two brothers.

Duncan had finally grabbed her and kissed her. It was the only way he could find to take her mind off the subject. It was also a very satisfying method.

Duncan told himself at least ten times a day that he couldn't be bothered with the mundane problems of his household. He had greater, far more important work to do. Aye, it was his duty to turn ordinary men into mighty warriors.

For that reason he tried to maintain a distance from his brothers, his sister, and most especially, his stubborn, undisciplined wife.

Yet while he could remove himself from the workings of his household, he couldn't seem to separate himself from the problem of Madelyne. He was too busy protecting her.

In truth, all his men took a turn saving Madelyne's life. She never offered a word of appreciation to any of them, yet Duncan knew it wasn't because his wife was a discourteous woman. Nay, the truth was far worse. Madelyne simply didn't realize how her own impulsiveness put her into constant jeopardy.

Madelyne was in such a hurry to get to the stables one afternoon, she ran right in front of a line of soldiers practicing with their bows and arrows. An arrow just missed the back of her head. The poor soldier who had shot the arrow immediately fell to his knees. He couldn't find his target the rest of the day, thanks to his brief encounter with Duncan's wife. Madelyne hadn't even realized the danger. She had hurried on, oblivious to the chaos she had created.

The incidents involving near tragedy were too many for Duncan to recount. He was fast approaching the point where he dreaded the evening report given to him by Anthony. His faithful vassal looked haggard from his duty. Though he never complained, Duncan was certain the vassal would have preferred a good battle to the death instead of trailing behind his leader's wife.

It had taken him time, but Duncan finally understood why Madelyne had become so carefree, so uninhibited. It was such a simple reason too. And it pleased him immensely. Madelyne felt safe. When the fever ruled her mind, Duncan had learned all about her childhood. She was a quiet child who tried to be as inconspicuous as possible. Madelyne's mother had sheltered her daughter from her father and her brother, but the two years Madelyne lived alone with Louddon after her mother's death had been cruel, painful years indeed. Madelyne had quickly learned not to laugh or to cry, or show spirit or anger, for to do so would have drawn attention to herself.

Though the years she spent with her uncle Berton were blessed years, Duncan doubted Madelyne acted like a normal little girl even then. Living with a priest would have taught her additional restraint. Duncan didn't believe she'd been mischievous when she had to answer to a fragile old man who probably depended on her more than she depended on him.

Madelyne had learned control from her uncle. Duncan knew the priest was trying only to help Madelyne survive. The uncle taught her how to hide her emotions from her brother, assuming she'd be returning to him soon. Neither Madelyne nor her uncle expected the visit to stretch into years. For that reason Madelyne lived in constant fear that Louddon would appear on her uncle's doorstep at any moment and take her back home.

With fear came caution. Now that Madelyne felt safe, she let go of all restraint.

Duncan understood Madelyne better than she understood herself. She appeared clumsy, but the simple truth was that she was in such a hurry to catch up with life, to savor each experience, she didn't have time for caution. That duty fell to her husband. Madelyne was like a young filly just testing her legs. She was a joy to watch, a nightmare to protect.

What Duncan didn't understand was his own feelings for his wife. He'd gone to Louddon's fortress to take Madelyne captive. His plan was revenge; an eye for an eye. And that had been reason enough.

Until she'd warmed his feet.

Everything had changed at that moment. Duncan had known with a certainty he couldn't deny that they were henceforth bound together. He could never let her go.

And then he'd married her.

The following morning, Louddon's army left Wexton land.

Each day Duncan would find a new reason for having made his impractical decision to marry her. Aye, he wanted to use his most logical mind to give reason to the feelings inside his heart.

On Monday he told himself he married her because he wanted her to have a safe haven, a place to live without being afraid. Her unselfish act of kindness in trying to rescue him merited such a reward.

On Tuesday he told himself he married her because he wanted to bed her. Aye, lust was a good enough reason.

Wednesday he changed his mind, deciding that he'd pledged himself to her because she was weak and he was strong. All his training conditioned him for such a response. Madelyne was just like a vassal, and though she hadn't knelt on the ground and given him her pledge, it was still his duty to protect her. And so, compassion was the true reason after all.

Thursday arrived and with it came another realization. Why, he'd married Madelyne not only to protect her but to show her how valuable she really was. The early years spent with Louddon had been cruel years indeed. His gentle wife had been taught she was unworthy. She didn't believe she had value. Louddon had abused her sorely for two years, then sent her to her uncle Berton for a visit. It was obvious, even to Duncan, that Louddon had forgotten her existence. It was the only reason he could find for Madelyne living with the old priest for nearly ten years.

When he gave Madelyne his name, Duncan was actually showing her just how worthy she really was.

It was unfortunate, but that reason didn't even make it through the day.

He stubbornly ignored the truth. Duncan actually believed he'd be able to make passionate love to Madelyne every night and then ignore her during the day. It sounded reasonable enough to him. After all, he'd been most successful in separating himself from his family. He was lord and he was brother. Neither duty conflicted with the other. Aye, it sounded easy enough. Madelyne had worked herself into his heart, but that didn't mean she was going to affect his way of life.

The truth nagged him all week long, as irritating as the first whispering sounds of thunder. On Friday afternoon, just two weeks to the day after he'd married Madelyne, the storm erupted. Violently.

Duncan had just returned to the upper bailey when Edmond's shout drew his attention. He turned, just in time to see Madelyne strolling toward the stables. The doors to the barn were wide open. Silenus had gotten free. The animal was galloping toward Madelyne, his head down, his hooves thundering. The huge stallion was about to trample her to death.

The stablemaster chased after the horse, holding a bridle in his hands. Anthony was right behind him. Both were shouting warnings to Madelyne, but Duncan decided the noise from the stallion's pace must have blocked out the sound, for his wife never even looked around her.

He was certain she was going to die.

"No!" The bellow came from the depths of his soul. Duncan's heart felt as though it were being ripped out of his chest. All he could think of was getting to Madelyne and protecting her.

Everyone was running toward Madelyne, trying to save her.

And there wasn't even need.

Madelyne was oblivious to the chaos surrounding her. She kept her attention directed on Silenus. She carried his treat in her hand and was on her way to visit him when he lurched out of the stables and headed for her. She assumed the animal was eager to meet her halfway.

Silenus came within a breath of killing her. Dust flew around Madelyne's face when the stallion stopped so abruptly a scant inch or two in front of her. She waved her hand in front of her face to clear the air. Silenus immediately nudged her hand. The animal was looking for his clump of sugar, Madelyne guessed.

Everyone was too stunned to move. They watched the

great stallion paw the ground and nudge Madelyne again. She laughed, delighted with his show of affection, finally holding her hand out for him to lick the sugar from her palm.

When the stallion was finished with his treat, Madelyne patted him. She noticed James and Anthony standing a short distance behind the animal then. Anthony was leaning against James for support.

Madelyne smiled at the men. "Is your injury bothering you, Anthony? You look a little pale to me," she said.

Anthony shook his head quite vigorously. Madelyne turned to James, took in his glassy-eyed stare. "Did my lamb finally tear the door down? He's been trying for the longest time."

When James didn't answer her, Madelyne decided Silenus must have given him a fright. "Come, Silenus, I believe you've upset James," she said. She slowly walked around the animal and headed for the stables. Silenus turned, quite docile now as he danced back toward his home. Her voice, crooning a soft melody, kept the beast trailing meekly behind her.

Duncan wanted to go after Madelyne. He was going to kill her for trying to scare him to death. But he'd have to wait, he knew, until his legs would let him walk again.

God's truth, he had to lean against the wall. His strength had deserted him. He felt like an old man with a weak heart. Duncan noticed Edmond was in much the same condition. His brother was kneeling on the ground. Duncan knew it wasn't by choice.

Anthony seemed to be the only one in control now. He strolled over to Duncan, whistling under his breath. Duncan wanted to kill him.

The vassal put his hand on Duncan's shoulder. It was probably meant as a sympathetic gesture. Duncan wasn't sure if Anthony was offering him condolences because he was wed to Madelyne or if the vassal was giving him understanding over the scene he'd just witnessed. Duncan didn't appreciate the action, no matter what the motive.

"There's something I've been meaning to tell you, Duncan."

Anthony's voice was mild but it captured Duncan's

attention. He turned to scowl at his first-in-command. "What is it?" he demanded.

"Your wife is determined to ride Silenus," Anthony said.

"When I'm dead and unable to witness it," Duncan roared.

Anthony had the gall to smile. He turned, a blatant attempt to shield his face from Duncan. "Protecting your wife is an unusually demanding challenge. When her mind is set on a plan of action, there's no stopping her."

"She has ruined my faithful horse," Duncan shouted.

"Aye," Anthony answered, unable to keep his amusement out of his voice. "She has."

Duncan shook his head. "God, I thought I'd lost her." His voice had turned into a harsh whisper. When he looked down at his hands, saw how they still shook, he was immediately furious again. "I'm going to kill her. You may witness the deed if you wish."

Duncan was back to shouting. Anthony wasn't intimidated. The vassal leaned back against the wall. He asked only curiously, "Why?"

"It would improve your day," Duncan announced.

Anthony did laugh then. "I didn't mean to ask you why I'd want to witness Madelyne's death, Baron. I meant to ask you why you'd want to kill her."

Anthony's laughter didn't sit well with his lord. "How would you like the new duty of seeing to the water?" he threatened. "Would you find it amusing to drag bucket after bucket to the kitchens? Would that duty be challenge enough, Anthony?"

It was an insulting suggestion for someone of Anthony's rank. Duncan thought his vassal would immediately show contrition over his lack of respect.

Anthony, however, didn't seem to be the least contrite. "'Tis a dangerous mission you give me, Baron. You've only to ask Ansel just how dangerous this duty is."

"What are you talking about?"

"Your squire nearly drowned the other day. He had climbed to the top of the steps to the rainwater vat, when a ball hit him square in the shoulders. He lost his balance, of course, and—"

Duncan held up his hand for silence. He didn't want to

hear any more of this tale. He closed his eyes, praying for patience. Though he didn't know the full story, he had an instinctive feeling his gentle little wife was behind Ansel's mishap. He'd also noticed her showing a new game to the children yesterday afternoon.

Edmond walked over to join Duncan and Anthony. "What is so amusing to you, Anthony?" Edmond asked. Duncan's brother was still too shaken by Madelyne's brush with death to find anything remotely humorous.

"Our lord is going to kill his wife," Anthony remarked.

Edmond looked exasperated. "For God's sake," he muttered. "Look at our leader now." A slow grin settled on his face before he added, "Why, Duncan couldn't kill a lamb."

Hell, it was humiliating. Edmond had obviously heard Madelyne call his stallion her lamb. Everyone probably heard, and if they hadn't, Edmond would certainly tell them.

"It would seem, Anthony, our captive has turned captor."

"I'm in no mood for your riddles, Edmond," Duncan muttered.

"You're in no mood for admitting you love Madelyne either. Look at your condition, brother, and the truth will hit you between the eyes."

Edmond shook his head, turned, and slowly walked away.

"Madelyne's an easy woman to love, Baron," Anthony commented when they were again alone.

"Easy? As easy as swallowing a mace."

They were completely ill suited for each other. He was as rigid as a trunk of an old tree. Madelyne was as flighty as the wind.

And he never stood a chance . . . not since the moment she touched his feet. Duncan knew that now. Lord, he did love her.

"I'll not have chaos in my life." Duncan made the proclamation as a fervent vow.

"Perhaps, in time, all will settle—"

"When Madelyne is too old to get out of bed," Duncan interrupted. "Then I'll have peace again."

"Peace can be boring," Anthony commented with a smile. "Your wife has given new life to your home, Duncan."

Anthony sought to appease Duncan with his argument.

He concluded, from the way Duncan scowled, that his plan wasn't working. Perhaps his lord had only just realized how much Madelyne meant to him. If that was the situation, Anthony decided his baron wasn't taking the realization well at all.

He decided to leave Duncan to his own thoughts, excused himself with a bow, and walked away.

Duncan was glad for the solitude. He kept picturing his stallion racing toward his gentle little wife, knowing he'd never forget the horror for as long as he lived.

She'd captured his horse just as she'd captured him. Duncan found his first smile when he realized what a feat Madelyne had accomplished. Edmond was right. Madelyne was captor now, for she owned his heart.

There was surprising strength with the truth. Duncan suddenly felt as though he'd just ended a forty-day fast. He wasn't going to have to ignore Madelyne any longer. Aye, he could feast on her. Besides, he admitted, it was past time he took a firm hand.

He started after his wife, thinking he would lecture her awhile, then kiss her. He was still angry. It was her fault, of course. She was the one who'd made his heart start pounding. She'd scared the hell out of him. He didn't like that feeling, not at all. He wasn't used to loving either. The first would take time to get over; the second would take time to adjust to.

Another shout stopped him. Fergus, soldier in charge of the south watch, called out a warning that a visitor was approaching the fortress. From the colors displayed on the banner waving in the breeze, the watchman knew that Baron Gerald and his assembly wished entrance.

It was all Duncan needed to turn his day completely black. Damn, he had sent a messenger to Gerald with the full explanation of Adela's condition. He assumed Gerald would have sent a messenger back with agreement to nullify the contract. Obviously, because Gerald had troubled to journey such a distance, there was still a problem to be solved before the betrothal could be set aside.

Hell, he was going to have to be diplomatic. And Adela would probably revert to her crazed condition when she learned her intended was here for a visit.

Duncan realized he might be jumping to conclusions.

Gerald was an old friend. There could be a number of reasons for the baron to visit. Lord, Madelyne was affecting him more than he'd realized. He was beginning to take on her flaws.

She was gifted with affecting his concentration too. Why, only two days ago he'd been in the middle of issuing an important command to his men, when his wife had strolled into his line of vision. Duncan suddenly found himself watching the gentle sway of her hips as she walked by, forgetting all about the order he was giving.

Duncan smiled over that memory. The soldiers had been staring at him so expectantly, and there he stood, without a glimmer of an idea what he was telling them, probably looking quite stupid, until Gilard stepped forward and reminded him of their topic.

Fergus shouted to Duncan again, interrupting his concentration. Duncan immediately gave the order to let Baron Gerald inside.

Madelyne was just coming out of the stables when Duncan intercepted her. Without giving her any sort of proper greeting, he abruptly stated his order.

"Adela's inside, Madelyne. Go and tell her Baron Gerald is here. She'll greet him at dinner."

Madelyne's eyes widened over Duncan's startling news. "Why is he here, Duncan? Did you send for him?"

"I did not," Duncan answered, irritated she didn't immediately pick up her skirts and run to do his bidding. He was standing close enough to kiss her, and that thought fully consumed him. "Now, do as I've instructed, wife."

"I always do what you instruct," Madelyne answered with a smile. She turned, started to walk toward the castle. "And good day to you too, Duncan," she called back over her shoulder.

It was a disrespectful comment meant to remind him of his lack of manners, Duncan supposed. He told himself it was too bad there wasn't time to throttle her senseless.

"Madelyne."

She stopped as soon as he called out to her, yet didn't turn around until he commanded it. "Come here."

Madelyne complied, frowning now, for her husband's voice had sounded very tender. "Yes, Duncan?" she asked.

Duncan cleared his throat, frowned, and then said, "Good afternoon."

He hadn't even meant to say that, had he? Duncan frowned all the more when Madelyne smiled. Duncan suddenly pulled her into his arms and kissed her.

She was too stunned to respond at first. Duncan had never touched her during the day. Why, he always ignored her. He wasn't ignoring her now, however. Nay, he was kissing her quite forcefully, and in clear view of anyone who might be passing by.

The kiss wasn't gentle either, but passionately arousing. Just when she was getting the way of it, Duncan pulled away.

He smiled at her. "Don't ever call my horse your lamb again. Do you understand me?"

Madelyne stared up at Duncan, looking confused and flushed.

Before she could form an answer, Duncan walked away from her. Madelyne picked up her skirts and chased after him. She grabbed hold of his hand, stopping him with her touch, and when he turned to look at her, he was still smiling.

"Are you ill, Duncan?" Madelyne asked. Fear sounded in her voice.

"Nay."

"Then why are you smiling so?" she demanded.

Duncan shook his head. "Madelyne, please go and tell Adela about Gerald's arrival," he said.

"Please?" Madelyne asked. She looked appalled. "You've told me to please—"

"Madelyne, do as I've ordered," Duncan said.

She nodded but didn't move. Madelyne just stood there, watching Duncan walk away from her. She was too stunned to go after him again. Duncan had always been so predictable. Now he was trying to change on her. She wrung her hands together while she worried about that. Had it been a hot summer day, she would have believed the sun had baked his head. Since it was January, however, and as cold as purgatory, Madelyne couldn't find any acceptable excuse for his sudden turnabout in attitude.

She needed time to think. Madelyne sighed and tried to

dismiss her husband's unusual behavior from her thoughts. She hurried in search of Adela then.

Trying to dismiss Duncan was easier said than done. Why, it would have been less difficult to walk across a bed of nails barefoot.

Adela did help take Madelyne's mind off her husband. Duncan's little sister was in her bedroom. She was sitting on the side of the bed, braiding her hair.

"We have company, Adela," Madelyne announced cheerfully.

Adela was happy to see Madelyne until she heard who company was. "I'm staying in this room until he leaves," Adela shouted. "Duncan gave me his word. How could he ask Gerald to come here?"

Madelyne could see how frightened Adela was. Her hands fell to her lap and her shoulders sagged.

"Duncan didn't invite Gerald. Don't get upset, Adela. You know your brother won't break his promise. In your heart you know I speak the truth, don't you?"

Adela nodded. "Maybe, if I act like I did when you first came here, then Gerald will be so disgusted he'll leave immediately."

"'Tis foolish talk," Madelyne announced, squelching the spark of eagerness in Adela's eyes. "Gerald will only think you're quite pitful. He just might think you haven't gotten over your incident," Madelyne said. "If you look as pretty as you can and greet him respectfully, well, then I do believe he'll know your mind is set and you simply don't want to marry him. Besides, Duncan is the one who'll have to answer to Gerald, not you, Adela."

"But Madelyne, I can't face Gerald, I just can't," Adela cried out. "He knows what happened to me. I'll die of shame."

"For heaven's sake," Madelyne answered, trying to sound exasperated. Inside, she ached for Adela. "What happened wasn't your fault. Gerald knows that."

Adela didn't look relieved by Madelyne's argument, so she decided to turn the topic a little. "Tell me what you remember about Baron Gerald. What does he look like?"

"He has black hair and hazel-colored eyes, I think," Adela answered, shrugging.

"Do you think he might be handsome then?" Madelyne asked.

"I don't know."

"Is he kind?"

"Barons aren't kind," Adela returned.

"Why not?" Madelyne asked. She walked over and started to rebraid Adela's hair.

"They don't have to be kind," Adela answered. "What does it matter if he's pleasing to look at or not, Madelyne?" She tried to turn around to look up at Madelyne.

"Be still, else your braid will be lopsided," Madelyne interjected. "I was just curious about the baron, that is all."

"I can't go downstairs," Adela said.

She started to cry. Madelyne wasn't sure what to do. "You don't have to do anything you don't want to do, Adela. Duncan did give you his word, however, and it would seem to me that the least you could do to show your appreciation is to stand beside your brother and treat Gerald as an honored guest."

Madelyne had to keep up her argument for quite a while. In the end she was able to sway Adela. "Will you go downstairs with me? Will you stay by my side?" Adela asked.

"Of course I will," Madelyne promised. "Remember, Adela. Together we can face any challenge."

Adela nodded. Madelyne sought to lighten her mood. "I'm afraid your braid is hanging over your ear," she said. "You'll have to redo it, then change your gown. I must see to dinner arrangements and change my own clothes."

Madelyne patted Adela on her shoulder. Her hands were shaking. She knew it was because Adela was so upset and had this new ordeal to go through.

She kept smiling until she shut the door behind her. Then she let her worry show. Madelyne began to pray for what she believed would take a miracle. She prayed for courage.

Chapter Sixteen

"Love conquers all; let us too yield to love."

VIRGIL, *ECLOGUES*, X

After Madelyne had given proper instructions to Gerty for dinner arrangements, she went up to the tower room.

It had been two weeks since Duncan had torn the door down and a week since it had been rebuilt. The loops were missing from the new door, however, and Madelyne smiled over that change every time she noticed it. Duncan must have given the order as a precaution so that Madelyne couldn't lock him out again.

Madelyne went through all her gowns and finally chose a royal blue chainse. The new ankle-length gown fit snugly and made a pretty contrast to the off-white knee-length bliaut she added. They were Wexton colors and a deliberate choice on Madelyne's part. She was Duncan's wife, after all, and hostess to Baron Gerald. She wanted Duncan to be proud of her tonight.

She brushed her hair a long while, until it curled against

the swell of her breasts. Since there was still ample time, she sat down on the bed and braided three long strips of blue ribbon into a pretty belt. She draped the braid around her waist but left it loose enough to fall against the tilt of her hips, as was the current fashion dictate, according to Adela, who knew far more on the subject of fashion than Madelyne did. She finished her dress by placing the small dagger she used for stabbing her meat inside the extra loop in the braid she had struggled to design.

Madelyne wished she had a mirror so that she could see how she looked, then decided it was vain of her to want such an unnecessary extravagance.

She was halfway down to Adela's room, when a sudden worry stopped her. Would Baron Gerald treat her as Duncan's wife or as Louddon's sister? God only knew he had sufficient reason to hate Louddon. Her brother had destroyed Gerald's future with Adela. Would Baron Gerald lash out at her because of his anger?

Madelyne pictured one horrible scene after another. When she pictured Baron Gerald grabbing hold of her throat, she forced herself to calm down. She was afraid, true, but that fear helped give her composure. Madelyne forced a serene expression.

She told herself she'd gotten through far more degrading encounters. That thought gave her strength. Besides, no matter how horrible Gerald treated her, Duncan wouldn't let him harm her.

Adela was ready when Madelyne finally knocked on her door. The little sister wore a rose-colored bliaut over a lighter-colored pink chainse. Her hair was braided into a coronet on top of her head. Madelyne thought she looked pretty. "Adela, dove, you look splendid."

Adela smiled. "You call me such funny names, as if I were younger than you are, when you know perfectly well I'm almost two years older."

"That is no way to acknowledge a compliment," Madelyne instructed, ignoring Adela's reminder of their age difference. After all, Adela might be older in years, but Madelyne felt far more worldly. She wasn't nearly as fragile as her friend, and she was a married woman.

"Thank you for telling me I look splendid," Adela said.

"Madelyne, you always look beautiful. Tonight you wear Duncan's colors. My brother won't be able to take his eyes off you."

"He probably won't even notice I'm in the room," Madelyne returned.

"Oh, he'll notice all right," Adela predicted with a smile. "Have you softened in your attitude toward your husband yet?"

Adela tried to sit down on the bed, as if she had all the time in the world for this discussion. Madelyne took hold of her hand and started tugging her toward the door. "I never know how to feel about your brother," she admitted once Adela was walking next to her. "One minute I pretend our marriage will work to both our satisfactions, and the next I'm certain Duncan would like to be rid of me. I'm no fool, Adela. I understand why your brother married me."

"To get even with your brother?" Adela asked, frowning.

"See? You've realized that fact too," Madelyne exclaimed.

Madelyne had ignored the fact that Adela asked the question and hadn't spoken a certainty. Adela thought to explain herself more fully because she really didn't think Duncan would go to such extreme measures to get even, but Madelyne started talking again, turning her concentration. "It would be a foolish hope to think Duncan would become accustomed to having me for his wife, and I know it will only be temporary anyway. The king is sure to demand that the church nullify our marriage."

Adela nodded. She'd also thought of that possibility. "I heard Gilard say that our king is in Normandy again, settling yet another rebellion."

"I've heard the same," Madelyne commented.

"Madelyne, what did you mean when you said you hoped Duncan would become accustomed?" Adela asked.

"Your brother has made a sacrifice when he married me. He gave up his Lady Eleanor. I just wish he wouldn't be unhappy. . . ."

"You see yourself as a sacrifice?" Adela asked. "Don't you realize how important you've become to all of us?"

When Madelyne didn't answer, Adela said, "Do you love my brother?"

"I'm not that foolish," Madelyne answered. "Everyone

I've ever loved has been taken from me. Besides, I'm not about to give my love to a wolf. I only wanted to live peacefully together for the time we're united."

Adela smiled. "Duncan isn't a wolf, Madelyne. He's a man. And I think you're not telling the truth."

"I always tell the truth," Madelyne returned, appalled Adela could suggest such a thing.

"Well then, you're lying to yourself and don't know it," Adela answered. You might be trying to protect your heart against losing Duncan, but I think you're beginning to love him all the same, else you wouldn't look so upset by my question."

"I'm not the least upset," Madelyne snapped. She immediately regretted her angry outburst. "Oh, Adela, life isn't as simple as it should be. Why, I almost feel sorry for Duncan. He had to change his future just to satisfy his lust for revenge, and now he's saddled with me for a wife. I believe he regrets his rash action now. He's just too stubborn to admit it."

"Duncan has never done anything you could call rash in his life," Adela argued.

"There's always a first time," Madelyne answered, shrugging.

"Maude saw Duncan kissing you outside," Adela whispered.

"And she immediately told you, didn't she?"

"Of course," Adela returned, laughing. "Maude and Gerty compete with each other. Each wants to be the first in telling the latest gossip."

"It was the strangest thing, Adela. Duncan kissed me in front of everyone." Madelyne stopped to sigh. "I think he might be coming down with a chill."

They reached the bottom step outside the entrance to the hall. Adela paused. "Lord, I'm so frightened, Madelyne."

"I am too, Adela," Madelyne admitted.

"You? Why, you don't look frightened at all," Adela said, so surprised by her friend's confession, her own fear lessened. "Why are you frightened?"

"Because Baron Gerald surely hates me. I *am* Louddon's sister. Dinner will probably be a trial to get through."

"Duncan won't let Gerald offend you, Madelyne. You're my brother's wife now."

Madelyne nodded but she wasn't at all convinced. When Adela took hold of her hand and squeezed it, she smiled at her friend.

They stopped again when they reached the entrance. Adela's grip on Madelyne became painful.

The reason was obvious. Duncan and Gerald were standing together in front of the hearth. They were both staring at Madelyne and Adela. Odd, but Madelyne thought they both looked a bit stunned. And neither appeared to be angry.

Madelyne smiled at Baron Gerald and immediately glanced over to look at her husband. Duncan was staring quite intently at her. He wasn't smiling. His gaze made her blush. She recognized the look. Duncan always wore that expression after he kissed her.

It soon became awkward, what with the four of them staring at one another. Madelyne was the first to remember her manners. She made a small curtsy, nudged Adela into doing the same, and then slowly walked into the hall. Adela trailed behind her.

Her expression was serene. She gave the appearance of being most tranquil.

Madelyne walked with a haughty, dignified, ladylike stride, and Duncan immediately knew something was wrong. He met his wife in the center of the room. He stood so close to her, his tunic brushed her arm. "What are you afraid of?" he asked, leaning down until his face was a breath away from hers. His voice was so low, she had to rise up on tiptoe to hear what he said.

She was surprised he knew she was frightened. "Does Baron Gerald know I'm Louddon's sister, Duncan?" she asked. Fear sounded in her whisper.

Duncan understood then. He nodded, giving Madelyne answer to her question, and then put his arm around her shoulders. When she was settled against his side, he introduced her to the baron.

Gerald didn't appear to be the least offended with her. He smiled, a true warm smile it was, and bowed after their introduction.

He was a nice-looking man, but Madelyne wouldn't have called him handsome, not when he was standing so close to Duncan. Why, her husband was much better looking. In truth, he probably overshadowed every other man in England.

Madelyne looked up at Duncan. She was going to ask him to help Adela, in a whisper, of course, so Gerald wouldn't chance to overhear, yet standing so close to her husband addled her thoughts and she could only stare at him. She couldn't even manage a smile. His eyes were the most amazing color of gray, with such beautiful chips of silver.

"Why are you looking at me like that?" Duncan asked. His nose almost touched hers. He was close enough to kiss.

"How am I looking at you?" Madelyne asked.

She sounded out of breath, and she was blushing enough for Duncan to surmise her thoughts. He suddenly wanted to carry her upstairs. Aye, he wanted to make love to her until tomorrow.

The tranquil expression was gone from his wife's face now. Duncan grinned with pleasure.

Edmond walked into the hall just as Duncan was about to kiss his wife. Adela was staring at the floor, Gerald was staring at Adela, and Madelyne seemed mesmerized by her husband.

"Good eve," Edmond bellowed out into the silent hall.

Everyone moved at the same time. Madelyne jumped, knocking Duncan's nose. Her husband took a step back, then hurried to grab hold of Madelyne before she fell to her knees. Adela turned, forcing a smile for Edmond. Baron Gerald nodded his greeting.

"'Tis a fine evening, isn't it, Duncan? Gerald, my God, you've aged to an ugly old man since I last saw you," Edmond stated in a loud, cheerful voice.

Duncan's head cleared. He still wanted to pick up his wife and leave the hall, but he found enough discipline to see dinner through first. "It's time for supper," he announced. Duncan grabbed hold of Madelyne's arm and guided her toward the table.

Madelyne couldn't understand his hurry. She'd thought they'd have a bit of conversation before dining. But the look in her husband's eyes decided her against arguing the matter.

Duncan sat at the head of the table, with Madelyne seated on his left. He showed his surprise when Ansel appeared at his other side and began to serve him. Though it was the custom for the squires to learn all about the duties required to serve their lord, Duncan had instructed the boy only in defense.

Another change instituted by Madelyne, of course, and without gaining his permission. He shook his head over her breach, nodded to Ansel, and then glared at his wife.

She had the audacity to smile at him. "Did you know, Duncan, this is the first meal we've shared together?" she whispered, trying to take his mind off the squire.

Duncan didn't seem inclined to answer her comment. In fact, he barely spoke during dinner. Gilard was late in arriving, which made Duncan frown. Madelyne was thankful though that Duncan didn't chastise his brother in front of their guest.

Father Laurance didn't come for dinner at all. Madelyne was the only one who wasn't surprised by his absence. She didn't believe he'd taken ill either, although Edmond had given that story. Madelyne thought the true reason was that the priest was frightened of Duncan. She couldn't blame the man. He was terribly young for the duty of advising Duncan on matters of God and church.

Edmond and Gilard kept up a constant chatter through dinner, taking turns questioning Gerald about his past year, for it had been that long since any of them had seen one another.

Madelyne listened to their conversation, fascinated by the easy way they badgered one another. They were insulting one another's looks, ability, too, but it didn't take Madelyne long to realize it was just their way of showing affection. She thought it a most interesting observation.

Baron Gerald was obviously a good friend of the Wexton brothers. He had a nice laugh. When Edmond called him a weakling and repeated a story of how Gerald had misplaced his sword during an important battle, Gerald shouted with laughter and then came up with a story of his own to prove Edmond's worthlessness.

Adela sat across from Madelyne. She stared at the table-top, yet Madelyne noticed there were a few instances when she smiled over the ridiculous remarks flying across the table.

Gerald didn't speak directly to Adela until dinner was

nearly finished. Edmond sat between the two. Madelyne was certain Gerald was going to have a permanent crick in his neck from tilting his head around Edmond in order to look at Adela.

Edmond finally took mercy on Adela's would-be suitor. He stood up and casually walked around the table, pretending to be fetching a jug of ale. No one was fooled by the ploy, least of all Adela. There was another jug right in front of Edmond's trencher.

"And how are you, Adela?" Gerald politely inquired. "I was sorry I missed you when you were . . ."

Gerald's face turned red, though not as red as poor Adela's. The baron had inadvertently mentioned the incident.

An awkward silence fell over the group. Duncan sighed and then said, "Adela was sorry she missed you in London, Gerald. Adela? The baron asked you how you were feeling," he reminded his sister.

Duncan's voice was tender, filled with understanding as he spoke to his sister. Lord, he was becoming an easy man to love. Too easy. Was she in love with her husband and just too stubborn to admit it?

Madelyne immediately began to worry. She sighed as well, a loud, unladylike sound she immediately regretted. Duncan turned and grinned at her. He surprised the worry right out of her when he gifted her with a slow, teasing wink.

"I am very well, Gerald," Adela said.

"You look well."

"I feel well, thank you."

Madelyne watched her husband roll his eyes heavenward, knew he thought all this talk about looking well and feeling well was ridiculous.

"Madelyne, I've never had such a fine meal," Gerald said in praise, drawing her attention away from her husband.

"Thank you, Gerald."

"I've eaten too much of everything," the baron told her. He turned to Adela then. "Would you like to walk with me in the courtyard after dinner, Adela?" He glanced over at Duncan and hastily added, "Gaining your brother's permission, of course."

Before Adela could deny the request, Duncan granted it. Adela immediately looked at Madelyne for help.

Madelyne didn't know what she could do, but determined to find a way to change Duncan's mind. She nudged his leg with her foot. When Duncan didn't even look over at her, she nudged him again, much more forcefully.

Her patience wore out when he still wouldn't look at her. Madelyne kicked him then, but all she gained from her effort was to lose her shoe under the table.

Yet while Duncan still pretended to ignore her, he did reach under the table and grab hold of her foot, pulling it up onto his lap.

Madelyne was mortified by her undignified position and thanked God no one seemed to notice how she gripped the table with her hands when Duncan began to stroke the arch of her foot. She tried to pull away but she lost her balance. She almost fell off the stool.

Gilard was sitting next to her. When she bumped him, he gave her a puzzled look and then grabbed hold of her arm and helped straighten her.

She knew she was blushing. Adela was staring at her, reminding her of the dreaded walk outside, Madelyne supposed. She decided it was high time she took control. Duncan might have hold of her foot so she couldn't kick him again, but he couldn't grab hold of her mind, now, could he? "What a wonderful idea, to stroll outside after dinner," Madelyne said.

She looked at her husband when she made the comment. Duncan frowned. Madelyne smiled, sensing victory. "Duncan and I would love to join you, wouldn't we, husband?" she asked.

One had to be on one's toes around Duncan, Madelyne thought, even when the toes were in his lap. He wouldn't dare deny her suggestion in front of their guest. Madelyne turned to Adela and shared a smile with her. Adela did look relieved.

"No, we wouldn't," Duncan announced to the group in a mild voice.

His denial forced frowns on both Madelyne's and Adela's faces. "Why wouldn't we?" Madelyne challenged.

Madelyne tried to smile at Duncan because she knew Gerald was observing the exchange.

Duncan smiled at her. His eyes, however, told a different

story. He was probably wishing he could throw her out a window, she supposed. She had noticed that Duncan didn't like his decisions questioned. Madelyne thought the trait was an irritating one. Aye, irritating for Duncan, she thought with a bit of sympathy, knowing full well she'd continue to question his orders whenever the mood came over her. She couldn't help herself.

"Because, Madelyne, I would like to speak to you in private after dinner."

"Speak to me about what?" Madelyne demanded with a disgruntled look.

"Men and their horses," Duncan told her.

Edmond snorted; Gilard laughed outright. Madelyne gave both of them a good frown before she turned back to Duncan. She didn't believe this nonsense any more than his brothers did. Men and horses, indeed. The real message was clear enough. He was going to strangle her for challenging him. Madelyne thought to give him a saucy retort, couldn't think of any, decided then she'd better not goad him further. He just might say something to embarrass her.

Madelyne decided to ignore him and all but turned her back on him. It was a rude gesture, a mistake as well, because she'd forgotten all about her foot resting in his lap. Gilard had to catch her again.

Duncan knew she was trying to dismiss him. The smile reached his eyes. When he turned to nod at Gerald, he realized his friend had also caught on to Madelyne's game. The baron was trying not to laugh.

"With Duncan's permission, I've a gift to give you, Adela."

"You do?" Adela was surprised by Gerald's thoughtfulness. "Oh, I couldn't accept anything from you, Gerald, though it was good of you to take the trouble to bring me something."

"What'd you bring her?" Gilard asked. It wasn't a polite question. Baron Gerald didn't seem offended though. He grinned and shook his head.

"Well?" Gilard demanded.

"A musical instrument," Gerald advised. "A psaltery."

"Catherine had one of those," Gilard said. He turned to Madelyne. "Our oldest sister couldn't seem to conquer the thing though. Thank God she took it with her when she married," he added with a grin. "She could set our teeth to grinding with one song."

Gilard turned back to Gerald and said, "It was a good gesture, Gerald, but it'll only gather dust here. Adela doesn't know how to work the strings and God help us all if Catherine comes back to teach her."

"Madelyne knows how," Adela blurted out. She remembered Madelyne had told her she played the instrument for her uncle every evening. Adela was embarrassed by the way her brother tried to denigrate the gift. "And she'll teach me the way of it, won't you, Madelyne?"

"Of course," Madelyne answered. "It was most kind of you to bring such a gift, Baron."

"Yes," Adela rushed out. "Thank you."

"Well then?" Gerald asked, looking at Duncan.

Duncan nodded, Gerald grinned, Adela actually smiled, and Madelyne sighed. "I shall go and get it for you now," Gerald announced. He stood up and started for the doorway and then called over his shoulder, "Perhaps we can persuade Madelyne to give us a song or two before we take our walk, Adela, if Duncan's talk about men and horses can wait a while longer."

Gerald heard Duncan's laugh before he left.

Gilard also stood up. "Where are you going?" Edmond asked.

"To get Madelyne another chair. There seems to be something wrong with this one," he added. "She keeps trying to fall off it."

Madelyne slowly turned to Duncan and glared at him. If he said one word, she was going to throw him out a window.

Adela thought it was a wonderful idea for Madelyne to play the psaltery. She was all for any plan that would delay her walk with Gerald. She pleaded with Madelyne to play for them all.

"Oh, Adela, I don't think tonight would be a good time—"

"Are you so eager to be alone with your husband?" Duncan asked in a soft whisper.

Madelyne turned to her husband again, frowned, and was rewarded with one of his heart-stopping smiles. The dimple

232

was back in his cheek too. And then he winked at her again, right in front of everyone.

Duncan was tearing a piece of bread in half and she very stupidly watched him, until it dawned on her that he wasn't holding her foot now. How long had both his hands been in plain sight?

She immediately removed her foot from his lap. "And if I sing like a frog, Duncan, and shame you?" she asked him.

"You could never shame me," Duncan answered.

It was such a kind thing to say. Madelyne didn't know how to respond. Was he teasing her or telling her the truth? "You're my wife, Madelyne. Nothing you could do would shame me."

"Why?" Madelyne asked, leaning toward her husband so they wouldn't be overheard.

"Because I've chosen you," Duncan answered. He also leaned toward his lovely wife. "'Tis a simple fact, even to a—"

"If you call me half witted, I shall be forced to take Adela's gift and knock you senseless with it."

Madelyne was more appalled by her threat than Duncan appeared to be. Duncan took hold of her hand and pulled her closer. "Stop touching me," Madelyne whispered.

She glanced over to the other Wextons. Gilard was telling an amusing story and both Adela and Edmond were listening to him.

"No."

She looked back at Duncan when she heard him deny her request. "I don't like it, Duncan."

"Yes, you do, Madelyne. When you're in my arms, you like everything I do to you. You moan and you beg me to—"

Her hand covered his mouth and she blushed as red as the fire in the hearth. Duncan laughed, a loud booming sound that filled the hall with warmth. Edmond and Gilard both demanded to know the cause. Duncan looked like he just might tell them. Madelyne started praying, and held her breath.

She started breathing again when Duncan merely shrugged and changed the subject.

Madelyne happened to notice Adela was straightening the sleeves of her gown. She patted her hair too.

And then it dawned on her. Lord, she really was simple-minded. Adela wanted to look pretty for Gerald. She was primping and squirming enough to give that impression at least.

Now that she thought about it, Madelyne realized Gerald was still attracted to Adela. The way he had stared at her said as much.

Madelyne's heart softened with the knowledge that Gerald might still want Adela. It made her feel great affection for the baron.

And then she immediately began to worry. Adela's mind was set on remaining with her family. Duncan had given his word. It was a complication.

"What has you frowning so, Madelyne?" Gilard asked.

"I was just thinking how complicated life becomes the older we get," Madelyne answered.

"We can't stay children forever," Edmond interjected with a predictable shrug that made Madelyne smile. She thought Edmond was as set in his ways as her uncle was.

"I'll wager you frowned your childhood away," she teased.

Edmond looked taken aback by the remark. He started to frown and then stopped himself. Madelyne laughed.

"I don't remember much of my childhood," Edmond said. "I do remember Gilard as a boy all too clear. Our brother was in constant mischief."

"Did you get into mischief when you were a little girl?" Gilard asked Madelyne, thinking to draw attention away from his embarrassing escapades. Madelyne didn't need to know about his wild inclinations. She might think less of him.

Madelyne shook her head. "Oh, nay, I never got into mischief, Gilard. I was very quiet. "Why, I never did anything wrong."

Duncan laughed as loud as his brothers. Madelyne took exception until she realized she'd made herself sound like a saint. "Well, I did have flaws," she stammered.

"You? Never," Edmond interjected, smiling.

Madelyne blushed. She wasn't sure how she should take Edmond's comment. She still didn't completely trust this Wexton, though she'd adjusted to his smiles. She turned to look at Duncan.

"Don't embarrass Madelyne," Duncan admonished his brother.

"Tell us one of your flaws, Madelyne," Adela asked, smiling with encouragement.

"Well, I know you'll find this difficult to believe, but I was a most awkward child, clumsy, in fact."

No one found it the least bit difficult to believe. Duncan shook his head at Gilard, who looked ready to shout with laughter over Madelyne's confession. Edmond started choking on a drink he was trying to swallow when Madelyne shyly admitted her flaw. Adela was giggling while she slapped her brother on his back.

Baron Gerald returned with the psaltery and placed it on the table in front of Adela just as Edmond controlled his fit of coughing. The triangular-shaped instrument was made of a light bleached wood. The strings numbered a dozen and Madelyne watched with envy as Adela ran her thumb across the wires.

"Father Laurance will have to bless this instrument," Adela said.

"Aye, at mass tomorrow," Gilard interjected. "I've instructed the priest to say the mass in the hall each morning until the chapel is repaired, Duncan."

Duncan nodded. He stood, giving the unspoken command that dinner was over.

Madelyne waited until everyone started to walk toward the chairs in front of the hearth. As soon as their backs were turned, Madelyne knelt down and searched under the table for her missing shoe.

Duncan lifted her by her waist, pulled her back against him, and then dangled her shoe in front of her face.

Madelyne turned and tried to grab her shoe.

"Why are you frowning at me?" Duncan asked. He lifted her onto the edge of the table, took hold of her foot, and put her shoe back on.

"I could have done that," Madelyne whispered. "And I'm frowning because you're teasing me, Duncan. I don't like it."

"Why?" Duncan lifted Madelyne back to the ground. He didn't let go of her waist, however, a fact that bothered Madelyne more than she cared to admit.

"Why?" she asked, wishing she could remember what she

wanted to say. It was all his fault, of course, because he was staring at her as though he'd like to kiss her, and how could she think of anything but kissing him back?

"Why don't you like me teasing you?" Duncan asked, leaning down toward her upturned face.

"Because you aren't predictable when you tease," Madelyne answered. "You're like a blade of grass in the winter, Duncan. Cold and stiff, aye, rigid." She tried to take a step back, but Duncan increased his hold and slowly pulled her closer, until she was touching his chest. "And now you're acting like the grass of summer, bending this way and that. . . ."

She looked so flustered, he didn't dare laugh. "I have never been compared to a blade of grass," he told her. "Now give me the truth and not another parable if you please."

"If you please?" She looked appalled by his suggestion. "Duncan, I don't like you teasing me because it makes me think you're being kind to me. I want you predictably angry," she muttered. "And I'm going to break my neck looking up at you like this."

The woman wasn't making sense. That shouldn't have surprised him, he told himself. Wives were more difficult to understand than he had suspected. "You don't want me to be kind to you?" he asked, sounding incredulous.

"I do not." Her voice increased in volume.

"Why the hell not?" Duncan didn't whisper his question. He had forgotten all about his family and his guest. All he could think about was getting this contrary woman into his arms, and making love to her.

Madelyne didn't want to answer him. She'd have to be honest.

"We'll stand here all night until you answer me," Duncan promised.

"You'll laugh."

"Madelyne, if I didn't laugh at your suggestion that I was like a blade of grass, I doubt I'll laugh at your next comment."

"Oh, all right," Madelyne said. "When you're kind to me, I want to love you. There, are you satisfied?"

He was very satisfied. And if Madelyne had been watching him, she'd have known how her words had pleased him.

Dear God, she'd actually shouted at him. Madelyne felt

like crying. She took a deep breath, stared at Duncan's chest, and whispered, "Then I'd get my heart broken, wouldn't I?"

"I would protect your heart," Duncan answered.

He sounded very arrogant. Madelyne gave him an exasperated look. Duncan couldn't stop himself. Her mouth was too close to deny. All his discipline evaporated. He leaned down and captured her mouth in a searing kiss.

"For God's sake, Duncan, we're all waiting for Madelyne to play the psaltery," Edmond shouted.

Duncan sighed into Madelyne's mouth before pulling away. His thumb slowly rubbed her lower lip. "I forgot we weren't alone," he told her with a grin.

"I also," Madelyne whispered back. She blushed and tried to catch her breath.

Duncan took hold of her arm and escorted her to the one vacant chair. "This is where you're supposed to sit," Madelyne told him. "It has the highest back," she explained.

When it became obvious Madelyne wasn't going to begin until Duncan sat where she thought he should, he complied with her order. He even smiled over it.

Edmond pushed another chair toward Madelyne. "You'll be more comfortable here," he told her when she reached for a stool.

Madelyne thanked him and sat down. Gerald handed her the psaltery. Her hands shook when she placed the instrument in her lap. Madelyne was terribly nervous now. She hated being the focus of everyone's attention. There was comfort in being inconspicuous.

Gerald stood behind Adela's chair. His arm was draped over the back. Both Gilard and Edmond stood, leaning against the hearth at opposite corners. And every one of them was staring at Madelyne.

"It has been such a long time," Madelyne said. She looked down at the instrument. "And I sang only for my uncle and his friends. I've had no true training."

"I'm certain your uncle and his friends thought you were wonderful," Adela interjected. She had noticed how Madelyne's hands trembled and tried to encourage her.

"Oh, they did think I was wonderful," Madelyne admitted, smiling at Adela. "But then, they were all quite deaf."

Duncan immediately leaned forward so that everyone could see him clearly. The look on his face suggested no one laugh.

Baron Gerald coughed. Gilard turned around to stare into the fire. Madelyne thought he was weary of waiting for her to begin.

"I could sing some of our Latin chant we use during Eastertime," she suggested.

"Do you know any songs about blades of grass?" Duncan inquired.

Madelyne looked startled. Duncan grinned.

"A blade in winter can be broken in half when you stomp on it," Madelyne told Duncan sweetly. "And a blade in summer can be smothered if you keep your boot on top of it long enough," she added.

"What are you talking about?" Gilard asked, puzzled.

"A sad tune," Duncan commented.

"Predictability," Madelyne answered at the same time.

"I'd rather you sang about Polyphemus," Edmond interjected.

"Who or what is a Polyphemus?" Baron Gerald asked.

"A one-eyed giant," Edmond answered, grinning at Madelyne.

"He was the leader of the Cyclops," Madelyne said. "Do you know the stories about Odysseus?" she asked Edmond.

"Bits and pieces," Edmond answered. He didn't add that everything he'd learned had come from Madelyne when she raged with fever.

"Gerald? Madelyne does tell the most wonderful stories," Adela said. In her enthusiasm she actually reached up and touched his hand.

"I've never heard of this Odysseus," Gerald announced. "Why is that, do you suppose?"

Madelyne smiled. Gerald sounded irritated that he was uninformed. He seemed to be looking for someone to blame.

"There's no shame in that admission," Madelyne returned. "Have you heard of Gerbert of Aurillac perchance?"

"The monk?" Gerald asked.

Madelyne nodded. She looked at Adela to give her explanation, certain Duncan's little sister couldn't have heard of the man. "Gerbert lived a long time ago, Adela. Almost a hundred years past, I believe. He left his monastery and went to study in Spain. When he returned to France, he led the cathedral school at Reims, and it was during that time that he gave his students some of the ancient stories he'd translated. It was another man named Homer who told the tales about the mighty warrior, Odysseus, and Gerbert who translated the tales from Greek to Latin."

"Were Homer and Gerbert friends, do you suppose?" Adela asked.

"No," Madelyne answered. "Homer lived in ancient times, in a place called Greece. He died hundreds of years before Gerbert was born. Homer's stories were kept safe in the monasteries. Some of them would make our church frown, but I mean no disrespect when I repeat the stories. In truth, they're really too foolish to believe as fact."

Everyone looked interested. Madelyne turned to Duncan, caught his nod, and then began to play the psaltery.

She made several ear-wincing mistakes in the beginning. And then the ballad of Odysseus meeting the Cyclops became the focus of her attention. Madelyne stared down at the psaltery, pretended she was sitting next to her uncle Berton and singing to him. Once she'd captured the pretext, her hands stopped shaking. Her voice grew in strength and purity as the tale about the warrior came to life.

The poem captured her audience. Duncan thought her voice was bewitching. It was a true reflection of the gentle woman he now claimed as his wife.

Madelyne spun a magical spell around all of them. Duncan, a man who wasn't given to linger, now leaned back in his chair and smiled with contentment.

She began the story when Odysseus and his men were taken captive by Polyphemus, since Edmond had specifically requested that tale. Polyphemus determined to eat every one of the soldiers. The one-eyed giant kept them imprisoned inside his cave by blocking the entrance with a large boulder. Since Polyphemus also kept his sheep in the cave every night, it was necessary for him to move the stone each morning to let his flock out into the fields to graze. Odysseus blinded the giant and then showed his men how to crawl under the sheep and cling to their bellies. Polyphemus let the sheep pass by but waved his arms higher into the air, trying to catch the soldiers. Odysseus's clever plan saved them all.

When Madelyne finished her recital, her audience begged to hear another.

Everyone took a turn telling their favorite part, interrupting one another in their enthusiasm.

"It was brilliant of Odysseus to tell Polyphemus his name was Nobody," Gilard stated.

"Aye," agreed Gerald. "And when the other Cyclops heard Polyphemus screaming because Odysseus had blinded him, they called into the cave to him, asking if he needed help and to give them the name of his tormentor."

Edmond's laugh joined the others. "And when he called out that Nobody was tormenting him, his friends left him alone."

Madelyne smiled, pleased with the enthusiastic reaction to her story. She turned to look at Duncan. Her husband was staring into the fire. He was smiling and had a satisfied look on his face.

He had a beautiful profile. As she continued to stare at him, a warm glow washed over her. And then she realized who Duncan reminded her of. Odysseus. Aye, Duncan was just like the mighty warrior she had dreamed about when she was a little girl. Odysseus had become her imaginary confessor, her friend, her confidant; she had whispered all her fears to him when she was frightened and lonely. She liked to pretend that one day Odysseus would magically appear and take her away with him. He'd fight for her, protect her from Louddon. And he'd love her.

When Madelyne became a woman, she put the childhood dreams away. And until this moment, she'd actually forgotten her secret dream.

Yet in this precious moment, while she stared at her husband, she realized that her dream had come true. Duncan was her Odysseus. He was her lover, her protector, her savior from her brother.

Dear God, she was in love with the man.

Chapter Seventeen

"The price of wisdom is above rubies."

OLD TESTAMENT, JOB, 28:18

"Madelyne, what ever is the matter with you? Are you ill?" Adela bounded to her feet and hurried over to her friend. She thought Madelyne looked ready to faint. Madelyne's face had lost all color, and if Adela hadn't reached out in time, the beautiful psaltery would have fallen to the floor.

Madelyne shook her head. She started to stand up, then decided her legs might not support her. In truth, she was still shaking over her realization. She was in love with Duncan. "I'm fine, Adela. Just a little tired, that is all. Please don't carry on so."

"Are you well enough to sing another song?" Adela asked. She immediately felt guilty for asking, but excused her conduct by telling herself she was desperate, after all, and would think of a way to repay Madelyne for her kindness if she'd only come to her aid now. Why, she'd carry a breakfast tray up to Madelyne in the morning.

Madelyne knew Adela was stalling. She sympathized with

241

her friend yet couldn't think of any plan to get her out of her walk with Gerald.

When Gerald walked over to stand beside Adela, Madelyne said, "'Tis a fine instrument you've given Adela. You've chosen with care, Gerald."

The baron smiled. "Duncan has also chosen with care."

Madelyne puzzled over his odd remark. Then Edmond and Gilard expressed their pleasure over her performance. She was soon blushing with embarrassment. In truth, she wasn't used to such praise. She thought the Wextons were the most unusual family. They threw out compliments so easily. They didn't think it detracted from their own value, Madelyne decided.

She'd never been called beautiful until she met the Wextons. Yet each one of them had given her that compliment more than once. It seemed to Madelyne that they believed she really was beautiful. "You're going to make me quite vain if you keep up this praise," she admitted with a shy smile.

She did notice, however, that Duncan hadn't offered her any comment and wondered if she'd pleased him.

Her husband still wasn't acting like himself. He'd behaved so strangely outside when he grabbed her and kissed her in front of the world. And he'd teased her during dinner. If she hadn't known better, she'd have to think the man had a sense of humor. That was ridiculous, of course.

Madelyne watched Gerald take hold of Adela's hand and escort her out of the hall. Duncan's little sister kept glancing back over her shoulder at Madelyne, giving her a pleading look.

"Don't stay outside long, Adela," Madelyne called out. "You'll get a chill."

It was the best she could do. Adela grasped the suggestion with a thankful nod before Gerald pulled her out of Madelyne's view.

Gilard and Edmond also left the hall. Duncan and Madelyne were suddenly alone.

Madelyne smoothed her gown to give her hands something to do. She wished she could go up to the tower room to spend a few minutes alone. Lord, there was so much to think about, so many decisions to make.

She could feel Duncan staring at her. "Would you like to tell me about men and their horses now, Duncan," Madelyne asked, "before you take your swim in the lake?"

"What?" He looked perplexed.

"You said you were going to talk to me about men and their horses," she explained. "Don't you remember?"

"Ah, that," Duncan replied. He gave her a warm smile. "Come closer, wife, and I shall begin my instructions."

She frowned over the request, thinking she was close enough. "You're acting very strange, Duncan," she remarked when she'd walked over to stand at his side. "And looking very relaxed too. You're not yourself at all," she added.

Madelyne nibbled on her lower lip while she stared down at her husband. She suddenly reached out and put the back of her hand to his forehead. "You don't have fever," she announced.

He thought she sounded disappointed. Her frown was fierce enough to give him that idea. Duncan grabbed Madelyne, pulled her into his lap.

Madelyne adjusted her gown and sat as primly as she could manage. She folded her hands in her lap.

"Are you worried about something?" Duncan asked. His thumb rubbed her lower lip away from her teeth.

Of course she was worried. Duncan was acting like a complete stranger. Wasn't that enough to worry any wife? Madelyne sighed. She brushed a lock of hair away from her eyes, accidentally bumping Duncan's chin with her elbow.

She apologized, embarrassed by her sudden awkwardness.

He nodded, thoroughly resigned to it.

"You don't sing like a frog."

Madelyne smiled, thinking it was the most wonderful compliment she'd ever received. "Thank you, Duncan," she said. "And now you'll instruct me in the ways of men and horses," she suggested.

Duncan nodded. His hand slowly moved upward along her back until it rested against her shoulder. The motion made Madelyne's skin tingle. Then he pulled her forward. Madelyne found herself settled against his chest.

"We men form a special attachment to our steeds,

Madelyne," Duncan began. His voice was as warm as the heat from the fire. Madelyne snuggled a little closer, yawned, and closed her eyes.

"Aye, we depend upon our mounts to obey our every command. A knight can't fight diligently if he has to take time to control his horse. It could mean his life if the battle is fierce and the animal unruly."

Duncan continued on with his explanation for several more minutes. "You, wife, have bewitched my stallion away from me. I should be furious with you. Now that I think about it, I am furious," Duncan muttered. The smile soured on his face as he mulled over the loss of his faithful mount. "Aye, you've ruined Silenus. You may protest now if that is your wish, but I've already made up my mind to give you Silenus. And so I will listen first to your apology for ruining my horse and next your appreciation for the gift I've given you."

Duncan didn't get either. Madelyne didn't apologize or thank him. He frowned over her stubbornness and then tilted her head back so he could look at her face.

She was sound asleep. She probably hadn't heard a word he'd said. He should have been angry with her. It was certainly disrespectful at the very least. Duncan kissed her instead of waking her. Madelyne snuggled closer. Her hands crept up around his neck.

Edmond walked into the hall just as Duncan placed a second kiss on the top of Madelyne's head. "She's asleep?" Edmond asked.

"My lecture frightened her into a faint," Duncan answered dryly.

Edmond laughed, remembered Madelyne was sleeping, and softened his voice.

"Don't worry about waking her, Edmond. She sleeps like a well-fed kitten."

"Your wife puts in a long day. The food at dinner was exceptional and all because Madelyne demands perfection from her staff. I ate four tarts," Edmond admitted. "And did you know it was Madelyne's own recipe given to Gerty?"

"Her staff?"

"Aye, they are loyal to Madelyne now."

"And you, Edmond? Are you loyal to Madelyne?"

"She's my sister now, Duncan. I would give my life to protect her," he added.

"I don't doubt you, Edmond," Duncan returned when he caught the defense in Edmond's voice.

"Then why did you ask?" Edmond said. He pulled up a chair and sat down, facing his brother. "Did Gerald bring news concerning Madelyne?"

Duncan started to nod but as soon as he moved his head, Madelyne took up the space under his chin. He smiled. "Gerald did bring news. Our king is still in Normandy, but Louddon is gathering his troops. Gerald lines with us, of course."

"I am bound to return to Baron Rhinehold in just three weeks," Edmond remarked. "Though he has my pledge of fealty, I'm vassal to our king first, you second, Rhinehold third. For that reason, Rhinehold would allow me to stay here as long as I'm needed."

"Rhinehold would also line up with Gerald and me against Louddon if it became necessary. Together we can muster over a thousand men."

"You forget your alliance with the Scots," Edmond reminded Duncan. "Catherine's husband could rally eight hundred, perhaps more."

"I haven't forgotten, yet I don't wish to bring Catherine's family into this feud," Duncan answered.

"And if the king sides with Louddon?"

"He won't."

"How can you be so certain?" Edmond asked.

"There are many misunderstandings about our king, Edmond. I've fought by his side many times. He's thought to have an uncontrollable temper. Yet, once in battle, one of his own men accidentally knocked our king to the ground. Soldiers surrounded William, each vowing to kill the careless vassal. The king laughed over the mishap, slapped the soldier on the shoulder who'd thrown him down, and then bade him to remount his horse and see to his defense."

Edmond mulled over the story. "It's said Louddon has an unusual hold over the king's mind."

"I doubt our king would let anyone rule his mind."

"I pray you're right, brother."

"There is another matter I wish to discuss with you, Edmond. The Falcon holding to be exact."

"What about it?" Edmond asked, frowning. The Falcon land was barren but thought to be rich farming land, owned by Duncan. It consisted of the southernmost area of the Wexton holdings.

"I would like you to oversee that domain, Edmond. Build yourself a fortress there. I would deed the land over to you if it were possible. The king wouldn't allow it, unless a way was found to gain his pleasure."

Duncan paused while he considered the complexities of the problem.

Edmond was stunned by his brother's comments. "'Tis unheard of, this plan you propose," he stammered. For the first time in his life, Edmond was actually rattled. And though it was highly improbable, a beacon of hope flamed in his heart. To own his own land, to rule as his own master, why, it was all too overwhelming to take in.

"Why would you want me to take over Falcon land?" Edmond asked.

"Madelyne."

"I don't understand."

"My wife listened to Gilard and me discussing the king's brothers. When Gilard left the hall, Madelyne pointed out how restless Robert and Henry were. She believes it's because neither was given sufficient responsibility."

"Good Lord, Robert was given Normandy," Edmond interjected.

"Aye," Duncan said, smiling. "But the king's youngest brother was given gold and a small, insignificant holding from his father and I can see the restlessness in him. He's a born leader, denied by birth the right to rule."

"If there is a parallel, I am eager to hear it," Edmond said.

"Madelyne did start me thinking. You're vassal to me and to Rhinehold, and those duties must remain intact, yet, if we could gain the king's grant, then you could take Falcon and make it profitable. You've a good head for turning one coin into ten, Edmond."

The brother smiled, pleased with the compliment. "If nought comes of our petition, you'll still build your home there and act as my overseer. The king will welcome the additional tithing and won't care which brother makes the contribution."

"I'm in agreement with your plan," Edmond announced, smiling now.

"Gilard will soon return to Baron Thormont to complete his forty days," Duncan interjected.

"Gilard has a way of leading others and will soon become first-in-command just as Anthony has became your first-in-command," Edmond said.

"Our brother will have to learn to control his temper first," Duncan commented.

Edmond nodded in agreement. "You've still to tell me what news Gerald brings us about Madelyne," he said then.

"Gerald is convinced that the king's brother, Henry, might be stirring up mischief. Gerald has been requested to speak with Henry."

"When? Where?"

"The Clares will have Henry as their guest. I don't know when the meeting will come about."

"Do you think Henry will ask Gerald's loyalty against our king?" Edmond asked. "And what of you? Are you also invited to this gathering?"

"Nay. He knows I'll stand beside my king," Duncan answered.

"You suggest Henry will turn against William then?"

"If I was convinced of that, I'd stand in front of our leader and give my life for him. I am honor bound to protect him."

Edmond nodded, satisfied. "Gerald said that the number of those becoming discontent is growing. There is more than one plot to kill him. That is not unusual. His father had just as many enemies."

When Duncan didn't comment, Edmond continued. "Gerald believes he's been invited to join this gathering because of his friendship to me. He thinks Henry wants to know if I'll honor him as king in the event of William's death."

"We wait to see what the outcome of this meeting brings?"

"Aye, we wait."

Edmond frowned. "There is much to consider, brother."

"Tell me this, Edmond," Duncan asked, changing the topic, "does Gilard still believe himself in love with Madelyne?"

Edmond shrugged. "He was having a time of it, adjusting to your marriage," he admitted. "But he's over the infatuation now, I believe. He loves Madelyne, yet she keeps calling him brother, and that puts a damper on his ardor. I'm surprised though that you noticed Gilard's affliction."

"Gilard wears his thoughts on his face," Duncan remarked. "Did you see the way he reached for his sword during the marriage ceremony, when he thought I was forcing Madelyne?"

"You were forcing her," Edmond returned with a grin. "And yes, I did witness the act. Madelyne also saw his reaction. I think that is the only reason she suddenly agreed to take you for husband."

Duncan grinned. "A true observation, Edmond. Madelyne will always try to protect anyone she believes weaker. At that moment she feared I would retaliate."

Duncan began to caress his wife's back. Edmond watched the way his brother stroked Madelyne and thought to himself that he probably wasn't even aware of what he was doing. "Does Madelyne want us gone then?" Edmond asked.

"Nay, Edmond. I imagine she'll become upset and blame me," Duncan answered. "My wife doesn't understand that your loyalty extends to Rhinehold too."

Edmond nodded. "I think Madelyne worries I'll keep you and Gilard under my control for the rest of your lives and won't allow either of you to act on any thought of your own."

"Your wife has strange ideas," Edmond remarked. "Yet she has changed your life, hasn't she, Duncan? And ours as well. This is the first time we've ever had such a long discussion on any issue. I believe Madelyne has made us a stronger family."

Duncan didn't respond to that comment. Edmond stood up and started to walk toward the entrance. "It's a shame you know," he called over his shoulder.

"What's a shame?" Duncan asked.

"That I didn't capture her first."

Duncan smiled. "Nay, Edmond, it was a blessing. God's truth, I would have taken her from you."

Madelyne awakened just as Duncan made his comment. She struggled to sit up and smiled shyly at her husband. "What would you have taken away from your brother, Duncan?" she asked him in a husky voice. She patted her hair and Duncan dodged her elbows before answering.

"Nothing for you to concern yourself with, Madelyne."

"You should always share what you have with your brothers," Madelyne instructed Duncan.

Edmond obviously heard her remark. His laughter trailed behind him.

Just then, Adela came tearing into the hall. As soon as Duncan's little sister spotted Madelyne, she burst into tears. "Gerald still insists that the contract is valid, Madelyne. What am I going to do? The man still wants to marry me."

Madelyne jumped off Duncan's lap just as Adela threw herself into her arms.

Duncan stood up and sighed in exasperation over his sister's near hysteria.

"You should be asking me that question, Adela," he snapped. He took hold of Madelyne's arm, ignoring the fact that Adela was clinging to her like a wet gown, and started pulling Madelyne toward the entrance.

"We can't just leave your sister in such a condition," Madelyne protested. Lord, she felt like she were in the middle of a tug-of-war. "Duncan, you're pulling my arm off."

Baron Gerald came rushing into the hall then, disrupting Duncan's bid to take Madelyne upstairs and deal with Adela's problem in the morning. Duncan wasn't in the mood for a long discussion and determined to resolve the matter immediately.

Before Gerald could say a word, Duncan asked, "Do you still want to marry Adela?"

"I do," Gerald answered. His voice challenged, as did his stance. "She will be my wife."

"I've given Adela my word she can stay here for as long as she wishes, Gerald."

Gerald's face showed his anger. Duncan felt like growling. "I was wrong to give her such a promise," he said, admitting the error in front of Edmond, Madelyne, Adela, and Gerald. It was an amazing confession coming from a man who never admitted any mistake. Duncan smiled over the way his confession stunned everyone.

He turned to Madelyne and whispered, "Your obsession with telling the truth has affected me, wife. Now, close your mouth, love. All will be well."

Madelyne slowly nodded. She gave her husband a smile, letting him know she trusted him. He was so pleased that when he turned back to confront Gerald, he was still smiling. Gerald knew Duncan well enough to wait until he was given a full explanation before openly challenging him. Duncan had always been a man of his word in the past.

"Adela," Duncan demanded, "quit screeching like a hen and tell Baron Gerald my exact promise to you."

His tone of voice didn't suggest argument. Adela straightened away from Madelyne and said, "You said I could live here until I died if that was my wish."

Gerald took a step toward Adela then, but Duncan's stare stopped him.

"Now then, Gerald? What promise did I give to you?"

Duncan's voice was mild, giving the impression he was bored with the conversation. Madelyne clutched his hand.

Gerald answered Duncan with a shout. "With the king's blessing, you agreed Adela would become my wife."

Edmond couldn't keep silent any longer. "How in God's name are you going to honor both pledges?" he asked Duncan.

"Gerald," Duncan said, ignoring Edmond, "my word to Adela is dependent upon her wish to remain here. I believe it is up to you to change her mind."

"Do you suggest . . ."

"You're a welcome guest in my home for as long as it takes," Duncan said.

Gerald looked startled, then a most arrogant grin transformed his face. He turned to Adela and smiled at her. "Adela, since you won't leave, then I shall stay here with you."

"You'll what?"

Adela was back to screeching, yet Madelyne couldn't see fear in her eyes, only disbelief, and anger.

"As your brother said, for as long as it takes me, Adela, to make you realize I mean to marry you," Gerald said. "Do you hear me?"

Of course she heard him. Madelyne thought the south watchman must have heard Gerald. He shouted his announcement loud enough.

Madelyne took a step toward Adela, fully intending to protect her from Gerald's anger, but Duncan suddenly took hold of her hand again. He jerked her up against his side, and when she opened her mouth to protest, his grip intensified, and Madelyne decided to save her protest for later.

Adela was too enraged to speak. She picked up her skirts and rushed over to Gerald. "You'll be old and gray and withered, too, before I change my mind, Gerald."

Gerald smiled at Adela. "You underestimate my abilities, Adela," he told her.

"You're the most stubborn man alive," Adela blurted out. "You . . . you plebeian." She turned her back on him then and left the hall.

It was all going to be all right. Madelyne felt it in her heart. Adela was furious, but she wasn't terrified.

"What's a plebeian?" Gerald asked Edmond.

Edmond shrugged and looked over at Madelyne. "Another one of your words?" he asked.

"Aye," Madelyne admitted.

"Is it as distasteful as Polyphemus?" Edmond asked.

Madelyne shook her head.

"At least Adela places higher value on you, Gerald, than Madelyne placed on me when we first met," Edmond said with a grin.

Madelyne didn't know what Edmond was talking about. Duncan bade everyone a good night and dragged Madelyne out of the hall before she could question Edmond.

Neither husband nor wife said a word to each other until they reached Duncan's bedroom. When he opened the door for her, Madelyne was waylaid from asking him about Adela or Edmond. The bedroom drew her attention first. Duncan had moved her possessions from the tower to his chambers. The two chairs now flanked his hearth, the cover now lined his huge bed, and her tapestry was hanging above his hearth.

Maude was just leaving the room and announced to the baron that Madelyne's bath was ready for her, as he'd instructed.

As soon as the door closed behind the servant, Madelyne said, "I can't bathe in front of you, Duncan. Please go and swim in your lake while I—"

"I've seen you often enough without your clothes on, Madelyne," Duncan said. He untied her braided belt, tossed it over one of the chairs, then proceeded to remove her bliaut and chainse as well.

"But always in bed, Duncan, with the covers and . . ." Her voice trailed off.

Duncan chuckled. "Get into your bath, love, before the water turns cold."

"You swim in a freezing lake," Madelyne reminded him. Her husband was slowly edging her chemise up over her shoulders. "Why do you do that?" she asked, blushing enough to feel the heat in her cheeks. "Do you like to swim when it's so cold?"

Madelyne thought to turn his attention away from undressing her. But Duncan seemed capable of answering her question and stripping her at the same time.

"I don't particularly enjoy it," Duncan answered. Duncan made short work of her undergarment, eager to get rid of the clothing that shielded her beauty from him. He knelt down in front of her and slowly removed her stockings and shoes, and then caressed a hot trail back to her waist.

His hands made her sigh with pleasure.

"Then why do you do it?" Madelyne stammered.

"To toughen my mind and my body."

He stopped touching her. Madelyne was disappointed. "There are easier ways to toughen your body," Madelyne whispered.

She thought she sounded hoarse. Madelyne tried to cover her breasts by pulling her hair forward, frowning when she realized the length didn't do an adequate job. She twisted the ends of her hair, conveniently blocking his view of her breasts.

Duncan wouldn't let her hide from him. He stood up and gently pushed her hands away. His palms cupped the fullness of her breasts while his thumbs made lazy circles around her pink nipples. Madelyne's toes curled into the rushes. She instinctively leaned forward, seeking more of his touch.

"If I kiss you, Madelyne, I won't let you have your bath. I can see the passion in your eyes. Can you feel how much I want you?" He whispered to her in a voice that caressed as tenderly as his hands.

Madelyne slowly nodded. "I always want you, Duncan." She forced herself to turn around and walk over to the tub.

Duncan tried not to watch his wife. He had vowed to go slowly this night. He was going to make love to her without rushing, no matter how much the urge to throw her on the bed and love her wildly challenged him.

He was going to gentle her with soft words too. His plan was to force her to tell him how much she loved him. Duncan was uneasy. He needed to hear the words now that he'd admitted to himself how much he loved her.

Duncan was determined to make her love him. And he was arrogant enough to believe that once he'd wooed her, she wouldn't be able to deny him anything.

Duncan smiled to himself. He was about to use her obsession with telling the truth to his advantage. He removed his tunic, then knelt down before the hearth to add another log to the fire.

Madelyne washed quickly, worrying that Duncan would turn and watch her doing such an intimate task.

And then she saw the humor in her predicament and laughed.

Duncan walked over to stand beside the tub. With his hands on his hips, he demanded to know what she found so amusing.

He wasn't wearing his shirt now. Madelyne's heart started racing. She suddenly became breathless too. Oh, how he could so easily arouse her. "I sleep beside you every night without a stitch of clothing and I really shouldn't be embarrassed now. That was why I was laughing," she added with a shrug that nearly drowned her.

Madelyne stood and faced her husband, proving to herself and to him she wasn't embarrassed any longer.

Droplets of water glistened against her skin. The ends of her hair were clumped together in wet locks. She had a mischievous look on her face. Duncan leaned down to kiss her once, on the top of her forehead, then again, on the bridge of her nose. He couldn't help himself. Madelyne was looking so magnificent and trying so nobly not to be shy with him.

When she shivered, Duncan reached for the cloth Maude had left on one of the chairs. He wrapped the material around Madelyne, lifted her from the tub, and carried her over to the hearth.

Madelyne stood with her back to the fire. She closed her eyes when Duncan's chest rubbed against her breasts. The heat from the blaze warmed her shoulders and Duncan's tender gaze warmed her heart.

She felt cherished. It was such a wonderful feeling, she didn't offer any protest when Duncan began to dry her. At first he used the cloth to pat her skin, but when he'd finished with her back, he suddenly pulled the edges of the material toward him, dragging her up against his chest. And then his mouth captured hers in a searing kiss. His tongue penetrated the treasure she offered him. Duncan let go of the cloth, cupped her buttocks, pulling her up against his hardness, his incredible heat.

She moaned with pleasure into his mouth, stroked his tongue with her own. Her hands carressed his back, but when her fingertips edged under the waistband of his pants, Duncan abruptly pulled away.

"Take me to bed, Duncan," Madelyne pleaded. She tried to capture his mouth for another kiss. But Duncan deliberately eluded her.

"In time, Madelyne," he promised her in a husky whisper. He kissed the tip of her chin, then slowly made his way down to her breasts. "You're so beautiful," he told her.

He wanted to taste all of her. Duncan stroked one breast with his hand while he worshipped the other with his mouth, sucking until the nipple was a hard nub.

His tongue felt like hot velvet. Madelyne could barely stand up. When Duncan knelt down and began to rain hot, wet kisses down the length of her belly, she took a deep breath and forgot to let it out. His hands rubbed her thighs, moved between them, driving her to the brink of losing her control. He kissed a path along the length of her scar as his hands continued their sweet torment, stroking, caressing, adoring the very heat of her.

254

He held her by her hips, and when his mouth began to kiss the soft mound of curls between her thighs, her knees did buckle.

Duncan wouldn't let her move. His mouth and his tongue tasted the moist heat he'd created in her. She was as sweet as honey and as intoxicating as a fine wine.

Madelyne thought she was going to die from the pleasure. Her fingernails dug into Duncan's shoulder blades. She moaned a soft whimper. The primitive erotic sound nearly drove Duncan mad.

He slowly lowered Madelyne to the floor. His mouth claimed hers just as his fingers penetrated her tight, wet sheath. Madelyne arched against his hand, cried out his name when the splendor erupted inside her. Wave after wave of incredible pleasure washed over her, and through it all, Duncan held her close, whispering words of love.

She felt like liquid gold in his arms, thought to tell him how much he pleased her, but couldn't seem to quit kissing him long enough to tell him anything.

Duncan pulled away and quickly removed the rest of his clothes. He stretched out on his back then and pulled Madelyne on top of him.

He knew he was about to lose control. Duncan pushed her legs apart, trying not to be rough, and when she was straddling him, his hand began to stroke her wild again. Madelyne moaned his name, begged him with her hands and her mouth to end this torment.

He lifted her hips and thrust into her with one powerful surge. She was more than ready for him.

She was so incredibly hot, so wet, so tight.

Duncan let her capture him then. Madelyne arched her back until she surrounded all of him, and then began to move, with slow, instinctive motions that drove him crazed.

He felt as weak as a squire and as powerful as a warlord. Duncan held her by the sides of her hips, demanding her to move more forcefully.

He found release before Madelyne did, but the sound and feel of him gave Madelyne her own blissful surrender.

Madelyne collapsed against his chest. Duncan groaned but Madelyne was too exhausted, too satisfied to apologize.

Long minutes passed before either was capable of speaking. Madelyne's fingers stroked Duncan's chest. She loved the feel of his crisp hair, his smooth, hot skin, his wonderful scent.

Duncan slowly rolled with Madelyne until she was trapped underneath him. He moved to his side then, propped his head up with one elbow, and casually draped one heavy thigh over her legs.

Madelyne thought he looked most arrogant. He stared at her with such a smug expression on his face. A lock of hair had fallen forward to rest against his forehead.

Madelyne was about to reach up and brush the hair back in place when Duncan spoke. "I love you, Madelyne."

Her hand froze in the air between them.

Madelyne's eyes widened and it was then that Duncan realized what he'd said to her.

It wasn't at all how he'd planned it. She was supposed to tell him she loved him. He smiled over his own blunder while he patiently waited for her to recover from his admission and tell him how much she loved him.

Madelyne couldn't believe he'd said the words. His expression turned solemn, telling her he meant what he said.

She started to cry. Duncan didn't know what to make of that. "Are you weeping because I've told you I love you?"

Madelyne shook her head. "No," she whispered.

"Then why are you so upset? I have just pleased you, haven't I?"

He actually sounded a little worried. Madelyne wiped the tears from her cheeks, bumping Duncan's chin. "You have pleased me," she told him. "I'm so frightened, Duncan. You shouldn't love me."

Duncan sighed. He decided he'd have to wait a few more minutes to get a decent explanation out of her. She was shivering too much to speak coherently.

He really held his patience, but once he'd carried Madelyne to their bed and they were under the covers, she snuggled up against him and didn't say a word.

"Why are you afraid?" he asked. "Is it so terrible for me to love you?"

His voice was filled with tenderness and that made Madelyne cry again.

"There can be no hope for us, Duncan. The king will—"

"Give us his blessing, Madelyne. Our king will have to approve this marriage."

He sounded so sure of himself. She drew comfort from his confidence. "Tell me why you think the king will side with you. Make me understand. I don't want to be frightened."

Duncan sighed. "King William and I have known each other since we were young boys. He has many flaws, but he has proven himself to be an able leader. You dislike him because of the stories you've heard from your uncle. And your uncle reflects only the attitudes of his church. The king has lost the support of the clergy because he took treasures from their monasteries. He has never been quick to replace any church official either. The clergy belittles our king because he doesn't bend to their dictates."

"But why do you think—"

"Do not interrupt me when I'm instructing you," Duncan said. He softened his command by giving her a gentle squeeze. "Though I don't mean to boast, in truth I've helped our king unite the Scots and maintain a peaceful coexistence. The king knows my value. I've a well-trained army he can call upon in time of need, Madelyne. He relies on my loyalty. I would never betray him. He knows that too."

"But, Duncan, Louddon is his special friend," Madelyne interjected. "Marta told me so and I've also heard rumors from my uncle's friends."

"Who is this Marta?"

"One of the servants assigned to my uncle," Madelyne answered.

"Ah, then she must surely be as infallible as the pope," Duncan returned. "Is that your way of thinking?"

"Of course not," Madelyne muttered. She tried to turn around to look at Duncan, but he wouldn't let her move. She settled back against his shoulder and said, "My brother even boasts of his power over William."

"Tell me, wife, what you mean by special," Duncan commanded.

Madelyne shook her head vehemently. "I cannot say the words. It would be sinful."

Duncan sighed in exasperation. He knew well enough

what the king's preferences were, had guessed long ago that Louddon was more than a clerk in William's court. He was surprised, however, that his innocent little wife would have such knowledge.

"You will just have to trust me on this, Duncan, when I tell you it's a sinful pact between my brother and our king."

"It will not matter," Duncan returned. "We'll not speak of this any longer, since it seems to embarrass you so. I know what you mean by special, Madelyne. Yet the king will not betray his barons. Honor is on my side in this feud."

"Are we speaking about the same honor that got you tied to a post in Louddon's fortress perchance?" Madelyne asked. "You're so honorable, you trusted Louddon to honor the temporary truce, didn't you?"

"It was a most carefully thought out plan," Duncan answered. His voice grated against Madelyne's ear. "I never trusted your brother."

"He could have killed you before your men gained entrance, Duncan," Madelyne returned. "As for that matter, you could have frozen to death. I, of course, saved you. Honor had little to do with it."

Duncan didn't argue with her. Madelyne was wrong in her assumptions, of course, but he didn't feel he needed to point out her error.

"Louddon will use me to harm you."

That comment didn't make any sense at all. "Madelyne, there isn't a baron in England who hasn't heard about Adela. If the king turns his back on the truth, he'll have made his first foolish mistake. There are other loyal barons who will stand by me. We are all honor bound to our leader, aye, but he must also act with honor toward each of us. Otherwise our pledge of fealty means nothing. Have faith in me, Madelyne. Louddon cannot win this war. Trust me, wife, to know what's to be done."

Madelyne thought about what he said for several minutes and then whispered, "I've always trusted you, ever since that night we slept together in your tent. You promised me you wouldn't touch me when I slept, and I believed you."

Duncan smiled over the memory. "Now do you realize how absurd it was for you to think I could take advantage without you knowing it?"

Madelyne nodded. "I am a very sound sleeper, Duncan," she teased.

"Madelyne, I'm not going to let you ignore our initial topic. I've just vowed my love for you. Have you nothing to say to me in return?" Duncan asked.

"Thank you, husband."

"Thank you?" He shouted the words back at her. His patience deserted him. Madelyne was supposed to tell him how much she loved him and why the hell she didn't know that infuriated him.

Madelyne suddenly found herself flat on her back with her husband looming over her. The muscle in the side of his jaw flexed, a true indication of his anger. He looked ready to do battle.

She wasn't the least intimidated. Madelyne gently stroked his shoulders, then let the palms of her hands slowly slide down his arms. His body was stiff, rigid. She could feel the strength of steel under her fingertips. Madelyne never took her gaze away from his as she caressed him. And though she could feel the power in him, she could also see the vulnerability in his eyes. It was a look she'd never seen before but recognized all the same. Duncan looked good and worried.

When she gifted him with a tender smile, Duncan immediately stopped frowning. He saw the sparkle in her eyes and responded to it. His body relaxed against her.

"You dare to tease me?"

"I'm not teasing you," Madelyne told him. "You've just given me the most wonderful gift, Duncan. I am overwhelmed."

He waited to hear more. "You're the only man to ever tell me you love me." Madelyne whispered. A wrinkle crossed her brow and she added, "How could I not love you in return?"

She looked as if she'd only just realized that fact. Duncan's sigh of exasperation all but parted her hair. "Then I suppose I'm damn fortunate Gilard didn't tell you he loved you first."

"He did," Madelyne announced, smiling over the startle that admission caused. "But I didn't count that pledge of love as being the first, you see, because it wasn't really true. Your brother had a small infatuation."

Madelyne suddenly stretched up and kissed Duncan. She

put her hands around his waist and squeezed him. "Oh, Duncan, I've loved you for the longest time. What a fool I've been not to have realized it sooner. Though I must confess, tonight, when we were sitting by the fire with your family and your guest, I did realize it then. You've given me value, Duncan. In my heart I know I matter to you."

Duncan shook his head. "You've always had value, Madelyne. Always."

Madelyne's eyes filled with tears. "It is a miracle, your love for me. You captured me to fulfill your plan of revenge against my brother. Didn't you?"

"Aye," Duncan admitted.

"That is why you married me," Madelyne said. She was suddenly frowning up at her husband. "Did you love me then?"

"I thought it was lust," Duncan answered. "I wanted to bed you," he added with a grin.

"Revenge and lust," Madelyne returned. "Sorry reasons at best, Duncan."

"You've forgotten compassion," Duncan informed her.

"Compassion? You mean you felt sorry for me, is that the way of it?" Madelyne asked, growing irritated. "Good Lord, you love me out of pity?"

"My love, you've just relisted all the reasons I gave myself."

She took exception to his laughter. "If your love is based upon lust, pity, and revenge then—"

"Madelyne," Duncan interrupted, trying to soothe her, "what did I say to you before we left your brother's fortress. Do you remember?"

"You told me it was an eye for an eye," Madelyne returned.

"You asked me if you belonged to Louddon. Do you remember my answer to that question?"

"Aye, though I didn't understand it," Madelyne said. "You said I belonged to you."

"I spoke the truth," Duncan told her. He kissed her just to rid her of her suspicious look.

"I still don't understand," Madelyne told him when he let her speak again.

"Neither did I," Duncan said. "I thought I'd keep you, but I didn't consider marriage until later. In truth,

Madelyne, it was your act of kindness that sealed your fate."

"It was?" Madelyne's eyes brimmed with tears again. The look on Duncan's face was so loving, so tender.

"It was inevitable from the moment you warmed my feet, though it took a while before I'd acknowledge the truth."

"You called me simpleminded," Madelyne told him, smiling over the memory.

The sparkle was back in her eyes. She wasn't angry any longer. Duncan pretended outrage over her remark just to gain her reaction. "I've never called you simpleminded. It was someone else and I will challenge him immediately."

Madelyne burst into laughter. "It was you, Baron. I've already forgiven you though. Besides, I've called you many unkind names."

"You have? I've never heard any of them," Duncan said. "When did you call me these names?"

"When your back was turned, of course."

She looked so innocent. Duncan's smile widened. "Your obsession for telling the truth will get you into trouble one day." He kissed her again before continuing. "But I'll be by your side to protect you."

"Just as I will always protect you," Madelyne told him. "It is my duty as your wife."

She laughed over his incredulous expression. "You don't worry me," she boasted. "I'll not be afraid of you anymore now that I have your love."

He thought she sounded smug. "I know."

Madelyne laughed because of his forlorn tone of voice.

"I would hear you tell me you love me once again," Duncan demanded.

"Such an arrogant command you give me," Madelyne whispered. "I love you with all my heart, Duncan." She kissed him on his chin. "I would give my life for you, husband." She rubbed his lower lip with the tip of her tongue. "I will love you forever."

Duncan growled his pleasure and proceeded to make slow, sweet love to her.

"Duncan?"

"Yes, love?"

"When did you realize you loved me?"

"Go to sleep, Madelyne. It's nearly dawn."

She didn't want to sleep. Madelyne never wanted this glorious night to end. She deliberately wiggled her backside against his stomach. Her toes curled against his legs. "Please, tell me exactly when it was."

Duncan sighed. He knew she wouldn't quiet until he answered her. "Today."

"Ha!" Madelyne announced.

"Ha what?" Duncan asked.

"Now you are beginning to make sense," Madelyne explained.

"You're not making any sense," Duncan returned.

"You're the one who has been acting so unpredictable all day. To tell you the truth, you had me a bit worried. When today?"

"When what?"

"When exactly did you realize you loved me?" Madelyne wasn't going to give up.

"When I thought my horse was going to kill you."

"Silenus? You thought Silenus would harm me?"

He heard the astonishment in her voice. He smiled against the top of her head. She still didn't have any idea of the terror she'd given him.

"Duncan?"

He liked the way she whispered his name when she wanted something from him. It was tender, coaxing, and terribly sexy. "You've ruined my stallion. I was telling you that downstairs when you fell asleep in my lap."

"I haven't ruined him," Madelyne protested. "I've only shown him kindness. Surely being affectionate can't be harmful."

"Affection might be the death of me if you don't let me rest," he answered with a yawn. "You've turned into an insatiable wench," he added with a mock sigh. "You've taken my strength."

"Thank you."

"You can have Silenus for your own."

"Silenus? Mine?" She sounded as eager as a child.

"The animal is loyal to you now. You've demoted my great beast from stallion to lamb. I'll never live it down."

"Live what down?"

Duncan ignored her question. He made her turn around

to face him. Then he gave her a good long stare. "Now listen to me well, wife. You're not to ride him until I've given you proper instruction. Do you understand me?"

"What makes you think I haven't had proper instruction?" Madelyne asked. She hadn't, of course, yet thought she'd hidden that flaw from him. But her husband was more astute than she'd realized.

"Just promise me," Duncan demanded.

"I promise." She began to nibble on her lower lip, when a sudden thought began to nag her. "You won't change your mind in the morning, will you?"

"Of course not. Silenus is yours now."

"I wasn't speaking of Silenus."

"What then?"

She looked worried. Duncan frowned until she whispered her fear to him. "You won't change your mind about loving me, will you?"

"Never."

He kissed her to give her proof of his pledge, then closed his eyes and rolled onto his back, fully intending to go to sleep. He was exhausted.

"You didn't remember to swim in your lake tonight. That was very unpredictable of you."

When he didn't comment, Madelyne prodded him. "Why didn't you?"

"Because it was too damn cold."

It was a sensible answer, yet strange coming from Duncan. Madelyne smiled to herself. Oh, how she loved him. "Duncan? Did you like making love to me by the fire? You know, when you kissed me . . . there?"

She sounded shy, curious as well. "Aye, Madelyne. You taste as sweet as honey."

The memory of her taste was making him aroused yet again. His lust for his wife astonished him.

Madelyne rolled to her side and looked at Duncan. His eyes were closed but he was smiling and looking very satisfied.

Her hand slowly stroked a path from his chin to his stomach. "Will I like the taste of you?" she asked him in a husky whisper.

Before Duncan could answer her, Madelyne leaned down and kissed his navel, smiling when she saw how his stomach muscles contracted. Her hand slowly moved lower, stroking a line for her mouth and her tongue to follow.

Duncan stopped breathing when her hand captured him. "You're so hard, Duncan, so hot," she told him. "Give me your fire."

Duncan forgot all about sleeping. He let his wife weave her magic spell over him. He thought he was surely the richest man in all the world, and all because his wife loved him.

And then he couldn't think at all.

Chapter Eighteen

"I proclaim that might is right, Justice the interest of the stronger."

PLATO, *THE REPUBLIC*, I

The harsh days of winter boasted unholy temperatures, led by a howling wind that gripped the countryside in its frozen, frostbitten jaws. Winter promised to hold the world in glacial splendor for eternity it seemed, until that gentle maiden, spring, came forth with a promise of her own. She carried the gift of rebirth, wrapped in the warm glow of the sun. Wooed by the promise, the wind lost its shivering edge and magically turned into soft breezes.

The trees were the first to show fulfillment of the promise. Branches were no longer brittle, but malleable with graceful motion when the breeze coaxed them. Fragile buds and green leaves fattened each limb. Forgotten seeds, blown into the earth by autumn's warning blusters, now bloomed into a riot of color and fragrance, heady enough to entice vain, flittering honey bees.

It was a magical time for Madelyne. And there was such joy in loving Duncan. She thought it was a miracle that

Duncan loved her. The first few weeks after his declaration, she had actually been uneasy, worried that he'd grow bored with her. She went to great lengths to please him. Yet the inevitable first fight occurred anyway. A simple misunderstanding that could easily have been resolved, blown out of proportion because of Duncan's black mood and her exhaustion.

In truth, Madelyne couldn't even remember what started the argument. She recalled only that Duncan had yelled at her. She had immediately retreated behind her safe mask of composure, but it didn't take her husband long to goad the perfected tranquility right out of her. She had burst into tears, told him he obviously didn't love her anymore, and then ran to the tower.

Duncan followed her. He still bellowed, but the topic had changed to her habit of jumping to incorrect conclusions. When she realized he was furious that she thought he'd stopped loving her, she hadn't minded the fierce frown or the shouts. After all, he was yelling that he loved her.

She'd learned an important lesson that night. It was quite all right to yell back. The rules had all shifted on her since meeting the Wextons. The freedom she was now allowed unlocked all the doors to her emotions. She didn't have to be restrained. When she felt like laughing, she laughed. And when she felt like yelling, she went right ahead, though she did try to maintain a ladylike, dignified manner.

Madelyne also realized she was taking on some of her husband's characteristics.

There was safety in predictability and she was beginning to dislike change as much as he did. When Gilard and Edmond both left to give their forty days to their overlord, Madelyne let everyone within shouting distance know of her displeasure.

Duncan pointed out the inconsistency of her reasoning, even reminded her she'd once argued in favor of giving his brothers more responsibility. Madelyne, however, didn't want to listen to reason. She had turned into a mother hen and wanted all the Wextons to stay right where she could keep an eye on them.

Duncan understood his wife far better than she understood him. His brothers and Adela had all become members of her family. She had been alone for so many years, the pleasure of having so many caring people surrounding her was too comforting to let go without protest.

She was a peacemaker too. Madelyne constantly interfered if she thought one was being picked on. She was each one's protector and yet was amazed when anyone sought to protect her.

In truth, she still didn't understand her value. Duncan knew she thought it was a miracle that he loved her. He wasn't a man given to proclaiming his feelings, but he quickly realized she needed to hear his vow of love often. There was an underlying sense of fear and insecurity, understandable because of her background, and he accepted that it would take time for her to gain confidence in her abilities.

The days spent with his new wife would have been idyllic if Adela hadn't been so determined to drive them all daft. Duncan tried to maintain a sympathetic manner toward his sister, but her behavior was enough to make him secretly want to throttle her.

He made the mistake of telling Madelyne how he felt about Adela's conduct and his urge to put a gag in her mouth. Madelyne was appalled. She immediately defended Adela. His wife suggested Duncan learn to be more compassionate, and why in God's name she thought he'd want to do that was beyond his comprehension.

Madelyne called him unsympathetic, yet the opposite was really the truth of the matter. Duncan was extremely sympathetic toward Baron Gerald. His friend had the patience of Job and the endurance of forged steel.

Adela was doing everything she could to dissuade her suitor. She mocked, she screamed, she cried. None of it mattered. Gerald wasn't the least deterred from his singular goal of winning her. Duncan thought Gerald was either as stubborn as a donkey or as stupid as a bull. He might have been a little of both.

Duncan couldn't help but admire Gerald. Such determination was praiseworthy, especially when one considered the prize Gerald was after had turned into a screaming shrew.

Duncan really would have preferred ignoring the whole situation. Madelyne, however, wouldn't allow him that privilege. She constantly dragged him into the middle of family squabbles, explaining it was his duty to set things right.

She told him, very matter-of-factly, he could be both lord and brother, but all that nonsense about keeping a cold, distant attitude toward his family was a habit of the past to be shed.

Madelyne also told him he could keep his brothers' respect and gain their friendship too. Duncan didn't argue with her. Lord only knew he hadn't won a single argument since they'd wed.

In this instance, however, she'd been correct. He didn't bother to tell her, of course, knowing she'd immediately point out some other "habit" he should discard.

He began to eat his evening meal with his family because he knew it would please Madelyne, and found he gained pleasure in the experience. He discussed various topics and enjoyed the lively debates that resulted. His brothers were both perceptive men and it wasn't long before Duncan began to value their suggestions.

He slowly removed the barriers he'd erected to separate himself from his family, found the rewards were far greater than the effort.

His father had been wrong. Duncan knew that now. His father might have ruled rigidly in order to protect his position as lord. Perhaps he thought he'd lose their respect if he showed his children affection. Duncan wasn't sure what his father's reasoning had been. He only knew he didn't have to follow the old ways any longer.

He had his wife to thank for the change in his attitude. She taught him that fear and respect didn't have to go hand in hand. Love and respect worked just as well, perhaps even better. It was ironic. Madelyne thanked Duncan for giving her a place in his family, when the reverse was really the truth. She had given him a place in his own home. She had shown him how to be a brother to Gilard, Edmond, and Adela. Aye, she'd dragged him right into the middle of the family circle.

Duncan did continue to maintain the same schedule with his men, but he set aside an hour each afternoon to instruct his wife in the proper way of riding. She was a quick learner and it wasn't long before he let her ride Silenus to the lower hill outside the walls. He followed behind her, of course, as a precaution. And he grumbled, too, over her stubborn habit of taking food to her imaginary wolf.

Madelyne asked him to explain why one side of the hill was barren while the other side was a forest of trees and wilderness.

Duncan explained that all the trees had been chopped down on the side of the hill that faced the fortress. The watchman couldn't see beyond the crest, so it wasn't necessary to chop the trees down on the other side. Anyone who wanted entry to his home would have to climb the lower crest first. The watchmen could see if it was enemy or friend then. And if it was an enemy, archers would have easy targets without the clutter of trees providing shelter and hiding places.

She'd been amazed by his explanation; it seemed everything he did had something to do with protection. He shook his head and pointed out to his wife that protection was his responsibility as lord of Wexton.

Madelyne smiled over his lecture. He had grown accustomed to her smiles too.

Duncan knew Madelyne worried about their future. She still didn't like to be reminded of her brother and everyone tried not to bring his name up in conversation. Since he couldn't seem to convince her that everything would be all right, both of them avoided the topic.

Spring was a time of enlightenment for Duncan. He had to leave Madelyne for nearly a month because of pressing business matters, and when he returned, his wife wept with happiness. They stayed awake all night, loving each other passionately, and would have stayed in bed the following day if the household hadn't intruded.

Madelyne hated it when Duncan had to leave her. He hated it just as much, and though he never would tell Madelyne, his thoughts were consumed with getting back to her side.

Spring left her cloak of sunshine and flowers behind her. Warm summer days at last came to Wexton land.

Travel was easier now. Duncan knew it was only a matter of time before he would be called to answer to his king. He hid his concerns from Madelyne while he quietly gathered his soldiers.

Baron Gerald returned to Wexton land in the last days of

June for yet another attempt to woo Adela. Duncan met his friend in the courtyard. Each had important news to give the other. Duncan had just received a messenger and had accepted a missive with the king's seal upon it. Baron Wexton could read, a fact his wife wasn't aware of, and the letter he'd just read made his manner brisk. He was too preoccupied to greet Gerald properly.

Gerald seemed to be of the same frame of mind and disposition. After giving Duncan a curt bow, he handed the reins of his stallion to Ansel and turned back to Duncan. "I've just returned from the Clares," he announced in a low whisper.

Duncan motioned Anthony over to his side. "There are many things to talk about and I would have Anthony included," he explained to Gerald.

Gerald nodded. "I was telling Duncan I've just returned from the Clare holding," Gerald repeated. "The king's brother, Henry, was there as well. He asked many questions about you, Duncan."

The three men slowly walked toward the hall. "I believe he was trying to come to some sort of understanding as to your position if he were to become our king," Gerald confessed.

Duncan frowned. "What questions?" he asked.

"The conversation was guarded. It was as if they were all privy to some information I lacked. I'm not making much sense, am I?" he asked.

"Is there need to defend William? Do you think Henry might challenge?"

"I do not," Gerald answered, sounding emphatic. "I thought it strange though. You weren't invited, yet all the questions asked me were about you."

"Were they questions about my loyalty?"

"Your loyalty was never an issue," Gerald answered. "But you command an army of the strongest fighting men in England, Duncan. You could easily challenge our king if you'd a mind to."

"Does Henry believe I'd turn against my liege lord?" he asked, clearly astonished by the possibility.

"Nay, everyone knows you to be an honorable man, Duncan. Still, the meeting made little sense to me. There was such an uneasy atmosphere." Gerald shrugged, then said, "Henry admires you, yet I could tell he was worried about something. God only knows what."

The three men climbed the steps to the main hall. Madelyne was standing beside the dining table, arranging a cluster of wildflowers into a fat jar. Three little boys were sitting on the floor next to her, eating tarts.

Madelyne glanced up when she heard the men approach. She smiled when she saw Gerald was once again visiting. With a curtsy she greeted all three. "Dinner will be ready in one hour's time. Gerald, 'tis good to see you again. Isn't it, Anthony? Adela will be pleased."

The men shouted with laughter.

"'Tis the truth I'm giving you," Madelyne insisted. She turned to the children then. "Go and finish your treats outside. Willie, please go and find Lady Adela. Tell her she has a guest. Can you remember that important duty?" she asked him.

The children bounded to their feet and ran out of the room. Willie suddenly rounded on Madelyne and threw his arms around her legs. Duncan watched his wife grab hold of the table with one hand and pat Willie on the top of his head with her other hand.

He was warmed by her gentleness. All the children loved Madelyne. They followed her wherever she went. Each was eager for her smiles and her words of praise. None of the little ones were ever disappointed. Madelyne knew each by name, a considerable accomplishment considering that there were well over fifty of them living inside the manor with their parents.

When Willie finally let go of Madelyne and ran toward the entrance, her gown was covered with the stains from the lad's face.

She looked down at the damage and sighed. Then she called out to the child. "Willie, you've forgotten to bow to your lord again."

The little one tripped to a stop, turned, and affected an awkward bow. Duncan nodded. The child smiled and started in running again.

"Who do the children belong to?" Gerald asked.

"The servants," Duncan answered. "They follow my wife."

A shout of distress interrupted their talk. Duncan and

Gerald sighed in unison. Willie had obviously just informed Adela of Gerald's arrival.

"Don't frown so, Gerald," Madelyne said. "Adela's been dragging around here ever since your last departure. I do believe she missed you. Don't you agree, Anthony?"

Duncan could tell from the look on his vassal's face that he didn't agree. He laughed when Anthony said, "If you think so, then I'll allow for the remote possibility."

Gerald grinned. "Playing the diplomat, are you, Anthony?"

"I don't wish to disappoint my mistress," Anthony announced.

"I pray you are correct, Madelyne," Gerald said. He sat down adjacent to Duncan and Anthony at the table. Madelyne handed him a goblet of wine, and Gerald took a long, thirsty swallow. "Are Gilard and Edmond here?" he asked then.

Duncan shook his head. He took the cup of wine Madelyne offered him but didn't let go of her hand. Madelyne leaned against his side and smiled at him.

"Duncan, Father Laurance is finally going to say mass for us," Madelyne announced. She turned to Gerald to explain her remark. "The priest burned his hands right after he wed Duncan and me. The poor man has taken the longest time healing. It was a terrible accident, though he hasn't explained the exact way it happened."

"If he'd allowed Edmond to see to his burns, it wouldn't have taken him such a long time to heal," Anthony remarked. "Now Edmond's gone, of course," he added with a shrug.

"I've been meaning to have a word with Father Laurance," Duncan muttered.

"You don't like the man?" Gerald asked.

"I do not."

Madelyne was surprised by her husband's comment. "Duncan, he's never around you. How can you like or dislike him? You barely know him."

"Madelyne, the man doesn't do his duty. He hides in his chapel. He's too timid to suit me."

"I didn't know you were such a religious man," Gerald interjected.

"He isn't," Anthony commented.

"Duncan just wants the priest to do what he was sent here to do," Madelyne said. She reached over and refilled Anthony's goblet with more wine.

"He insults me," Duncan announced. "This morning a missive arrived by messenger from his monastery. I've requested his replacement. Madelyne wrote the petition for me," he ended with a boastful tone of voice.

Madelyne nudged Duncan's arm, nearly upsetting his cup of wine. Duncan knew she didn't want him telling anyone she could read or write. He smiled at her, amused she was ashamed of such a remarkable talent.

"What did the missive say?" Madelyne asked.

"I don't know," Duncan answered. "I've had other pressing matters to attend to, wife. It can wait until after dinner."

Another bellow stopped the conversation. Adela was obviously working herself into a fine state. "Madelyne, for God's sake, go and make Adela cease her screams. Gerald, I'm beginning to dread your visits," Duncan told his friend.

Madelyne rushed to soften the rebuke. "My husband didn't mean to sound rude," she told Gerald. "He has many important matters on his mind."

Duncan sighed, long enough to make his wife turn back to look at him. "You needn't excuse my behavior, Madelyne. Now see to Adela."

Madelyne nodded. "I shall also invite Father Laurance to our dinner table. He won't come, but I'll invite him all the same. If he does give us his presence, please be polite to the man until supper is over. Then you may yell at him."

It was phrased as a request, yet given in a voice that reeked of command. Duncan scowled at Madelyne. She smiled at him.

As soon as Madelyne left the hall, Gerald said, "Our king is back in England." His voice was a low whisper.

"I'm ready," Duncan answered.

"I'll go with you when the petition arrives," Gerald said.

Duncan shook his head. "Surely you can't believe our king will ignore your marriage, Duncan. You'll have to give an accounting for your actions. And I've as much right to challenge Louddon as you have. Perhaps more. I'm determined to kill the bastard."

"Half of England would like to kill him," Anthony interjected.

"The petition has already arrived," Duncan commented. His voice was so mild, it took a moment for the other men to react.

"When?" Gerald demanded.

"Just before you arrived," Duncan answered.

"When do we ride?" Anthony asked.

"The king demands I leave for London immediately," Duncan said. "The day after tomorrow will be soon enough. Anthony, you will stay behind this time."

The vassal showed no outward reaction to his lord's decision. He was puzzled, however, for he usually rode by his lord's side.

"Will you take Madelyne with you?" Gerald asked.

"No, she'll be safer here."

"Safe from the king's wrath or from Louddon?"

"Louddon. The king would protect her."

"You have more faith than I do," Gerald admitted.

Duncan looked at Anthony now. "I leave my greatest treasure in your hands, Anthony. This could all be a trap."

"What do you suggest?" Gerald asked.

"That Louddon has access to the king's seal. The instructions in the missive weren't given in the king's voice. That is what I'm suggesting."

"How many men will you take and how many will you leave to guard Madelyne?" Anthony asked. He was already thinking about the protection of the fortress. "This could be a plan to get you away from here so that Louddon can attack. He knows you won't take Madelyne with you, I'm thinking."

Duncan nodded. "I've considered that."

"I've only a hundred men with me now," Gerald interjected. "I'll leave them here, with Anthony, if that is your wish, Duncan."

Gerald and Anthony discussed the issues of numbers while Duncan stood up and walked over to stand in front of the fire. He happened to turn just in time to see Madelyne go around the corner. She was probably going to speak to Father Laurance now, he thought. The little boy, Willie, had hold of her skirt and was running to keep up.

Duncan dismissed his wife from his mind when Anthony and Gerald joined him again. A good ten minutes elapsed in heated debate over the defense of Wexton fortress. Anthony and Gerald both pulled up chairs and Duncan also sat down in the chair Madelyne had declared belonged to him.

All of a sudden, Willie came running into the hall. The child skidded to a halt when he saw Duncan. Willie had a wild, terrified look in his eyes.

Duncan thought the boy looked as though he'd just seen the devil. He never took his gaze off the child. Willie timidly walked over to stand beside Duncan's chair.

"What is it, lad? Do you wish to speak to me?" Duncan asked. He kept his voice soft so the little one wouldn't become any more frightened.

Anthony started to ask Duncan a question, but his baron held up a hand for silence.

Duncan turned in his chair until he was facing the child. He leaned down and motioned Willie closer. Willie started whimpering, but he edged between Duncan's legs, sucking on his thumb while he stared up at his lord.

Duncan's patience was wearing thin. Suddenly Willie pulled his thumb out of his mouth and whispered, "He's hitting her."

Duncan bounded out of the chair, overturning it, and was halfway across the room before Gerald and Anthony knew what was happening.

"What's going on?" Gerald asked Anthony when the vassal started after his lord.

Gerald was the last to catch the fear. "Madelyne." Anthony shouted her name. Gerald jumped to his feet and chased after Anthony. His sword was drawn before he reached the steps.

Duncan reached the chapel first. The door was barred against him but he made quick work of ripping it apart. Rage gave him added strength.

The sound he made alerted Father Laurance. When Duncan rushed into the vestibule, the priest was using Madelyne as his shield. He held her in front of him and pointed a dagger against the side of her neck.

Duncan didn't look at Madelyne. He didn't dare. His rage would explode then. He kept his attention totally focused on the demented man challenging him.

"If you come any closer, I'll slit her throat," the priest screamed. He was slowly backing away, half dragging, half pulling his hostage.

Each step the priest took in retreat, Duncan measured with a step in advance.

The priest backed up against a small square table laden with burning candles. He dared a quick look behind him, obviously judging the distance around the obstacle to the side door, and that was the miscalculation Duncan was waiting for.

Duncan attacked. He wrenched the knife away from Madelyne's face, forcing the blunt side of the blade through the priest's neck in one swift, deadly motion. The priest was propelled backward just as Duncan jerked Madelyne free.

Father Laurance was dead before he hit the ground.

The table crashed against the far wall, overturning the candles. Flames immediately began to lick the dry wood.

Duncan ignored the fire. He gently lifted Madelyne into his arms. She sagged against his chest. "You took the longest time getting here," she whispered against his neck. Her voice was ragged and she was weeping softly.

Duncan took a deep, settling breath. He was trying to rid himself of his anger so that he could be gentle with her. "You are all right?" he finally managed, though his voice was as harsh as his fury.

"I've seen better moments," Madelyne whispered.

Her lighthearted answer calmed him. Then Madelyne looked up at him. When he saw the damage to her face, he was furious again. Her left eye was already swollen. The corner of her mouth was bloody and there were numerous scratches on her neck.

Duncan wanted to kill the priest all over again. Madelyne could feel the tremor that passed through her husband. His eyes mirrored his anger. She reached up, touched his cheek with her fingertips. "It is over, Duncan."

Gerald and Anthony rushed into the church. Gerald saw the fire and immediately ran back outside, shouting an order for aid to the gathering men.

Anthony stood next to his leader. When Duncan turned and started out the doorway, his vassal lifted one of the boards out of the way, the only remnant of the door Duncan hadn't destroyed.

Madelyne could see how worried Anthony was. He was frowning as ferociously as Duncan was. She tried to give him comfort, to let him know she was still fit enough.

"Have you noticed, Anthony, how my husband likes to walk through doors?" she asked him.

Anthony looked startled for a moment, and then a slow grin settled on his face.

Duncan bent down, guarding Madelyne's head as he walked through the opening. She rested her cheek against his shoulder. It wasn't until they'd reached the doors of the castle that she realized she was still crying. A leftover from the fright she'd just had, she thought with a shiver.

By the time they reached Duncan's room, Madelyne's teeth were chattering. Duncan wrapped her in blankets and held her on his lap while he tended to her bruised face.

He was sweating from the heat of the fire he'd started in the hearth for Madelyne. "Duncan? Did you see the crazed look in his eyes?" Madelyne shivered over the memory. "He was going to . . . Duncan? Would you still love me if he'd raped me?"

"Hush now, my love," Duncan soothed her. "I'll love you forever. That was a foolish question."

She was comforted by his gruff answer. Madelyne rested quietly against his chest for several minutes. There was much she needed to tell Duncan and she needed strength for the duty.

Duncan thought she might have fallen asleep, when she suddenly blurted out, "He was sent here to kill me."

Madelyne turned in his arms until she was facing him. The look in his eyes chilled her again. "He was sent?" His voice was soft. Madelyne thought he might be trying to keep his anger hidden. It wasn't working, but she didn't tell him that.

"I went to the church to tell Father Laurance he was invited to dinner. I caught him unawares because he wasn't dressed in his robes. He was dressed just like a peasant, but of course you must have noticed that too. Anyway, his hands weren't covered with bandages either."

"The rest," Duncan instructed when Madelyne stared at him so expectantly.

"There weren't any scars. The priest was supposed to have burned his hands, remember. He couldn't say mass because of his injuries. Only there weren't any scars."

Duncan nodded for her to continue. "I didn't say anything about his hands. I pretended I didn't even notice, but I

277

thought to remember to tell you. Anyway," she continued, "I told him we'd received a letter from his monastery and that after dinner you wanted to speak to him. That was my mistake, though at the time I didn't know why," she added. "The priest went into a rage then. He told me Louddon had had him sent here. His duty was to kill me if the king granted you his favor instead of Louddon. Duncan, how could a man of God have the soul of the devil? Father Laurance knew his game was up, I guess. He told me he was going to get away but not before he killed me."

Madelyne sagged against Duncan's chest again. "Were you frightened, Duncan?" Madelyne asked in a whisper.

"I am never frightened," Duncan snapped. He was so incensed over the priest's treachery, he could barely concentrate.

Madelyne smiled over her husband's statement. "I meant to ask you if you were concerned, not frightened," she amended.

"What?" Duncan asked. He shook his head, forcing his anger aside. Madelyne needed his comfort now. "Concerned? Hell, Madelyne, I was furious."

"I could tell you were," Madelyne answered. "You reminded me of my wolf when you were stalking my captor."

Duncan let her sit up so he could kiss her. He was very gentle, for her lips were too bruised to allow true passion.

Madelyne pushed herself off his lap. She took hold of his hand, tugging until he stood up and followed her across the room. She sat down on the bed and patted the space next to him.

Duncan took off his tunic. He was drenched from the heat in the room. He sat down beside his wife, put his arm around her shoulders, and pulled her against him. He wanted to hold her close and tell her how much he loved her. God's truth, he thought he needed to say the words more than she needed to hear them. "Madelyne, were you frightened?"

"A little," Madelyne replied. She would have shrugged, but the weight of his arm wouldn't allow the gesture. Her head was inclined and she was tracing circles around his thigh, trying to distract him, he supposed.

"Only a little?"

"Well, I knew you'd come for me, so I wasn't terribly frightened. Yet I was beginning to get a bit irritated when you didn't appear at the door right away. The man was tearing my gown . . ."

"He could have killed you," Duncan said. His voice was shaking with anger.

"Nay, you wouldn't have let him kill me," Madelyne told him.

Lord, she had such faith in him. Duncan was humbled by it.

The slow circles Madelyne was making with her fingertips were moving toward the junction of his legs. Duncan grabbed hold of her hand, settled it against his thigh. His wife was probably so distraught, she didn't realize what she was doing, or how it was beginning to affect him.

"Lord, it's gone warm in here," Madelyne whispered. "Why would you want to start a fire in this weather, Duncan?"

"You were shaking," Duncan reminded her.

"I'm better now."

"Then I'll go downstairs and get this letter from the monastery. I am curious to learn what his superiors have to tell us," Duncan announced.

"I don't want you to go downstairs just yet," Madelyne said.

Duncan was immediately solicitous. "You must rest for an hour or so," he told her.

"I don't want to rest," Madelyne answered. "Will you help me out of these clothes?" she asked her husband in such an innocent voice, Duncan was immediately suspicious.

Madelyne stood between her husband's legs and didn't help at all while her husband pulled her clothes off her. "What made you come to the church when you did?" she suddenly thought to ask him.

"Maude's boy saw the bastard hit you. He came to tell me," Duncan answered.

"I didn't know Willie followed me into the church. He must have run back out before the priest barred the door. Willie must have been terrified. He's only five summers. And you must reward him for coming to fetch you."

"Damn, this is all my fault," Duncan stated. "I should have seen to my household as thoroughly as I see to my men's training."

Madelyne put her hands on Duncan's shoulders. "'Tis my duty to see to your home. Though, now that I think about it, none of this would have happened if—"

His sigh stopped her. "I know, none of this would have happened if I'd been there to protect you," he interjected.

His voice was filled with anguish. Madelyne shook her head. "I wasn't going to say that," she told him. "You mustn't jump to conclusions, Duncan. It's a sorry trait. Besides, you have more important matters to attend to."

"You come before everyone and everything else," Duncan stated quite emphatically.

"Well, I was only going to tell you that this wouldn't have happened if I'd known how to protect myself."

"What are you suggesting?" Duncan asked. He really didn't have a clue as to what was going on inside her mind. He smiled then, for he had just realized he rarely *did* know what she was thinking.

"Father Laurance wasn't much bigger than I am," she said. "Ansel is just my height."

"How did my squire get into this conversation?" Duncan asked.

"Ansel is learning about defense," Madelyne announced. "Therefore, you must instruct me in the ways of defending myself also. You see the way of it, don't you?"

He didn't, but decided not to argue with her. "We'll speak of this later," Duncan announced.

Madelyne nodded. "Then you must now see to my needs, Duncan. I order it."

Duncan reacted to the teasing tone in her voice. "And what is this order you dare give your husband?" he asked.

Madelyne explained by slowly pulling the ribbon free that kept her chemise in place. The garment edged off her shoulders. Duncan shook his head, trying to deny her. "You're too bruised to think of—"

"You'll think of a way," Madelyne interrupted. "I know I don't look very pretty now. I do look a fright, don't I?"

"You're bruised, as ugly as one of your Cyclops, and I can barely stand to look at you."

His words made her laugh. She knew he was teasing

because he was trying to pull her down on top of him and take her chemise off at the same time.

"Then you'll have to close your eyes when you make love to me," Madelyne instructed Duncan.

"I'll suffer through it," he promised.

"I can still feel his touch," Madelyne whispered. Her voice had a tremor in it now. "I need you to touch me now. You'll make me forget. I'll feel clean again, Duncan. Do you understand?"

Duncan answered her by kissing her. Madelyne soon forgot everything but kissing him back. Within moments only the two of them mattered.

And she was cleansed in body and heart.

Chapter Nineteen

"Ye shall know the truth, and the truth shall make you free."

NEW TESTAMENT, JOHN, 8:32

Though it was ironic, the attack Madelyne suffered helped to reconcile Gerald and Adela.

Madelyne had insisted on eating dinner with the family and their guest. When she and Duncan walked into the hall, Adela was already seated at the table. Gerald was pacing in front of the fireplace, looking lost in thought.

Duncan sighed, letting Madelyne know he wasn't in any mood for another one of Adela's scenes. Madelyne started to tell him to please be patient and then decided against it. She wasn't in the mood for dissension either.

When Adela saw Madelyne, she let out a loud gasp. She completely forgot Gerald. "What has happened to you? Did Silenus finally unseat you?" she asked.

Madelyne turned to frown at Duncan. "Just before we left our room, I specifically remember you telling me I looked all right," she whispered to him.

"I lied," Duncan answered, grinning.

"I should have looked in Adela's mirror," Madelyne returned. "Adela looks like she's going to be sick. Will I ruin everyone's appetite, do you suppose?"

Duncan shook his head. "An invasion wouldn't wreck my hunger. I've just used up all my strength trying to satisfy your—"

She nudged him to be quiet, for they were close enough for Adela to overhear. "I needed you to love me," she whispered. "I've forgotten all about the priest's foul touch now. It was the only reason I was a little . . . bold."

"Bold?" Duncan chuckled. "Madelyne love, you turned into a—"

She nudged him again, more forcefully, then turned to watch Gerald and Adela.

It was Gerald, in fact, who gave Adela explanation about Madelyne's injuries.

"Oh, Madelyne, you look terrible," Adela confessed in a sympathetic voice.

"It's a sin to lie," Madelyne said to Duncan, glaring at him.

Duncan demanded Father Laurance's name not be mentioned during dinner. Everyone complied. Adela went back to ignoring Gerald too. The baron offered Duncan's sister a compliment when everyone stood to leave the table. Adela made a rude comment back to him.

Duncan's patience was gone. "I would speak to both of you," he demanded. His voice had a hard edge to it.

Adela looked frightened, Gerald looked puzzled, and Madelyne looked like she was going to smile.

Everyone followed Duncan over to the hearth. Duncan sat in his chair, but when Gerald started to take a chair for his own, Duncan said, "Nay, Gerald. Stand next to Adela."

He turned to Adela then and demanded, "Do you trust me to know what's best for you?"

Adela slowly nodded. Her eyes were as large as trenchers, Madelyne thought.

"Then let Gerald kiss you. Now."

"What?" Adela sounded appalled.

Duncan frowned over her reaction. "When my wife was attacked by Laurance, she wanted me to wipe the memory away. Adela, you've never been kissed or touched by a man who loves you. I suggest you let Gerald kiss you now and then decide if you are repelled or enlightened."

Madelyne thought it was a wonderful plan.

Adela was turning red with embarrassment. "In front of everyone?" she asked. Her voice sounded like a squeak.

Gerald smiled. He took hold of Adela's hand. "I would kiss you in front of the world if you'd allow it," he told her.

Duncan thought Gerald was going a little overboard, telling Adela she could allow or disallow, yet he kept his thoughts to himself.

Besides, his command was finally being carried out. Before Adela could back away, Gerald leaned down and placed a chaste kiss on her lips.

Duncan's sister looked up at Gerald in confusion. And then he kissed her again. His hands never touched her but his mouth held her captive all the same.

Madelyne felt foolish watching the pair. She walked over and sat on the arm of Duncan's chair and tried to stare at the ceiling instead of the two people kissing each other so thoroughly.

When Gerald took a step back, Madelyne looked at Adela. Duncan's sister looked flushed, embarrassed, and truly astonished.

"He doesn't kiss like Mor—" The color immediately drained from her face over her near blunder, and she looked at Madelyne for help.

"He'll have to know, Adela."

Gerald and Duncan shared a frown. Neither knew what Madelyne was talking about. "I cannot tell him," Adela whispered. "Would you do this one terrible duty for me? Please, Madelyne. I beg of you."

"If you'll let me tell Duncan as well," Madelyne said.

Adela looked at her brother. He could see the worry in her gaze.

Adela finally nodded. She turned back to Gerald then and said, "You'll not ever want to kiss me again when you know the full truth of what happened to me. I'm sorry, Gerald. I should have . . ."

Adela started to cry. Gerald reached out to take her into his arms but she shook her head. "I think I do love you,

Gerald. And I am so sorry." With those parting words, Adela rushed out of the room.

Madelyne had little liking for the promise she'd made. She knew she was about to cause her husband and Gerald pain. Both men loved Adela.

"Gerald, please sit down and listen to me," Madelyne asked. Her voice sounded strained. "Duncan, promise you won't be angry with me for keeping this from you. Adela made me promise to share her secret."

"I'll not be angry," Duncan announced.

Madelyne nodded. She couldn't bear to look at Gerald while she told the full truth about Adela, so she stared at the floor through the recitation. She stressed the fact that Adela was so disappointed that Gerald hadn't joined her in court and for that reason was easy prey for Louddon's deceptions. "She was really trying to punish you, I think," Madelyne told Gerald. "Though I doubt she realizes that."

Madelyne dared a look over at Gerald, caught his nod, and then looked at Duncan. She told the rest then, leaving nothing out, and when she told of Morcar's treachery, she fully expected one or both men to shout in anger.

Neither baron said a word.

When the telling was finished, Gerald got up and slowly walked out of the hall.

"What will he do?" Madelyne asked Duncan. She realized she was crying, brushed the tears away from her face, wincing when she knocked her bruises.

"I don't know," Duncan answered. His voice was soft, angry too.

"Are you upset with me for not telling you sooner?"

Duncan shook his head. A sudden thought occurred to him then. "Morcar is the man you wanted to kill, isn't he?"

Madelyne frowned. "You told me you were going to kill a man. Remember? It was Morcar you meant, wasn't it?"

She nodded. "I couldn't let him get away with his treachery, yet I was honor bound to keep Adela's secret," she whispered. "Duncan, I didn't know what to do. It is God's duty to see to sinners. I know that well enough. And I shouldn't want to kill him. I do, though, God help me, I do."

Duncan pulled her into his lap. He held her tenderly. He understood his gentle wife's torment.

Each lapsed into silence for several minutes. Madelyne was worrying about Gerald. Would he leave now or would he continue to pursue Adela?

Duncan used the time to gain control of his emotions. He didn't blame Adela for her infatuation with Louddon. His sister was such an innocent, she couldn't be faulted. But Louddon had deliberately preyed on that innocence.

"I'll take care of Morcar," Duncan said to Madelyne.

"You will not."

It was Gerald who bellowed the denial. Both Madelyne and Duncan watched Gerald rush over to stand in front of them. His anger was most evident. He was shaking with it. "I'll kill him, and you as well, Duncan, if you dare deny me this right."

Madelyne gasped. She looked up at Duncan. His expression didn't tell her if he was insulted or angry.

Duncan stared at Gerald a long moment. Then he slowly nodded. "Aye, Gerald, it is your right. I'll stand behind you when you challenge him."

"As I'll stand behind you when you challenge Louddon," Gerald answered.

The fight went out of Gerald then. He sat down in the chair facing Duncan.

"Madelyne? Would you please tell Adela I'd like to speak to her?"

Madelyne nodded. She hurried to comply but had worried herself sick before she reached Adela's bedroom. She still didn't know what Gerald was going to do.

Adela had already made up her mind Gerald was going to leave her. "It's all for the best," she told Madelyne between sobs. "Kissing is one thing, but that is all I could ever allow. I could never let him come to my bed."

"You don't know if you could or couldn't," Madelyne returned. "Adela, it won't be easy but Gerald is a patient man."

"It doesn't matter," Adela said. "He's going to leave me."

Adela was wrong. Gerald was waiting for her at the bottom of the steps. Without saying a word, he took hold of her arm and led her down the next staircase.

Duncan walked over to Madelyne and lifted her up into his arms. "You look exhausted, wife. 'Tis time for bed."

"I'd better wait until Adela comes back. She might need

me," Madelyne protested when Duncan started up the steps.

"I need you now, Madelyne. Gerald will take care of Adela."

She nodded. "Madelyne, I have to leave you tomorrow. It will be for a short time only," he added before she could interrupt.

"Where are you going?" she asked. "Do you have important matters to attend to?" she asked then, trying her best to sound interested and not disappointed. She couldn't expect him to spend every minute with her. Duncan was an important man, after all.

"I do have a matter that calls for attention," Duncan answered, deliberately keeping his explanation to a minimum. Madelyne had been through enough torment today. Duncan didn't want to add another worry, and he knew if he told her about the king's petition tonight, she wouldn't get any rest.

Maude was just coming down the steps when Duncan turned the corner. She said she'd see to the baroness's bath right away, but Duncan shook his head. He told Maude he'd take care of the task.

Maude made a curtsy. "Maude, your son has done a courageous thing today."

The woman beamed. She'd already heard all about her son's brave act. The lad had made his parents proud. Why, he saved the baroness's life.

"I'll have to think of a suitable reward for such bravery," Duncan said.

Maude looked too overwhelmed to speak. She made another curtsy, then stammered out her gratitude. "I do thank you, milord. My Willie took a fancy to the baroness. He's a bit of a nuisance, running after her all the time, but she don't seem to mind it and always has a kind word for my boy."

"He's an intelligent lad," Duncan said in praise.

His flattery, an unusual event to be sure, added to the fact that he was actually speaking to her, made Maude feel giddy. She thanked her lord again, picked up her skirts, and went flying down the steps. Gerty would be wanting to hear this tale to be sure. Maude was bent on being the first to tell her.

Madelyne brushed her hand against her husband's cheek. "You're a good man, Duncan," she whispered to him. "'Tis yet another reason I love you so much."

Duncan shrugged, forcing Madelyne to grab hold of his shoulders to keep her balance. "I do only my duty," he commented. Madelyne smiled. She thought her husband was as awkward with praise as Maude appeared to be.

"I've been denied my bath," she said, teasing him. "Perhaps I'll swim in your lake. What say you to that?" she added.

"I say it's a good plan, wife. I will swim with you."

"I was only teasing you," Madelyne rushed out. "I don't want to swim in your lake."

She shivered. "When I was little, I jumped into the pond. It wasn't deep, and I did know how to swim, you understand. But my toes squished in the mud and my gown weighed ten stone, at least, before I could drag myself out. Why, I needed another bath then and there. Mud was even caked in my hair."

Duncan laughed. "First of all, my lake has a rock bottom in most places," he said. "And you aren't supposed to swim with your clothes on, Madelyne. I'm surprised you didn't drown."

She didn't look too convinced of the merits of his lake. "The water is clear. You can almost see to the bottom," Duncan told her.

They reached their bedroom. Madelyne was undressed and waiting for Duncan in their bed before her husband had removed his tunic.

"You don't want to swim with me?" he asked her with a grin.

"No," Madelyne said. "There are soldiers outside. Good Lord, Gerald and Adela are outside too. It wouldn't be decent to parade in front of them without my clothes on. Whatever could you be thinking of, Duncan, to suggest such—"

"Madelyne, no one goes to the lake at night. Besides, the moon isn't bright enough to—"

She interrupted him with a startled gasp. "Duncan, what are you doing?"

It was obvious, even to her. Duncan was standing next to

the bed, holding her cloak up. "Wrap yourself in this. I'll carry you to the lake," he suggested.

Madelyne nibbled on her lip in indecision. She really did want to swim. It was hot and sticky tonight. Yet the thought of being seen by anyone was a worry to be considered.

Duncan patiently waited for Madelyne to make her choice. He thought she looked terribly appealing right now. Only a thin blanket covered her, and the tips of her breasts were nicely revealed.

"You said I looked exhausted," Madelyne stalled. "Perhaps . . ."

"I lied."

"'Tis a sin to lie to me," Madelyne commented. She pulled the blanket up, holding it like a shield against him. "My soap is in your chest," she told him.

Madelyne thought to send him on an errand so she could wrap the cloak around her in privacy. She still wasn't used to parading around him naked.

Duncan grinned. He walked over to the chest to get the soap. Madelyne tried to grab her cloak before he turned, but she wasn't quick enough.

Her husband returned to the side of the bed. Her cloak was draped over his arm. The packet of soap was in one hand and a small circular mirror in the other.

He handed the mirror to Madelyne. "You've a black eye to match the one you gave Edmond," he remarked.

"I never gave Edmond a black eye," Madelyne protested. "You're teasing me."

She turned the mirror over and looked at her face.

Madelyne screamed.

Duncan laughed.

"I do look like a Cyclops," she shouted. She dropped the mirror and began to pull her hair forward over the injured side of her face. "How can you stand to kiss me?" she asked. "I've a black circle around my eye and . . ."

She sounded like she was wailing. Duncan's smile faded when he leaned forward. With the palm of his hand he forced her chin up to make her look at him. His expression was most serious now. "Because I love you, Madelyne. You're everything I've ever wanted, and much, much more. Do you think a bruise or two could sway my heart? Do you believe my love could be so shallow?"

Madelyne shook her head. She slowly edged the blanket away and then stood up next to her husband.

She wasn't shy with him anymore. Duncan loved her. That was all that mattered.

"I would like to go to your lake now, Duncan. But we better hurry, before I begin to beg you to make love to me."

Duncan cupped her chin with his hands and kissed her. "Oh, I am going to love you, Madelyne."

She was warmed by the promise and the dark look in his eyes. She heard herself sigh, felt a warm knot in her stomach begin to spread inside of her.

Duncan wrapped the cloak around her, lifted her into his arms, and carried her out of their room.

They didn't encounter anyone on their route to the lake. Duncan was right, too, for the moon wasn't bright tonight.

Duncan took her to the far side of the lake. Madelyne tested the water with her toes, declared it was too cold.

He told her to suffer through it. She stood next to Duncan, her cloak held around her in a firm grip while she watched him casually strip out of his clothes.

Duncan made a clean dive into the water. Madelyne sat down on the bank, then edged into the water. She would have taken her cloak with her had Duncan allowed it. Her husband surfaced next to her, jerked the cloak out of her hands, and tossed it onto the grass.

The water took a few minutes to get used to. It was such an erotic feeling to swim without a stitch of clothing. Madelyne felt quite wanton, told Duncan so, admitting shyly that it was a pleasant sensation.

Madelyne hurried through her bath. She washed her hair and rinsed it by dunking herself under the water. When she surfaced a third time, Duncan was standing in front of her.

He was only going to talk to her, but Madelyne was smiling up at him with such a bewitching look in her eyes. The water lapped against her breasts. The nipples were hard, beckoning him. His hands covered them.

She leaned into him, tilted her head back for his kiss. It was a temptation he didn't want to resist. Duncan took her mouth hungrily. His tongue thrust into her mouth. Wet. Wild. So predictably undisciplined.

Duncan would have allowed only the one kiss, then

carried her back to their chambers to make love to her, but Madelyne's stomach rubbed against him then and her hands boldly moved into the water to capture his arousal.

Duncan wrapped his arms around her, roughly pulling her up against him. The kiss deepened, became consuming.

She was as rough as he was. Her hands moved to his shoulders, stroking him wild. Duncan lifted her higher, until her breasts were rubbing against his chest. Her legs moved restlessly against him. Her sweet whimper of longing drove him wild.

He whispered instructions to her, his voice gruff with need. When Madelyne wrapped her legs around his thighs, he entered her slowly, cautiously, thoroughly.

She pushed against him, demanded with her fingernails. "Duncan," she begged.

He kissed her temple. "I'm trying to be gentle with you, Madelyne," he whispered, sounding hoarse.

"Later, Duncan," Madelyne moaned. "Be gentle later."

Duncan gave in to his need. He was forceful, giving her as much pleasure as she gave him. When he felt Madelyne arch against him in fulfillment, he covered her mouth to catch her moans. His seed filled her and he clung to her as the tremor of bliss exploded.

Madelyne sagged against him, weak with satisfaction. Her breath warmed his neck. Duncan smiled with arrogant pleasure. "You are a wild woman, Madelyne."

She laughed, delighted with his compliment, until she remembered where they were. "Good Lord, Duncan. Do you think anyone saw us?"

She sounded so appalled. She buried her face into the crook of his neck. Duncan chuckled. "Love, no one saw us," he whispered.

"You're certain?"

"Of course, the light isn't sufficient."

"Thank God for that," Madelyne answered.

She was thoroughly relieved, until Duncan spoke again. "You did make enough noise to wake the dead though. You're a moaner, my love. The hotter you get, the louder your moans."

"Oh, God." Madelyne tried to sink under the water. Duncan wouldn't let her. He laughed, a husky, deep sensual sound, and then continued to tease. "I'm not complaining, sweetheart. As long as your fire is for me, I'll let you moan all you want."

Just when she was about to tell him how sinfully arrogant he sounded, Duncan deliberately fell backward. She had time only to hold her breath.

He kissed her again, under the water. She pinched him when she needed new air.

Madelyne didn't know how to play in the water. When Duncan splashed her, she took immediate offense. He had to tell her to splash him back. She thought it a silly game to try to drown each other, but she was laughing by the time she finished her comment, and trying to overturn him by nudging him with her foot.

She was the one who lost her footing. When Duncan pulled her up, she was sputtering, coughing, and trying to lecture him at the same time.

They stayed in the lake for almost an hour. Duncan taught her how to swim properly, though he'd begun his instructions by insulting her. "You look like you're about to drown when you swim."

She wasn't too offended, even kissed him to let him know her feelings weren't injured.

When Duncan finally carried her back to their bedroom, Madelyne was exhausted.

Duncan, however, was in the mood to talk. He was in bed, his hands folded behind his head, watching his wife brush her hair. Both were naked, and neither was shy about it.

"Madelyne, I've been invited to speak to my king," Duncan commented. He kept his voice controlled, trying to give Madelyne the impression he was bored with the request. "That is where I'm going tomorrow."

"Invited?" The brush was discarded when Madelyne turned to frown at Duncan.

"A summons then," Duncan admitted. "I would have told you sooner, but I didn't want you to worry."

"I'm in the middle of this, aren't I? Duncan, I won't be ignored or pushed aside. I've a right to know what is happening."

"I've neither ignored you nor pushed you aside," Duncan answered. "I was only trying to protect you."

"Will it be dangerous?" He wasn't given time to answer her. "Of course it will be dangerous. When do we leave?"

"We don't leave. You're staying here. It will be safer for you."

She looked ready to argue. Duncan shook his head and said, "If I have to worry about you, my concentration will be compromised. My mind is made up, Madelyne. You're staying here."

"And will you come back to me?"

He was surprised by her question. "Of course."

"When?"

"I don't know how long this will take, Madelyne."

"Weeks, months, years?"

He saw the fear in her eyes, remembered the time she'd been ignored by her family. Duncan pulled Madelyne on top of him. He kissed her. "I'll always come back to you, Madelyne. You're my wife, for God's sake."

"Your wife," Madelyne whispered. "Whenever I become frightened, or begin to fret about the future, I remember that I'm bound to you." Duncan smiled. She didn't look frightened any longer. "If you get yourself killed, I'll find your grave and spit on it," she threatened.

"Then I'll take every care."

"You promise me?"

"I promise you."

Madelyne tenderly cupped the sides of her husband's face. "You take my heart with you, my loving captor."

"Nay, Madelyne. I am your captive in body and soul."

And then he fulfilled his vow by making love to her again.

Duncan was dressed before the full light of dawn reached the sky. He called for Anthony and then waited for him in the hall.

When his vassal entered the room, Duncan was just breaking the seal on the neglected missive from the monastery.

Anthony sat down across from Duncan at the table, waiting for him to finish reading. Gerty intruded with a tray filled with bread and cheese.

The vassal had eaten a fair portion of his meal before Duncan finished the letter. The news obviously didn't please his lord. Duncan threw the parchment across the table and then slammed his fist down on the tabletop.

"The news displeases you?" Anthony asked.

"It is as I suspected. There is no Father Laurance."

"But the man you killed . . ."

"Sent from Louddon," Duncan said. "I already knew that much, yet I still believed he was a priest."

"Well, at least you didn't kill a man of the cloth then." Anthony made the observation with a shrug. "He wasn't able to report back to Louddon either, Duncan. He hasn't left this fortress since his arrival. I'd have known of it."

"If I'd been paying attention, I'd have noticed his odd behavior sooner. My lack of attention nearly cost my wife her life."

"She doesn't blame you," Anthony commented. "It didn't get as ugly as it could have either, Duncan. He could have been hearing all our confessions." Anthony shuddered over that obscene thought.

"I didn't get married either," Duncan said, slamming his fist on the table again.

The parchment bounced and settled against the bottom of the jar of wildflowers.

"Good God, I hadn't thought of that."

"Madelyne hasn't either," Duncan answered. "She will though. She'll have a fit. If there was time, I'd find a priest and wed her before I leave."

"It would take weeks . . ."

Duncan nodded. "Have you told Madelyne where you're going?" Anthony asked.

"Aye, but I'm not going to tell her about our impostor. When I return, I'll bring a priest with me. I'll tell her we aren't married a minute or two before I marry her again. Hell, what a mess."

Anthony smiled. His lord was right. Madelyne would have a fit.

Duncan forced himself to put aside the matter of Laurance's deception. He went over his plans with his vassal, trying to cover every eventuality.

"You've been trained by the best. I have complete faith in your ability," Duncan said when he'd finished his instructions.

It was an attempt to lighten his mood, a self-serving remark as well, since it was Duncan who trained Anthony. The vassal grinned.

"You're leaving enough soldiers to conquer England," Anthony remarked.

"Have you seen Gerald yet?"

Anthony shook his head. "The men are gathering in front of the stables," he remarked. "He could be there, waiting."

Duncan stood and walked with his vassal to the stables. The baron addressed his soldiers, cautioning them all that they could well be riding into a trap. He turned to the men who would remain behind and spoke to them. "Louddon could well be waiting for me to leave to attack the fortress."

When he finished addressing his men, Duncan returned to the hall. Madelyne was just coming down the steps. She smiled at her husband. Duncan took her into his arms and kissed her.

"Remember your promise to take every care," Madelyne whispered when he released her.

"I promise," Duncan answered. He put his arm around her shoulders and walked outside. They had to pass the church on their way to the stables. Duncan paused to stare at the damage from the fire. "I'll have to rebuild the vestibule," he said.

The mention of the church reminded Madelyne of the letter. "Duncan, do you have time to show me the letter from Father Laurance's monastery? I am most curious, I confess."

"I've already read it."

"You can read! I'd suspected as much, but you've never boasted of your skill. Why, just when I think I know you quite well, you say or do something to surprise me."

"So I'm not as predictable as you imagined?" he asked, smiling.

She nodded. "In certain matters you're always predictable. Oh, I wish you weren't leaving. I wanted you to teach me defense. If I could protect myself as well as Ansel does, you'd probably let me come with you."

"I would not," Duncan answered. "I promise, though, to begin your instructions as soon as I return." He made the comment to placate Madelyne. There *were* a few tricks every woman should know about, he decided. Perhaps it wasn't such a ridiculous request after all. Madelyne wasn't very strong but her determination impressed him.

Duncan noticed that Baron Gerald still hadn't arrived. Since he had a few more minutes with his wife, he turned to her and said, "I'll give you your first lesson now. Since you use your right hand, you must carry your dagger on the left side of your body." He removed her dagger and placed it in a loop of her belt on the tilt of her left hip.

"Why?"

"Because it is much easier to pull the weapon free. Sometimes, wife, every second counts."

"You carry your sword on the right side of your body, Duncan. I know you favor holding your sword with your left hand. The steps! Does this lesson have anything to do with the steps being built on the left side of the wall instead of the right?"

He nodded. "My father also favored his left over his right. When an enemy invades, he comes from below, not above. My father had added advantage. He could use his right hand to balance himself against the wall, and fight with his left hand."

"Your father was cunning," Madelyne announced. "Most men use their right hands, don't they? What a wonderful idea to go against tradition and build his home to his specifications."

"In truth, my father borrowed the idea from one of his uncles," Duncan said.

Duncan thought he'd successfully turned her attention away from the letter. He was mistaken, however, for Madelyne came right back to that topic. "What did the letter say, Duncan?"

"It was nothing significant," Duncan returned. "Laurance left the monastery when he was assigned to Louddon's fortress."

It was difficult lying to his wife. Yet his intent was good-hearted. He was trying to keep her from worrying while he was away.

"He was probably a good man until my brother got hold of him," Madelyne commented. "I'll see that his body is sent back to the monastery immediately, Duncan. They'll want to give him a proper burial."

"No." He realized he'd shouted. "I mean to say that arrangements have already been made."

Madelyne was puzzled by Duncan's abrupt manner. Baron Gerald walked over to greet them, turning her attention.

"Adela and I will be married when this task is finished," Gerald announced. "She has finally agreed."

Madelyne smiled. Duncan slapped Gerald on his shoulder. "Where is Adela?" he asked.

"In her room, crying. I've already said my farewell," Gerald added with a grin.

"You're certain you want to wed her, Gerald? My sister spends most of her days weeping."

"Duncan!" Madelyne protested.

Gerald laughed. "I'm hoping she'll use up all her tears before we're married."

Duncan suddenly turned and grabbed Madelyne. He kissed her before she knew what he was going to do. "I'll be home before you notice I've left," he told her.

Madelyne struggled to smile. She wasn't about to cry. It wouldn't be dignified, what with the soldiers filing past.

She stood in the center of the courtyard and watched her husband leave.

Anthony walked over to stand beside Madelyne. "He'll come back to us," Madelyne said. "He gave me his word, Anthony."

"He's a man of honor, Madelyne. He won't break his promise."

"I shall have to keep busy," she told the vassal. "Duncan has promised to teach me defense methods."

"Defense methods?" Anthony repeated, showing his confusion.

"Aye. He would like me to know how to protect myself," Madelyne explained. She deliberately made it sound as though it had all been her husband's idea. Madelyne knew it would be easier to gain Anthony's cooperation if he believed Duncan wished it. She didn't think she was being deceitful. "Perhaps you could give me a lesson or two. What do you think, Anthony? Could you spare me a little time each day to show me the way of defense?"

The way of defense? Anthony was at first too incredulous

to speak. He stared at Madelyne and realized she was quite serious.

Madelyne didn't think Anthony looked too thrilled by her request. "I believe I'll go and speak to Ned. He could fashion a nice bow for me, arrows, too, of course. If I apply my mind to the task, I believe I could become very accurate in no time at all."

Anthony felt like making the sign of the cross. He couldn't, of course, because his mistress was looking up at him with such a hopeful expression.

He was too weak-hearted to deny her. "I shall speak to Ned," he promised.

Madelyne thanked him profusely. The vassal bowed and walked away.

Anthony had a new problem to consider. His primary duty was to keep Duncan's wife safe. Now another duty had been thrust upon him. He was going to have to protect his men from Madelyne.

His sense of humor saved him from despair, however. By the time he reached the smith's hut, he was laughing. Heaven help them all. By week's end they'd probably all be wearing arrows in their backsides.

Chapter Twenty

Duncan was the first to catch the scent of danger. He gave the signal to stop. The soldiers lined up behind him. Not a word was spoken, and once the horses had settled down, an eerie silence descended upon the woods.

Baron Gerald was on Duncan's right. He waited, as did his men, deferring to Duncan's judgment. Duncan's reputation was legendary. Gerald had fought by his side in the past. He recognized Duncan's superior ability, and though they were nearly the same age, Gerald considered himself the student and Duncan his trainer.

When Duncan raised his hand, several soldiers fanned out to scan the area.

"It's quiet, too quiet," Duncan said to Gerald.

Gerald nodded. "'Tis not the place I would have chosen for a trap, Duncan," he admitted.

"Exactly."

"How do you know? I've seen nothing," Gerald said.

"I feel it," Duncan answered. "They're there, below us, waiting."

A faint whistle sounded from the forest to the left. Duncan immediately turned in his saddle. He motioned to his soldiers to split into sections.

The soldier who'd given the sound rode back to the gathering. "How many?" Duncan asked.

"I couldn't tell, but I spotted several shields."

"Then add that many a hundred times," Gerald said.

"By the bent crossing," the soldier announced. "They hide there, milord."

Duncan nodded. He reached for his sword but Gerald stayed his hand. "Remember, Duncan, if Morcar be one of them . . ."

"He is yours," Duncan acknowledged. His voice was harsh, controlled.

"As Louddon is yours," Gerald said.

Duncan shook his head. "He won't be there. The bastard hides behind his men or in William's court. Now I have my answer, Gerald. It was a false letter sent by Louddon and not the king. 'Tis the last game of deceit I play with Louddon."

Duncan waited until a third of his contingent had spread in a semi-circle on the western slope. The second third followed the same order, though they fanned in a half circle on the eastern bridge. The last third of their troops waited behind the barons. They were chosen to mount the direct assault.

Gerald was pleased with Duncan's plan. "We've trapped them inside their own trap," he said proudly.

"And now we close our circle, Gerald. Give the call."

It was an honor he bestowed on his friend. Gerald lifted himself in his saddle, raised his sword into the air, and shouted the battle cry.

The sound echoed throughout the valley. The soldiers who had circled the enemy now began their downward descent.

The net closed. The battle belonged to the fittest; might ruled this day, conquered.

Those cunning men who hid like women behind trees and rocks, waiting to pounce upon their unknowing victims, soon found themselves trapped.

Duncan's men showed their superiority now. They took command from the outset, fought with valor, and quickly claimed victory.

They took no prisoners.

It wasn't until the battle was nearly finished that Gerald spotted Morcar. Their gazes locked in challenge across the valley. Morcar sneered and then turned to mount his steed. He thought he had adequate time to make his escape.

Gerald's mind snapped. He began to fight like a man possessed, desperate to get to Morcar before he got away. Duncan protected Gerald's back more than once, shouted to his friend to regain control.

Duncan was furious. He was a man who demanded discipline from himself and his soldiers. Yet his equal, Baron Gerald, had cast off all the rules of training. His friend was out of control.

Gerald was beyond hearing any warnings. His eyes were glazed over with fury. Rage, so raw and wild, ruled his mind and body now.

Morcar sat on his mount and watched Gerald struggle to get to him. He wasted precious seconds, but he felt safe enough. Baron Gerald was on foot.

His smirk turned into a bellow of laughter when Gerald stumbled and fell to his knees. Morcar seized the opportunity. He charged his horse down the slope. Leaning to the side of his saddle, he waved his curved sword at Gerald.

Gerald feigned weakness. His head was bowed and he knelt on one knee, waiting for his enemy to come close enough.

Morcar lashed out with his sword just as Gerald jumped to the side.

Gerald used the flat of his own weapon to knock Morcar to the ground.

Morcar fell on his side, rolled onto his back, thinking to regain his weapon and leap to his feet.

He was never given the chance. Gerald's foot trapped his hand. When Morcar looked up, he saw the baron standing over him with the tip of his sword pointed at his neck. When the blade pricked his skin, Morcar squeezed his eyes shut, whimpering in terror.

"Will there be women in hell for you to rape, Morcar?" Gerald asked.

Morcar's eyes flew open. And in those last seconds before he died, he knew Gerald had learned the truth from Adela.

Duncan hadn't witnessed the fight. When the battle was finished, he walked among his own men, gaining numbers of those who had been killed. He saw to his injured as well.

Several hours later, when the sun was fading from the sky, he went looking for Gerald. He found his friend sitting on a boulder. Duncan spoke to Gerald, but didn't receive an answer.

Duncan shook his head. "What the hell's the matter with you?" he demanded. "Where's your sword, Gerald?" he asked, almost as an afterthought.

Gerald finally looked up at Duncan. His eyes were red and swollen. Though Duncan wouldn't ever comment on it, he could tell his friend had been weeping. "Where it belongs," Gerald said. His voice was devoid of emotion and as flat as the expression on his face.

Duncan didn't understand what Gerald was talking about until he found Morcar's body. Gerald's sword was embedded in Morcar's groin.

They made camp up on the ridge above the battleground. Gerald and Duncan ate a meager offering and didn't speak to each other until darkness was upon them.

Gerald used the time to rid himself of his rage.

Duncan used the time to fuel his anger.

When Gerald began to speak, he poured out his anguish. "I've lived a pretense all this time with Adela," Gerald said. "I thought I'd come to terms with all that happened to her. When I vowed to kill Morcar, it was a logical decision. Until I saw him, Duncan. Something broke inside me. The bastard laughed."

"Why do you give me these excuses?" Duncan asked. His voice was soft.

Gerald shook his head. He smiled faintly. "Because I've the feeling you're wanting to run your sword through me," he said.

"You fought like a fool, Gerald. If I hadn't been there, you never would have made it up that hill. You'd be dead now. Your lust for revenge almost destroyed you."

Duncan paused a moment to give Gerald time to think

about what he'd just said. His anger over his friend's undisciplined conduct was blown out of proportion. Duncan realized that now. He was infuriated with Gerald because he saw the flaw in his friend's character and now admitted he carried the same mark.

"I have acted the fool. I'll give you no more excuses," Gerald said.

Duncan knew the admission was difficult for his friend to make. "I don't demand excuses. Learn from this, Gerald. I'm no better than you are. I, too, have been ruled by my thirst for revenge. Madelyne was injured in battle because I took her captive. She could have been killed. We have both taken a turn acting the part of a fool."

"Aye, we have," Gerald returned. "Though I'm not about to acknowledge it in front of anyone else but you, Duncan. You tell me you almost lost Madelyne. You would have been denied her magic and never known your loss."

"Her magic?" Duncan smiled over the flowery comment. It wasn't usual for Gerald to speak in such a manner.

"I cannot explain it," Gerald said. He blushed, obviously embarrassed by what he'd said. "She's so untarnished. And though you regret taking her captive now, I'm grateful. She was the only one who could give Adela back to me."

"I've never regretted taking Madelyne. I'm only sorry she was involved in my battle with Louddon."

"Ah, my sweet Adela," Gerald said. "I could have been killed today. Adela would have forever been denied the bliss only I can give her."

Duncan smiled. "It's still undecided in my mind, Gerald, if Adela would have mourned your passing or celebrated your death."

Gerald laughed. "I will tell you something, and if you repeat it, I'll cut your throat. I had to make Adela a promise before she would agree to marry me."

Duncan was highly curious. Gerald was looking embarrassed again.

"I had to vow I wouldn't bed her."

Duncan shook his head. "You feast on punishment, Gerald. Tell me, do you plan to honor your vow?" he asked, trying not to laugh.

"I will," he announced, surprising Duncan.

"You plan to live as a monk in your own home?" Duncan sounded appalled.

"No, but I've learned from you, Duncan."

"What are you talking about?" Duncan asked.

"You told Adela she could live with you for the rest of her days, remember? And then you suggested I move to Wexton fortress and change her mind. It was a clever ploy and I am parroting it."

"I see," Duncan said with a nod.

Gerald laughed. "No, you don't," he said. "I've promised Adela I wouldn't bed her. She, however, can bed me anytime she wishes."

Duncan smiled, understanding at last.

"It will take time," Gerald admitted. "She loves me, but she still doesn't trust me yet. I accept the conditions, for I know she won't be able to resist my charms forever."

Duncan laughed.

"We best get some rest. Do we ride to London tomorrow?" Gerald asked.

"No, we ride to Baron Rhinehold. His fortress is central to my plan."

"And what is your plan?"

"To gather my allies, Gerald. The game is over. I'll send word from Rhinehold's home to the others. If all goes well, we'll gather in London within two weeks, three at the most."

"Do you call up their numbers as well?" Gerald asked, thinking of the huge army Duncan could so easily amass. Though the barons were inclined to fight among themselves, and constantly jostled for a more significant position of power, they all were quite equal in their respect and admiration for Baron Wexton. Each sent their fittest knights to train under Duncan. None were ever turned away.

The barons deferred to Duncan's judgment. He'd never asked their backing before. Yet none among the bickering group would turn his back on Duncan.

"I don't want their armies at my side, only my equals. I'm not going to challenge our leader, only confront him. There is a difference, Gerald."

"I will stand by your side as well, though I'm sure you know that," Gerald announced.

"Louddon has played his last game of deceit. I don't believe the king knows about Louddon's treachery. I plan to enlighten him, however. He cannot continue to ignore this problem. Justice will be served."

"You'll enlighten our leader in front of the other barons?"

"I will. Every one of them knows about Adela," he said. "They might as well hear the truth."

"Why?" Gerald's face showed his anguish. "Will Adela have to stand before—"

"No, she'll stay at my home. There isn't any need to put her through the ordeal.

Gerald immediately looked relieved. "Then why are you—"

"I'll present the truths to our king, in front of his barons."

"And will our leader act with honor over this issue?" Gerald asked.

"We'll find out soon enough. There are many who believe our king is incapable of that. I'm not one of them." Duncan's voice was emphatic. "He has always acted with honor toward me, Gerald. I'll not judge him so easily."

Gerald nodded. "Madelyne will have to go with us, won't she?"

"It is necessary," Duncan answered.

Gerald could tell from the look on Duncan's face that his friend didn't want Madelyne to go to court any more than he wanted Adela to.

"Madelyne will have to recount what has happened. Otherwise it will be Louddon's word against mine."

"Does the outcome depend upon Madelyne then?" Gerald asked. His frown matched Duncan's.

"Of course not," Duncan answered. "But she has been a pawn in all of this. Louddon and I have both used her. It isn't easy for me to acknowledge that, Gerald."

"You saved her from Louddon's abuse when you took her with you," Gerald pointed out. "Adela told me a little about Madelyne's past."

Duncan nodded. He was weary of conflicts. Now that he'd discovered the joy of loving Madelyne, he wanted to spend every minute with her. He smiled when he realized he was mimicking Madelyne's imaginary hero, Odysseus. She had told him all about the warrior who was forced to endure one challenge after another, for ten long years, before he could return home to his beloved.

It would be another two weeks before he could hold her in

his arms again. He sighed once more. He was beginning to act quite pathetic. "At least there will be time before we reach London—"

"Time for what?" Gerald asked.

Duncan hadn't realized he'd spoken his thought aloud until Gerald questioned him. "To marry Madelyne."

Gerald's eyes widened. Duncan turned and walked into the wilderness, leaving Gerald to wonder what in heaven's name he was talking about.

Duncan's home underwent a few subtle changes while he was away. They were necessary precautions, and every one of them because of the baroness.

The courtyard was always deserted in the morning hours now. Though the heat should have beckoned the staff out into the upper bailey to do their daily chores of washing the linens and braiding fresh rushes, everyone preferred to work indoors. They waited until late afternoon to go outside and gain a few minutes of fresh, cooling air.

More specifically, they waited for Madelyne to finish her target practice.

Madelyne was determined to gain accuracy with her new bow and arrows, and toward this end she drove Anthony to distraction. He tutored her, yet couldn't understand why his mistress didn't get any better. Her determination was admirable. Her accuracy, however, was a different story. She was consistently three feet above her target. Anthony kept commenting on that fact, but Madelyne didn't seem to be able to correct her aim.

Ned kept Madelyne supplied with new arrows. She'd gone through a good fifty of them before she corrected her aim enough to keep the arrows below the top of the wall. She was then able to retrieve her arrows to use again, arrows that had speared the trees, the huts, and hanging linens.

Anthony was patient with his mistress. He understood her goal. She wanted to learn to protect herself, true, but she also wanted to make her husband proud of her. The vassal wasn't guessing Madelyne's second motive. No, she told him her quest several times a day.

Anthony knew why she repeated herself. His baroness worried he'd get disgusted with her poor performance and

306

stop tutoring her. The vassal wouldn't, of course, deny Madelyne anything.

A messenger from the King of England arrived at Wexton fortress late in the afternoon. Anthony received him in the hall, fully expecting to be given a verbal message. The king's servant handed Anthony a parchment scroll. The vassal called for Maude, directing her to give the soldier food and drink.

Madelyne walked into the room just as the soldier followed Maude into the buttery. She noticed the scroll immediately. "What news is there, Anthony? Does Duncan send us word?" she asked.

"The message comes from the king," Anthony said. He walked over to a small chest located against the wall opposite the buttery. An ornately carved wooden box sat on top of the chest. Madelyne had thought it was merely a decorative piece of work, until Anthony lifted the top and placed the scroll inside.

She was close enough to see other pieces of parchment inside. The box was obviously where Duncan kept his important papers. "You're not going to read it now?" she asked Anthony when he turned back to her.

"It will have to wait until Baron Wexton returns," Anthony announced.

Madelyne could tell from the look on his face that Anthony wasn't pleased about waiting. "I could send for one of the monks at—"

"I would read it for you," Madelyne interjected.

Anthony looked astonished by her remark. Madelyne felt her cheeks heat, knew she blushed. "It's true, I can read, though I would appreciate it, Anthony, if you didn't tell anyone. I've no wish to be the topic of ridicule," she added.

Anthony nodded. "Duncan has been gone over three weeks now," Madelyne reminded him. "And you told me he could be away another month. Do you dare wait that long to fetch a priest to read the message for you?"

"No, of course not," Anthony returned. He opened the box and handed the scroll to Madelyne. Then he leaned on the edge of the table, folded his arms in front of him, and listened to the message from his overlord.

The letter was written in Latin, the preferred language for official communications.

It didn't take Madelyne any time at all to translate the message. Her voice never quavered, but her hands trembled when she'd finished reading the missive.

The king gave no greeting to Baron Wexton. His anger was as evident as his breach in manners, Madelyne thought. He demanded, from the first word to the last, that Madelyne appear before him.

She wasn't as upset over that command as she was over the announcement that King William was sending his own troops to fetch her.

"So our king sends soldiers to take you," Anthony said when she finished reading. His voice shook.

Anthony was caught in the middle, Madelyne thought. His loyalty belonged to Duncan. Aye, he'd pledged fealty to him. Yet Anthony and Duncan were both vassals to the King of England. William's command would have to take precedence over all others.

"Was there anything else, Madelyne?" Anthony asked.

She slowly nodded. And then she braved a smile for him. "I was hoping you wouldn't ask," she whispered. "It would seem, Anthony, in our king's mind, there are two sisters, two barons. William wants the feud ended, suggesting that perhaps . . . aye, he uses just that word, perhaps each sister be returned to the rightful brother."

Madelyne's eyes brimmed with tears. "The other alternative is for Duncan to wed me," she whispered.

"The king obviously doesn't know you're already wed," Anthony interjected. His frown intensified, for he knew Madelyne wasn't aware of the fact she really wasn't married to Duncan yet. "And if Duncan weds me, then Adela will become Louddon's bride."

"God help us," Anthony muttered with disgust.

"Adela mustn't know about this, Anthony," Madelyne rushed out. "I will tell her only the king demands my presence."

Anthony nodded. "Can you write as well as read, Madelyne?" he suddenly asked.

When Madelyne nodded, he said, "Then perhaps, if the king hasn't already dispatched his troops, we might gain a little time."

"Time for what?" Madelyne asked.

"Time for your husband to return to you," Anthony told her.

The vassal hurried over to the chest, picked up the oblong wooden box, and carried it over to Madelyne. "There is parchment and dye inside," he told Madelyne.

Madelyne sat down and quickly prepared for the task ahead. Anthony turned his back on her. He began to pace while he decided what he'd tell his king.

Madelyne noticed the rolled missive on the table then, next to the jar of flowers. The torn seal was from Roanne monastery. Out of curiousity, she took the time to read the letter from Father Laurance's superiors.

Anthony turned back to Madelyne just as she was finishing the missive. He recognized the seal, knew then the pretense was over. "He didn't want you to worry," Anthony said to Madelyne. He put his hand on her shoulder, offering her comfort.

Madelyne didn't make any comment. She tilted her head up to look at him. Anthony was stunned by the amazing change in his mistress. She looked very serene. He knew then how terrified she really was. Aye, it was the same expression she wore those first few weeks she'd been Duncan's captive.

He didn't know how to help her. If he tried to explain that Duncan meant to marry her as soon as he returned, he might just make the situation worse. They both knew the baron had lied to Madelyne. "Madelyne, your husband loves you," he said, sorry he couldn't keep the harshness out of his voice.

"He isn't my husband, is he, Anthony?"

She didn't give him time to answer but turned her back on him. "What is it you wish me to say to our king?" she asked. Her voice was mild, almost pleasant.

Anthony admitted defeat. He'd have to leave the explanation to Duncan, he decided. He turned his attention to his dictation.

In the end, it was a simple message, giving only the notification that Baron Wexton hadn't returned to his fortress, and therefore had no knowledge of the king's demand.

Anthony made Madelyne read the message twice. When

he was satisfied, she fanned the parchment dry, then oiled the back until it was pliable enough to roll into a scroll.

Anthony gave the message to the king's soldier and commanded him to make haste returning to his king.

Madelyne went to her room to pack her gowns. It was a precaution, for Madelyne knew the king's soldiers could arrive at any moment.

She went and explained to Adela what had happened, using most of the afternoon to visit with her friend. She didn't tell Adela the exact wording of the king's message. Nay, Madelyne deliberately left out any mention about Adela possibly going to Louddon.

Madelyne wouldn't ever let that happen. Nor would she put Duncan in the position of having to choose.

She didn't eat dinner that night but went up to the tower room instead. Madelyne stood in front of the window for over an hour, letting her emotions control her mind.

Laurance really should have been found out sooner. Madelyne blamed herself for being too preoccupied to notice all the little oddities. Then she blamed Duncan. If he hadn't frightened her so much during that wedding ceremony, she'd have caught on to Laurance's deception.

She never considered the possibility that Duncan knew all along. No, she was certain he thought Laurance had truly married them. She was still angry. He had blatantly lied to her about the contents of the letter from the Roanne monastery. Duncan knew how much she valued the truth. She never lied to him. "Just you wait until I get my hands on you," she muttered. "Adela isn't the only one who knows how to scream."

Her burst of anger didn't help her mood much. She started to cry again.

By midnight she had exhausted herself. She leaned against the window. The moon was bright. Madelyne wondered if it was shining down on Duncan now. Did he sleep outdoors tonight or in one of the king's chambers?

Madelyne's attention turned to the crest of the hill outside the wall. A movement had caught her eye, and she looked just in time to see her wolf climb the ridge.

It really was a wolf, wasn't it? Maybe even the same one she'd seen months before. The animal looked large enough.

She wished Duncan were here, standing beside her, so she

could prove to him that her wolf did exist. She watched the animal lift the meaty bone she'd left there for him, turn, and disappear down the other side of the hill.

Madelyne was so exhausted, she decided she was getting fanciful again. It was probably just another wild dog after all, and not even the one she'd seen before.

Duncan was her wolf. He loved her. Madelyne never doubted him on that issue. Aye, he lied to her about the letter, yet she instinctively knew he'd never lie to her about his love for her.

It was a comforting admission. Duncan was too honorable to deceive her in such a manner.

She tried to sleep. Fear made it impossible though. How content she'd been to let Duncan take care of the future. She felt so safe because she carried his name. Aye, she was bound to him.

Until today.

Now she was terrified again. The king demanded her attendance in court. She was going back to Louddon.

Madelyne began to pray. She pleaded with God to keep Duncan safe. She asked favor for Adela's future, Gerald's, too, and even prayed for Edmond and Gilard.

And then she whispered a prayer for herself. She begged for courage.

Courage to face the devil.

Chapter Twenty-one

"Answer a fool according to his folly, lest he be wise in his own conceit."

OLD TESTAMENT, PROVERBS, 26:5

Duncan knew something was wrong the minute he rode into the lower bailey. Anthony wasn't there to greet him, and neither was Madelyne.

A feeling of dread settled around his heart. He goaded his stallion forward, galloped over the bridge and into the courtyard.

Adela came rushing out of the castle just as he and Gerald dismounted. She hesitated a short distance away from the two men, finally seemed to make up her mind, and then ran and threw herself into Gerald's arms. When she embraced him, she started to cry.

It took patience and several long minutes to gain any information from Adela.

Duncan's second-in-command, a large but soft-spoken man by the name of Robert, came running up to give his accounting. While Gerald sought to hush Adela, Robert explained that the king's soldiers had come for Madelyne.

"Was the king's seal on this missive?" Duncan asked.

Robert frowned over the question. "I do not know, Baron. I didn't see the summons. And your wife insisted that she take the letter with her." Robert lowered his voice to a whisper when he added, "She didn't want anyone to read the contents of the summons to your sister."

Duncan wasn't sure what to make of his wife's action. He concluded the directive must have included some sort of threat toward Adela and that Madelyne was trying to protect his sister from worry.

The king wouldn't have threatened. Nay, William wouldn't treat his loyal barons in such a way. Duncan had sufficient faith in his leader to believe his king would wait to hear all the explanations.

Louddon's hand was in this treachery. Duncan would stake his life on it.

He immediately shouted the order to prepare to ride again. Duncan was so angry, he could barely think logically. The only calming thought was the fact that Anthony had gone with Madelyne. His loyal vassal had taken a small contingent of Duncan's fittest warriors with him. Robert explained that Anthony dared not take too many soldiers, lest the king think he was being distrustful.

"Then Anthony believes the summons came directly from our king?" Duncan asked.

"I was not privy to his thoughts," Robert answered.

Duncan called for a fresh mount. When the stablemaster led Silenus to him, Duncan asked why Madelyne hadn't chosen his stallion to carry her to court.

James, unaccustomed to speaking directly to his lord, stammered out his reply. "She worried her brother would abuse the horse if he found out Silenus belonged to you, milord. Those were her true words."

Duncan nodded, accepting the explanation. How like his gentle wife to be concerned about the horse. "She demanded one of the king's horses," James added.

Adela actually begged to go along with them. Duncan had already gained his saddle but was forced by his sister's hysterics to wait precious minutes while Gerald disengaged himself from his intended.

After declining Adela's plea to go with them, Gerald had to vow on his mother's grave he'd return to her unscratched, a vow Duncan knew to be false since Gerald's mother was still alive. He certainly didn't comment on the contradiction, for he saw how Gerald's promise had calmed his sister.

"Will you be able to catch up with milady?" James dared to ask his lord.

Duncan turned to look down at the stablemaster. He saw the frightened look in the man's eyes and was warmed by his concern. "I'm at least a week late," Duncan said. "But I will bring your mistress back, James."

Those were the last words Duncan spoke until he was halfway to London. If the horses hadn't needed rest, Gerald thought Duncan wouldn't have stopped at all.

Baron Wexton separated himself from his men. Gerald left him alone for a few minutes and then went over to speak to him. "I would offer you a word of advice, friend."

Duncan turned to look at Gerald. "Remember my reaction when I saw Morcar. Don't let your rage control you, though I vow I'll try to defend your back while we are in court."

Duncan nodded. "I'll be under control as soon as I see Madelyne. She's been in court at least a week now. God only knows what Louddon has done to her. I swear to God, Gerald, if he has touched her, I'll . . ."

"Louddon has too much at stake to harm her, Duncan. He needs her support, not her anger. Nay, there will be too many people watching him. Louddon will play the loving brother."

"I pray you're right," Duncan answered. "I . . . worry about her."

Gerald patted him on the shoulder. "Hell, man, you're scared of losing her, just as I was scared of losing Adela."

"What an arrogant pair we make," Duncan announced. "Don't worry about my anger. When I see my wife, I'll be disciplined again."

"Yes, well, there is another issue that needs discussion," Gerald confessed. "Adela told me about the letter you received from the monastery."

"How could she know about the letter?" Duncan asked.

"Your Madelyne told her. It seems she found the letter and read it."

Duncan's shoulders sagged. His worries had just multiplied. He wasn't sure what his wife would do. "Did Adela tell you how Madelyne reacted? Was she angry. God, I hope she was angry."

Gerald shook his head. "Why would you want her angry?"

"I lied to Madelyne, Gerald, and I would hope she's angry over the lie. I don't want her to think that I . . . used her in ill faith." Duncan shrugged. It was difficult for him to put his feelings into words. "When I first met Madelyne, she tried to convince me Louddon wouldn't come after her. She told me she wasn't worthy of his attention. Madelyne wasn't trying to deceive me, Gerald. God's truth, she really believed what she said. Louddon made her feel that way, of course. She was under his thumb for nearly two years."

"Two years?"

"Aye, from the time her mother died until he sent her to her uncle, Louddon was Madelyne's sole guardian. You know as well as I what cruelty Louddon is capable of, Gerald. I've seen Madelyne grow stronger each day, but she is still . . . vulnerable."

Gerald nodded. "I know you wish you'd been the one to tell her that Laurance wasn't a true man of the cloth, but consider how unprepared she would have been if Louddon had been the one to explain it."

"Aye, he would have caught her unprepared," Duncan admitted. "Do you know that Madelyne asked me to teach her how to defend herself. There wasn't time. Nay, I didn't make time. If anything happens to her . . ."

Duncan was a man tormented. His innocent wife was back in the devil's hands. The thought chilled his soul.

Gerald didn't know what words to offer to give Duncan solace. "The moon gives us sufficient light to continue on through the night," he suggested.

"Then we will take advantage of the light."

The barons didn't speak again until they'd gained their destination.

Madelyne tried to sleep. She was locked inside the chamber next to her sister Clarissa's room. The walls were parchment-thin. Madelyne tried not to listen to the discussion Louddon was having with Clarissa.

She'd already heard enough. Madelyne was so sickened by her sister and her brother, she'd made herself ill. Her stomach wouldn't keep any food down and her head pounded with pain.

Louddon had been very predictable. He greeted her in front of the king's soldiers, kissed her on the cheek, even embraced her. Aye, he played the role of loving brother, especially in front of Anthony. As soon as they were alone in her chambers, however, Louddon had turned on her. He raged accusations, ending his tirade by knocking Madelyne to the floor with a powerful fist against her cheek. It was the same cheek he'd kissed in greeting.

Her brother regretted his outburst immediately, for he realized Madelyne's face was going to bruise. Since he knew some of his enemies would conclude he was responsible, he kept Madelyne locked in her room and gave everyone the excuse that his sister had been through such an ordeal in the hands of Baron Wexton that she would need a few days to regain her strength.

Yet, while Louddon had been predictable, Clarissa had proven to be a devastating disappointment to Madelyne. When she had time to think about it, Madelyne realized she'd built up a fanciful picture of her older sister. Madelyne wanted to believe Clarissa cared about her. Yet every time she sent messages to both her sisters, neither Clarissa nor Sara ever bothered to answer her. Madelyne had always made excuses for their behavior. Now she realized the truth. Clarissa was every bit as self-serving as Louddon.

Sara hadn't even come to London. Clarissa explained her absence by telling Madelyne that Sara was newly married to Baron Ruchiers and didn't wish to leave his side. Madelyne hadn't even known Sara was betrothed to anyone.

Madelyne gave up trying to rest. Clarissa's voice grated like a shrill rooster's call. The sister was prone to whine, was doing so now as she complained to Louddon about the humiliation Madelyne had caused her.

A snatch of conversation drew her over to the connecting door. Clarissa was talking about Rachael. Her voice was filled with loathing as she so easily defamed Madelyne's mother. Madelyne knew Louddon hated Rachael, yet never thought his two sisters felt the same way.

"You wanted the bitch from the day she walked through the door," Clarissa said.

Madelyne edged the door open. She saw Clarissa sitting on a padded cushion in the window well. Louddon was standing next to his sister. His back faced Madelyne. Clarissa was looking up at her brother. Both held goblets in their hands.

"Rachael was very beautiful," Louddon said. His voice was harsh. "When Father turned against her, I was amazed. Rachael was such an appealing woman. Father forced the marriage, Clarissa. It was assumed that Baron Rhinehold would wed her."

Clarissa snorted. Madelyne watched her take a long drink from her cup. Dark red wine spilled down the front of her gown, but Clarissa seemed oblivious to the mess and poured another cupful from the jug she held in her other hand.

The sister was as pretty as Louddon, with the same white-blond hair and hazel eyes. Her expression, when she was angry, was also just as ugly as her brother's. "Rhinehold was no match for our father back then," Clarissa said. "But Father was played the fool, wasn't he? In the end Rachael mocked him. I wonder, Louddon, if Rhinehold knows Rachael was carrying his child when she wed our father?"

"No," Louddon answered. "Rachael was never allowed to see Rhinehold. When Madelyne was born, Father wouldn't even look at her. Rachael was punished for her folly."

"And you hoped Rachael would turn to you for comfort, didn't you, Louddon?" Clarissa asked. She laughed when Louddon turned to glare at her. "You were in love with her," she goaded. "Rachael thought you were disgusting, though, didn't she? If she didn't have her brat to look after, I think she really might have killed herself. God knows I suggested it to her often enough. Perhaps, brother dear, Rachael didn't fall down those steps. She might have been pushed."

"You were always jealous of Rachael, Clarissa," Louddon snapped. "Just as you're now jealous of her daughter, illegitimate or not."

"I'm not jealous of anyone," Clarissa screamed. "God, I'm looking forward to getting this over and done with. Then I swear I'm going to tell Madelyne about Rhinehold. I might even tell her you killed her mother."

"You will say nothing," Louddon screamed. He slapped the goblet out of Clarissa's hand. "You're a fool, sister. I didn't kill Rachael. She did slip and fall down those steps."

"She was trying to get away from you when she fell." Clarissa sneered.

"Let it be," Louddon yelled. "And no one must ever know Madelyne isn't one of us. The shame would affect you and me."

"Will the little bitch do as you demand? Will Madelyne perform before our king the way you have decided? Or will she turn against you, Louddon?"

"She'll do whatever I tell her to do," Louddon boasted. "She obeys me because she's afraid. What a coward she is. She hasn't changed in temperament since she was a child. Besides, our little Madelyne knows I'll kill Berton if she displeases me."

"'Tis a shame about Morcar's death," Clarissa said. "He would have paid handsomely for Madelyne. Now no one will want her."

"You're wrong, Clarissa. I want her. I won't let anyone marry her."

Madelyne shut the door on Clarissa's obscene laughter. She made it to the chamber pot just in time to throw up the bile from her stomach.

She wept for her mother, Rachael, and the hell Louddon and his father had put her through. She'd been appalled to learn that Rachael had gone to her marriage bed carrying another man's child. And then the full truth dawned on Madelyne. She wept tears of joy next, for she'd just realized she wasn't blood relative to Louddon after all.

She'd heard the name Rhinehold from Duncan, knew they were allies. She wondered if Baron Rhinehold was in court. She wanted to see what he looked like. Had he ever married? Louddon was right; no one must ever know . . . and yet, Madelyne knew she'd tell Duncan the truth. Why, he'd probably be as pleased as she was.

She was finally able to force her emotions under control. She would need her wits about her. Aye, she must try to protect Father Berton and Duncan. Louddon believed Madelyne would willingly betray one to save the other. There was also the problem of Adela, of course, but Madelyne wasn't concerned about Duncan's sister now.

Nay, Gerald would marry Adela soon, and when that happened, the king couldn't very well threaten to give Adela to Louddon.

Madelyne spent most of the night formulating her plan. She prayed Louddon would stay predictable, that Duncan would remain safe, and that God would give her courage for the battle ahead.

She finally closed her eyes to sleep. And then she played the same pretense she used to play when she was a little girl. Whenever she was frightened that Louddon was going to take her back home, she'd pretend Odysseus was standing over her, guarding her. The pretense changed, however. It was not Odysseus but Duncan standing guard now.

Aye, she'd found someone more powerful than Odysseus. She had her wolf to protect her now.

The following afternoon Madelyne accompanied Louddon to meet with their king. When they neared the king's private chambers, Louddon turned to Madelyne and smiled at her. "I am counting on your honesty, Madelyne. You need only tell the king what has happened to your home and to you. I'll do the rest."

"And the truth will damn Duncan, is that what you believe?" Madelyne asked.

Louddon's smile abruptly soured. He did not like the tone his sister used with him. "Dare you find your backbone now, Madelyne? Remember your precious uncle. Even now I have men ready to ride. If I give the word, Berton's throat will be slit."

"How do I know you haven't already killed him?" Madelyne argued. "Aye," she added when Louddon grabbed hold of her arm in a threatening manner. "You can't control your temper, Louddon. You never could. How do I know you haven't already killed my uncle?"

Louddon proved her comment about his temper was accurate. He lashed out, striking her face. The bejeweled ring he wore cut the edge of her lip. Blood immediately began to trickle down Madelyne's chin. "Look what you've made me do," Louddon bellowed. He arched his hand again to inflict another blow, and suddenly found himself slammed up against the wall next to Madelyne.

Anthony had appeared out of the shadows. He now had

Louddon by his neck, and was giving Madelyne every indication he was going to strangle her brother.

Madelyne had deliberately provoked her brother into losing his temper. God's truth, she wasn't even thankful for Anthony's interference. "Anthony, unhand my brother," Madelyne commanded. Her voice was harsh but she softened the order by placing her hand on the vassal's shoulder. "Please, Anthony."

The vassal shook off his anger, let go of Louddon, and calmly watched the baron crumble into a coughing fit to the floor.

Madelyne took advantage of her brother's weakened condition. She leaned up and whispered into Anthony's ear. "'Tis time for me to put my plan into action. No matter what I do or say, do not argue with it. I am protecting Duncan."

Anthony nodded so that Madelyne would know he'd understood her. He longed to ask her if her plan was to goad Louddon into killing her. And why was she thinking to protect Duncan? It was obvious to the vassal that his mistress wasn't the least bit concerned about her own safety.

It took all of Anthony's determination not to show any reaction when Madelyne helped Louddon to his feet. He didn't want Madelyne to touch the bastard.

"Louddon, I don't believe you haven't harmed Uncle Berton," Madelyne said when her brother tried to drag her away from Anthony. "We will solve this problem here and now."

Louddon was astonished by Madelyne's boldness. His sister wasn't acting timid or frightened now. "What do you think to tell the king when he notices the marks on my face, Louddon?"

"You aren't going to see the king," Louddon bellowed. "I've changed my mind. I'm taking you back to your chambers, Madelyne. I'll speak to our leader on your behalf."

Madelyne pulled out of her brother's grasp. "He'll want to see me and hear my explanation," she said. "Today, tomorrow, or next week, Louddon," she added. "You have only extended the wait. And do you know what I'll tell our king?"

"The truth." Louddon sneered. "Aye, your honesty will trap Baron Wexton." He actually laughed over his own announcement. "You can't help yourself, Madelyne."

"I would tell the truth if I spoke to the king. But I'm not going to say a word. I'll simply stand there and stare at you when the king asks me his questions. God's truth, I'll not say one word."

Louddon was so enraged by Madelyne's threat, he almost hit her again. When he raised his hand, Anthony took a menacing step forward. Louddon's urge to retaliate was immediately pushed aside.

"We'll speak of this later," Louddon said. He gave Anthony a meaningful glare before he continued. "When we are alone, I promise you I'll change your mind."

Madelyne hid her fear. "We're going to speak of this now, Louddon, else I'll send Anthony to our king to tell him how you are mistreating me."

"You think William would care?" Louddon shouted.

"I am as much his subject as you are," Madelyne returned. "I will also instruct Anthony to tell the king how concerned I am that you are going to kill Uncle Berton. I doubt William would like the church's reaction to a baron murdering one of their own."

"The king wouldn't believe you. And you know damn well your precious priest is alive. But if you persist in this rebellion, I will have him killed. Goad me further, bitch, and I'll—"

"You'll send me back to live with Uncle Berton. That is what you'll do."

Louddon's eyes widened and his face turned a blotchy red. He couldn't believe this radical change in his sister's disposition. She was standing up to him, and in front of a witness too. Worry edged into Louddon's mind. It was imperative that he have Madelyne's cooperation if he was going to sway their king into ruling against Duncan. Aye, he'd counted on Madelyne to tell how Duncan had destroyed his fortress and taken her captive. Suddenly Madelyne had become unpredictable.

"You expect me to answer only certain truths, don't you? What if I begin my accounting by telling how you tried to kill Baron Wexton?"

"You will answer only those questions put to you," Louddon bellowed.

"Then give in to my request. Let me go to my uncle. I'll stay with him and let you take care of this problem with Baron Wexton."

Madelyne felt like weeping over her deliberate choice of words. Problem, indeed. Louddon was out to see Duncan destroyed. "I swear to you, I could do your petition far more damage if I'm called before the king. The truth might damn Duncan, but my silence will damn you."

"When this is over . . ."

"You'll kill me, I suppose," Madelyne announced with a forced shrug of indifference. Her voice was devoid of emotion when she said, "I don't care, Louddon. Do your worst."

Louddon didn't need to think about Madelyne's threat. He concluded immediately that she should be removed from court. There simply wasn't time to beat her into submission.

Just two days past he'd learned of Morcar's failure to kill Duncan. Morcar was dead, and Duncan would surely arrive in London anytime now.

Perhaps he should let his sister have her way. Her departure would serve his purpose well, he decided.

"You will leave within the hour," Louddon announced. "But my men will escort you, Madelyne. Wexton's men," he added, staring at Anthony now, "have no reason to follow after you. The baron no longer has a say in your affairs. He has his sister back and you now belong to me."

Madelyne agreed before Anthony could offer argument. The vassal exchanged a look with his mistress and then nodded his acceptance.

He didn't have any intention of honoring the agreement, of course. Anthony would follow Madelyne no matter where Louddon sent her. He would be discreet, however, and let Louddon believe his duty was done. "Then I'll return to Wexton fortress," he announced before he turned and walked away.

"I must go and have a few words with the king," Louddon muttered. "He is expecting us. I'm giving in to your whim, Madelyne, but you and I both know the time will come when you must report what happened to William."

"I will give him my honesty," Madelyne returned. When Louddon looked suspicious, she hastily added, "And that will, of course, support your cause."

Louddon looked slightly appeased. "Yes, well, perhaps the visit to your uncle is best after all. Seeing him again will remind you of your tenuous position."

The bitch needs reminding of how important her uncle is to her, Louddon decided. She'd obviously forgotten what an old, frail man Berton was, and how impossible it would be for him to protect himself. Aye, she needed to see the priest again. Then he'd have his fearful, timid sister back where he wanted her.

"There is always the chance that I'll have taken care of Duncan before you're asked to return to court, Madelyne. Return to your rooms now and get your puny possessions. I shall send soldiers to escort you to the courtyard."

Madelyne pretended humility. She bowed her head and whispered her appreciation. "I have truly been through such an ordeal," she told her brother. "I hope the king does not argue with your request that I leave . . ."

"My request?" Louddon laughed, an obscene sound that grated. "He won't even know, Madelyne. I need not request anything from William on such minor issues."

Louddon turned and walked away after making his odious boast. Madelyne watched him until he'd disappeared around the curve in the corridor. She turned then and started back toward her chambers. Anthony waited in the shadows and was quick to intercept her. "You take too many chances, milady," Anthony muttered. "Your husband will be displeased."

"We both know Duncan isn't my husband," Madelyne said. "It is important that you not interfere, Anthony. Louddon must believe he truly has his sister back."

"Madelyne, I know you think to protect Adela, but Gerald's duty—"

"Nay, Anthony," Madelyne interrupted. "I am only thinking to gain time. And I must go to my uncle. He is like a father to me. Louddon will kill him if I don't protect—"

"You must protect yourself," Anthony argued. "Instead, you try to protect the world. Will you not listen to reason? You'll be vulnerable if you leave the castle grounds."

"I am far more vulnerable here," Madelyne whispered.

She patted Anthony's hand and then said, "I'll be vulnerable until Duncan has righted this problem. You will tell Duncan where I've gone, Anthony, and then it will be his decision."

"What decision?" Anthony asked.

"Whether to come after me or not."

"You actually doubt . . ."

Madelyne let out a long sigh. "Nay, I do not doubt," she said, shaking her head for emphasis. "Duncan will come after me, and when he does, he'll leave soldiers to guard my uncle. I only pray he is quick about it."

Anthony couldn't fault Madelyne's plan. "I'll keep you in my sight at all times," he vowed. "You've only to cry out and I'll be there."

"You must stay here and tell Duncan—"

"I'll leave another to see to that duty," Anthony said. "I gave my word to my lord to protect his wife," he added, placing force on the word *wife*.

Though she didn't admit it, Madelyne was relieved to have Anthony's guard. When she'd finished gathering her clothing, she hurried to the courtyard adjacent to the king's stables. Three of Louddon's soldiers had escorted her. They left her standing alone now while they prepared their mounts.

Madelyne was thankful she hadn't run into Clarissa again. And Louddon was still in conference with their king . . . filling his head full of lies about Duncan, Madelyne knew.

A curious crowd had gathered to watch the departure. The marks on Madelyne's face were quite noticeable, and she couldn't help but overhear the speculative comments behind her back.

A tall red-headed woman separated herself from the group and rushed over to Madelyne. She was a beautiful woman, with a regal, elegant manner, a good deal taller than Madelyne, and a bit more filled out as well. She didn't smile at Madelyne but gave her a look of hostility.

Madelyne met her stare and asked, "Is there something you wished to say to me?"

"'Tis a risk I take in speaking so openly to you," the woman began. "I must think of my reputation, you see."

"And speaking to me will tarnish it?" Madelyne asked.

The woman looked surprised by the question. "But of course," she admitted. "Surely you realized that you are no longer a desirable—"

Madelyne cut off the veiled insult. "Say what you wish to say and be gone then."

"I am Lady Eleanor." Madelyne couldn't hide her surprise. "Then you've heard of me? Perchance Baron Wexton has spoken of—"

"I have heard of you," Madelyne whispered. Her voice shook. She couldn't help but feel a bit inferior standing next to the woman. Lady Eleanor was dressed splendidly, while Madelyne wore a simple traveling gown of faded blue.

Duncan's intended appeared to be everything Madelyne believed she wasn't. She was so composed, so dignified. Madelyne doubted the woman had ever been clumsy, even when she was a little girl.

"My father has still to come to formal agreement with Baron Wexton regarding our wedding date. I just wanted to tell you that you have my compassion, poor child. I don't place any blame on my future husband though. He was merely retaliating in kind. But I did wonder if Baron Wexton mistreated you."

Madelyne heard the worry in Lady Eleanor's voice and was furious. "If you must ask me that question, then you don't know Baron Wexton well at all."

She turned her back on the woman and mounted the horse one of the soldiers had led over to her. When she was settled, she looked down at Lady Eleanor and said, "He did not mistreat me. Now you have your question answered and it is my turn to ask you something."

Lady Eleanor agreed with a curt nod.

"Do you love Baron Wexton?"

It became obvious after a long silent moment that Lady Eleanor wasn't going to answer Madelyne. She did raise an eyebrow, and the look of disdain on her face told she had little liking for the question.

"I am not a poor child, Lady Eleanor," Madelyne announced, letting her anger sound in her voice. "Duncan won't marry you. He won't sign the contracts. He'd have to give up his greatest treasure in order to marry you."

"And what be that treasure?" Lady Eleanor inquired, her voice mild.

"Why, I'm Duncan's greatest treasure. He'd be a fool to give me up," she added. "And even you must know that Duncan is anything but a fool."

Madelyne then goaded her mount forward. Lady Eleanor had to jump out of the way, else be pounded into the ground. Dust flew up in the silly woman's face.

She didn't look so superior now. Aye, Lady Eleanor was clearly furious. Her anger pleased Madelyne considerably. She felt as though she'd just won an important battle. It was victory to Madelyne's way of thinking, childish, born of rudeness, true, but a victory all the same.

Chapter Twenty-two

"We walk by faith, not by sight."

NEW TESTAMENT, II CORINTHIANS, 5:7

She told him everything.

The retelling of all that had happened to Madelyne took almost two full days. The dear priest demanded to hear every word, every feeling, every outcome.

Father Berton had wept tears of joy when Madelyne walked into his tiny cottage. He admitted he'd missed her terribly and couldn't seem to gain control of his emotions for most of that first day. Madelyne, of course, did a fair amount of weeping too. Her uncle declared that it was fine enough to be so undisciplined because they were all alone, after all, and no one could witness their emotional display. Father's companions were off to visit another old friend who'd suddenly taken ill.

It wasn't until she'd prepared their supper and they were seated side by side in their favorite chairs that Madelyne was finally able to begin her recitation. While the priest ate his dinner, Madelyne told her story. She thought only to give her uncle Berton a brief summary, but he wouldn't allow a skimpy accounting.

The priest seemed to savor every detail. He wouldn't let Madelyne continue until he'd memorized each word. His training as both a translator and a guardian of the old stories was the reason Madelyne gave for this familiar peculiarity.

When Madelyne first greeted her uncle, she began to worry about his health. He seemed to be failing. Aye, she thought his shoulders slumped a little more now. His back appeared to be a bit more bent, too, and he didn't seem to move about the cottage as quickly. Yet his gaze was just as direct, his comments just as sharp. Father Berton's mind was as keen as ever. When he confessed that his companions wouldn't be returning to live out their last years with him, Madelyne surmised it was loneliness and not his advanced years of fifty summers that accounted for the changes she'd noted.

Madelyne was confident Duncan would come for her. Yet when three full days had passed, and still not a sign of Duncan, her confidence began to evaporate.

Madelyne admitted her fears to her uncle. "Perhaps, once he was again acquainted with Lady Eleanor, he changed his mind."

"'Tis foolish talk you're giving me," Father Berton announced. "I've as much faith as you, child, that Baron Wexton didn't know Laurance wasn't a priest. He thought he'd married you, and for a man to take such a step, there'd be a true commitment in his heart. You've told me his declaration of love. Have you no faith in his word then?"

"Oh, of course I do," Madelyne returned. "He does love me, Father. I know he does, inside my heart, yet a part of my mind does try to make me worry. I awakened during the night and my first thought was a frightening one. I asked myself what I would do if he doesn't come for me. What if he did change his mind?"

"Then he be a fool," Father Berton answered. A sparkle appeared in the priest's eyes. "Now tell this old man again, child, what were your very words to Lady Eleanor with the pretty red hair and the regal bearing?"

Madelyne smiled over the way he teased her with her own

description of Lady Eleanor. "I told her I was Duncan's greatest treasure. It wasn't a very humble remark, was it?"

"You spoke the truth, Madelyne. Your heart knows it well enough, but I'm agreeing there's a wee portion of your mind that needs some convincing."

"Duncan isn't a fool," Madelyne said then. Her voice was firm with conviction. "He won't forget me." She closed her eyes and rested her head against the cushion on the back of the chair. So much had happened to her in such a short time. Now, as she sat beside her uncle, it seemed as though nothing had really changed at all.

The old fears were trying to get the better of her. She'd soon be weeping and feeling pity for herself if she didn't guard against it. Madelyne decided she needed rest. Aye, it was only because she was so exhausted that she tended to worry now. "I do have value," she blurted out. "Why has it taken me so long to know it?"

"It doesn't matter how long it took," her uncle said. "What's important is that you've finally realized it.'

The rumble of thunder drew her uncle's attention. "Sounds as though we'll be having a good rain in a few minutes," he remarked as he stood and started for the window.

"Thunder's close enough to pull the roof apart," Madelyne remarked, her voice a sleepy whisper.

Father Berton was about to agree with his niece's comment when he reached the window and looked outside. The sight he beheld so startled him, he had to brace his hands against the window's ledge, else lose his balance and surely collapse to his knees.

The thunder was silent now. But Father could see the lightning. It wasn't in the sky though. Nay, it was on the ground . . . for as far as his eyes could see.

The sun forced the pretense, deflecting the shards of silver bolts as they bounced from chest plate to chest plate.

A legion it be, united behind one warrior, all armored, all quiet, all waiting.

Father squinted against the magnificent sight. He nodded once to the soldier's leader and then turned to walk back to his chair.

A wide smile transformed the old priest's face. When he was again seated beside Madelyne, he forced his smile

329

aside, dared to affect a disgruntled sound to his voice, and said, "I believe there's someone here to see you, Madelyne. Best see who it be, child. I'm too weary to get up again."

Madelyne frowned over his request. She hadn't heard anyone knock on their door. As a measure to placate him, she stood up to do his bidding. She remarked over her shoulder that she supposed it could be Marta paying a call to give them fresh eggs and old gossip.

The priest gained such a chuckle over her comment, he actually slapped his knee.

She thought it was a strange reaction from a man who'd just protested weariness.

And then she opened the door.

It took a minute or two for Madelyne to comprehend what she was seeing. She was so astonished, she couldn't move. She simply stood there, in the center of the doorway, with her hands clenched at her sides, staring up at Duncan.

He hadn't forgotten her after all. The realization settled in Madelyne's mind once the numbness had worn through.

He wasn't alone either. Nay, over a hundred soldiers were lined up behind their lord. All were still on horseback, all were wearing their full glorious battle armor, and every one of them was looking at her.

A silent signal brushed through the legion. As one, they suddenly raised their swords in salutation. It was the most magnificent show of loyalty Madelyne had ever witnessed.

She was overwhelmed. Madelyne had never felt so cherished, so loved, and so very, very worthy.

And then she understood the reason Duncan had called up so many of his soldiers to make this journey. He was showing her how important she was to him. Aye, he was proving her value.

Duncan didn't move. He didn't say a word for a long time. He was content to stay on Silenus's back and look upon his beautiful wife. Duncan could feel his worry, his uncertainty, ebb from his heart. God's truth, he thought he was the most content man in all the world.

When he noticed the tears streaming down Madelyne's face, he finally gave her the words he thought she needed to hear. "I've come for you, Madelyne."

Was it coincidence that Duncan now repeated the very first words he'd ever spoken to her? Madelyne didn't think so. The look in Duncan's eyes made her believe he did remember.

Madelyne straightened away from the door, tossed her hair over her shoulder, and then very deliberately put her hands on her hips. "'Tis high time, Baron Wexton. I have waited the longest while for you."

She thought her arrogant remarks pleased Duncan, but she couldn't be certain. He moved too quickly for her to see his face. One minute he was seated atop Silenus, and the next he was pulling her into his arms.

When he leaned down to kiss her, Madelyne threw her arms around his neck. She clung to him as his mouth feverishly settled on hers with almost frantic possessiveness. His tongue thrusted inside to reconquer what belonged to him.

Madelyne felt as though she was being swept away by a tide of arousal rushing through her. She met Duncan's demand by giving him all she knew how to give. Aye, she was just as savage in her quest to devour him. She was just as hungry for his touch, just as frantic.

The noise finally penetrated Duncan's mind. Reason was slow to return, however. He pulled his mouth away only to immediately return to her bruised lips a second time.

Madelyne also caught the sound. When Duncan finally lifted his head away from hers, she realized the soldiers were cheering. Good Lord, she'd quite forgotten they were there.

She knew she blushed and told herself she didn't care. Duncan didn't seem the least concerned, but he was so covered with dust and grime, and a full week's worth of whiskers, it was difficult to see any reaction.

He kissed her again, a quick, hard kiss it was, that told her he wasn't the least concerned about their audience. Madelyne's arms circled his waist. She leaned the side of her face against his chest and squeezed with all her might.

He sighed, pleased with her enthusiasm.

Madelyne remembered her duty, when she heard a discreet cough sound behind her. She should introduce Duncan to her uncle. The problem, of course, was that she couldn't get the words past her throat. And when Duncan leaned down and whispered, "I love you Madelyne," she became too preoccupied with weeping to speak at all.

Duncan motioned for his men to dismount and turned to

look over Madelyne's head to the old man waiting a short distance behind her. He pulled Madelyne into his side, unwilling to let her move away from him for even a short time, and then said, "I am Baron Wexton."

"I would certainly hope so," Father Berton answered. The priest smiled over his own jest and then started to bow. He was stayed from the formal show of respect by the baron's hand.

"'Tis I who should kneel before you," he told the priest. "I'm honored to meet you at last, Father."

The priest was humbled by the baron's speech. "She is your greatest treasure, is she not, Baron?" he asked. He was looking at Madelyne now.

"Aye, she is," Duncan admitted. "I will be forever in your debt," he added. "You have protected her for me all these years."

"She isn't yours yet," Father Berton announced. He was pleased to see the surprise that remark caused. "Aye, I've still to give her to you. 'Tis a marriage I'm speaking of, a true marriage, Baron, and the sooner done the better for this old man's peace of mind."

"Then you will wed us in the morning," Duncan dictated.

Father Berton had witnessed the passionate kiss between the baron and his niece. He wasn't at all sure tomorrow would be fast enough. "You'll not be sleeping next to Madelyne tonight then," he warned. "I'll continue to guard her well, Baron Wexton."

Duncan and Father Berton exchanged a long, hard stare. Then Duncan smiled. For the first time in a very long while, he found he couldn't intimidate someone. Nay, the priest wasn't going to back down.

He nodded. "Tonight."

Madelyne witnessed the exchange. She knew full well what the two men were talking about. She thought she might have looked as red as a sunburn. It was, after all, an embarrassment for her uncle Berton to know she'd slept with the baron.

"I would also like to wed Duncan tonight, but I do not—" Madelyne paused in her explanation when she saw Anthony walk over to stand by her side. "Father, this is the vassal I told you about," she said, smiling now.

"You are the one who placed yourself between my niece

and Louddon when he tried to strike her again?" the priest asked, moving forward to grasp Anthony's hand.

"I was," Anthony admitted.

"Again?" Duncan shouted. "She wasn't in the king's protection?"

"It was nothing," Madelyne protested.

"He would have killed her," the priest interjected.

"Aye, he wanted to harm her," Anthony said.

Madelyne could feel the tension in Duncan's grip around her waist.

"It was nothing," Madelyne protested again. "A mere slap . . ."

"She carries the bruises still," Father Berton announced with a vigorous nod.

Madelyne gave her uncle a good frown. Couldn't he tell his comments were upsetting Duncan?

When Duncan tilted her face up so that he could see the marks, Madelyne shook her head again. "He'll never touch me again, Duncan. That is all that matters. Your loyal vassal did protect me," she added before turning back to look at her uncle. "Uncle, why do you incite Duncan's anger?"

"There are marks on her shoulders and back, Baron," Father Berton said, ignoring Madelyne's question.

"Uncle!"

"You did not say a word to me," Anthony said to Madelyne. "I would have—"

"Enough. Father, I know you well. What game do you play now?" Madelyne demanded.

"You were about to tell Baron Wexton you'd like to marry him tonight, child, but you didn't finish your comments, now, did you? The truth of the matter, Baron," the priest said, turning to Duncan, "is that my niece will try to delay this marriage. Won't you, Madelyne? You see, child," he added, giving Madelyne a tender smile, "I know your mind better than you think I do."

"Does he speak the truth?" Duncan asked, frowning. "You have not changed your feelings, have you?" Before Madelyne could answer, he said, "It will not matter. You belong to me, Madelyne. 'Tis a fact you cannot turn your back on."

Madelyne was so astonished that Duncan would feel such insecurity. She realized then that his feelings were just as vulnerable as her own. It seemed that he needed to hear the words of her love as often as she did. "I love you, Duncan," she said, loud enough for both Anthony and Father Berton to hear.

"I'm aware of that," Duncan returned, sounding arrogant again. His grip lessened, though, and he did relax against her.

"There is much to be seen to," Anthony commented. "I have need to speak to you in private, Baron." The vassal turned and started to walk away.

"And you must surely be in need of a meal," the priest added. He turned to walk back inside his cottage. "I shall begin preparations immediately."

"A bath is first," Duncan said, giving Madelyne a good squeeze before releasing her. He was following her uncle, when Madelyne's words stopped him cold. Anthony and Father Berton also paused.

"We cannot marry just yet, Duncan."

She could tell, from the look on all three faces, that none of them cared for her announcement.

Madelyne clasped her hands together. Her words were hurried, for she wanted to make Duncan see reason before he bellowed at her. "If only we could wait until Gerald is wed to Adela, then Louddon cannot use the argument . . ."

"I knew it," Anthony muttered. "You still try to protect the world. Baron, that is only one of the announcements I've need to explain to you."

"She always would protect those she believed needed it," the priest said.

"You don't understand," Madelyne said, rushing up to face Duncan. "If we marry now, you'll be going against your king. He'll give Adela to Louddon. That's what the missive suggested, Duncan."

Madelyne would have continued her argument but for look in Duncan's eyes. She couldn't stop wringing her hands, but she was able to close her mouth.

Duncan stared at Madelyne a long moment. She couldn't tell if he was pleased or angered with her now. "I have but one question to put to you, Madelyne. Do you have faith in me?"

She didn't need time to think about it. Her answer was quick and forceful.

"I do."

Her answer pleased him. Duncan embraced her, placed a chaste kiss on her forehead, and then turned away again. "We marry tonight."

He stopped then, but didn't turn around. Madelyne knew what he waited for. Aye, he sought her agreement.

"Yes, Duncan, we'll marry tonight."

It was, of course, the correct answer. Madelyne knew that well enough when her uncle started chuckling, Anthony started whistling, and Duncan turned to give her a firm nod.

He wasn't smiling. That didn't bother her, however, when she realized Duncan had never doubted her. Her answer was but a reaffirmation. Nothing more.

The next hour was a blur of activity. While Duncan and Anthony sat at the small table inside the cottage and ate their supper, Father Berton went to explain the situation to his host, the Earl of Grinsteade.

The earl was still hanging on to life, and though he didn't have the strength to attend the ceremony, Duncan would pay a formal visit as soon as the wedding was over.

Duncan and his vassal walked to the lake behind the earl's home to bathe and speak to each other in private. Madelyne used the time to change her gown. She brushed her hair until it curled to her satisfaction, then decided to forget fashion and leave it unbound. She knew Duncan preferred it that way.

She wore his colors again, of course. Her shoes and chainse were a pale cream in color, and partially covered by the hand-stitched royal blue bliaut. She'd worked nearly a month on the yoke circling the neckline of the bliaut, making minute stitches, all the color of cream, of the design she wished to effect. In the center of her artwork was the outline of her magical wolf.

Duncan probably wouldn't even notice, she thought. Warriors of his stature didn't take time to note such things. "It's just as well," she admitted out loud. "He'd think me fanciful again and surely tease me."

"Who will tease you?" Duncan asked, standing in the doorway.

Madelyne turned, a smile on her face, and looked at her warrior. "My wolf," she immediately answered. "Is something amiss, Duncan. You look . . . unsettled."

"You grow more beautiful with each passing hour," Duncan whispered. His voice felt like a caress.

"And you more handsome," Madelyne said. She smiled at Duncan, then dared to tease him. "I'm wondering why my intended would wear black attire to his wedding though. Such a grim color," Madelyne announced. "And one used for mourning. Could you be mourning your fate, milord?"

Duncan was taken aback by her comments. He shrugged before answering. "It is clean, Madelyne. That is all that should matter to you. Besides, it is the only other clothing I carried with me from London." He started toward her, his intent obvious in his dark gaze. "I'm going to kiss you senseless enough not to notice my attire."

Madelyne ran to the other side of the table. "You cannot kiss me until we are wed," she said, trying not to laugh. "And why didn't you shave?"

Duncan continued to stalk his quest. "After."

Now, what did he mean by that? Madelyne paused to frown. "After?"

"Aye, Madelyne, after," Duncan answered. His hot stare confused her almost as much as his odd remark.

She deliberately hesitated long enough to be captured. Duncan pulled her into his arms. He was about to take her mouth, when the door opened. A loud cough gained his attention.

"We're waiting to begin," Father Berton announced. "There is one worry, however."

"What is that?" Madelyne asked once she'd wiggled out of Duncan's arms and righted her appearance.

"I would like to walk by your side, but I can't be in two places at the same time. And who be the witnesses to this act?" he added, frowning.

"Can you not walk with Madelyne to the altar and then proceed with the mass?" Duncan asked.

"And when, as priest I ask who gives this woman in holy matrimony, I should then run to Madelyne's side to answer my own question?"

Duncan grinned, picturing the scene.

"It will be an oddity, but I could manage," Father Berton announced.

"My soldiers will all bear witness," Duncan said. "Anthony will stand behind Madelyne. Is that good enough for you, Father?"

"So be it," Father Berton decreed. "Go now, Baron, wait by the makeshift altar I have fashioned outside. You'll be wed under the stars and the moon. 'Tis God's true palace to my way of judging."

"All right then, let's get this over and done with."

Madelyne took exception to his choice of words. She chased after Duncan, claiming his hand to get his attention. "Over and done with?" she asked, frowning.

When he looked down at her, Madelyne decided he'd been teasing her. And then he spoke, and her frown disappeared altogether. "We have been bound to each other since the moment we met, Madelyne. God knew it, I knew it, and if you'll only reflect upon the truth, you'll admit it too. We've pledged ourselves to each other, and though Laurance was not a priest and couldn't give us his true blessing, we are still wed."

"From the moment I warmed your feet," Madelyne whispered, repeating his past explanation.

"Aye, from that moment."

She looked as if she were going to weep. What an emotional woman his gentle wife had turned out to be. While her reaction pleased him, he knew she wouldn't wish to appear so undisciplined in front of his men. He immediately sought to repair her control. "You should be thankful, you know."

"Thankful for what, Duncan?" Madelyne asked, dabbing at the corners of her eyes.

"That it wasn't summer when we met."

She didn't understand at first. And then she laughed, a full, lusty sound that warmed his heart. "So it's the weather that gave you to me, is that your way of thinking?"

"You wouldn't have had to warm my feet if it had been summer," he said. He gave Madelyne a quick wink.

She thought he looked most arrogant. "You would have found another reason," she said.

Duncan would have responded to that comment if Father Berton hadn't started pushing him toward the door. "The men are waiting on you, Baron."

As soon as Duncan left, Father Berton turned to

Madelyne. He spent several minutes advising her on her duties as wife. When that task was done, he spoke from his heart, telling her how very proud he was to claim her for his family.

And then he offered his arm to the woman he'd baptized, seen raised, and loved as a daughter.

It was a beautiful ceremony, and when it was finished, Duncan presented his wife to his vassals. The men knelt before Madelyne and gave her their vow of loyalty.

Duncan was exhausted and impatient. He left his wife to pay an official call on the Earl of Grinstead, and returned to Father Berton's cottage less than twenty minutes later.

The priest had already gone to sleep. His pallet was across the room. Madelyne's bed was on the opposite wall, with only a curtain to protect her privacy.

Duncan found his wife sitting on the edge of the narrow bed. She was wearing the gown she'd been married in.

After he'd removed his clothing, he stretched out on top of the covers, drawing Madelyne down upon his chest. He kissed her soundly and then suggested she get ready for bed.

Madelyne took her time with the task. She kept pausing to peek around the curtain to see if her uncle was sleeping. Then she finally leaned down to tell Duncan that she really thought they should find a private place outside to sleep together. After all, it was their wedding night, and it had been a long time since they'd touched each other. Surely he could see the way of it, couldn't he, for once she started kissing him, she knew she'd be frightfully wild about it. God's truth, she knew she'd be loud. Why, she was ready to scream now.

Duncan didn't even try to hush her. She realized then that she really needn't have bothered with her explanation. Her husband was sound asleep.

The frustrated bride snuggled up against her husband, gritted her teeth together, and tried to fall asleep.

The sounds of Father Berton moving around the room awakened Duncan. He was instantly alert, feeling something was amiss and not immediately understanding what it was.

He started to stand up, his mind clearing now, only to realize he almost stepped on Madelyne. Duncan smiled over the absurdity of it. His wife was sleeping on the floor, a thick blanket her only covering.

Lord, he'd fallen asleep on their wedding night.

Duncan sat on the side of the bed, staring down at his lovely wife, until he heard the door open and then close behind the priest. He glanced out the window on the other side of the bed in time to see Father Berton walk toward the castle doors. The priest was wearing his church vestments and carrying a small silver chalice.

Duncan turned back to Madelyne. He knelt beside her and lifted her into his arms. Then he placed her on the bed. Madelyne immediately rolled onto her back, kicking the cover aside.

She wasn't wearing her sleeping gown. Dawn's light, streaming through the window, dappled her skin a golden hue. Madelyne's glorious hair was transformed by the rising sun into the color of fire.

Duncan's desire intensified until he was aching with need. He sat down on the side of the bed and began to make love to his wife.

Madelyne awakened with a sigh. She felt wonderfully lethargic. Duncan's hands were caressing her breasts. Her nipples strained for more. Madelyne moaned and moved her hips restlessly in sleepy invitation to her husband.

She opened her eyes and looked up at Duncan. His hot gaze made her shiver with desire. She reached up to him, trying to draw him down upon her, but Duncan shook his head, denying her.

"I'll give you what you want," he whispered to her. "And much, much more," he promised.

Before Madelyne could answer him, Duncan leaned down and took one breast into his mouth. He sucked the nipple while his hands stroked the flat of her stomach.

Madelyne's moans became wilder, louder. The sounds she made in the back of her throat pleased him, though not nearly as much as the taste of her.

His hand moved between her legs. He found the treasure he sought, thrust his finger inside, and was nearly driven beyond reason by her hot, wild response.

He wanted it all.

Duncan abruptly rolled to his side. Madelyne turned to

her husband. The side of her face rested on Duncan's warm thigh.

His mouth was driving her wild. She couldn't seem to draw a breath, her stomach indrawn as her husband placed wet kisses around her navel. His fingers continued his sweet torture. Madelyne whimpered when Duncan gently nudged her thighs apart. She knew what he wanted to do and opened herself to him, begging him to kiss her there.

Duncan moved lower, until he was tasting the heat of her. His tongue teased, tormented. And his beard drove her mad. His whiskers were excitingly abrasive against the sensitive skin of her inner thighs.

She wanted to taste him. All of him.

There was no warning of her intent, no tender kisses leading up to her quest. Madelyne arched her hips against Duncan as she captured him and took him into her mouth.

She was given her moans then. Her hands and mouth were just as pleasing, just as erotic as Duncan's. Aye, he told of his pleasure by moving forcefully against her.

And then he was suddenly pulling away from her. He turned, settled himself between her thighs, and penetrated her. His seed immediately spilled forth, his climax seemingly unending. The force of his surrender gave Madelyne her own release to the same splendor.

She was too weak to move, couldn't even summon the strength to let go of her husband's shoulders.

He was content. He thought to kiss his wife, to tell her how very satisfied he was, but he couldn't seem to make the effort. Aye, he was too content to move.

They stayed as one for long, pleasing minutes.

Madelyne recovered her wits before her husband did. She suddenly remembered where they were. When she tensed against Duncan, he guessed her thoughts. "Father Berton has gone to say mass," he whispered.

Madelyne relaxed against him. "Of course, you were loud enough for my army to hear," he added.

"You were just as loud," Madelyne whispered back.

"Now I'll shave," Duncan told her.

Madelyne started to laugh. "I understand what you meant by telling me you'd shave after, Duncan. You knew your beard would drive me mad."

Duncan braced himself on his elbows and looked down into Madelyne's eyes. "Do you know how much you please me, wife?"

"I do," she whispered. "I love you, Duncan, now and forever."

"Did you love me when you realized Laurance wasn't a true priest and I lied to you?"

"Aye, though I did want to throttle you for not telling me. Lord, I was angry."

"Good," Duncan remarked, smiling over the startle that comment caused. "I worried you would have thought I'd lied to you about other things," he admitted.

"I've never doubted your love, Duncan," Madelyne said.

"But you doubted your worth," he reminded her.

"No longer," she whispered. She drew him down to kiss him and then demanded that he make love to her once again.

It was a much more leisurely union the second time, but just as satisfying.

Father Berton returned to his home to find both Madelyne and Duncan dressed. The baron sat at the table, his gaze never leaving his wife's figure as she went about the task of preparing their breakfast.

"I've need for a priest, Father," Duncan said. "Would you like the duty of looking after my soul? I could request your attendance immediately."

Madelyne was so pleased with Duncan's suggestion, she clapped her hands together.

Father Berton smiled, then denied the request with a shake of his head. "The earl has taken me in all these years, Duncan. I cannot abandon him now. He depends upon my council. Nay, I can't leave him."

Madelyne knew her uncle was doing the honorable thing. She nodded. "I would suggest that you come to us after the earl is put to rest, but God's truth, I do think he's going to outlive us all."

"Madelyne! Do not speak so unkindly of the earl," Father Berton admonished.

Madelyne immediately looked contrite. "I didn't mean to be unkind, Uncle. And I am ashamed, for I understand your duty to the earl."

Duncan nodded. "Then we will come to visit you, and when you are finished with this duty, you will come to live with us."

He was much more diplomatic than she was. Madelyne saw how her uncle smiled and nodded his agreement. "How long will we be staying here?" she asked her husband then.

"We must leave today," Duncan announced.

"We could stay here until the summer's end," she suggested before she could stop herself.

"We leave today."

Madelyne sighed. Duncan was trying to stare her down, she realized. "Then today it is," she said.

Father left the cottage then, pretending an errand to fetch bread from the cook. As soon as the door closed behind him, Madelyne walked over to her husband. "You must allow me to have an opinion, husband. I'll not always bow to your dictates."

Duncan grinned. "I know that well enough, Madelyne. You are my wife and will rule by my side. But your argument to stay here is most—"

"Unreasonable," Madelyne interjected with a sigh. She sat down on Duncan's lap and put her arms around his neck. "I'm putting off the inevitable. You might as well know the full truth about your wife, Duncan. I am a bit of a coward on occasion."

Duncan thought his wife's confession was quite amusing. He laughed, uncaring that Madelyne wasn't looking too pleased with his conduct. When he gained control, he said to her, "You have more courage inside you than all my men put together. Who dared death to release her brother's enemy?"

"Well, I did, but—"

"Who stood behind Gilard's back and saved him?"

"I did, Duncan, but I was so frightened and I—"

"Who took on the task of caring for my sister? Who conquered Silenus for her lamb? Who—"

"You know it was me," Madelyne said. She put her hands on Duncan's cheeks and then said, "But you've still to understand. Each time I did any of those tasks you believe are honorable, I was so afraid inside. Why, I was terrified just standing up to you."

Duncan pushed Madelyne's hands away and drew her

down for a long kiss. "Fear doesn't mean you're a coward, love. Nay, in my mind it means you are mortal. Only a fool puts caution aside."

When he finished his speech, he had to kiss her again.

"You'll have to tell me what to do when we return to court, Duncan," Madelyne said next. "I don't want to displease you or say the wrong thing in answer to the king's questions. He'll question me, won't he, Duncan?"

He caught the fear in her voice, shook his head over it. "Madelyne, nothing you do will ever displease me. And you've only to tell the truth to the king's questions. That is all I would ever ask of you."

"'Tis what Louddon said to me," Madelyne muttered. "He thinks my truths will trap you."

"This is my battle, Madelyne. Tell the truth and leave the rest to me."

Madelyne sighed. She knew he was right.

Duncan tried to lighten her mood. "I must shave before we leave for court," he announced.

Madelyne started to blush. "I would prefer that you never shave again. I have come to . . . appreciate your beard, milord."

Duncan fully appreciated his wife's honesty. His forceful kiss told her so.

Duncan and Madelyne arrived in London two days later. Gilard, Edmond, and Gerald met them at the gates. They all wore grim expressions.

After giving Madelyne a welcoming embrace, Edmond told Duncan the other barons had already settled in their chambers.

Gilard next embraced Madelyne. He took his time with the greeting, and when he turned to speak to Duncan, his arm was still circling Madelyne's waist. "Do you go to the king tonight?"

Duncan decided Gilard wasn't quite over his infatuation with Madelyne. He pulled his wife into his side before he answered his brother. "I go now."

"Louddon thinks Madelyne is with her uncle. He's probably hearing of her return right this minute, Duncan. I must remind you that Louddon knows you're not married," Gerald interjected.

"We are married now," Duncan said. "Father Berton officiated, with my vassals as witnesses to the act, Gerald."

Gerald couldn't help but smile over that news.

"The king's going to be angry," Edmond predicted with a scowl. "Marrying before this matter is righted will be taken as a personal insult."

Duncan was about to respond to Edmond's comments, when his attention was drawn to the king's soldiers. Led by William's brother, Henry, the men marched in union to stand directly in front of Duncan.

Henry motioned to the soldiers to wait and then said to Duncan, "My brother sends his guard to escort Lady Madelyne to her chambers."

"I'm going to William now to give him my accounting, Henry. I'm uneasy letting Madelyne go anywhere without me. She was mistreated when last under our king's protection," he added, his voice grim.

Henry didn't show any reaction to Duncan's harsh voice. "'Tis doubtful the king even knew she was here, Duncan. Louddon . . ."

"I'll not have her placed in jeopardy again, Henry," Duncan argued.

"Then you wish this dear lady to be placed in the middle of your tug-of-war with her brother?" Henry inquired.

Before Duncan could answer, Henry said, "Come, walk with me. There is something I wish to say to you."

Out of deference to his position, Duncan immediately obeyed the order. He walked by Henry's side to a secluded area of the courtyard.

Henry did most of the talking. Madelyne had no idea what he was saying, but she could tell from the look on her husband's face that Duncan wasn't too pleased with the conversation.

As soon as Duncan and Henry returned to the waiting group, Duncan turned to his wife. "Madelyne, go with Henry. He'll see you settled."

"In your chambers, Duncan?" Madelyne asked, trying not to sound worried.

Henry answered her question. "You'll have your own rooms, my dear, under my guard. Until this matter is settled, neither Louddon nor Duncan will be allowed near you. 'Tis a fact that my brother has a fierce temper. Let us not fire the timber just yet. Tonight will be soon enough."

Madelyne looked at Duncan. When she received his nod, she bowed to Henry. Duncan took her aside then, leaned down, and whispered into her ear.

Everyone became highly curious over this conversation, for when Madelyne turned back to Henry, she was looking quite radiant.

Gilard watched Madelyne take Henry's arm and walk toward the entrance. "What did you say to her, Duncan? One minute our Madelyne was looking ready to weep and the next she was smiling and looking most content."

"I merely reminded her of an ending to a certain story," Duncan said with a shrug.

It was all he was going to say on the matter. Edmond suggested he go refresh his appearance and even sleep for a few hours.

Though Duncan thought it ludicrous for Edmond to suggest sleep, he did follow his advice about changing his tunic.

"I believe I'll follow Madelyne," Edmond commented then. "Perhaps I'll find Anthony standing outside her door and stay with him until this evening."

Duncan nodded. "Don't let Henry think you doubt his guard," he warned.

With those parting words Duncan walked away.

Gilard turned to Baron Gerald then. "We've averted a battle. Duncan would have charged into the king's chambers and demanded immediate justice."

"A temporary condition," Gerald answered. "The battle is still to come. The other barons will call on Duncan this afternoon. He'll be kept busy enough. Henry interceded and deserves his due for it. One day Duncan will thank him."

"Why would Henry be concerned over this matter?" Gilard asked.

"He wants Duncan's loyalty," Gerald answered. "Come, Gilard, find me a cool drink and toast my coming marriage to your sister."

Gilard looked pleased. "She has agreed then?"

"She has. I'm going to marry her before she changes her mind."

Gilard laughed over Gerald's announcement. Gerald smiled. He was pleased because he'd successfully turned Gilard's attention away from Henry's motives. Gerald didn't feel Gilard needed to be privy to the secret meeting he'd attended, nor Henry's odd questions about Duncan's loyalty. His reasons were easy enough to understand. Gilard might ask questions of the wrong barons, inadvertently causing trouble that wasn't needed now. Aye, the Wexton brothers had enough problems to solve.

"After we've toasted your marriage, I believe I'll go and stand with Edmond."

"It's going to be crowded in the corridor outside Madelyne's rooms," Gerald commented. "I wonder what Louddon will do, Gilard, when he learns his sister is back."

The baron under question had gone hunting in the king's forest. Louddon didn't return to the castle grounds until late that afternoon. He was immediately informed of Madelyne's return.

Louddon was, of course, furious. He went to claim his sister.

Anthony stood alone outside Madelyne's door now. Both Edmond and Gilard had gone to change for the coming dinner and confrontation.

When the vassal saw Louddon approaching, he lounged against the wall and gave Madelyne's brother a look of disgust.

Louddon ignored the vassal. He pounded on the door, shouting for entrance.

Henry opened the door. He greeted Louddon politely and then announced that no one was allowed to speak to Madelyne.

Before Louddon could argue, the door slammed shut in his face.

Madelyne watched the scene with bewilderment. She didn't know what to think of Henry's behavior. The king's brother hadn't left her side for more than a few minutes when she'd gone into the sleeping chamber to change her dress for her meeting with the king.

"Your brother's face is as red as my brother's," Henry announced after closing the door against Louddon. He walked over, took hold of Madelyne's hand, and led her over to the window, a considerable distance from the door.

"The walls have ears," he whispered. His voice, Madelyne noticed, was very kind.

She decided then and there to discard the rumors about Henry. He wasn't a very handsome man, small in size when compared to Duncan. It was said that Henry was greedy for power, a manipulator as well. He was known to have a lusty appetite, too, having fathered over fifteen bastard children. Because he was being so kind to her, Madelyne decided she wasn't going to judge him.

"I thank you again for aiding my husband this day," Madelyne said when Henry continued to look at her so expectantly.

"Something has been prickling my curiosity all afternoon," Henry confessed. "If it not be a private matter, I would like you to tell me what Duncan said to you before you left him. You seemed very pleased."

"He told me to remember that Odysseus is home."

When she didn't continue the explanation, Henry commanded her to give him the full story.

It sounded like an arrogant demand, yet Madelyne wasn't bothered by it. "I told my husband a story about a warrior named Odysseus. He was away from his wife a long time, and when he finally returned, he found his home infested with evil men who were trying to harm his wife and rob him of his treasury. Odysseus sent his wife the message that he was home. He cleaned his house of these terrible infidels too. Duncan is reminding me that he'll take care of Louddon."

"Your husband and I are alike in character then," Henry announced. "Aye, the time for cleaning this house has arrived."

Madelyne didn't understand. "I worry Duncan will do something to anger our king," she whispered. "You have said how fierce the king's temper is."

"I've another matter to take up with you," Henry suddenly said. His voice had gone hard.

Madelyne tried not to look startled. "Are you my husband's friend as well as his ally?" she asked.

Henry nodded. "Then I will do anything I can to help you," Madelyne said.

"You're as loyal as Duncan," Henry remarked. He seemed pleased with his observation. "If I intercede on your behalf with the king, will you do whatever is decided. Even if it means your exile?"

Madelyne didn't know how to answer. "You could be saving your husband's life," Henry said.

"I will do whatever is necessary."

"You'll have to trust me as much as you trust your husband," Henry warned.

Madelyne nodded. "My husband believes you're the most clever of the three—" She gasped when she realized what she'd just said.

Henry laughed. "So he knows my value, does he?"

Madelyne blushed. "He does," she said. "I'll do anything to keep my husband safe. If it means my own death, so be it."

"So you think to sacrifice yourself?" Henry asked. His voice was kind now. He smiled, too, confusing Madelyne. "I don't imagine Duncan will go along with your plan."

"This matter is most complicated," Madelyne whispered.

"You've told me you trust me. I will aid your cause, my dear."

Madelyne nodded. She started to curtsy and then decided to kneel. "I thank you for your help."

"Stand, Madelyne. I am not your king."

"I wish that you were," Madelyne confessed. Her head was bowed but she let Henry help her to her feet.

Henry didn't respond to her traitorous remark. He walked over to the door. Before he opened it, he turned back to Madelyne. "Wishes do come true, Madelyne."

Madelyne frowned over Henry's odd comment. "Show loyalty to neither side when we walk into the hall, Madelyne. Let everyone speculate until you're called to speak. I'll stay by your side."

With those words Henry left.

Two hours passed before the king's brother came back to fetch her. She walked next to him, her hands down at her sides, her back stiff. She prayed she gave a serene appearance. And she thought she'd die if she didn't see Duncan soon. She needed to know he was near.

When she and Henry walked into the main hall, she realized they were late. Most of the guests had already eaten and servants were clearing the tables.

She could feel everyone staring at her. Madelyne met

their curious gazes with a tranquil expression. It was the most difficult pretense, and all because she'd slowly looked around the room and couldn't find Duncan in the crowd.

Her husband stood against the far wall. Gilard and Edmond stood by his side. Duncan watched his wife walk into the hall. She looked composed, and very, very beautiful. She was wearing the gown she'd been married in. The memory of that blessed event saved Duncan from charging after her.

"She holds herself like a queen," Gilard whispered.

"She isn't awkward now," Edmond lamented.

"She's terrified."

Duncan made that announcement as he started forward. Gilard and Edmond immediately blocked his path. "She'll come to you, Duncan. Give Henry time."

Louddon was speaking to Madelyne now. Henry had turned to speak with an old acquaintance.

"I'll thrust my blade into your back if you take one step toward Baron Wexton," Louddon threatened. "And give the order to kill your precious priest as well."

"Tell me this," she asked, surprising her brother with the anger in her voice. "Will you also kill Duncan and his brothers, and all his allies too?"

Louddon couldn't restrain himself. He grabbed hold of Madelyne's arm. "Don't test me, Madelyne. I've more power than any other man in England."

"More power than our king?" said Henry.

Louddon jumped visibly. He turned to confront Henry, twisting Madelyne's arm in the process. "I'm your brother's humble advisor, nothing more, nothing less."

Henry showed his displeasure over Louddon's remark. He took hold of Madelyne's hand, knocking Louddon's own away. Henry then stared at the red marks on Madelyne's arm a long, silent minute. When he looked back at Louddon, his eyes seemed to mirror his disgust. "I'm going to introduce your sister to a few of our loyal friends."

His voice was hard, challenging. Louddon backed away. He gave his sister another threatening glare and then nodded to Henry.

"What did he say to you?" Henry demanded.

"He promises to kill my uncle Berton if I take one step toward Duncan."

"He bluffs, Madelyne. He can't do anything now, not in front of his peers. And tomorrow it will be too late. You'll have to trust me to know what I'm talking about."

Clarissa had obviously seen Louddon dismissed by Henry. She strolled over to greet Madelyne.

"I was going to show Madelyne my brother's impressive gardens," Henry told her.

"Oh, I'd love to see the garden as well," Clarissa announced.

Her plan to stay by Madelyne's side was easily seen through. Henry immediately foiled her. "Another time, perhaps?" he said.

Clarissa wasn't able to hide the hatred from her gaze. She turned without saying another word and walked away.

Madelyne walked by Henry's side toward the doors leading onto the terrace. "Who is that man speaking to Edmond?" she asked then. "The one with the bright hair. He has the most unsettled look on his face."

Henry quickly located the man. "He is Baron Rhinehold."

"Is he married? Does he have a family?" Madelyne asked, trying not to sound too curious.

"He never took a wife," Henry said. "Why do you take this interest in Rhinehold?"

"He knew my mother," Madelyne answered. She continued to look at Baron Rhinehold, waiting for him to glance her way. When he finally looked at her, Madelyne gave him a smile.

Though she knew it wasn't possible, she wished she could spend a few minutes alone with the baron. According to Clarissa, Rhinehold was Madelyne's father, and the reason Rachael's husband hated her.

Madelyne was a bastard. The truth didn't shame her. No one would ever know the truth, except Duncan, of course, and . . . dear God, she'd forgotten to tell him.

"Does Duncan call Baron Rhinehold his friend?" Madelyne asked Henry.

"He does," Henry answered. "Why do you ask?"

Madelyne didn't know how to answer him, and so she sought to change the topic. "I wish I could speak to Duncan for just a moment. I've just remembered something I have need to share with him."

"Luck is on your side, Madelyne. Did you not just see Louddon leave with his friends? He's no doubt going to try one last time to sway our king before the meeting is called. Wait on the terrace and I'll send Duncan to you."

She wasn't kept waiting long.

"Madelyne, it will be over soon," Duncan said as way of greeting. He took her into his arms and kissed her tenderly. "Soon, love, I promise you. Have faith in me, my sweet—"

"Have faith in me, Duncan," Madelyne whispered. "You do, don't you, husband?"

"I do," Duncan answered. "Come, stand by my side when we speak to the king. He should arrive at any moment."

Madelyne shook her head. "Louddon believes I'll trap you. Henry wants my brother to continue to feel confident until the last moment. For that reason I cannot stand by you. Don't frown so, Duncan. It will be over soon enough. And I've the most wonderful news to give you. Why, I've known the truth for several days but there's been so much going on I quite forgot to tell you when I first—"

"Madelyne."

She realized she was rambling then. "I am illegitimate. What think you of that news, husband?"

Duncan did look surprised. "I'm a bastard, Duncan. Doesn't that please you? God's truth, I am pleased, because it means I'm not related to Louddon at all."

"Who has called you bastard?" Duncan demanded. His voice was soft, yet filled with rage.

"No one. I heard Louddon talking to Clarissa. I always wondered why Louddon and his father had turned against my mother. Now I know the truth. She was carrying a child when she married. She was carrying me." Duncan stared at Madelyne. She thought he might be worried. "Will it matter to you that I'm a bastard?"

"Stop that talk," Duncan told her. He shook his head. But he was smiling and Madelyne's heart was warmed with love. "Wife, you're the only woman in this world who would welcome such news." He tried, yet couldn't contain his laughter.

"Louddon won't tell anyone," Madelyne whispered. "He has freed me and doesn't even know it. Will it matter to you?"

"How can you ask such a question?"

"Because I love you," Madelyne said with a mock sigh. "It doesn't matter if you're upset or not. You have to love me forever, husband. You gave me your word."

"Aye, Madelyne," Duncan answered. "Forever."

The trumpets sounded behind them just as Duncan leaned down to kiss his wife again. "Do you know who is your father perchance?" he asked when he saw the fear return to Madelyne's eyes.

"Rhinehold," Madelyne announced, nodding vigorously when Duncan smiled at her. "You are pleased," she said. "I can see that you are."

"Very pleased," Duncan whispered. "He is a good man."

Henry made the interruption from behind Duncan's back. "It's time," he called out. "Madelyne, come with me now. The king waits."

Duncan could feel Madelyne tremble. He gave her a squeeze before releasing her. When she started to walk away, his mind worked to find something, anything, to ease her worry.

Madelyne had just reached the doorway when Duncan called out to her. "Rhinehold has red hair, wife. As red as fire."

She didn't turn around. "'Tis more brown than red, Duncan. Surely you can see that."

And then her laughter reached him and he knew she was going to be all right.

Chapter Twenty-three

"... The just is blessed, but the name of the wicked shall rot."

OLD TESTAMENT, PROVERBS, 10:7

Silence descended upon the gathering as William II made his way to his chair positioned atop a platform. When the king sat down, everyone lowered their heads.

The laughter was gone from Madelyne's eyes now. She stood alone in the center of the room. Henry had left her unattended and was now speaking to his brother.

Whatever Henry was saying to the king didn't seem to sit well. She watched as King William suddenly shook his head and waved his hand in front of his brother's face. It was an obvious dismissal.

Madelyne closed her eyes and prayed for courage. Henry had told her that Louddon would present his side of the debate first, Duncan second, and she last of all.

She opened her eyes and found Duncan across the room. He stared at her as he slowly made his way over to her side. Neither said a word, but each looked at the other for a long time. Madelyne felt as though Duncan were giving her some of his strength. She rose up on tiptoe and kissed her husband, in plain sight of anyone who might be watching.

Oh, Lord, how she loved him. Duncan looked so confident, so unconcerned. He even winked at her when the soldier shouted his name.

"Stay here until you're called," Duncan said. He brushed his hand against her cheek before he turned and went to his king.

Madelyne didn't want to obey him. She started to follow, and hadn't gotten very far when she suddenly found herself completely surrounded on all sides by Edmond, Gilard, Gerald, and a number of barons she didn't even know. They made a complete circle around her.

The crowd parted as Duncan and Louddon made their way to stand before their leader. The two men faced each other a good thirty feet apart.

The king spoke, addressing the crowd. He told of his displeasure over these two warring barons, the pity and anger he felt because of slain soldiers, his frustration over hearing so many different accountings of what had truly taken place. The king ended his tirade by demanding the truth. He then nodded to each baron and motioned for Louddon to begin.

Louddon immediately protested innocence of any wrongdoing. He accused Duncan of treachery, stating that the baron had destroyed his fortress, killed as many as two hundred good, loyal men, taken his sister captive, and nearly destroyed her.

Louddon then took the defense, stating that Duncan blamed him for something another man had done to his sister, Adela. He spun a web of lies around the king, reeking with sincerity as he claimed he hadn't even known Baron Wexton was going to challenge him. How could he? He was in court when Duncan and his soldiers attacked his fortress and had witnesses ready to testify to that fact.

Louddon ended his persuasive argument by insisting that Duncan had no evidence of any wrongdoing, while he had plenty of evidence regarding Duncan's foul deeds.

He was as slick as an eel and lied like a whore to his king. He turned cunning next. Louddon explained he understood the king's difficulty in knowing which one to believe and therefore called forth three men to give testimony on his behalf.

When the king nodded, each man Louddon called knelt before their leader and told their lies. Madelyne didn't recognize any of the faces, but she knew their names well. They all shared the same. Aye, each one was Judas.

The last witness finished his obviously rehearsed story and moved to stand behind Louddon. Madelyne grabbed hold of the back of Edmond's tunic and was twisting the edge. Edmond turned, pulled his garment free, and then took hold of Madelyne's hand. Gilard grabbed hold of her other hand.

They offered her their comfort. Neither brother had expected the king to allow witnesses. Both were furious, and worried too. And both tried to hide their feelings from Madelyne.

Louddon stepped forward again. He bowed, added a few more of his obscene truths, and finished his version by dramatically pleading for true justice.

It was Baron Wexton's turn to speak. The king was obviously on good terms with his vassal, for he called him Duncan when he commanded him to tell his version.

Duncan was a man of few words. He quickly stated the facts. He didn't call any witnesses but explained that Louddon had abused Adela, tried to kill him, and he had retaliated in kind. It was evident to everyone in the hall that Duncan wasn't pleading for justice. He was demanding it.

"You have witnesses to bring forth to verify your accounting?" the king asked.

"I have given you the truth," Duncan answered. His voice was hard, controlled. "I need no witnesses to verify my honesty."

"You have each charged the other with ill conduct. There are still questions to be settled in my mind."

"He is caught in the middle," Gilard whispered to Edmond.

Edmond nodded. Each man did contradict the other. Edmond thought the king wanted to rule in Duncan's favor. Yet Louddon had balanced the scale in his favor by bringing witnesses to lie on his behalf. Duncan was a loyal vassal, a warrior as well, who could become a threat if he felt his king had betrayed him.

It was an insult to ask Duncan to have others testify on his behalf. He had told the truth. The king would either believe him or not.

Edmond let out a ragged sigh. Duncan wouldn't play the game now. He was stubborn in his belief that he'd acted honorably in the past and that the king would believe him now.

Yet Louddon had also made a valid point in his maze of lies. Duncan had married Madelyne without gaining permission. That was an insignificant breach, but destroying another baron's fortress and killing over two hundred soldiers was a more serious charge.

Duncan had stated that Louddon had tried to trap him twice, but those charges couldn't be proven. Gilard could testify to one battle, true, yet he couldn't state for fact that Louddon had been behind the attack.

Gerald could also testify against Louddon when the second trap was set, but Morcar could be blamed. Louddon hadn't been there either.

Edmond cleared his mind when Madelyne's name was called. He turned to look at her.

Madelyne straightened her shoulders, composed her expression, and slowly walked toward the king. She stopped when she reached the platform and then knelt down with her head bowed.

"Your brother has convinced me that you have been through too much pain to give me your accounting now," the king announced. "I therefore release you from this duty."

Madelyne took to her feet and stared in astonishment at the king. She understood now why Louddon was looking so confident all evening. He'd already made certain that she wouldn't be allowed to speak.

"I am one of your loyal subjects," Madelyne announced. She could tell she had the king's full attention, for his eyes did seem to widen. "Though I do not have an army of vassals to give you aid, I would do anything within my power to serve you. I would like to answer your questions."

The king immediately nodded. "You do not seem distraught, as your brother has indicated," he announced. He leaned forward and said in a lowered voice, "Would you prefer that I empty the hall before you tell me all that has happened to you?"

Madelyne was surprised by the gentle tone the king used with her. "I do not prefer it," she whispered.

"Then tell me what you can about this puzzle."

Madelyne obeyed. She folded her hands in front of her, took a calming breath, and then began her recounting.

It was quiet enough to hear a mouse nibble on cheese. "I would begin with the night of the attack on my brother's fortress if you wish," she said.

"That would be good enough," the king said. "I know it will be difficult for you, gentle lady, but I would have more light shed on this problem."

Madelyne wished the king weren't being so kind to her. It made her task all the more difficult. "My husband says you are an honorable man," she whispered.

William leaned forward in his chair again. He was the only one who heard what she said. "I am many things to many people," he boasted. He kept his voice as low as Madelyne's, wishing only to share his comments with her. "I believe I am honorable to everyone, even gentle ladies who have no armies to help my cause."

Madelyne gifted the king with a smile.

"Now, begin your tale," the king commanded, his tone loud enough for all to hear.

"I was on my way up to my chambers when one of my brother's soldiers announced to Louddon that Baron Wexton wished to speak with him."

"Louddon was there?" the king asked.

"He was," Madelyne said. "I heard him tell the soldier to let Duncan inside the gates under the sign of truce. It was a trap, of course, for as soon as Duncan rode inside the fortress, he was taken captive. My brother told his vassal he was going to kill Duncan. He thought himself very clever, you see, because he'd come up with a plan to kill the baron by freezing him to death."

Louddon let out a gasp. He started toward Madelyne, but stopped when he noticed Duncan reach for his sword. "She doesn't know what she's talking about," Louddon stammered out. "Madelyne is too distraught to know what she's saying. Release her from this ordeal!"

The king waved his hand for silence. Louddon took a deep breath. He calmed himself when he realized that the rest of Madelyne's story would be in his favor.

"There will be no more interruptions," the king shouted. He turned back to Madelyne, gave her a curt nod. "Continue, if you please, by explaining this clever plan to freeze my baron to death. I do not understand."

"Louddon didn't want to use a weapon on the baron. Once he'd died from the freezing temperature, the men would take his body to a remote area and leave it there until someone found him or until wild animals got to him. They stripped him of his clothes and tied him to a post in the courtyard."

Madelyne paused to take another deep breath. "Louddon left for London. He left some of his men to guard Duncan, but they couldn't take the cold, and finally went inside. As soon as they left, I untied Duncan."

"And did his soldiers attack the fortress then?"

"They gained entrance by climbing over the walls. Their duty was to protect their lord," Madelyne said.

"I see."

Madelyne didn't know what that meant. She glanced over to look at Louddon, saw him smirk, and then looked over at Duncan. Her husband nodded encouragement to her.

"They came inside, you say?" the king asked after a long minute.

"A fight began," Madelyne said.

"And then you were taken captive?"

"In truth, I was given freedom from my brother's mistreatment. He did like to hurt me, and as God is my witness, I tired of his abuse."

A surprised murmur rolled through the crowd. "Baron Wexton took me with him. I was afraid of Louddon and I confess again to you that for the first time in my life, I really felt safe. Duncan is an honorable man. He treated me well. I never feared he would hurt me. Never."

The king glared at Louddon a long minute and then turned back to Madelyne. "Who burned his home to the ground? Or was it burned at all?"

His voice had risen in volume.

"Duncan destroyed my fortress," Louddon shouted.

"Silence," the king roared. "Your sister is giving her

accounting and she's the only one I wish to hear. Answer this question," he added to Madelyne.

"Louddon destroyed his own home when he dishonored the sign of truce," Madelyne announced.

The king sighed. He looked weary now. "Then I can assume your virtue wasn't taken from you?"

Madelyne all but shouted her answer. "He didn't touch me."

Another low murmur escaped the crowd. Everyone was quite spellbound by the strange tale unfolding.

Until that moment Madelyne hadn't actually spoken a lie. "Duncan didn't touch me, but I've promised to speak the full truth and so I'll confess to you that I did try to take advantage of his good nature. 'Tis the truth that I did eventually seduce him."

A gasp replaced the murmur now. Madelyne thought she heard Duncan groan. The king looked ready to scream. Duncan was suddenly standing next to Madelyne, and his hand covered her mouth. She guessed he wanted her to stop.

When she nudged him, Duncan moved his hand back to rest on her shoulder.

"Do you realize how you defame yourself, my dear woman?" the king bellowed.

"I love Duncan," Madelyne answered. "And I wasn't able to seduce him until we were married."

The king turned to scowl at Louddon again. "Your charge that your sister was defiled I now deny. I've only to look at her to see she speaks the truth."

The king then asked Madelyne, "What about your husband's charge that Louddon defiled his sister?"

"It is true," Madelyne said. "Adela told me what happened to her. Morcar attacked her, but Louddon was there too. It was his plan and he was therefore just as responsible."

"I see." The king looked furious. He continued to question Madelyne a long while. She fenced with her answers, yet always spoke the truth.

"My husband acted with courage, my brother with deceit," Madelyne said.

She sagged against Duncan's side when she was finally finished.

"Do you have anything further to say to me?" the king asked Louddon.

Louddon could barely speak. His face was mottled with fury. "My sister boldly lies to you," he stammered.

"Isn't this the same sister you praised to me as always speaking the truth?" he yelled.

Louddon didn't answer him. The king turned back to Madelyne. "You are loyal to your husband. An admirable trait. Do you tell me truths now or do you protect Duncan?"

Before Madelyne could answer, the king turned to Duncan. "Do you have anything further to add to this?"

"Only that it was an equal seduction," Duncan commented. His voice was mild now. "And thoroughly satisfying."

A roar of approval echoed through the hall. The king smiled.

He stood then and gave his decision. "Louddon, you have betrayed my confidence in you. You are now stripped of all duties and forever banned from my court."

He turned to Duncan next. "My brother, Henry, has suggested a time to cool your anger. I am displeased over the havoc caused and the lives lost, but I accept that you were retaliating in measure for your sister's honor. Perhaps a month with the Scots would be sufficient time."

Madelyne felt Duncan stiffen against her. She took hold of his hand and squeezed it, begging him to keep silent.

"If, when you return, you still wish to challenge Louddon and the men who stand with him in this matter, I will allow a fight to the death. The choice of confronting will belong to you."

Duncan didn't immediately accept or reject the order. He didn't like waiting to challenge Louddon.

He felt Madelyne tremble. Her fear made the decision for him. "I will leave immediately."

The king nodded. "I've released Louddon from his duties, Duncan. I've given him a month to hide from you," he admitted.

"I'll find him."

The king smiled. "Of that I have no doubt."

Duncan bowed to his king. William then left the room, with Louddon chasing after him.

"I would have a few words with you, wife," Duncan whispered.

Madelyne tried to smile at her husband. His face was masked. She couldn't tell if he was angry or just irritated. "I am very tired, Duncan. And you did tell the king we would leave immediately."

"We?"

"You wouldn't leave me here, would you?" she asked, clearly appalled.

"I would not."

"Do not tease me," she muttered. "I have been through an ordeal."

Baron Rhinehold interrupted the discussion. "Your wife equals you in courage, Duncan. She faced our king and told him her story. Why, her voice never wavered."

"And what did she tell him?" Duncan asked, his voice mild.

Baron Rhinehold smiled. "That is the question, isn't it? I listened to her explanation and am still confused as to who burned what, who attacked and who retreated . . . and still I haven't the faintest idea of what happened."

"You have just described my life with Madelyne," Duncan announced. His voice sounded pained now.

Duncan looked down at Madelyne and saw how she stared at the baron. "I've forgotten to introduce you," he realized out loud. "Baron, this is my wife, Madelyne. I understand that you knew her mother?"

The baron nodded. "Your wife looks like Rachael," he said. "It is a pleasure to meet you, Baroness."

He had such a nice smile. Madelyne could feel herself getting emotional. She forced a smile and said, "I would like to speak to you about my mother, Baron. Perhaps, when we return from our temporary exile, you would pay us a visit."

"I would be honored," Rhinehold said.

There wasn't any more time to talk with the baron. The other allies came to express their pleasure over the outcome. Madelyne stood by Duncan's side, holding his hand, wishing he'd tell her what he thought about this encounter.

Duncan ignored her. He turned when Gerald joined them and stated that they would ride in one hour's time.

"Duncan? Is there time for me to gather my things from my room?" Madelyne asked.

"You wear the clothes on your back, wife."

Madelyne sighed. "You're angry then?" she asked.

Duncan looked down at his wife. Her eyes were misty and she chewed on her lower lip. He slowly shook his head. "Seduce me? My God, you told the king you seduced me. When you decide to tell a falsehood, you aren't the least timid." He grinned at her while he rebuked her.

"It wasn't a falsehood," Madelyne said. "I did want you to kiss me and I never liked it when you stopped. That is a bit of a seduction, isn't it, Duncan? And I kissed you that first night. You only responded in kind, husband. Aye, it was the truth. I did seduce you."

"If you'd told the full truth, I would have been able to challenge Louddon now," Duncan pointed out.

"Oh, I know how that works," Madelyne said. "You both contradicted each other. The king would have put you in a lake, with your hands and feet tied to stones. And if you sank to the bottom, then he'd know you spoke the truth. Of course you'd be dead, but your honor would be intact. Well, I don't want to go to bed at night with your honor for company. I want you alive and well. What say you to that, husband?"

Though she tried, she couldn't help the tears that escaped.

Duncan was staring at her with the most astonished expression on his face.

"Madelyne," he said, drawing her name out in an exaggerated sigh, "warriors are not put to such trials. The church uses that method, not the king."

"Oh."

Duncan felt like laughing. He took Madelyne into his arms, smiled when he heard her mutter, "I have been through an ordeal."

"You have a heart of gold," he said. "Come, wife. I have the urge to let you seduce me."

Madelyne was in complete agreement with his plan.

They made camp almost four hours later. Madelyne was weary. Clarissa had intercepted her just as she was leaving with Duncan. The vile, angry words she'd yelled at Madelyne still echoed in her mind.

Duncan left her by a stream he'd found while he saw to protecting his camp. Madelyne was in his sight at all times, however. As long as Louddon was alive, Duncan wasn't going to leave Madelyne's side.

Madelyne washed as best she could under the circumstances and then returned to the campsite. Duncan had just finished building a tent for the two of them. It was a short distance away from the contingent of men traveling with them.

"Will Father Berton be safe enough? Or do you think you should increase the number of men guarding him?" she asked Duncan.

"He will be fine," Duncan said. "I left the fittest men in charge. Don't worry, love."

Madelyne nodded. "Do you remember the first night we slept together?"

"I remember it well."

"I thought the fire was too close and worried our tent would catch flame," she said.

"You worried about everything," Duncan told her. He untied the roped belt resting against her hips. "You slept with your clothes on that night."

"I protected my virtue," Madelyne said. "I hadn't known then that I really wanted to seduce you." She laughed over the disgruntled look on her husband's face.

"I protected your virtue," Duncan countered.

Madelyne settled herself on top of the animal skins. It was a cool, accommodating evening. The breeze refreshed and the bright moon gave them a soft light.

"Take your clothes off, Madelyne," Duncan told her. He'd already stripped out of his tunic and his boots.

Madelyne wanted to do just that, but she worried about the men. She tugged Duncan's hand. When he was leaning over her, she whispered to him, "We can't make love this night. Your soldiers would see us."

Duncan shook his head. "No one can see us, wife. I want you. Now." He showed her he meant what he said by kissing her soundly. Madelyne sighed into his mouth as she wound her arms around his neck. She opened her mouth, rubbed her tongue against his, instinctively arching against him.

"You make too much noise," Madelyne whispered when Duncan ended the kiss and began to nibble on her earlobe.

She shivered in reaction to the pleasure he gave her. Duncan chuckled. "You're the one who screams for fulfillment, love," Duncan told her. "I'm too disciplined to make a sound."

"Is that the truth?" Madelyne asked. Her hand slowly caressed a line to his throbbing arousal.

Duncan forgot what they were talking about. He caught her mouth again while he roughly pulled on the hem of her gown. He wanted her heat, and when his fingers probed the satin folds shielding the very core of her femininity, he knew she wanted him. She was moist with heat, and arched against him when he thrust his fingers inside.

Their clothes were discarded in wild abandon. Duncan didn't want to calm his ardor. He needed Madelyne now, and he could tell from her uninhibited response that she didn't want tenderness. Aye, she needed him to forget all restraint.

Duncan silenced her moans by covering her mouth with his. He settled himself between her thighs, penetrated her. She drove him to the brink of fulfillment with her erotic whimpers of pleasure, goaded him toward spilling his seed into her with her pleas and her nails digging into his shoulders. When Duncan couldn't hold back any longer, he slid his hand between their bodies and stroked her into climax.

Duncan wanted to shout with his release. He couldn't, of course, and claimed Madelyne's mouth again, trapping her own scream.

"I love you, wife," he whispered later, when she was cuddled up against his side.

"I love you too, Duncan," Madelyne said. She was content to rest against her husband for several more minutes. Then she asked, "Did I embarrass you in court when I said I seduced you?"

Duncan smiled against the top of her head. Madelyne turned, bumping him.

"I do not get embarrassed," he announced. His voice was laced with arrogance. "Women become embarrassed."

Madelyne smiled. "What do warriors become?"

"Tired," he said. "They become exhausted after making love to their wives."

"Are you suggesting I go to sleep now?"

"I am."

"Then I will, of course, obey your suggestion after just

one more question." She heard him sigh but ignored it. "Who were those men who lied for my brother? Were they barons?"

"They were not barons, only men who have joined your brother against me," Duncan said.

"Then they have no following? No armies of their own?"

Duncan hesitated a long minute. "They have no armies, Madelyne. Yet there are many unscrupulous men who would join them if given enough incentive. Louddon doesn't have enough gold at his disposal now to cause much of a threat."

Madelyne was content with his answer. She put the worry of Louddon aside. "Duncan? You'll be able to meet my cousin, Edwythe, when we go to Scotland. I was going to live with her. That was the plan I'd formed before I met you."

"You'll be able to meet my sister, Catherine," Duncan said. His voice sounded sleepy.

"Your sister is married to a Scot?" she asked. Her voice sounded incredulous.

"She is."

"Does her husband . . ."

"No, he doesn't have red hair," Duncan interjected.

"I wasn't going to ask that," Madelyne protested. "I just wondered if Catherine and her husband might know Edwythe."

Duncan's deep, even breathing told her he'd fallen asleep. When he began to snore, she was certain. Madelyne snuggled up against him.

She had the most wonderful dreams that night. They were dreams of the innocent.

Chapter Twenty-four

Love and honor, treasures above value . . .

The following month was a calming period for Duncan, a blissful time for Madelyne.

Madelyne was enchanted with the Scots. She thought they were the most amazing warriors in all the world, save for her husband, of course. The Scots reminded Madelyne of the ancient Spartans because of their stark existence and their fierce loyalty.

They treated Duncan as one of their own. Catherine was also happy to welcome Madelyne into her home. Duncan's sister was very pretty and very much in love with her husband.

Madelyne wasn't able to see Edwythe, though Catherine promised to send a message of greeting to her for Madelyne. Edwythe lived in the highlands, a considerable distance from Catherine's home, too far, in fact, to go for a visit.

They stayed with Duncan's relatives a full thirty days.

Duncan remembered his promise to teach his gentle wife how to defend herself. He was patient with her until she reached for her bow and arrows. He left her on her own then, fearing he'd lose his temper if he had to watch her make the same error over and over again. She was consistently off target. Anthony had warned him about that flaw. Madelyne was always three feet, a little less perhaps, above the mark she wished to hit.

Duncan and Madelyne returned to Wexton fortress the end of August. It was then that they learned of King William II's death. The accounts were milky, but everyone who had witnessed the tragedy vowed it had truly been an accident. William, with his brother and his friends, had gone hunting in his forest. A soldier shot his arrow toward a stag, it was said, but the king's neck got in the way. The king died before he hit the ground.

The most accepted and least believed account came from an eyewitness who claimed he'd seen the whole of it, from start to finish. He stated that the loyal subject had truly aimed his arrow at the stag, but when the arrow was flying toward the animal, the devil's red hand suddenly reached up out of the earth. The arrow was caught in the devil's fist and redirected toward the king.

The church blessed the account as accurate. Aye, it was written down immediately. Satan had ended the king's short life, and certainly none of those who witnessed it were responsible.

Henry immediately claimed the treasury and became king.

Madelyne was thankful she and Duncan had left court before the tragedy. Her husband was just as angry that he hadn't been there. He thought he might have been able to save his leader's life.

Neither believed the story about the devil's hand, and neither would admit that Henry might have had something to do with his brother's accident.

Though Madelyne wasn't as knowledgeable as Duncan in matters of state, she remembered that Henry had suggested to King William that Duncan spend a month with the Scots. She believed he wanted Duncan away from London, believed, too, that Henry might have given Duncan his life by sending him away. She never spoke such thoughts to her husband, however.

Gerald and Adela were married on the first Sunday of October. Father Berton had only just arrived with his baggage to take up the task of saving Wexton souls. The Earl of Grinsteade had died five days after Madelyne's wedding ceremony.

Duncan had sent soldiers throughout England, searching for Louddon. Since Henry was now king, Louddon was an outcast. Henry had made no pretension about his dislike for Louddon.

Madelyne believed Louddon had left England. Duncan didn't argue with her, but he was convinced Louddon was hiding, waiting for his chance for revenge.

A summons arrived requesting that Duncan kneel before his new king and give him his pledge of fealty. Duncan couldn't refuse the order, yet found he was uneasy leaving Madelyne.

He sat in the hall, the petition from Henry still in his hands, when Madelyne finally came down for breakfast. Duncan had already eaten his midday meal.

His wife looked rested, but he knew in just a few hours she'd need a nap. She tired easily these days. Madelyne tried to hide the fact from Duncan, but he knew she was sick every morning.

He wasn't the least upset over her sickness. No, he waited for her to realize she carried his child.

Madelyne smiled when she saw her husband sitting in his chair by the hearth. It had turned chilly and the fire beckoned her. Duncan pulled her into his lap.

"Duncan, I must speak to you. It's almost noon and I've just gotten out of bed. I believe I'm ill, though I don't wish to worry you. I did ask Maude for a potion yesterday."

"And did she give it to you?" Duncan asked. He tried not to smile, for his wife's expression was close to brooding.

Madelyne shook her head. She pushed her hair away from her shoulder, hitting Duncan's chest in her haste. "No, she didn't," she said. "She just smiled at me and walked away. What am I to think about that I ask you?"

Duncan sighed. He was going to have to tell her. "Will you be very upset if our son has red hair?"

Madelyne's eyes widened and her hand instinctively moved to her stomach. Her voice shook when she finally answered his question. "She'll have brown hair, like her mother. And I will be the most wonderful mother, Duncan."

Duncan laughed and then kissed Madelyne. "You have taken on my arrogance, wife. You'll give me a son and that's the end of this discussion."

Madelyne nodded, pretending agreement while she pictured the beautiful baby girl she would hold in her arms.

She was so overwhelmed with joy, she thought she might weep.

"You can't feed your wild animals anymore. I don't want you going outside the walls."

"It's my wolf," Madelyne teased. She still hadn't admitted to Duncan that she really thought it was a wild dog. "Today will be the last time I leave food for him," she promised. "Is that good enough for you?"

"Why today?" Duncan asked.

"Because it's been exactly one year since I arrived here. You may walk with Anthony and me if you wish." She gave a mock sigh. "I shall miss my wolf."

Duncan saw the sparkle in her eyes.

"I will stop feeding him only because you order it, husband."

"I don't believe that for one minute," Duncan returned. "You obey me because you feel like it."

Duncan finally promised to accompany Madelyne. She waited for him but when she'd finished her target practice, the sun was beginning to fade, and Duncan still hadn't finished his other duties.

Madelyne collected her arrows, slipped them into the cloth carrier Ned had fashioned for her, and then strapped the carrier on her back.

Anthony carried the food for her in the burlap sack she always used for the task. She carried her bow, boasting to the vassal that she just might catch at least one rabbit for their dinner.

Anthony thought it impossible.

When they reached the crest of the hill, Madelyne took the food from Anthony. She spread the cloth on the ground, kneeling now, and placed the food into a pile. A large bone, fat with meat, topped her pyramid. Since Madelyne knew she wouldn't be feeding the wild animals any longer, she thought to leave them one last filling treat.

Anthony was first to catch the noise behind him. He turned, scanning the trees behind Madelyne, just as an arrow whistled through the air and lodged in his shoulder. The vassal was knocked to the ground. He tried to catch his balance and then saw his enemy raise his bow a second time.

The watchman shouted the warning as soon as Anthony fell. Soldiers lined the walkway along the wall, their arrows raised to their bows. They waited for the enemy to show himself.

Duncan had just mounted his horse. He had thought to please his wife by joining her and carrying her back. He heard the shout, then goaded his horse into a full gallop. His bellow of rage could be heard throughout the fortress. Men ran to their horses to follow their lord.

Madelyne knew she didn't have time to run. A half circle of almost twenty men slowly came from their hiding places behind the trees. She knew, too, that the watchman and the archers wouldn't be able to see them until they reached the crest.

She wasn't given any choice. Madelyne reached for one of her arrows, adjusted the indented edge to her bow, and took careful aim.

She recognized the man closest to her. He was one of the three who had testified to Louddon's lies. She knew then that Louddon was close by.

The knowledge made her more furious than frightened. She shot the arrow and was reaching for another before the enemy fell to the ground.

Duncan didn't climb the crest. He rode around the base of the hill, motioning for the others to take the opposite side. He thought to cut off the enemy by placing himself between them and his wife.

Within bare minutes Duncan's soldiers were engaged in battle with the enemy. Madelyne dropped her bow and turned, thinking to help Anthony. The vassal had rolled halfway down the hill but was standing now and slowly making his way back up to her.

"Madelyne, get down," Anthony suddenly shouted.

She heard his order, started to do as he commanded, when she was grabbed from behind. Madelyne screamed as she turned, and came face-to-face with Louddon.

He had a crazed look in his eyes. His grip was excruciating. Madelyne stomped her foot down on his, causing him to change balance. Remembering Duncan's lessons in defense, she slammed her knee into his groin. Louddon went crashing to the ground, pulling Madelyne with him.

She rolled to her side just as Louddon staggered to his knees. He hit Madelyne with his fist, his aim right below her jaw. The pain proved too intense to endure. Madelyne fainted.

Louddon jumped to his feet when Madelyne went limp. He looked to the bottom of the hill, saw his men running away. They deserted him, trying to escape Duncan's wrath.

Louddon knew then he couldn't get away from Duncan this time. "You'll watch me kill her," he screamed.

Duncan was on foot now. He started running up the hill. Louddon knew he had only seconds left. He frantically searched the ground for his knife. He would plunge it into Madelyne's heart before Duncan could stop him.

Louddon shouted with obscene laughter when he spotted his dagger on top of a pile of garbage. He knelt down and reached for his weapon.

He made the mistake of touching the food.

Louddon's hand rested on the handle of his dagger. He was turning, when a low growl stopped him. The sound intensified until it was earthshaking.

Duncan also heard the sound. He saw Louddon throw up his hands in front of his face. And then a streak of brown lightning leapt at his throat.

Louddon fell backward, strangling to death on his own blood.

Duncan motioned to his men to stand where they were. He kept his gaze on the mighty wolf as he slowly reached for his bow and arrow. The wolf stood over Louddon. The animal's teeth were bared and a low, threatening growl permeated the stillness.

Duncan prayed Madelyne wouldn't wake up. He started forward so he could gain a clear shot at the beast.

The wolf suddenly moved to stand over Madelyne. Duncan stopped breathing.

Her scent must have been familiar to the animal, Duncan decided, for the wolf quickly ended his curiosity and went back to the food. Duncan watched the wolf take the bone between his teeth, turn again, and disappear down the other side of the hill.

Duncan threw down his bow and arrow as he ran to his wife. Madelyne was just waking up when he knelt down beside her. He gently lifted her into his arms.

She rubbed her jaw, testing her injury. She was able to move it, yet thought it throbbed enough to make her think it should be broken. She realized then that Louddon was there.

"Are they gone?" she asked Duncan. She was squeezed so tightly against his chest, she could barely whisper her question.

"Louddon's dead."

Madelyne closed her eyes and said a prayer for his soul. She didn't think it would do him much good, but she said it all the same.

"Is Anthony all right? We must see to his injury, Duncan," Madelyne said, trying to struggle out of her husband's hold. "He's wearing an arrow in his shoulder."

Duncan stopped shaking. Madelyne was deliberately talking without pause. She knew he needed a few minutes to recover. When he eased up on his hold, Madelyne smiled at him. "Now is it over?" she asked.

"It is over," Duncan said. "Your wolf saved your life."

"I know you did, love, you will always protect me," Madelyne answered.

"Madelyne, you misunderstand," Duncan said, frowning. "Your wolf killed Louddon."

Madelyne shook her head. How like her husband to become fanciful in her moment of fear. She knew he teased her just to lighten her worry.

"Are you strong enough to stand?" Duncan asked. "Do you feel—"

"I am fine. *We* are fine," she amended. She patted her stomach for emphasis. "I can't feel her yet, Duncan, but I know she's safe."

When Duncan helped her to her feet, she tried to look at Louddon. Duncan moved in front of her, effectively blocking her view. "You needn't look at him, Madelyne, it would only distress you," he told her. Louddon's throat had been shredded by the wolf's jaws. It was not a sight Madelyne would soon forget if she saw it, Duncan decided.

Anthony came to stand with them. He looked more incredulous than pained.

"Anthony, your shoulder—"

"'Tis only a flesh wound," Anthony said. "Baroness, you shot one of them right through his heart," he stammered.

Duncan didn't believe him. "It was her arrow?"

"It was."

Both men turned to stare at Madelyne. They looked quite astonished. Madelyne was a little irritated by their lack of faith in her ability. For a fleeting second she thought she just might keep silent. The truth, however, won out. "I was aiming for his foot."

Both Duncan and Anthony thoroughly enjoyed her admission. Duncan lifted Madelyne into his arms and began to walk down the hill.

"The wolf saved your life," he told her once again, thinking to explain the full truth.

"I know, dear."

He gave up. He'd have to explain it all to her later, when her mind wasn't so stubbornly set on believing he was her savior. "You'll never feed the beast again, Madelyne. I'll see the duty done. The wolf deserves to live an easy life now. He has earned it."

"Will you stop teasing me, Duncan?" Madelyne announced, clearly exasperated. "I've been through an ordeal."

Duncan smiled. Such a bossy bit of goods she was, and such a delight. He rubbed his chin against the top of her head while he listened to her complain about her new bruise.

Baron Wexton was eager to get Madelyne home, as eager, he thought, as Odysseus must have been to get home to his wife.

The future belonged to them. Madelyne liked to call him her wolf, but he was only a man, yet a man more powerful than the magical Odysseus.

For though Duncan was a mere mortal, flawed as well, he'd accomplished a daring feat. Aye, he'd captured an angel. And she belonged to him.

Visit

JULIE GARWOOD

online!

For a preview excerpt of Julie Garwood's
upcoming hardcover, *Heartbreaker*, go to:

www.SimonSays.com/juliegarwood

Read excerpts from her other books,
find a listing of future titles, and
learn more about the author!

SIMON & SCHUSTER
A VIACOM COMPANY
www.SimonSays.com

POCKET
BOOKS

POCKET BOOKS
PROUDLY PRESENTS

Mercy

JULIE GARWOOD

Now available in paperback
from Pocket Books

The following is a preview of
***Mercy*. . . .**

Theo Buchanan couldn't seem to shake the virus. He knew he was running a fever because every bone in his body ached and he had chills. He refused to acknowledge that he was ill, though; he was just a little off-kilter, that was all. He could tough it out. Besides, he was sure he was over the worst of it. The god-awful stitch in his side had subsided into a dull throbbing, and he was positive that it meant he was on the mend. If it was the same bug that had infected most of the staff back in his Boston office, then it was one of those twenty-four-hour things, and he should be feeling as good as new by tomorrow morning. Except, the throbbing in his side had been going on for a couple of days now.

He decided to blame his brother, Dylan, for that ache. He'd really nailed Theo during a family football game on their parents' lawn at Nathan's Bay. Yeah, the pulled muscle was Dylan's fault, but Theo figured that if he continued to ignore it, the pain would eventually go away.

Damn, he was feeling like an old man these days, and he wasn't even thirty-three yet.

He didn't think he was contagious, and he had too much to do to go to bed and sweat the fever out of his body. He'd flown from Boston to New Orleans to speak at a law symposium on organized crime and to receive recognition he didn't believe he deserved for simply doing his job.

Tonight was the first of three black-tie affairs. He'd promised to attend a fund-raiser, and he couldn't back out. Dinner was going to be prepared by five of the top chefs in the city, but the gourmet food was going to be wasted on him. The thought of swallowing anything, even water, made his stomach lurch. He hadn't eaten anything since yesterday afternoon.

He sure as certain wasn't up to pointless chitchat tonight. He tucked the room key into his pocket and was reaching for the doorknob, when the phone rang.

It was his brother Nick calling to check in.

"What's going on?"

"I'm walking out the door," Theo answered. "Where are you calling from? Boston or Holy Oaks?"

"Boston," Nick answered. "I helped Laurant close the lake house and then we drove back home together."

"Is she staying with you until the wedding?"

"Are you kidding? Tommy would send me straight to hell."

Theo laughed. "I guess having a priest for a future brother-in-law does put a crimp in your sex life."

"Five more weeks and I'm gonna be a married man. Hard to believe, isn't it?"

"It's hard to believe any woman would have you."

"Laurant's nearsighted. I told her I was good-looking and she believed me. She's staying with Mom and Dad until we all head back to Iowa for the wedding. What are you doing tonight?"

"I've got a fund-raiser I have to go to," he answered. "So what do you want?"

"I just thought I'd call and say hello."

"No, you didn't. You want something. What is it? Come on, Nick. I'm gonna be late."

"Theo, you've got to learn to slow down. You can't keep running for the rest of your life. I know what you're doing. You think that if you bury yourself in work, you won't think about Rebecca. It's been four years since she died, but you—"

Theo cut him off. "I like my life, and I'm not in the mood to talk about Rebecca."

"You're a workaholic."

"Did you call to lecture me?"

"No, Laurant's been bugging me to call you."

"Is she there? Let me talk to her," he said. He sat down on the side of the bed and realized he was feeling better. Nick's fiancée had that effect on all the Buchanan brothers. She made everyone feel good.

"She isn't here. She went out with Jordan, and you know our sister. God only knows what time they'll get home. Anyway, I promised Laurant that I'd track you down and ask . . ."

"What?"

"She wanted me to ask you but I figure I didn't need to," he said. "It's understood."

Theo held his patience. "What's understood?"

"You're gonna be my best man in the wedding."

"What about Noah?"

"He's in the wedding, of course, but I'm expecting you to be best man. I figured you already knew that, but Laurant thought I should ask you anyway."

"Yeah?"

"Yeah, what?"

Theo smiled. "Yeah, okay."

His brother was a man of few words. "Okay, good. Have you given your speech yet?"

"No, that's not until tomorrow night."

"When do you get your trophy?"

"It's a plaque, and I get it right before I give my speech."

"So if you blow it and put all those armed officers to sleep, they can't take the trophy back, can they?"

"I'm hanging up."

"Hey, Theo? For once, stop thinking about work. See the sights. Get laid. You know, have a good time. Hey, I know . . . why don't you give Noah a call. He's in Biloxi for a couple of months for a training conference. He could drive over to New Orleans, and the two of you could have some fun."

If anyone knew how to have fun, it was Noah

Clayborne. The FBI agent had become a close friend of the family after working on several assignments with Nick and then later assisting Theo with his investigations as a federal attorney for the Justice Department. He was a good man, but he had a wicked sense of fun, and Theo wasn't sure he could survive a night out with Noah just now.

"Okay, maybe," he answered.

Theo hung up the phone, stood, and quickly doubled over from the pain that radiated through his right side. It had started in his belly, but it had moved down, and, damn, but it stung. The muscle he'd pulled felt like it was on fire.

A stupid football injury wasn't going to keep him down. Muttering to himself, he grabbed his cell phone from the charger, put it into his breast pocket with his reading glasses, slipped his gun into his belt holster, and left the room. By the time he reached the lobby, the pain had receded and he was feeling almost human again. That, of course, only reinforced his own personal golden rule. Ignore the pain and it would go away. Besides, a Buchanan could tough anything out.

It was a night to remember.

Michelle had never attended such an extravagant affair before, and as she stood on the steps overlooking the hotel ballroom, she felt like Alice about to fall through the looking glass into Wonderland.

There were flowers everywhere, beautiful spring flowers in sculptured urns on the marble floors and in crystal vases on all the white linen tablecloths. In the very center of the ballroom, beneath a magnificent crystal chandelier, was a cluster of giant hothouse-nurtured magnolia trees in full bloom. Their heavenly fragrance filled the air.

Waiters moved smoothly through the crowd carrying silver trays with fluted champagne glasses while others rushed from table to table lighting long, white tapered candles.

Mary Ann Winters, a friend since childhood days, stood by Michelle's side taking it all in.

"I'm out of my element here," Michelle whispered. "I feel like an awkward teenager."

"You don't look like one," Mary Ann said. "I might as well be invisible. I swear every man is staring at you."

"No, they're staring at my obscenely tight dress. How could anything look so plain and ordinary on a hanger and so—"

"So devastatingly sexy on you? It clings in all the right places. Face it, you've got a killer figure."

"I should never have spent so much money on a dress."

"For heaven's sake, Michelle, it's an Armani . . . *and* you got it for a song, I might add."

Michelle self-consciously brushed her hand down the side of the soft fabric. She thought about how much she'd paid for the dress and decided she would have to wear it at least twenty times to make it cost-effective. She wondered if other women did that—rationalized a frivolous expense to appease the guilt. There were so many more important things she could have used the money for, and when, in heaven's name, was she ever going to have another opportunity to wear this beautiful dress again? Not in Bowen, she thought. Not in a million years.

"What was I thinking? I never should have let you talk me into buying this dress."

Mary Ann impatiently brushed a strand of white blond hair back over her shoulder. "Don't you dare start in complaining about the cost again. You never spend any money on yourself. I'll bet it's the first really gorgeous dress you've ever owned, isn't it? You're absolutely beautiful tonight. Promise me you'll stop worrying and enjoy yourself."

Michelle nodded. "You're right. I'll stop worrying."

"Good. Now let's go mingle. There's hors d'oeuvres and champagne out in the courtyard, and we've got to eat at least a thousand dollars' worth each. That's what the tickets cost. I'll meet you there."

Her friend had just gone down the stairs, when Dr. Cooper spotted Michelle and motioned for her to join him. He was the chief of surgery at Brethren Hospital, where she had been moonlighting the past month. Cooper was usually reserved, but the champagne had rid him of his inhibitions, and he was quite affectionate. And effervescent. He kept telling her how happy he was that she was using the tickets he'd given her and how pretty she looked all dressed up. Michelle thought that if Dr. Cooper got any happier, he was going to pass out in the soup.

A few minutes later, Cooper's wife joined them with another older couple in tow. Michelle used the opportunity to sneak away. She walked around into the adjacent hallway with the bank of elevators.

And that's when she noticed him. He was leaning against a pillar, hunched over, tilted protectively to one side. The man was tall, broad-shouldered, well built, like an athlete, she thought. But there was a sickly gray pallor to his complexion, and as she walked toward him, she saw him grimace and grab his stomach.

He was definitely in trouble. She touched his arm to get his attention just as the elevator doors opened. He staggered upright and looked down at her. His gray eyes were glazed with pain.

"Do you need help?"

He answered her by throwing up all over her.

She couldn't get out of the way because he'd grabbed hold of her arm. His knees buckled then and she knew he was going to go down. She wrapped her arms around his waist and tried to ease him to the floor, but he lurched forward at the same time, taking her with him.

Theo's head was spinning. He landed on top of the woman. He heard her groan and desperately tried to find the strength to get up. He thought he might be dying and he didn't think that would be such a bad thing if death would make the pain go away. It was unbearable now. His stomach rolled again, and another wave of intense agony cut through him. He wondered if this was what it felt like to be stabbed over and over again. He passed out then, and when he next opened his eyes, he was flat on his back and she was leaning over him.

He tried to bring her face into focus. She had pretty blue eyes, more violet than blue, he thought, and freckles on the bridge of her nose. Then, as suddenly as it had stopped, the fire started burning in his side again, so much worse than before.

A spasm wrenched his stomach, and he jerked. "Son of a bitch."

The woman was talking to him, but he couldn't understand what she was saying. And what the hell was she doing to him? Was she robbing him? Her hands were everywhere, tugging at his jacket, his tie, his shirt. She was trying to straighten out his legs. She was hurting him, damn it, and every time he tried to push her hands away, they came back to poke and prod some more.

He felt her open his jacket, knew she could see the gun holstered above his hip. He was crazed with pain now, couldn't seem to think straight. He only knew he couldn't let her take his weapon.

She was a damned talkative mugger. He'd give her that. She looked like one of those J. Crew models. Sweet, he thought. No, she wasn't sweet. She kept hurting him.

"Look, lady, you can take my wallet, but you're not getting my gun. Got that?" He could barely get the words out through his gritted teeth.

Her hand pressed into his side. He reacted instinctively, knocking her back. He thought he might have connected with something soft because he heard her yell before he went under again.

Theo didn't know how long he was out, but when he

opened his eyes, the bright lights made him squint. Where the hell was he? He couldn't summon up enough energy to move. He thought he might be on a table. It was hard, cold.

"Where am I?" His mouth was so dry, he slurred the question.

"You're in Brethren Hospital, Mr. Buchanan." The man's voice came from behind him, but Theo couldn't see him.

"Did they catch her?"

"Who?"

"J. Crew."

"He's loopy." A female voice he didn't recognize made the comment.

Theo suddenly realized he wasn't in any pain. He felt good, in fact. Real good. Like he could fly. Odd, though, he didn't have the strength to move his arms. A mask was placed over his mouth and nose. He turned his head to get away from it.

"Are you getting sleepy, Mr. Buchanan?"

He turned his head again and saw her. Blue Eyes. She looked like an angel, all golden. Wait a minute. What the hell was she doing here? Wait . . .

"Mike, are you going to be able to see what you're doing? That eye looks bad."

"It's fine."

"How'd it happen?" the voice behind Theo's head asked.

"He clipped me."

"The patient decked you?"

"That's right." She was staring into Theo's eyes when she answered. She had a green mask on, but he knew she was smiling.

He was in such a happy daze now and so sleepy, he was having trouble keeping his eyes open. Conversation swirled around him, but none if it made any sense.

A woman's voice. "Where did you find *him,* Dr. Renard?"

"At a party."

Another woman leaned over him. "Hubba, hubba."

"Was it love at first sight?"

"You decide. He threw up all over me and ruined my new dress."

Someone laughed. "Sounds like love to me. I'll bet he's married. All the good-looking men are married. This one's sure built. Did you check out the goods, Annie?"

"I hope our patient is sleeping."

"Not yet," a male voice said. "But he isn't going to remember anything."

"Where's the assist?"

"Scrubbing."

There seemed to be a party going on. Theo thought there were at least twenty or thirty people in the room with him. Why was it so damned cold? And who was making all the clatter? He was thirsty. His mouth felt like it was full of cotton. Maybe he ought to go get a drink. Yeah, that's what he would do.

"Where's Dr. Cooper?"

"Probably passed out in the dessert by now." Blue Eyes answered the question. Theo loved the sound of her voice. It was so damned sexy.

"So you saw Cooper at the party?"

"Uh-huh," Blue Eyes answered. "He wasn't on call tonight. He works hard. It was nice to see him having a good time. Mary Ann's probably having a great time too."

"You." Theo struggled to get the word out. Still, he'd gotten her attention because when he opened his eyes, she was leaning over him, blocking out the glaring light above him.

"It's time for you to go to sleep, Mr. Buchanan."

"He's fighting it."

"What . . ." Theo began.

"Yes?"

"What do you want from me?"

The man hiding behind him answered. "Mike wants your appendix, Mr. Buchanan."

It sounded good to him. He was always happy to accommodate a beautiful woman. "Okay," he whispered. "It's in my wallet."

"We're ready."

"It's about time," the man said.

Theo heard the chair squeak behind him, then the stranger's voice telling him to take deep breaths. Theo finally figured out who the man behind him was. Damn if it wasn't Willie Nelson, and he was singing to him, something about Blue Eyes cryin' in the rain.

It was one hell of a party.

Theo slept through recovery. When he awoke the following morning, he was in a hospital bed. The side rails were up, and he was hooked to an IV. He closed his eyes and tried to clear his mind. What the hell had happened to him? He couldn't remember.

It was past ten o'clock when he opened his eyes again. She was there, standing beside the bed, pulling the sheets up around his waist. Blue Eyes. He hadn't imagined her after all.

She looked different today. She was still dressed in surgical scrubs, but her hair wasn't hidden underneath a cap. It was down around her shoulders, and the color was a deep, rich auburn.

She was much prettier than he remembered.

She noticed he was awake. "Good morning. How are you feeling? Still a little drowsy?"

He struggled to sit up. She reached for the controls and pushed a button. The bed slowly rose. Theo felt a tugging in his side and a mild stinging sensation.

"Tell me when."

"That's good," he said. "Thanks."

She picked up his chart and started writing while he blatantly stared at her. He felt vulnerable and awkward sitting in bed in a hospital gown. He couldn't think of anything clever to say to her. For the first time in his life he wanted to be charming, but he didn't have the faintest idea how to go about it. He was a die-hard workaholic, and there simply wasn't room for social graces in his life.

"Do you remember what happened last night?" she asked, glancing up from her notes.

"I had surgery."

"Yes. Your appendix was removed. Another fifteen minutes and you definitely would have ruptured."

"I remember bits and pieces. What happened to your eye?"

She smiled as she started writing in his chart again. "I didn't duck fast enough."

"Who are you?"

"Dr. Renard."

"Mike?"

"Excuse me?"

"Someone called you Mike."

Michelle closed the folder, put the lid back on her ink pen, and tucked it into her pocket. She gave him her full attention. The surgical nurses were right. Theo Buchanan was gorgeous . . . and sexy as hell. But none of that should matter. She was his physician, nothing more, nothing less, yet she couldn't help reacting to him as any woman naturally would react to such a fit specimen. His hair was sticking up and he needed a shave, but he was still sexy. There wasn't anything wrong with her noticing that . . . unless, of course, he noticed her noticing.

"You just asked me a question, didn't you?" She drew a blank.

He could tell he'd rattled her, but he didn't know why. "I heard someone call you Mike."

She nodded. "Yes. The staff calls me Mike. It's short for Michelle."

"Michelle's a pretty name."

"Thank you."

It was all coming back to Theo now. He was at a party, and there was this beautiful woman in a slinky black evening gown. She was breathtaking. He remembered that. She had killer blue eyes and Willie Nelson was with her. He was singing. No, that couldn't be right. Obviously, his head hadn't quite cleared yet.

"You were talking to me . . . after the surgery," he said.

"In recovery. Yes," she agreed. "But you were doing most of the talking." She was smiling again. "And by the way, the answer's no. I won't marry you."

He smiled, sure she was joking. "I don't remember being in pre-op. I remember the pain though. It hurt like a son of a . . . "

"I'm sure it did."

"You did the surgery, didn't you? I didn't imagine that?"

"Yes, I did the surgery."

She was backing out of the room. He didn't want her to leave just yet. He wanted to find out more about her. "You don't look old enough to be a surgeon." Stupid, he thought, but it was the best he could come up with at the moment.

"I hear that a lot."

"You look like you should be in college." That statement, he decided, was worse than stupid.

She couldn't resist. "High school, actually. They let me operate for extra credit."

"Very funny."

"Dr. Renard? May I interrupt?" A male aide was standing in the hallway, shifting a large cardboard box under his arm.

"Yes, Bobby?"

"Dr. Cooper filled this box with medical supplies from his office for your clinic," the young man said. "What do you want me to do with it? Dr. Cooper left it at the nurses' station, but they wanted it moved. It was in the way."

"Would you mind taking it down to my locker?"

"It's too big, Dr. Renard. It won't fit. It isn't heavy, though. I could carry it out to your car."

"My father has the car," she said. She glanced around, then looked at Theo. "Would you mind if Bobby left my box here? My father will carry it down to the car for me just as soon as he arrives."

"I don't mind," Theo said.

"I won't be seeing you again. I'm going home today, but don't worry. You're in good hands. Dr. Cooper's Chief of Surgery here at Brethren, and he'll take good care of you."

"Where's home?"

"In the swamp."

"Are you kidding?"

"No," she said. She smiled again, and he noticed the little dimple in her left cheek. "Home is a little town that's pretty much surrounded by swamp, and I can't wait to get back there."

"Homesick?"

"Yes, I am," she admitted. "I'm a small-town girl at heart. It isn't a very glamorous life, and that's what I like about it."

"You like living in the swamp." It was a statement, not a question, but she responded anyway.

"You sound shocked."

"No, just surprised."

"You're from a big, sprawling city, so you'd probably hate it."

"Why do you say that?"

She shrugged. "You seem too . . . sophisticated."

He didn't know if that was a compliment or a criticism. "Sometimes you can't go home. I think I read that in a book once. Besides, you look like a New Orleans kind of woman to me."

"I love New Orleans. It's a wonderful place to come for dinner."

"But it won't ever be home."

"No."

"So, are you the town doctor?"

"One of several," she said. "I'm opening a clinic there. It's not very fancy, but there's a real need. So many of the people don't have the resources to get regular medical care."

"Sounds like they're very lucky to have you."

She shook her head. "Oh, no, I'm the lucky one." Then she laughed. "That sounded saintly, didn't it? I am the lucky one, though. The people are wonderful, at least I think they are, and they give me far more than I can give them." When she spoke, her whole face lit up. "You know what I'm going to like best?"

"What's that?"

"No games. For the most part, they're honest, ordinary people trying to scrape a living together. They don't waste a lot of time on foolishness."

"So, everyone loves everyone else?" He scoffed at the notion.

"No, of course not," she replied. "But I'll know my enemies. They won't sneak up behind me and blindside me. It isn't their style." She smiled again. "They'll get right in my face, and I'm going to like that. Like I said, no games. After the residency I just finished, that's going to be a refreshing change."

"You won't miss the big beautiful office and all the trappings?"

"Not really. There are rewards other than money. Oh sure, it would be great to have the supplies and equipment we need, but we'll make do. I've spent a lot of years getting ready for this . . . besides, I made a promise."

He kept asking her questions to keep her talking. He was interested in hearing about her town but not nearly as much as he was fascinated with her expressions. There were such passion and joy in her voice, and her eyes sparkled as she talked about her family and friends and the good she hoped she could do.

She reminded him of how he had felt about life when he had first started practicing the law, before he'd become so cynical. He too had wanted to change the world, to make it a better place. Rebecca had changed all that. Looking back, he realized he had failed miserably.

"I've worn you out, going on and on about my hometown. I'll let you rest now," she said.

"When can I get out of here?"

"That's Dr. Cooper's call, but if it were up to me, I'd keep you another night. You had quite a nasty infection. You need to take it easy for a couple of weeks, and don't forget to take your antibiotics. Good luck, Theo."

And then she was gone, and he'd lost the only chance he had to find out more about her. He didn't even know where her home was. He fell asleep trying to figure out a way to see her again.